Hawaii
PEARL

Jena Nix

ISBN 978-1-0980-8442-4 (paperback)
ISBN 978-1-0980-8443-1 (digital)

Christian Faith Publishing, Inc.
832 Park Avenue
Meadville, PA 16335
www.christianfaithpublishing.com

Printed in the United States of America

Dedication

Hawaii Pearl is dedicated to Jesus Christ who was with me every step of the writing process. He has shown me that there is no need to place limits on what I can do when He is by my side.

Contents

Acknowledgements

Writing a novel was an idea that originated from my love of reading. But as I began, I saw I could write a scene, describe emotions, and develop characters on how they experienced their daily walk with Christ. That skill came with extensive mentoring from those in my life who read my work throughout the writing process and provided much needed and appreciated constructive feed back.

I would like to start by thanking my husband, Michael, for supporting and believing in me through the years of writing.

Matthew, my son, was circumspect with his comments but told me exactly what I needed to know to improve the story.

My mother-in-law, Rose Marie, received the first home printed manuscript in its entirety and upon reading it, gave it a big thumbs-up. Her positive response was a huge balm to my soul.

Thank you, Emily and Karen G., for providing me your assessment on each new story segment.

Mahalo, Kathy, for the weekly hours and hours you spent with me to fine-tune and enhance the sentence structure, grammar, and word usage. I literally could not have finished without you!

Bosnia, 1994

Oskar knew he couldn't use the torch in his hand, and since it was a new moon, walking through the forest was becoming increasingly difficult. They had picked this time of the month for that very reason without understanding how truly dark the park was without moonlight. Sutjeska National Park was huge, and once they traversed it, they still had to cross Croatia to get to Dubrovnik. His finger played with the on-off switch, but he knew he could not click it on yet. He heard Kim behind him praying.

Oskar slowed as he saw a dark obstacle ahead. *What is that?*

Kim came upon Oskar and whispered in his ear, "What do you see?"

Oskar couldn't hear the words but knew the meaning. He shook his head. Hanadie and Axle were further behind but would soon catch up. It was unlikely that anyone was out in this part of the park this late, but the war had definitely taught Oskar to expect the unexpected. He took one small step at a time. Even in the bitter cold, sweat was trickling down his back. During the five minutes Oscar watched, he detected no movement so he moved closer and saw the obstacle was a partially fallen tree. He took a huge breath and whispered to Kim, "Let's go." The faint rustling behind him he took to be Hanadie and Axle.

They all trudged through the park with one goal in mind: getting to Dubrovnik for the boat pick up in three days. After walking for three days since leaving Sarajevo, they were now coming close to leaving the park. Croatia was an unknown entity, so they were not sure what to expect when arriving at the border. There were Bosnian Serbs on one side and Croatians on the other; Oskar was planning on avoiding both.

Oskar looked up and realized dawn was almost upon them. He flashed his light once, and all movement stopped.

"Let's look for somewhere to rest."

They continued walking the trail until a treeless dark space was revealed. He again flashed his light. Making his way slowly to it, he found the dark space was shown to be an opening to a cave. Clicking on his torch again, Oskar quickly checked around the entrance of the cave. Light from the torch was failing, but that was probably for the best so they would remain undetected. He stepped cautiously into the opening, aiming the light so he could see inside. He was relieved when his inspection proved the cave empty. With a slight movement of the flashlight, Oskar motioned the others over. They lowered their backpacks and sat.

No one said anything initially, but once they had each pulled a piece of bread from the loaf Oskar handed them, Axle spoke up.

"How far have we come do you think?"

"After three days? Forty kilometers maybe?"

Hanadie looked up. "I would say closer to 50. We're almost halfway there."

Oskar thought about the numbers. "We should be further along. We need to make seventy more kilometers in three days. Can we do it?"

Kim lay down with his backpack as a pillow, and soon they heard his soft snores.

Axle said to the others, "If we want to speed up, we'll have to use our torches."

Hanadie piped up, "You know you'll have to call those flashlights when we get to the US, right?"

Oskar snorts. "That's the least of our worries right now, but Axle is right. While we skirt the edge of the park, we should be safe from the Serbs or Croats. I bet we can double our speed with light."

Hanadie's demeanor changed dramatically as he narrowed his eyes and remembered his cousin Luka and wife Ena lying in a pool of blood on the floor of their Bosnian home. "I still wish we had chosen a different destination than the US!" His thoughts take a grim direction thinking of the weak US president and his cowardice in not taking a stand early in the conflict.

With impatience, Oskar responded to Hanadie, "We've had this conversation too many times to count. The US provides the easiest avenue for us to assimilate and get jobs. The economy is booming, and acceptance of immigrants from here is more welcoming than any place else. I can't believe I'm repeating myself. *Again*, we have a long treak tomorrow so let's get some sleep."

*****

That evening, as the four men packed up their gear in the cave, Kim said, "Let's pray."

They all knelt.

"Father, thank You for the safety of our journey thus far. We ask for continued protection and increased speed to Dubrovnik. We pray this war will end soon, and there will be unity among all the peoples affected. In Jesus's name, we pray."

Having had a decent rest during the day, the men arranged their backpacks and started their walk as the sun set. Oskar shook his flashlight and turned it on. Luckily, the beam shown brighter than the previous night, so he continued to lead the way.

After several hours, the men stopped at a stream to take a short break.

"The light has been worth the risk. I bet we've doubled our distance already, and I actually see some lights ahead. Do you have the map, Hanadie? I want to find our exact location."

Hanadie hands Oskar the map. "How are we going to get through the fence gate the Croats built to monitor who comes into the city? I hear there are still some pockets of Serbs hanging around that may not take kindly to us sneaking out of Bosnia! It's crazy, Croats don't want us in Dubrovnik, and the Serbs don't want us leaving Bosnia."

Oskar points to a location on the map. "See this gate? My thought is we won't go through the gate but traverse outside the fence for a distance where we can either cut or climb the fence to sneak into the city."

Axle looks up from washing his face in the stream. "It might be easier to walk through the gate with others."

Oskar folded the map and answered, "I don't want to take the chance of getting stopped at the gate. We've come too far to get way-laid at this point. Let's go. We won't get there tonight anyway."

As Oskar again nervously plays with the flashlight's on-off switch, he feels thankful for his three *drugari* who are closer than *brats*. *I have to stop thinking in Bosnian. My three friends who are closer than brothers.* Taking a breath, he smiles as he and his buddies continue their trek to freedom.

CHAPTER 1

Hopefully a New Beginning

D riving along 290 West near Stonewall, Ruth's thoughts are jumbled.

This seems longer than a forty-five day journey—no, not the road trip from Austin to Kerrville but all these changes in my life. All those days ago I was making this same trip to Kerrville with Mark, scared to death about the future and yet hopeful, believing the Lord was leading us down this path.

When I think of all the joy of Mark's life before his dad passed away five years ago, it's hard to reconcile the young man he is today at twenty-two to the happy, energetic boy of his youth. Although Mark is still a handsome, green-eyed, muscular athlete with dark curly hair, his dad would not recognize this alternately hyper and lethargic individual with significant skin breakouts.

I keep thinking back to forty-five days ago when I came home from work early and found Mark in full-blown opiate withdrawal. There's no other way to describe how I felt that day but shell-shocked in a war zone—or at least in the wrong house!

The scene plays out vividly in her mind.

I'm walking in the front door of the house that day when normally I come inside through the side garage. My plan is to leave again shortly, so I park out front. The first thing I hear as I cross the threshold is Mark moaning from his room next to the entrance.

I knock on his door and get no answer, so I walk into his room and see him lying in bed, tossing from side to side.

"Mark, what's wrong?" I ask, and he tells me, "I'm drug sick."

"Drug sick?" I say. "What's that?"

"Mom, I'm sick because I haven't had any heroin in over two days."

Of course, I stand there like the biggest ninny, not truly comprehending what he's telling me, and say something inane like, "When did you start using heroin?"

Mark doesn't even answer the question but says, "Call a doctor or clinic or something, Mom. Can't you see I'm suffering? There are special places that can give me something to help with the detox! Hurry, Mom!"

Again, I stand there thinking back, and all the puzzle pieces start fitting together. I knew Mark smoked pot and had harassed him mercilessly about it, but heroin! I remember the hypodermic needle I had recently found in the driveway. I had asked Mark about it, and he told me he had a friend who was diabetic and must have dropped it after using it in the house.

And this is the second time my life turned upside down. I didn't think I would make it back from Luke's death. Now I'm picking Mark up from rehab. This is a milestone that I could use Luke's help with right now because even Luke would be perplexed with what Mark has done with his life.

Unfortunately, her memory goes to the day the officer came to her house to tell her of Luke's death in a car accident. She tries not to get emotional, but the tears come anyway. After five years, the pain feels fresh and thinking about Luke and how she needs him overcomes her. Grabbing a tissue from her console, Ruth wipes her eyes before she's unable to drive. Surprisingly, Ruth smiles as she realizes Luke would have trusted God to help in this tumultuous time.

Ruth sighs deeply and decides to stop for some lemonade at The Confectionery in Fredericksburg before going into Kerrville.

I definitely need a pick-me-up. I still have a little bit of time before the noon pick-up time Tranquillo Ranch recommends.

Gee, Fredericksburg is packed with tourists today. Main Street is clogged with traffic for one of their many festivals. Why am I surprised it's so busy? Heck, the shopping is incredible and the German architecture make it immensely appealing. Hmmm, I should have taken the route on the edge of town rather than succumb to my sweet tooth. Ahh, there's The Confectionery. What the heck, I can pick up a couple of the pecan lemon bars to go along with my lemonade.

Grinning, she feels blessed that someone is pulling out right in front of the bakery.

Ruth pulls into the just-opened space, grabs her wallet, pushes her purse under a sweater, and gets out of her trusty ten-year-old BMW 3 series.

As Ruth expected, it's packed inside the sweet shop. As she breathes deeply of all the incredible smells, she looks to see if any clerks are available. She thinks, *I may not be able to get away with only lemon bars. That smell of baking chocolate in itself will have me gaining at least a pound.* Of course, no clerk is available so as she waits in this small old-fashioned bakery; she returns to her meandering thoughts.

Should I continue to go by Ruthie now? It does seem incongruent that at forty-seven years of age my friends still call me Ruthie. Ruth would certainly have a more mature sound. Ruthie Max or Ruth Max? I don't know, Ruth Max almost sounds like a drain cleaner. Well, as earth shattering a thought as that may be, I should be thinking more about how I'm going to tell Mark that we are moving to Hawaii. I know I should have told him before that I was entertaining the idea, but it seemed premature to mention it when I didn't know if I'd be able to procure a job there.

"Ma'am, ma'am, may I help you?"

Ruth comes out of her reverie, shaking her head as if clearing the cobwebs from her brain and says, "Yes, please. Lemonade and two pecan lemon bars, and add a brownie as well."

The clerk smiles and goes to the case to get Ruth's confections. Pulling out a ten and hoping it will cover the cost, she grabs a couple of napkins from the dispenser in front of the cash register.

Sue returns with the order and rings it up. "That will be $10.01."

Ruth rolls her eyes and digs through her wallet for a penny, which she doesn't have, but a nickel will work. She hands Sue $10.05 and walks out to her car.

Putting the sweets in the glove box and her lemonade in the broken drink holder, she starts the car. Driving on Highway 16 out of Fredericksburg, she realizes she is only thirty minutes away from Kerrville and had better plan her Hawaii conversation with Mark.

"Lord, please help me convey this move in an encouraging way that will entice Mark to want to go. Please provide Mark a guardian angel during this critical time in his recovery. In Jesus's name, I pray, Amen."

Ruth takes a deep breath, feeling better able to cope. Her mind continues to go in many different directions, but she is mostly excited to see her sober son and take that next big step in their lives.

The Pickup

Ruth sees the entrance sign for Tranquillo Ranch, the drug rehab center Mark has been living in for the last forty-five days. The guard at the gate waves her in, so Ruth pulls into the parking lot. The facility has not only been Mark's refuge but hers in a way too as it provided her time to prepare for Mark's return home.

She locks the car and goes to sign in at the registration office and sees Mark walking toward her. Ruth's eyes light up, and she walks faster to meet him. They both hug tightly, and Mark says, "Right on time, as always."

"Are you all packed?"

"Yep, took me about five minutes."

"Let's go sign you out then."

After signing out, the two quickly walk to the car. Ruth checks her watch and asks Mark, "Are you hungry for some lunch?"

"Actually, I crave a burger. Can we pick one up on the way home?"

"Yes, let's do that. On the way, you can check out the brownie I bought at The Confectionery." She grins. "Plus I need to talk to you about something."

Mark raises his eyebrows. "That sounds ominous."

"Nope, not ominous, but I think a change of scenery is what we need right now." Ruth smiles at the guard as she exits Tranquillo.

Ruth looks over at Mark, "Look, let me explain what I mean before you say anything else."

"Okay. Look, there's a Whataburger."

*****

Mark starts on his burger as the car pulls out of the parking lot.

Ruth begins to explain, "Once I dropped you off at Tranquillo that first day, I went home and started looking for a new job far away. I think distance will help in your long-term recovery."

"How much distance?"

"About 3,500 miles," Ruth mutters.

"Mom, are we talking about Hawaii? I know we've taken our last two vacations there, but isn't this a little extreme?"

"Mark, when I came to the family days here at Tranquillo, I learned a significant amount about the disease. The odds of you relapsing if you return to your old environment are high. I want us to do everything we can to prevent a relapse. One way is for us to move completely away from your old friends and your usual haunts. Moving to Hawaii may be extreme distance wise, but based on what we've been through these last few weeks, I think it will be a wonderful new start for me and for you too. I looked online for a position and found one with Oahu National in Kailua. Do you remember when I told you I went out of town for work? I actually went to Honolulu for an interview. They offered me the position while I was there last week."

"Mom, are you kidding me? What am I going to do? You can't really expect me to go!"

Hmmm, this is not quite the direction this conversation was supposed to go. "Mark, I'm not trying to force you, but because I love you so much and want the very best for you, I thought I could offer you this chance for a fresh start. When I thought of what you were leaving behind, all I saw was drugs and undesirable friends. I can see now that this is a shock for you. You've lived in Austin your entire life, and I know I've dropped a bombshell on you with this plan to move to

Hawaii. But please consider it. I've made all the arrangements. Come on, give it a chance. You know we both need to get away from here."

"It seems to me you're punishing me by making this change before asking me first!"

"Why do you think that? Because I'm moving us to a tropical paradise?"

Mark jams the last of his fries in the burger bag. "You always twist everything to make your opinion or decision to be best."

"Actually, I prayed at length about this, Mark. The Lord is directing us to make this move, but at the time I didn't think you were in a place mentally to choose."

Mark sinks down in his seat. "If you say so."

"All I'm asking is you give this plan serious consideration."

Ruth prays to herself, "Father, I know this is your will. Please help Mark see it as well. In Jesus's name, Amen."

Chapter 2

The Move

R uth and Mark deplane in Honolulu. As they wait for their
bags, Ruth's phone vibrates. She answers it,
"Hi, Maria, we're just now getting our bags."

"Great, Ruth. I'm a little rushed for time, so I won't be able to meet you at the garage apartment, but Meylani will let you inside. I'll call you later to make sure the two of you have set up a cleaning schedule."

"Sounds good, Maria. You're such a lifesaver. I was beginning to think we'd be sleeping on the beach!"

"This works great for me since you and Mark are remodeling the garage apartment where you guys will be living."

Ruth recalls with a bit of guilt her conversation with Mark on the move and hopes she can make good on this remodeling task. Ruth watches for the suitcases on the baggage carousel.

"With housing costs here, I'm happy we actually found a place! Thanks again." *I've got to figure out how to tell Mark he'll be remodeling the garage apartment where we'll be living in Kailua. Luckily, our new home is close to the bank and in fact, I'll actually be able to walk to work, which is great since the Beemer hasn't arrived in Honolulu yet.*

A cab pulls up, and Mark drags their four suitcases over to be stuffed in the trunk. Determined to release all the recent stress, Ruth takes a deep breath and absorbs the amazingness of Hawaii. This is God's plan. It'll work out.

Mark's New Friend

The taxi driver jumps out of the car and rushes to help Mark with the suitcases, all four gigantic ones.

"*Aloha*, bro, let me get those."

Mark looks up and stares motionless at our driver. Ruth nudges him. Mark smiles, and says, "Sure."

The cabbie is average in height but muscular and looks like his picture most likely graces Hawaii post cards. He's tan from many hours in the sun, and his hair is thick and could use a good brushing! His name tag shows his name as "Leek."

"Bro, with all them bags only one of you will fit in the back seat. Do you mind sitting up front with me?"

"Nah, I'm fine with that."

"My name is Alika Ihohali, but everyone calls me Leek." He stretches his hand toward Mark.

"My name is Mark Max, and I go by Mark."

"Funny guy, huh? Where can I take you guys?"

Making a face, Mark says, "To our new home in Kailua."

"Are you saying you are not happy about moving to Kailua? There are people who would love to be in your shoes."

"Well, they can have 'em."

Leek smiles as he chats with Mark. Ruth sees that Mark continues to be bummed by the move. She sighs as she listens to their conversation.

"Bro, you will be living near one of the best beaches in the world! I windsurf there all the time. Would you like me to teach you?"

Mark's countenance changes immediately. "I would like to learn. Do you surf as well?"

"Yep, I practically live on the North Shore, and in my spare time, I scuba as well. Are you going to work or go to school?"

"Oh, I'll have to work to help my mom out. There's probably not going to be much time for surfing."

"Mark, I'm changing your name to Kanuha."

"Why?"

Leek looks pointedly at Mark, "It's Hawaiian for 'one who sulks.'"

"Hey!" But Mark laughs anyway.

"Okay, Canoe, where in Kailua are we going?"

"Leek, I thought my name was Kanuha."

"I am shortening it to Canoe. Easier. Oh, perfect, here's the highway we need."

Ruth thinks, *who would have thought a cabbie named Leek could get Mark out of the doldrums? The Lord always has a surprise waiting.*

Ruth hears Leek talking about Kailua. "Kailua is a pretty cool town. Close to beaches, shopping, and restaurants. It has everything tourists and locals love."

Mark responds, "That sounds right up my mom's alley. She was excited too because her new bank job is within walking distance."

"Oh, which bank?"

"Oahu National."

"That's definitely the biggest bank in Kailua, Canoe. Now I have a good idea where we're going."

"Can we drive by it on our way to the house so I can see it? I know Mom would like that."

"Sure. Now, which street in Kailua are we going? Kailua is our next exit."

"Mom, tell Leek the street name."

"It's on South Kalaheo Avenue."

Leek asks Ruth, "Is it oceanfront?"

"It's actually a garage apartment in front of a beachfront vacation rental. A friend of ours manages it and is letting us stay there while we remodel it. Or I should say, while Mark remodels it." *Uh-oh, this is not how I was planning to tell Mark.* Ruth looks apprehensively at him.

"You have construction experience, Canoe?"

"Mom, this is the first I've heard of this! You know my construction ability is practically nil! I haven't had much construction experience!"

Leek interjects, "Actually, I do some construction myself, if you'd like some help."

"Well, yeah…how about you just do it! I can't believe you, Mom!"

"Mark, I know this is a surprise, but Maria offered it, and since it's so expensive to live here, I jumped on the opportunity. Okay, so I didn't think it all the way through."

"Yeah, exactly."

Leek doesn't comment as he looks for the street. As he turns, he asks Ruth to give him the number.

"Here it is. The bank is about three blocks southwest of here. Let me take you there before I drop you off."

Leek points out the beautiful Oahu National branch building on Kuulei Road. "It's a small replica of the Iolani Palace. If you notice, it's right on the edge of the Kailua Elementary. The school district made an agreement with the bank, and so the bank was able to lease the lot here. It's rather crammed up next to the school, and the parking garage is in the basement. As you drive through the school parking lot, you see the bank first, which includes the drive-through and garage parking entrance. Plus, I'm told the vault is actually in the basement as well and is quite impressive. Customers take an elevator down to access their safety deposit boxes."

Ruth stares at the palace replica and mentions, "That's unusual. Most recently built banks have smaller vaults as most no longer offer safety deposit boxes. They're not as popular these days. I can't wait to start my job there tomorrow and see it."

"Well, let's get you guys to your new home. It's right up here."

Meylani

The garage to the big beachfront residence is right on the street, literally. Unlike most garage apartments, this one is on the side rather than over the garage. Leek's cab can barely fit on the driveway without hanging into the street.

22

As they grab their suitcases, a young Hawaiian woman steps from the apartment to greet them. She has hair tied in a pony tail that hangs to her waist. She's wearing denim cutoffs and an orange tank top. Mark stares at her as she walks up.

Ruth steps up to her with her hand out and says, "You must be Meylani. I'm Ruth Max. This is my son, Mark, and this is our new friend, Leek."

Shaking Ruth's hand, Meylani answers, "Hi, Leek. Long time no see. Ruth, so glad to meet you guys. Let me show you your place. I've just finished cleaning it."

Ruth smiles, "What a nice welcome. We certainly appreciate it."

"Yes, I'm happy to help out. Maria said you may also be helping me to clean the vacation rentals until she can hire someone. I understand you're only available at night. Usually, there are one to three to do daily, and each house takes two to four hours to clean. Ruth, I'll try and leave you the ones that only take two hours."

"Oh, well, yes, that's what Maria and I discussed." Ruth crosses her fingers. "Mark can help as well when I'm unavailable." *Cleaning and bank work? What was I thinking?*

"Good to know. Let me show you your new home."

Leek winks at Meylani as he and Mark drag the suitcases across the threshold. All but Meylani stare at the place with surprised looks. Everything looks like a throwback to 1960 and not in a good way! The floors are covered with a stained and cracked, possibly gray, linoleum. There is an old, also possibly gray, couch and a dining chair in the front room. To the right, what appears to be the kitchen must be walked through to get to the tiny bathroom. The kitchen has one stainless steel counter with an old refrigerator and freestanding stove. A tiny table with one chair (the mate is in the small living room!) rounds out the space.

As they walk into the tiny bedroom, Mark says, "Where's my room, Mom?"

Ruth says cheerfully, "Your room is the living room we walked through."

Mark drops the suitcases and storms out of the apartment.

Ruth sighs, "Sorry, guys, this move has been difficult for Mark. He'll come around." *I hope*, she thinks.

Leek gently sets down the two cases he's been carrying. "Let me go talk to him."

He walks out, and Ruth looks at Meylani and shrugs.

Meylani says, "Why don't you get settled? The closet does have a small chest where you can place some of your things. Believe it or not, there are many people who would adore living here. Maria must like you immensely to offer you this opportunity."

"I've told her many times how much I appreciate this, Meylani. You don't have to convince me. It's Mark that will take some convincing."

"Maybe it will help if I pick you guys up some lunch. There's a great plate lunch place a few blocks from here. My car is just down the street at another vacation rental, so it will only take me a short time to pick up the food. I'll get the barbeque plates and bring them back. Maybe that'll get Mark in a better frame of mind."

"You're a lifesaver. Would you get an extra one for yourself and Leek as well? Maybe we can go eat it on the beach." Ruth hands Meylani some money.

"Sure. I'll be back in a minute."

Ruth takes a deep breath. She opens the first suitcase and thinks, *Well, I might as well start now putting our things away.*

The Showdown

Leek walks past the vacation rental home knowing it's quite the opposite of the tiny garage apartment. He sees a soaring roofline and double teak entry doors. He goes around the side of the house and sees the pool but doesn't see Mark. He keeps walking, passing the bushes surrounding the pool and steps on the sand. It's a beautiful setting with waves crashing on the beach just thirty feet in front of him.

He looks down Kailua Beach searching for Mark in his black Hurley hat. Smiling sadly, he thinks he has an inkling of why Mark is unhappy. He sees Mark only a few yards away sitting in the sand, sifting it through his fingers.

Leek walks up and sits down next to Mark.

Mark jerks his head toward Leek. He doesn't say anything.

Leek looks at Mark, takes a deep breath and says, "Getting sober can be a challenge, bro."

Looking away from Leek, Mark growls, "Look, *bro*, no offense, but you don't know me."

"You're right, I don't, but I've been there. I feel like I can recognize the reactions of a fellow addict."

Still sifting the sand, Mark looks up at Leek. "Okay-y-y, I hear you, but I've got this."

"If you say so. You may not be ready to hear my experience, but I can tell you what helped me get a handle on my using. My life is clean and sober because of Jesus."

Mark raises his eyebrows. "Now, you sound like my mom. She's always talking about Jesus. Where was He when I was using? Why didn't He stop me?"

"I'm thinking he probably did nudge you, but you didn't pay any attention. You have free will to make your own choices. You can either take the good choice or the bad choice."

Mark grumbles, "Look, I know you mean well, but just give me a break, okay?"

Ruth and Meylani are walking toward them with some to-go Styrofoam containers that Ruth hands to Leek.

Leek lifts the lid of one of the containers, "This smells so good. Is this from Kailua BBQ?"

Meylani hands Ruth her change. "It sure is. Ruth thought it would be nice to eat on the beach."

The containers are passed around, and food establishes a new comradeship of four *disparate* souls.

CHAPTER 3

A New Chapter

Ruth is up early for her first day on the job at Oahu National. She's nervous and excited as she steps out of the shower, which continues to leak as she towels herself dry. She grimaces, thinking of the huge challenge she has accepted in remodeling this place.

It actually needs gutting. I agree with what Mark said last night that Maria may possibly be taking a little advantage of us by having us do the remodel, but I realize I never mentioned we don't have any construction skills. That wasn't smart. I better get Mark to call Leek today, and hopefully, he can at least steer us in the right direction.

Ruth dresses in khaki slacks and a navy blazer. *This looks smart but not too dressy.* She brushes her short dark hair, puts on her favorite coral lipstick, and looks closely in the mirror at the new wrinkles by her eyes and mouth. *If I didn't dye my hair, I would look ten years older. Of course, I am forty-seven. In the past, my friends complemented me frequently on my youthful looks and compared me to Holly Hunter. They wouldn't think that now! Isn't it funny? Of all the difficulties of Mark's addiction, looking older is hitting me the hardest. I never realized how vain I've become!*

Ruth walks into the kitchen to make coffee. She looks out to the other room and sees Mark sleeping on the couch, an empty ice cream container on the floor. Ruth sighs and catches herself. *I need to stop doing that if I'm going to meet this challenge optimistically.*

She smiles and places the Kona coffee in the coffeepot. As it brews, she thinks about her new position at the bank.

My title is operations administrator, and I'll be handling all customer service issues. It's interesting my new manager didn't mention the safe deposit box vault. Well, I'm sure I'll get to see it today. It'll be interesting to see the basement setup for it.

Ruth pours her coffee in an old Starbucks mug, grabs her purse, and heads out the door for her walk to work. She stops at the couch, leans over, kisses Mark's hair, and steps out to officially start her new life.

Oahu National

Ruth walks into the lobby of the impressive Iolani branch of Oahu National. It has a rich tropical feel with koa wood surfboards hanging on the walls, amazing paintings of Kailua and Oahu scenes plus elaborately carved wooden couches in the customer waiting area. She steps up to the teller counter with five teller windows and asks for Daniel Chen. As she's speaking to the teller, Daniel walks around the teller counter toward her.

"Ruth, welcome to Oahu National. I see you've met Katrina. Let me introduce you to everyone, then I can go over your duties with you."

Ruth shakes hands with Daniel. "I'm excited to be here. This building is incredibly beautiful both outside and inside."

"I'll give you the full tour as I introduce you around. This branch has only been open a year because it took three full years to build. The small lot size created some building challenges for us that continue to cause some issues even after completion."

"A new friend of mine mentioned the parking garage and the safe deposit box vault are both underground. He even mentioned the vault is quite large. It seems the building already has people fascinated."

Daniel smiles at Ruth's comments and takes her behind the teller line. He introduces her to two additional tellers, Sharon Lipscomb and Brenda Smith. Both ladies nod at Ruth as they place their cash in their teller drawers.

"You mentioned to me previously we have three full-time tellers and one part-time. Correct?"

"That's correct. Daniel Barlow works through lunch. He has classes in the late afternoon. He should arrive by 9:00 a.m."

"Wow, two Daniels. Does that get confusing?"

Daniel smiles. "Sometimes."

He and Ruth leave the teller line and walk to the office next to it. It's a woodframed glass enclosure with more of the beautiful carved teak furniture.

Ruth remarks, "This furniture is amazing. Where is it made?"

"Actually, it was all made in Bali. We had it all custom made to fit each of the offices and lobby. This office is used by one of our commercial loan officers, Mike Cunningham, who's currently at a client meeting. I'll introduce you to him later."

Ruth caresses the desk with her hand. "Is this a dragon carved into the desk?"

"Yes, it's quite detailed, isn't it?"

Ruth nods but feels her stomach tighten. Anything with dragons makes her uncomfortable. The first thing that comes to mind is Revelation 12:9, "This great dragon—the ancient serpent called the devil, or Satan, the one deceiving the whole world—was thrown down to earth with all his angels." *Remember, this is just a desk. Don't overreact! You would think the place was crawling with demons or something.*

As they keep walking, Ruth looks back one more time, takes a deep breath and whispers a short protection prayer. *It couldn't hurt, could it?*

Daniel shows her four more offices including his own. They all look alike except Daniel's. As he is the president of the Kailua branch, his is big and imposing. They step out of Daniel's office and he points to the nearest desk.

"This is where you'll be working, Ruth. I have many projects in which I'll need your assistance, so being near to one another will be helpful."

Daniel's office is to the right of the teller line with a full view of the lobby. Ruth thinks the location will be great to facilitate her ability to assist customers. "Great, may I put my purse in the desk?"

"Sure. Would you like to see the safe deposit box vault?"

"Absolutely!"

Daniel walks Ruth to the elevator. He pushes the *B* button, and down they go. The elevator door opens, and thirty feet ahead is the biggest vault door Ruth has ever seen. It's round and must be ten feet in diameter with a big wheel for opening it.

As they step off the elevator, Daniel describes the basement layout. "As I mentioned, in addition to the vault in front of us, immediately to the right a hallway takes you to the two restrooms. Before the restrooms, an additional hallway branches left. All the rooms down that hallway open to the right starting with the security officer's office, followed by the break room, and the conference room."

With her head jerking from forward to right and back again, Ruth feels like Linda Blair in *The Exorcist*. "There is more branch space down here than I would have thought. Seems like a good use of space."

"I'll get you a vault combination. That way, you; Mike, the loan officer; Axle; and I will be the only ones able to open it and assist customers with their safe deposit boxes. Two people open the vault at 9:00 a.m. The branch security officer, Axle Besic, is most likely in the break room getting himself a cup of coffee."

Ruth is thinking it strange with four other employees, Daniel only allows three to assist customers with their boxes. *And why is the security officer assisting customers? That could get awkward should Daniel and Axle both be out of the branch simultaneously.*

"Here comes Axle now."

Ruth is taken aback by the man approaching them. *Axle doesn't look like any banker I've ever seen. He must be six foot three, at least, and is a blonde Arnold Schwarzenegger look-alike. In fact, they could be twins. At least his smile is welcoming.*

"Axle, I'd like you to meet my new assistant, Ruth Max. Ruth, this is Axle Besic."

Axle extends his hand to Ruth, and they shake. As big as he is, for some reason, he's not intimidating. "With Mike out so much with clients and meetings in Honolulu, it'll be nice to have someone available to help open the vault. Good to meet you, Ruth. I'm head of security for the branch."

"Wow, I've never worked for a bank with its own in-house branch security. Is it because the neighborhood is not safe that we have full-time security?" Ruth directs her question to Daniel.

"No, the neighborhood isn't a problem. As you've seen, we have some expensive artwork and our insurance carrier lowered our premiums significantly once we hired Axle."

"Daniel, do you want me to show Ruth how the vault works now, or should we do that later?"

"There's no time like the present."

"Ruth, as with most bank vaults, two combinations are needed to open the door. We'll need to have the vault service company come to program the one you choose to use." Axle inputs his code. "Also, the vault door is on our alarm system." Daniel walks up and inputs his combination as well, turning the round handle to the left until he hears a loud clink. The vault slowly opens.

Amazed at the size of the door, Ruth holds her breath as she imagines the size of the interior.

Daniel pushes the open door against the wall. "We have two hundred safe deposit boxes in the vault, most of which are rented. We have a few of the large ones available, but all others have been leased."

Ruth looks at the vault and is surprised it's so small. *Why have they put this huge vault door on a normal-sized vault?* She notices a door at the back of the vault. *It must lead to a supplies area, but I'm only guessing.* She's tempted to scratch her head but figures Daniel may think she has dandruff, so she keeps her hand to her side.

Daniel looks toward Axle. "Would you please call Jantzen Security and have them come today if possible to set Ruth's combination?"

"Sure. I'll get on the phone right now." As he steps a few feet away, he pulls his cell phone from his pocket and pushes a preprogrammed number.

"So what do you think, Ruth? Pretty impressive, huh?" Daniel asks.

"Actually, I was curious. Why such a large vault door?"

"Originally, they had intended the vault to be larger. They had planned to allow customers to store larger items such as paintings and sculptures. The large door was ordered, but the city would not allow the amount of concrete needed for the larger space thus the door remained and the vault itself became smaller."

"Well, the door will certainly keep everything safe. The door in the back of the vault, what's behind that?"

"We were able to take some of the space for the safety deposit box files. There are file cabinets holding those as well as some of Mike's loan files. We plan to scan them soon, eliminating the need for storing the paper here. Let's go to the break room and get a cup of coffee to take upstairs so we can talk more about things you need to know."

Ruth steps into the big room. "Nice break room. That's a super big coffee machine. It looks like one I would see in a fancy coffee shop."

"Yes, it does. I'll show you how to operate it before we go back upstairs. When the big wigs come here for their monthly board of directors meetings, the next of which is tomorrow, they want lots of coffee and this machine will do the job. We have all the great add-ins as well. We have cream delivered each week as well as chocolate syrup. I can make you a mocha if you like."

"I would love that. This place is getting better and better!"

Daniel laughs and prepares two mochas to take back to his office.

CHAPTER 4

Mark and Meylani

Mark rubs his eyes. *I actually slept well considering how upset I was when I went to bed. Mom doesn't understand the strain I'm under trying to stay sober and now dealing with this move and remodeling. I don't even know what she wants me to do today. Well, I'm not calling her. She can call me and let me know.*

He looks at the ceiling painted light blue and thinks about the old Texas tradition of painting outside porch ceilings blue to prevent birds from nesting.

Were they trying to do the same here? he asks himself with a smirk. He hears something vibrating and realizes it's his phone. He digs around on the floor for his jeans and grabs his phone from the back pocket.

"Hello."

"Hey, Canoe, you up?"

"Not really, Leek."

"I thought I could come by after my shift today, and we can do some work on the apartment. And if you're good, maybe I'll bring my windsurf board."

Mark's eyes light up a little. "When?"

"How about three o'clock?"

"Sure."

"Well, if you don't want me to come…"

Mark sits up on the couch. "No, no, I do. I'm still half asleep. I'll see you at three o'clock."

"Good, see you then, bro."

Mark stretches, and there's a knock on the door. "What is this, Grand Central Station? Who is it?"

"Meylani."

Mark jumps up, trips over his jeans, and almost flies into the kitchen. He takes a deep breath. "Just a minute." He pulls his jeans up and opens the door and greets his visitor. "Hey."

"Hey to you too, sleepyhead." Meylani has on another comfy-looking turquoise tank top and denim cutoffs. "I thought you could go with me on two of my cleaning jobs today to see how it works."

Realizing he's staring, Mark quickly says, "Oh, I'd be thrilled. Let me eat a bowl of cereal real quick and brush my teeth. Come in, and I'll hurry." Mark rushes into the kitchen.

"Don't worry about wearing a shirt on my account," Meylani quips as she lays her cleaning supplies on the kitchen counter. "Are you really just now getting up?"

"Yeah, the jet lag, you know," he mumbles as he pours milk over his Cocoa Pebbles.

"Sure, it is. Your mom didn't seem to have any problem. I saw her walking to work on my way here. Anyway, you should be getting up with the chickens coming from Texas with a four-hour time difference."

Mark grimaces knowing he wasn't making the greatest impression on Meylani. After inhaling his cereal, he dashes to the tiny bathroom to brush his teeth. "I'll only be two shakes."

Mark grimaces again. *I can't get over this tiny place Mom and I are sharing. Was she crazy agreeing to us living here? Of course, she was crazy. She just had us move halfway across the world, didn't she?* Mark looks in the mirror as he brushes his teeth and sees a man with no future and a drug-soaked past. *What am I doing here? I could have stayed back in Texas, but no-o-o, I came here thinking I could run away from my past. Maybe the big book from AA that Tranquillo made me read was right. I'll take it one day at a time.* He takes a deep breath and concedes to his image in the mirror. *I know Mom's only trying to help me!* He feels a twinge of guilt. *Maybe I'll even ask Leek about going to an AA meeting. That would certainly please Mom.* Mark washes his face, grabs a T-shirt, and opens the door right into Meylani.

"Oops, sorry. I'm ready."

"I wondered if you fell in the toilet or something. Come on, Canoe, let's go over to the big house."

"I guess that nickname is going to stick," Mark says under his breath.

Meylani unlocks the big house back door, and the alarm beeps as they walk to the wall by the washing machine. Meylani enters the alarm code, and the beeping stops.

"As you can see, we're going through the utility room. Each vacation rental has clothes washing soap and cleaning supplies, but I also bring some of my own things that I like to use, like polishing clothes. Let's start in the bedrooms. We'll take the sheets off the beds and grab all the dirty towels so we can start washing. Hey, Canoe, you with me?"

"Wow, this house is amazing—and big! It will take us all day to clean this place."

Meylani laughs a big belly laugh, "And you have somewhere else to be? With my experience and your help, we can get it done in three hours."

"Well, I could be at the beach," Mark mutters as he runs to the next bathroom and grabs some towels. Mark has never paid much attention to architecture or building styles, but he's awestruck by the beauty of this house. Each bathroom of the five total is fancier than the last. As he picks up the towels from the last one, he thinks his mom would absolutely love this place. Right then and there, he promises himself he will start working hard because his mom deserves something this beautiful to live in. He rushes to the utility room and runs into Meylani. He smiles for the first time in weeks and says the proverbial, "We have to stop meeting like this."

Meylani looks at him, amazed at what a difference his smile makes, and feels her chest tighten and her heart beat a little faster. "I agree."

They both smile and cram towels into the washer.

A Change in Attitude

"Canoe, I truly believe this is a record time in getting this house cleaned since we finished it in only two and a half hours. Thanks for listening to my instructions and following them to the letter. Everything looks spic and span, and it's much easier having a helper! Here, I have an extra key, so I'm going to give it to you should I need you to clean this for me on your own. Don't come into the house again until after the new renters leave because we don't want any dirt getting tracked in. I spoke to Maria, and she wants me to assign houses to you and your mom. I'll let you know when and where. She even said she would offer you a permanent job since her other cleaner quit today."

Mark thinks about what Mey said. "That's pretty cool. I could certainly use the money. Hey, Mey, Leek is coming over at three to talk remodel and show me how to windsurf. Do you have time to come to the GA and give us your suggestions? You see these fabulous houses all day long. I bet you have some great suggestions that will help us."

She smiles, "You're calling your place GA?"

"Yeah, garage apartment."

"GA, huh? Well, okay, I can spare a few minutes. You probably need to write and draw a plan so Ruth can show it to Maria. She will need to make the final approval before you actually start work."

Mark looks deflated. "I was hoping we could start tearing down stuff today."

"Talk to your mom, but I would say wait."

"Well, let's get to the GA!"

Mark starts running and Mey lets him. As they get closer, they see Leek sitting cross-legged at the entrance of the GA, pushing in a number on his phone.

"I was just texting you. I thought you might be at the beach."

"Hey, Leek. Mey is going to come in with us and give us some ideas on what she thinks would work well in a vacation rental."

"Good idea. I see you have been doing some manly cleaning!"

Mark grabs one of Meylani's rags and pops Leek with it. "I'd rather work with Mey than drive an old cab around."

"Hmmm, you have me there."

They all three walk into the GA. No one is smiling at this point. Mark's things are scattered on the couch and floor. Mey sets her cleaning supplies on the kitchen counter again since there really is nowhere else to place them. Leek pulls out a measuring tape.

"This probably needs to be the first order of business. Help me measure every square inch. We're going to need it."

And just like that, a trio is formed for the GA project.

Mey pulls out a small notebook from her cleaning carrier. She walks through the apartment and goes into the one bedroom. Opening the closet door, she raises her eyebrows at the amount of space and gets an idea.

"Guys, come in here."

Mark and Leek come inside the bedroom. As Mark really looks at it, he notices it's not quite as tiny as he thought. For some reason, it has a king-size bed that takes up most of the space. Mey motions the guys over to the closet.

"This place actually has a walk-in closet. All the storage is in here. If you make the closet smaller, you could add some space to the bathroom."

Leek and Mark start measuring.

Leek says, "That might work. This closet is seven by ten feet. That's bigger than the kitchen and bathroom together."

"Maybe we could have a small closet, add some space to the bathroom and a little more space to the kitchen. The other thought I have concerns the garage. We could bump a wall out into the garage and also get more space there. It's not as though the vacation renters need a three-car garage."

"Canoe, has Maria ever said what the budget is for this remodel? We're talking some major changes here."

"She may have told Mom, but I haven't heard a number. I'll call her." Mark pulls out his cell. He pushes Ruth's name in his address book and hears it ringing. It goes to voice mail, and Mark leaves a message. "She doesn't answer, but hopefully, she'll text or call me back."

"Leek's right, Canoe, before we even start the process, we need a dollar figure to work from. I have to go to my next house anyway. You and Leek are going windsurfing, right?"

Mark's eyes light up, and he looks at Leek who has a sheepish expression on his face.

"Uh, Canoe can we do a rain check? My boss just texted me and asked me to do another shift today. Sorry, bro."

Mey jumps in and says, "Why don't you come with me to my next house? You can earn some more money, and I can finish earlier, so we might be able to spend an hour at the beach."

"Sure, that sounds great, all except the cleaning part!"

Mark's phone buzzes, and he looks down. "My mom says the amount she was told is $25,000."

Both Leek and Mey look shocked. They both start to speak at once. Leek stops, and Mey says, "That's such a paltry sum for what it will take to make this nice. That's so sad. Maria must be thinking of doing the minimal, floors, paint, and possibly countertops. I'll talk to her about it. The homeowners are obviously footing the bill, so hopefully, Maria can get them to up the number."

"They must be thinking they're saving lots on the labor cost since we get the GA free until the remodel is finished."

Leek again looks at Mey, and they both nod slightly, understanding the enormous cost of doing anything in Hawaii!

"Probably so. I've got to get going. Mey, let me know what Maria tells you, and I can come again tomorrow to help write up what materials will cost. We can do two plans, one with what we want and a second one on what the cheapest route will cost. Canoe, don't get discouraged. Once the homeowners see our idea, they may decide to go big."

"It's okay, Leek, as long as we get it nicer. I sure appreciate you guys helping out."

Leek and Mey exchange an amused glance, surprised by Mark's change of attitude.

"No, problem, bro. We are bros now, right?"

With a nod, Mark smiles, waves, and walks with Mey to the next house while Leek backs his cab out of the driveway.

1994: The Escape Continues

As they pick up their gear, Kim lowers his head and the others follow suit.

"Lord, thanks for being with us every step of this journey. We seek your protection, Jehovah Shamah, as we take the most critical step in our travel over into Croatia. We ask for guidance and direction for each step. Amen."

Looking out toward the horizon, Kim is mesmerized by the beauty of the sunrise. The gray skies slowly begin to change to blue as the sun brightens the skyline.

Oskar adjusts his backpack and explains, "We're only a few miles from the gate. It's best we don't walk long once the sun rises. We'll walk one mile further to see if we can find a place away from the crowds. I have wire cutters so we can cut through the fence rather than climbing. When we actually cross over, one of us will need to watch behind us, one to watch for anyone on the other side of the fence, and one to help the person going through the fence. Any questions?"

"Wire cutters, that's a good idea. I was thinking we would have to climb over it. Do we know if it's electrified?" Hanadie asks.

Oskar pulls the wire cutters from his backpack and hands them to Hanadie. "When I last visited with Zoran, the inspector for the last apartments we built, he told me the cost was expensive so the fence was not electrified. There are guards walking the fence line on a sporadic basis. Let's hope today isn't the day for that."

"Amen to that. Although I wouldn't mind watching a few Serbs fry as they try to climb after us." Hanadie spits as he hands the wire cutters back to Oskar, who doesn't bother to argue the idiocy of that statement.

They continue walking without speaking. After about twenty minutes, the sky darkens as storm clouds move in. They see people on a road through the trees.

Oskar holds his hand up. All stop. Oskar looks up the hill as Axle walks up with the map. He whispers, "We can hide until dark. We've got until midnight to get to the water. How far is it once we cross over into Dubrovnik?"

"About eleven kilometers, so still about three or four hours of walking. If we leave right at dusk, we should be able to make it, but it'll be close. Let's move up the hill to those bushes and sit behind them next to the cliff. We can stay dry and watch the crowds this afternoon, then we can leave."

CHAPTER 5

A New Friend for Ruth

aniel sticks his head out of his office. "Ruth, I had planned to take you on a first day lunch, but something has come up requiring me to go to Honolulu. Do you mind if Axle takes you instead?"

Ruth turns around in her chair to face Daniel. "No, that will be fine. Is everything okay? Is there anything I can do for you?"

"No, but thanks. Axle is on his way up, so I'll see you later this afternoon. Why don't you observe the tellers after lunch? It will give you a good introduction to our systems."

"Sounds great, Daniel. I'll see you when you return."

Ruth sees Axle walking across the lobby, twirling his car keys. "How does Hanadie's sound as a place to take Ruth to lunch?"

Daniel raises his eyebrows, "Well, it's a good thing Oskar approves your expenses. Oh, and it's been pretty quiet in the lobby so Mike shouldn't have to worry about customers coming in to access their safety deposit boxes."

"Oh, it won't be that expensive for me 'cause I know the owner. You ready, Ruth?"

Ruth shuts down her computer. "Sure. Thanks for agreeing to take me on short notice."

Axle smiles, "I never want to miss an opportunity to take a pretty lady to lunch."

Ruth laughs. *Axle is certainly more laid-back than he first appeared.* "Well, I'm pretty hungry, so let's get going."

Walking into Hanadie's, Ruth and Axle are led to a table on the patio. Ruth looks perplexed, and Axle asks her, "Is something wrong?"

"No, this place is nice, but it actually doesn't look much like a five-star restaurant."

"Don't let the simple surroundings fool you. This may be the best restaurant on the entire island. It usually takes weeks to get a reservation, but as I mentioned earlier, I know the owner." Axle waves a tall man over to their table. Standing up, Axle shakes the owner's hand, "Hanadie, I'm so glad you're here today. Good to see you. Let me introduce my new coworker, Ruth Max. Ruth, this is my cousin and one of my very best friends, Hanadie Besic."

Ruth's mouth is hanging open, for sure catching flies. She takes in Hanadie's good looks at a glance—blue eyes, patrician nose, slightly graying blond hair, and an interesting dent in his left eyebrow ridge. As she stands to shake his hand, she realizes he's even bigger than Axle and is in awe as he leans down to kiss her cheek. He smells as good as he looks and is wearing a stunning silk aloha shirt with dress slacks and what looks like a pair of thousand dollar shoes. *Things must be going well in the restaurant world!*

"It's a pleasure having you visit my humble business. I'll have the waiter bring you the best items on the menu. Did Axle tell you we've been friends since we were children? He and I immigrated to the US together as young men during the Bosnia conflict."

Ruth feels goose bumps as she sees Hanadie's look of anger while he rubs his eyebrow scar. It's so fleeting, she might have imagined it. Nonetheless, she feels rather unsettled and turns to look at Axle as he answers Hanadie. "Yes, it was Hanadie, Kim, Oskar, and myself. We were the best of friends and helped each other during our first years in a new country."

Hanadie asks, "Has Ruth met Kim yet?"

"No, she and I only met this morning. This is her first day on the job, which is why I'm bringing her to the best restaurant in all of Hawaii."

Again the goose bumps as Hanadie places his hand on Ruth's shoulder. "Ruth, it has definitely been a pleasure. Anytime you need reservations, call me directly. I must get back to the kitchen to place your order." He hands Ruth his business card and reaches to punch Axle in the arm. "Later, buddy."

As they sit, Axle says, "So tell me what brought you to Hawaii, besides the job, of course."

"My son, Mark, is twenty-two and was having some difficulties with drugs. He went to rehab near where we lived in Austin, Texas. I felt he and I both needed a change of scenery, and we had fallen in love with Hawaii on previous visits, so this seemed the perfect choice. My husband died five years ago, and Mark has been deeply depressed since then. Both our hearts were broken. I'm hopeful this place will start the healing process for both of us. So how did you get here all the way from Bosnia?"

"Well, we've been blessed since we arrived in the US. All of our families were killed during the Bosnian conflict in 1994, so Oskar helped us escape by sneaking us out of Bosnia across to Croatia. He paid for someone to ferry us to Italy. The boat dropped us off at night, so we were able to sneak into Rome and get to the US embassy. We sought asylum and were able to get a rush on the immigration process. Oskar did all the work. It's actually a miracle we made it to the States. He's the owner of the bank, so you should meet him at tomorrow's board of directors' meeting. I'll have him tell you the story if he will."

Ruth leans back in her chair, "Wow, that's an incredible story. Getting the group of you out of Bosnia was an impressive feat. He's obviously focused and committed to achieving his goals. I will be honored to meet him. Plus with him being the big boss, I better be on my best behavior! You and Oskar work at the bank, Hanadie has this lovely restaurant, and your other friend, Kim, right? What type of work is he doing now?"

"You're new to Kailua, but have you heard of Ho'omaika'i Church?"

"No, how do you pronounce it again?"

"Ho-o-mika-e."

"That's a mouthful. I haven't heard of it. Mark and I need a church to attend, so tell me about it."

"It's a mouthful for sure. The name means 'bless' in Hawaiian, and as you can imagine, most people shorten it to Ho'o. It's Kim's church, even though he wouldn't say that at all, but would tell you it's God's church. Kim is the human light of the church. The congregation is quite big and in fact thousands attend each Sunday."

Ruth spills her tea. "Thousands! That would intimidate me. I'm more comfortable with a smaller congregation."

"Why don't you let me take you and your son this next Sunday, and you can decide how you feel? This will give me an opportunity to introduce you to Kim as well. The music itself is worth the visit."

Ruth regards Axle thoughtfully. She was moved by Axle's story and doesn't see a reason to say no. "Sure, what time is the service?"

"At 10:30 a.m. I can pick you guys up. Ho'o is only twenty minutes from the bank. How far is your place from the bank?"

"I'm super close. It's been great since my car won't be here for probably another month. I walked today."

"Boy, I would love it if I could walk to work! But doing it every day would get old, I imagine. E-mail me your address and phone number, and I'll pick you up at 9:30 a.m. Will that work?"

"Yes. I look forward to it. It'll be interesting to experience a service with so many parishioners."

Two waiters walk to the table, each carrying a tray full of delectable food, and the aromas start their mouths watering. The plates are placed on the table, and Ruth and Axle immediately make their choices.

This has been a great day so far, Ruth is thinking as she stuffs a piece of the broiled *ahi* in her mouth.

Can This Be My Son?

Ruth walks into the apartment, turns around, and walks back outside to make sure she's in the correct location. It certainly seems the right place. She walks back inside and is still dumbfounded. The place is spotless. She smells something good coming from the kitchen as well. The first thing she does is take her shoes off realizing she should have known better than to wear her dressy flats while walking. Her feet will do better tomorrow wearing her walking shoes. She checks the kitchen to determine what's making the fabulous smell and opens the oven. There are hamburger patties staying warm, and buns and chips are ready on the counter. She walks dazedly to her room and places her shoes in the closet. As she changes into capris and a T-shirt, the screen door slams.

"Mom, you home?"

Ruth walks into the kitchen and sees Mark making cheeseburgers.

"Mark, this is so great, and I'm starving. The place looks amazing as well. How was your day?"

"Let me finish making our burgers, and I'll tell you all about it." Mark points his finger at Ruth. "Sit down, Mom, and rest your feet. I almost have yours ready."

Ruth sits and sighs—as she has been doing too much lately—and smiles. Mark places a plate with her cheeseburger and all the fixings in front of her.

"I have a treat for you. One of the houses I helped Mey clean today left a couple of diet drinks in the fridge, and Mey said I could bring them home to you."

"Mark this is a feast, and the drink tops it off!" Ruth has mayonnaise dripping down her chin and starts to speak as Mark laughs. "So you call Meylani Mey now?"

As Mark sits down with his burger, he says, "Yeah, it seemed natural to shorten her name. I found out she spells her name, M-e-y-l-a-n-i, which looks like you'd pronounce it Meelani, but *e* in Hawaiian is pronounced like a long *a*." He takes a huge bite of his burger and takes a large chip and tries to cram it into his mouth with his burger bite.

Ruth laughs as well and continues to eat. She hasn't felt this good in a long time. It feels wonderful. *Thank you, Lord.*

"Mom, I made $200 cleaning houses today! Maria offered me a paying job because one of her cleaners quit recently. It isn't fun work, but doing it with Mey makes the time go quickly. Leek had planned to take me kiteboarding, but he ended up having to work an extra shift today, so we had to postpone for another time. Plus, he, Mey, and I did some planning for the remodel. You probably guessed that from my text today."

"You did have a full day! Mark, thank you for cleaning the GA. I couldn't believe how quickly we trashed the place! It looks good, and this burger ain't bad either! That walk home helped me build up my appetite. The walk in the morning is enjoyable but not so much walking home in the evening. I'll be glad when the car arrives."

"When's that going to happen? It'll be nice to have our own transportation."

"I'm thinking another few weeks, but it could happen sooner if there was room on the ship going out the day we dropped it off in LA. I'll call the shipping company after we finish eating. Once it comes, you could actually drop me off in the mornings and pick me up in the afternoons so you can have the car during the day."

"That's a great idea, Mom. I'll be able to pick up supplies for the remodel. I hope it shows up tomorrow!"

Ruth is flabbergasted by Mark's demeanor. *Where is the sulking guy from yesterday? Lord, of course, this is from you. Thank you for providing Mark with Your shalom peace so he can enjoy our new home.*

"Mom, both Mey and Leek think the $25,000 Maria quoted you is too low for what needs to be done at this place. Mey was going to talk to Maria, but do you think she can get the owners to increase the budget?"

"Not having seen the place, I didn't question the amount. After seeing it, I can see how the costs could add up. Why do Leek and Mey think the amount is too low?"

"Mey had a great idea on how to enlarge the place by pushing the bedroom wall into the garage. It might allow an additional bedroom and, of course, a bigger bath and kitchen."

"That would be great, but I'm not sure the homeowner cares about that."

Mark looks disappointed.

"I'm glad Mey is talking to Maria though. They have a long-term working relationship, so Mey may be able to convince Maria to talk to the homeowner. Let's pray about it." Mark is eating his food, so Ruth prays, "Lord, we wish to follow your will in this. We look to you for the remodel provision of this apartment. We thank you for this and all your blessings. In Jesus's name, Amen."

Marks says, "Amen!" simultaneously.

Ruth smiles again. *God is good.*

CHAPTER 6

Meeting Oskar

The next afternoon, as Ruth finishes preparing coffees in the break room, she hears the elevator doors open.

Axle leads a group into the conference room and barks, "Where are the five different coffees I need for our esteemed board?"

Ruth jumps and sees him smirk. "You almost gave me a heart attack! I have them all on this tray. If I tell which one is which, can you remember or do you need for me to follow you into the conference room?"

"Definitely, I need you to come with me. It'll be a great opportunity for you to meet everyone."

Ruth's nerve meter jumps up. "Okay," she says with a crack in her voice.

"Come on, it'll be fine. I promise they won't bite too hard."

"Nice."

Axle carries the coffee tray while Ruth walks behind him with another tray holding cookies. Most of the board are already sitting except for two individuals, a man and a woman. The man looks up and grins when he sees Axle. The lady does the same.

Ruth notices the lady likes Axle, really likes him. She looks more interested in Axle than the coffee and the cookies.

Axle sets the coffee tray down and introduces Ruth. "Good afternoon, everyone. I'd like you to meet the new addition to our team here in Kailua, Ruth Max. She's our operations administrator and works with Daniel."

47

Beaming, Ruth says, "Hello, everyone. Axle gave me directions on your coffee preferences, and hopefully, I prepared it just the way you like it! Let me hand them out to each of you as Axle introduces you."

The standing gentleman walks over to Ruth with an appraising look. He's shorter than Axle and stocky with white hair, a dark tan, and dark eyes. Everything about him seems dark except his white hair.

"Hi, Ruth. I'm Oskar Soto. I'm the chairman of the board." Oskar looks toward the woman on the other side of him. "Sara Chin is the comptroller."

Ruth hands both Oskar and Sara their coffees. "Mr. Soto, here's your mocha, and Ms. Chin, here is yours, black."

Sara takes hers and saunters over in her Manolo Blahnik shoes and long sweeping black hair to speak to Axle without acknowledging Ruth.

Oskar takes his coffee and sips it. "Ruth this is an excellent mocha. I look forward to coming to Kailua just for the coffee. You make it much better than Axle! But, just an FYI, I've started drinking my coffee black. Less calories." He stares at length into Ruth's eyes.

Ruth can't put her finger on it, but even though he's smiling and friendly, the eyes seem to convey the opposite. Ruth's nerve meter jumps up again. *What is it with my nerves today?* She reaches for a coffee to hand out, but Oskar reaches for it simultaneously. His hand surrounds hers, and she gasps. She takes a breath and says, "This one is for Daniel."

"Great, I'll hand it to him."

There are two coffees and one water left on the tray: one for Axle and one each for the two additional board members. Oskar introduces the two additional men.

"Ruth, this gentleman is Tom Kawahee, who is over the lending department of the bank. He prefers black coffee as well."

Ruth picks the cup up and hands it to Tom, who thanks her.

Oskar introduces the other gentleman as Frank Jantzen. "Frank owns the security company we use."

Ruth smiles, "Mr. Jantzen, I understand you drink water." Ruth hands him a bottle of Fiji water with a glass. "Your technician got me set up yesterday with all my security codes. He was quite efficient."

"Please call me Frank." He sits down and says to Oskar, "I need to get back to the office. Are we starting the meeting or what?"

Oskar pulls out the chair next to Frank, and Ruth picks up the drink tray and walks out.

Church

"Mark, I'm finished in the bathroom. I'm sorry I took so long. My hair was uncooperative after being at the beach this morning."

Mark looks up from the kitchen where he's eating his toasted waffle. He sees his mom put barrettes in her hair to keep it off her face. "Well, I'm finishing my breakfast. I was hoping you changed your mind about church." Mark thinks, *Wait just a second, and…*

"Mark, when have we missed church?"

Mark laughs. "Practically never!" He grabs his jeans from the other kitchen chair and walks two steps to the bathroom.

Ruth smiles. She picks out her navy Keds, which should go well with her white ankle slacks and sleeveless aqua blouse. She goes into the kitchen, rinses Mark's breakfast plate, and hears a car pull up outside. She peeks out the window and sees a Chevy Tahoe pull into the tiny driveway.

"Mark, please hurry. Our ride is here."

Ruth walks outside and meets Axle on the path to the door.

"Good morning, Axle. Mark is finishing up and should be ready in a few minutes. Why don't you come in and see our humble abode?"

"Good morning to you as well. You certainly live in a great neighborhood. I think I'm jealous!"

"You are correct. The neighborhood is amazing as is the beach that's only 150 feet from our door, but our little place is not what you would expect."

They walk inside, Ruth first. Axle tries to not look shocked by the "humbleness" of the apartment.

Ruth quickly states, "We truly were blessed with this place. The homeowner needs it remodeled. And the vacation rental manager, Maria, negotiated a deal for us that if we do the remodel, we can live here rent free until the work is finished."

"That's a wonderful friend you have to provide this opportunity for you. You seem to have many skill sets!"

"Oh, Mark and I are going into this with no remodeling skills. Crazy, huh? We actually met someone our first day here, Leek Ihohali. He has remodeling skills and is going to help us. What an amazing blessing."

Axle is trying to follow everything Ruth is saying while he nods. "It certainly is a small world. Actually, I know Leek from church. He attends Ho'o."

"Really? That's great. I hope Mark and I get a chance to talk to him while we're there."

Mark walks through the kitchen tucking his Western shirt into his jeans. He walks up to Axle and offers his hand.

Axle grabs it and says, "Hi, I'm Axle, a coworker of your mom's. You ready to go hear some great music? Your friend, Leek, is on the worship team."

Mark smiles with anticipation as they exit the apartment and walk toward Axle's SUV. "Cool. I didn't know Leek was a musician."

Ruth turns to Mark in the back seat. "Since Leek is on the worship team, we should see him today if we can find him among the thousands of parishioners."

"Thousands? Mom, we've never attended a church that big. The building must be like huge to hold that many people."

Ruth looks toward Axle to explain.

"We conduct services in the Blaisdell Center on Ward Avenue. Originally, we were located at Aloha Stadium because, initially, it seemed the best place for the number of people who attended and the growth of the congregation. The downside of going there is it's an open stadium, so last year we moved to the Blaisdell. Have you been to either location?"

"We did go to the stadium on previous visits for the swap meet in the parking lot but never to the other place you mentioned. Did you say it was called the Blaisdell Center? It must be big as well if it can accommodate the large congregation. Don't let us get lost from you, or we'll never find you!"

"Don't worry, I have my phone and your number. And yes, it's quite large, and yes, it's the Blaisdell, but it only holds around eight thousand where as the stadium holds fifty thousand! So the Blaisdell actually works out better as we tend to have four thousand to six thousand attend each Sunday." Looking in his review mirror, Axle changes subjects. "So, Mark, tell me what you've been up to your first week in Kailua."

"I've been cleaning houses with a friend of mine. She, Leek, and I are working together on remodeling the apartment where Mom and I are living. We were hoping the owner would up their $25,000 allotment for the remodel, but they won't." Mark frowns, but then smiles. "Leek and Mey put together a plan for us, and I think it looks great. Mey is having her manager take it to the owner for approval, so once we receive that, we'll get started."

The big SUV is comfortable, and Mark and Ruth sit back and enjoy the ride as Axle drives them to the Blaisdell.

As they pull into the parking lot, Ruth is amazed at the crowd already there. Axle finds a space, pulls into it, and they all get out and walk together to the entrance.

Axle directs them to the area where the worship team has their equipment. Mark spots Leek tuning his ukulele and hastens over to greet him.

Axle calls out to Mark, "Your mom and I are going to meet the pastor. Our seats are right over there on the first row. We won't be gone long." Axle turns back to Ruth. "While Mark visits with Leek, let me introduce you to Kim." Axle takes Ruth's elbow and directs her to a door down the hall outside the sanctuary where he knocks and walks inside without permission.

A man is sitting on a small couch reading his Bible but stands up and steps toward Axle, and they hug.

"Ruth, I would like you to meet Jokim Zec or Kim as we call him, the pastor of Ho'o church. Kim, Ruth is a new coworker of mine, and I have brought her and her son here for the service."

Kim smiles at Ruth and reaches his hand to clasp hers. His eyes are the most startling green she has ever seen. He also has a major scar on the right side of his temple. The hair does not grow around it, so it gives the appearance of a receding hairline. A white section of hair from the scar up through to the crown of Kim's head is a startling contrast with his thick black head of hair.

Ruth returns the smile and says, "Hi." She thinks, *What is it about these Serbian men with their scars? The trip out of Bosnia must have been pretty rough.*

"Ruth, thank you for coming to Ho'o today. The worship team will be starting in a few minutes, and I know you'll enjoy hearing them. Axle, why don't you take Ruth to your normal seats? I'll visit with you guys after the service."

"Sounds good, Kim. Ruth, let's go get Mark and find our seats."

Ruth and Mark follow Axle to three front row seats. The lights are bright and showcase the worship team warming up on the stage. The group starts with Hillsong United's "Oceans," and Ruth feels certain this is going to be a great place to worship Jesus. Axle shakes hands with a gentleman already seated. Ruth notices its Oskar and nods. Since the music is starting, Axle doesn't introduce Mark to the owner of the bank.

After playing three songs, the worship team plays their last note, and Kim jogs to the podium. The crowd stays standing and claps for at least a minute. Kim nods and speaks.

"This is the day the Lord has made, let us rejoice and be glad in it! He made this paradise for us to enjoy, and it truly is a blessing to be here with you all. Let's talk about grace. It's my favorite topic, and I want to explain the amazing grace God showed me when I left Bosnia with my three best friends.

One of the dictionary definitions for 'grace' is forgiveness, charity, and mercy. God provides us full grace, which includes forgetfulness. Once we repent, God no longer remembers our sin. I think for most of us we can't conceive of such a merciful God. Do we forget when our boss reprimands us in front of a coworker, or when our spouse forgets our birthday, or when someone crashes into our car while texting? We desire to do so, but bitterness may intrude, getting in the way of us forgiving and forgetting. God is so much bigger than our past, his shalom peace has been my saving grace. I go back again and again to Ephesians 2:8–9 in the NIV. *'For it is by grace you have been saved, through faith and this is not from yourselves, it is the gift of God.'* Let me dissect this for you so you truly can feel the blessing of what Jesus has done for you."

Kim expands his discussion using Ephesians as his starting point. He goes more in depth and realizes as he's closing his remarks, a great feeling of freedom has come over him.

Kim stops for a moment and bows his head. Looking back up, he takes a breath.

"When Axle, Hanadie, Oskar, and myself escaped Bosnia, we saw many atrocities that still haunt us. I actually had to kill a fellow Serbian when he attacked me as we were cutting through a fence near the border of Croatia and Bosnia. He didn't understand why we were escaping. Even though he had his gun aimed at Hanadie at the time, I still feel great remorse over what occurred. This is when I truly began to experience God's grace and love. So I can tell you from my own life that believing and receiving forgiveness that the Bible talks about is the beginning of freedom." He looks to where his friends are seated and smiles.

Ruth looks toward Axle, and his face is white and drawn, but she notices he returns Kim's smile. *It's hard understanding war when one has not lived through it.* She looks over at Oskar, who looks uncomfortable for a moment but his face calms. As she starts looking around, many in the congregation are looking at Kim with sympathy on their faces. They continue to listen.

"God spoke to me that day in Bosnia." Kim pauses. "He said, 'I'm with you. Do not be afraid.' I know many of you have not heard this full story. I can understand the horror you may feel because I lived it. I've told you in order to help you know that God has an amazing plan for each of us. My struggle has brought me closer to Jesus, who has given me joy. He's waiting right now to provide you the same. Today, I wish to provide prayer for all those hurting so Hanadie, Axle, and I, and the rest of our prayer team will be down on the floor. And all are welcome to come for prayer."

Ruth notices Hanadie coming from the back of the auditorium, moving toward Axle at the front of the stage. Han steps next to Axle, immediately speaking to him loudly in a foreign language. Axle shakes his head, steps away, and greets another who comes forward. Han narrows his eyes, looking out toward the audience, and nods at Ruth.

Ruth hesitantly responds with a small wave as she and Mark wait in their seats. They hear many of the comments from others as they leave.

"Wow, Kim actually killed someone. I didn't understand the Bosnian conflict much. Who were the good guys and who were the bad guys?"

"I don't know either. Let's look it up."

Mark turns to Ruth with a serious look on his face. "It really gives you a perspective on what they experienced, huh, Mom?"

"Yes…" Ruth watches as Oskar walks down the aisle for prayer.

"Who's the man with the white hair?"

"He's the owner of Oahu National."

Mark's eyebrows rise a half inch. "He looks like a Mafia type to me."

Ruth looks at Oskar again. *He does have that slick appearance with his expensive tailored clothes plus his tan and the white hair.* She wonders how he acquired all his wealth and decides to ask Axle at the bank the next day.

Death in Bosnia

As the sun sets, Axle nudges Oskar to wake him from a deep sleep.

"Should we take our chances crossing into Croatia? I've been watching for the last two hours, and I haven't seen one guard walk down this section of the fence."

Not quite awake, Oskar jerks up, knocking Axle back into Kim. Oskar grabs at Axle's arm to keep him from falling.

"Sorry, I was having a nightmare about Ena and Luka. I can't stop thinking of their last hours and it's driving me crazy. Damn the Americans!"

Kim places his hand on Oskar's shoulder. "Remember, Ena and Luka are in heaven now and live a perfect life. Harboring this hatred in your heart is making you sick, Oskar. We're going to a free society so we can worship and live as we please. That's something, isn't it?"

Oskar looks through bloodshot eyes at Kim. "But, Kim, you know if the Americans had become involved before now, Ena and Luka might still be alive."

Hanadie adds to Oskar's words. "Yeah, Kim, how can you be so forgiving of the Americans' nonchalance?"

Kim squeezes Oskar's shoulder as he looks at Hanadie. "I must forgive, Han, or I will not be able to move forward with my life." Kim's eyes tear up. "Don't forget who the real villains are, those who murdered them. I miss them too, guys. Shall we try cutting through the fence as Axle suggests?"

Oskar groans as he stands. "Of course. No more lollygagging, as the Yanks say."

Everyone stands with their packs, looking to Oskar for direction.

"Let's walk a little further up the fence line in a more wooded area so we can have more cover."

As they walk a hundred feet or so, Oskar asks, "Who brought a knife? I believe we need to trim some of this dead vine so we can get to the fence."

Kim steps up as he pulls a large knife from his pack. He looks around but doesn't see anyone and starts hacking at the overgrown foliage.

Axle places his hand on Kim's arm to stop him. "Sh-h-h."

They all stand perfectly still but hear nothing.

"I thought I heard something besides the cutting of the vine."

Hanadie growls, "You're just being paranoid. We're running out of time. Kim, do you want me to take over?"

Kim thankfully hands the knife over. "Han, my hand is already sore." Kim massages his hand as he walks into the trees away from the camp to "take care of business" and Hanadie laughs. "You always were a wimp!"

Only two minutes pass when they hear, "Halt!"

As Hanadie jerks back, his forehead is scraped by the jagged edge of the fence. He steps back, still holding the knife, blood flowing down his face as the hostile Bosnian guard advances cautiously with his gun aimed directly at Hanadie's heart.

"Drop the knife!"

The knife drops to the ground as the guard begins waving the gun at Hanadie and, in Bosnian, says, "All of you line up together so I can see you."

Hanadie, Axle, and Oskar stand closely to one another as Kim noiselessly steps up behind the guard, presses a knife to his neck and nervously states in the same language, "Drop the gun, and I won't hurt you. We only want to cross the border."

The other three men look in shock at Kim while the guard responds, "If you don't drop the knife, I'll kill at least one of your friends before you can even make the first cut."

Axle mouths in English, "You're going to have to kill him."

The guard pulls the trigger, but the bullet goes wide as Kim struggles to cut the guard, who jerks back, headbutting Kim. Without further thought, Kim stabs the guard in the side. The guard drops his gun as he falls to the ground; and Kim, in shock, stands there. Wiping the blood from his face, Hanadie picks up the gun as Axle grabs Kim and touches his eyebrow. "You okay?"

Kim jerks back from pain; and not answering, he bends over to pick up his pack, unzips a pocket, and pulls out the wire cutters. Hanadie stuffs the gun in his backpack as Oskar grabs the wire cutters and steps to the fence.

"We have to make this quick. It won't be long before someone starts searching for this guy. Check his pockets, Hanadie in case he has something we can use. Is he still alive?"

Hanadie places his fingers on the guard's neck, "I'm no doctor, but I don't feel anything. Should I shoot him to make sure? Does someone else want to check?"

Oskar looks in shock at Hanadie but responds as he cuts the wires of the fence, "We don't have time for all of that. Hanadie, get over here and help me."

Hanadie moves the guard to have access to the knife. He pulls it from the body and watches blood gush from the wound. In a swift move, he uses the knife to slit the guard's neck from ear to ear and mumbles, "All my restaurant training came in handy." He wipes the knife on the grass and adds it to his pack, and with one more swipe to his face, he steps over to assist Oskar.

Axle whispers to Kim, "How come you had two knives?"

Dazed and in shock, Kim responds, "They were my dad's, and I didn't want to leave them behind."

CHAPTER 7

Back to the Bank

R uth looks at the clock on the wall. *The research of this issue on a customer's safety deposit account is taking me way too long.* She picks up her papers and heads to the basement for Axle's thoughts on setting up the box contract with a trust as owner.

As she takes the elevator down and walks to the break room, she's thinking a mocha sounds pretty good about now. Amazingly enough Axle is making one as she enters and he hands it to her.

She smiles. "How did you know I was coming down here?"

"I heard the elevator and guessed it was you." He starts preparing an additional one for himself.

Ruth leans against the counter. "I saw Oskar and Hanadie at church yesterday."

"Yes, Oskar's been involved since the beginning. Leasing the Aloha Stadium seemed a good idea, but the staggering price was daunting even though Oskar gave Kim the money to pay it. Once our lease agreement was up, we moved over to the Blaisdell Center. As I mentioned on Sunday, the stadium was really too large, and with the open roof, it was uncomfortable the few times it rained. We're blessed now because we have enough tithes coming in, so Oskar no longer needs to supplement Ho'o to pay expenses."

"Axle, how did Oskar get in the banking business?"

Axle sips his coffee and adds some sugar. "In Bosnia, he was in the construction business as a foreman for an apartment complex construction company. His father had a little bit of money when he died, which provided Oskar with funds to start his own company there. He gave that company to a friend when we left. When he got to the US, he started doing basic construction work, and once the company where he worked saw his work ethic and skill, they promoted him into management roles. He learned how the construction business worked in the States and started his own company, Soto Construction. He moved into commercial construction and eventually started building bigger and bigger commercial buildings. We were in Salt Lake at the time. When he took all of us on vacation to Hawaii in 2005, he was mesmerized by the water and the history here. After researching the construction situation, he saw he could get involved in commercial remodeling jobs in Honolulu, and he talked all of us into moving here. The rest, as they say, is history."

"Okay, and the bank?"

"He did some remodeling of the Honolulu branch location and became friendly with the previous bank owner, Richard, who was ready to retire. They became good friends and spent time going out on Oskar's outrigger together. Oskar asked a lot of questions and became educated about the bank and the profit that Richard was making. Over time, both Richard and Oskar came to the conclusion that Oskar would make a good banker. Oskar sold Soto Construction in Salt Lake and here. He decided to focus all his energy on the bank."

"That was a major change. Is the bank doing well then?"

"It certainly doesn't have the profit margin the construction company had, but it does well enough. I almost see this as a hobby for Oskar. He lets his executives do most of the work."

"And you!"

"Yeah, yeah, that's true, but I like the many nuances of the bank. If I was doing strictly security, I'd get bored."

Ruth drinks the very last drop of her mocha. "Axle, could you help me with this contract I'm working on?"

"Sure. I can give you a few minutes. Oskar has asked me to run an errand and pick up some supplies for the outrigger he's building."

"Wow, what can the man not do?"

"Not much. He continually amazes me. I'm sure you've noticed the wood surfboards hanging in the branch. He made those himself and is now working on his second outrigger."

"I'm surprised he has time for that, but you said he leaves most of the management of the bank to the execs."

"Yes. He loves hanging out at the bank and particularly loves the Kailua branch. Getting it established has been his main focus. Now he likes doing his woodworking and keeping tabs on the bank on a more low-key basis."

"Does he have a big workshop at his home then?"

Axle hesitates. "He does have a workshop at his home at Ewa Beach. Here, let me look at your contract quickly before I leave."

Ruth hands it to him. She compiles in her mind all the Oskar details and decides to look at the wooden surfboards upstairs when she returns to her desk.

"The contract looks fine, Ruth. I have to leave so I'll see you tomorrow."

Axle walks Ruth to the elevator. "Ruth, Hanadie is creating a new dish at the restaurant tomorrow night and suggested I bring you and Mark by to try it. Would you both like to come?"

"Wow, that is an unexpected pleasure! Sure, Axle. Let me check with Mark and make sure he doesn't have plans. That is super of Hanadie to think of us."

As Axle leaves the branch, he calls out, "Let me know."

"Will do."

Ruth hurries to her desk as her customer will be coming in soon to sign the contract. She's thinking of Oskar and how great it is for her that he opened the Kailua branch.

Daniel sees Ruth and calls to her from his office, "Ruth, Daniel is out of balance in his teller drawer. Could you please help him? Mike and I have a loan committee meeting that I need to attend."

Ruth looks at her watch and answers, "Sure." She runs over to the teller line. "Daniel, let me help you."

"Thanks, Ruth. Hey, did you order cash for the branch today? We were balancing the branch vault today, and I noticed it was getting low in hundreds."

"I did, and I barely made it by the deadline too! I did it in the middle of completing a safety deposit contract that I just discussed with Axle."

Daniel steps aside for Ruth to count his cash. "I need to tell you my fall school schedule is changing. Do you think going forward I could close instead of working through lunch? I have a noon class every day but Friday."

Ruth really wants to sigh but says instead, "Daniel, let me talk to Katrina and see if she's willing to work the early shift so you can close. I'll let you know tomorrow."

"Ruth, I don't know what we did before you came. Honestly, we had to run things with just the four of us most days."

Ruth blows her hair out of her eyes. "Let's count your cash again, and see what we find."

CHAPTER 8

What's Happening at the GA?

Ruth drags herself the last few steps to the GA. She shuffles inside and calls out to Mark. There's no response, so she goes to the refrigerator and opens the door. She grabs a soft drink and thanks Mark's new job as a house cleaner.

As she sits on the couch and puts her feet up, she can see some work has been started in the bedroom. The sheet rock has been removed from the closet wall by the bathroom.

I guess Maria received the final plan approval. Mark and Leek didn't lose any time getting started.

Ruth lays her head back against the couch and starts thinking about all the new men in her life. The first one to come to mind is Axle.

Gee, when I first started working there, I thought he was only the security officer. He seems to be as knowledgeable about operations as security, which is a good thing for me since Daniel spends all his time on lending. It's nice to have a friend when you're new at work. I learned so much today about Oskar. The skill used to carve the wooden surfboards hanging in the lobby is off the charts. Oskar is a true artist, which doesn't correlate somehow to his bank demeanor. I'm going to ask him how he became interested in woodworking next time I see him.

Daniel is so darn busy with lending I would be floundering without Axle's help. I thought Daniel and I would be working closely with one another, but that hasn't happened at all. I understand what my part-time teller Daniel meant today about what it must have been like at the branch before I arrived. I get the impression Axle didn't help much in the lobby before I got here, so the tellers constantly called the main Honolulu branch with questions. At least I know I'm needed!

Ruth's eyes shut, and she immediately falls asleep.

Outside, a few houses down the street, Mark and Leek are putting Leek's tools in the back of his cab. Leek asks Mark, "How is Ruth liking her work at the bank?"

"I guess okay. I hardly see her. She leaves at seven and gets home around the same time. She's so exhausted, she eats and basically falls asleep on the couch every night. I've been sleeping in the bedroom because I hate to wake her up. Leek, let's go to an AA meeting tonight. I feel super stressed, and I'm not sure why. Let me go check and see if she's back at the GA, and I'll let her know our plans."

Leek rubs his neck and moves it side to side. Thinking for only a moment of his exhaustion, he takes a deep breath, smiles, and nods in assent.

Mark walks into the GA and sees Ruth snoring on the couch. *Dang it. How am I ever supposed to talk to her when she is always asleep! I'm going to have to wake her up though.* Mark steps over to the couch and gently touches Ruth's shoulder, "Mom, you awake."

Ruth's mouth turns into a smirk. "Yes-s-s-s."

"Good, Leek and I are going to an eight o'clock meeting. He'll bring me back home."

"Okay, be good. Don't drink up all their coffee." Ruth turns over and pulls her shoeless feet up on the couch.

Mark takes a beach towel and lays it over her. "Don't worry, Mom, I'll drink all the booze instead."

Ruth's eyes fly open, and Mark starts laughing.

"Hey, brat, that wasn't funny."

"It was until you freaked out. I was only kidding!" Mark stomps out the door, yelling to Leek. "Let's get going."

Ruth slumps on the couch. She's thinking she will have to apologize to Mark. *The brat.* She smiles. *Darn, I forgot to ask him about going to Hanadie's tomorrow night. He's going to love it when I wake him up in the morning to ask him.* Ruth pulls the towel back over her and snuggles under it and is immediately back asleep.

*****

The next morning, Ruth drags herself off the couch and tip-toes into the bedroom to get her clothes. She steps up to the bed and stands for a moment watching Mark as he sleeps. A tear slides down her face as she prays, "Father, you have blessed us both with this move. Thanks for Mark's sobriety. He's a changed person. Please guide me, Holy Spirit, on the best way to continue to help him and to help our relationship blossom. In Jesus's name, I pray. Amen."

Ruth realizes the remodel has required her clothes be moved out of the closet. She speaks up. "Mark, where did you put my clothes?"

Mark mumbles, "In the bin behind the couch."

"Since you're awake, I need to ask you something. Mark!"

"What, already?"

"You don't have to get pithy. Hanadie has invited us to try a new dish at the restaurant tonight. Would you like to go?"

"No."

"I thought you would enjoy that. Why don't you want to go?"

"Mom, did you forget I meet with my sponsor on Friday nights?"

"When did you start doing that, brat?"

"Now who's getting pithy? I told you several days ago. Don't you remember?"

Ruth looks at Mark blankly, "Are you sure?"

He groans, "Yes, remember you and Leek and I were sitting on the beach when I told you. You were all excited I was getting involved in AA."

"Oh, sure. What time will you be home?"

"What do you care? You'll be gone anyway."

Ruth winces. "Mark! I'm sorry I've been featherbrained lately, but I have been so busy at work…"

"Yeah, too busy. I'll be home at 10:00 p.m. I'll go to the 8:00 p.m. meeting, then meet my sponsor for an hour afterwards at that Kailua Coffee place. How about you? When are *you* getting home?"

Ruth takes a deep breath and says, "Listen, brat, I'll be home before you! I gotta go so let me get in the shower."

Mark puts his pillow over his head and mumbles something Ruth is pretty sure she's glad she didn't hear.

At the bank, Ruth disengages the alarm. She checks around the branch to ensure everything is okay before setting the all-clear signal. Normally, she would not open the branch without another employee waiting on her in the parking lot, but having seen Sharon on Kainalu Street, she knew she would arrive at the bank soon. Ruth goes down to the basement to ensure the conference room is prepared for the afternoon monthly meeting. Daniel had invited her to attend because he wanted her to take notes and e-mail them to all the board members. She likes that he invited her although she already has so much other work to do as well. The good news is he trusts her to be at the meeting. *I'm really looking forward to seeing Sara Chin again.* And laughing, she says, "I really crack myself up."

She notices a couple of lights on that she had turned off when leaving the previous night. It unnerves her at first, but she thinks, *it must have been the cleaning crew. I'll have to remind them of the lights that should be off and those that should be left on.* She turns on the light in the conference room and starts setting the table with place mats, pads, and pens. *Oskar wants to protect the table from scratches so the mats should please him. A few brownie points couldn't hurt!* She notices dust on the table and thinks of the cleaning crew again. She realizes this is Friday and the cleaning crew came on Tuesday. Now she's super concerned. *Who came into the branch last night?* She hears Sharon open the door upstairs and hurries to take the elevator up. *I better call Daniel because those lights should not have been on.*

Ruth walks toward her desk to call Daniel and sees the light on in his office. She walks to the doorway and sees him speaking on his phone.

"Sure, Oskar, I'll make sure the lights are turned off." He puts his phone down and greets Ruth. "You look upset. What's wrong?"

"Daniel, I went down to set up the conference room for the board meeting, and the lights were already on in the basement. The cleaning crew didn't come last night, and I was the last one out of the building yesterday, so it got me worried. Should we review the security camera footage?"

"Don't worry, it was Oskar who came by the branch last night. Remember, I told you he has a key?"

"Oh-h-h, I didn't think of that possibility."

"Actually, he comes frequently at night. He usually remembers to turn out the lights, though."

Ruth has a questioning look on her face but shrugs her shoulders and asks, "May I ask what he does here after hours?"

"It isn't a big deal. He loves this branch and uses the conference room to work sometimes."

"Oh, okay."

"Look, I'm glad you were concerned, but there's nothing to worry about. Could I get you to pull up the credit report on Mr. Koohouli? I want to give him an answer on the home improvement loan he and I spoke about yesterday afternoon."

"Sure. Let me open the teller vault so Sharon can get her teller drawer, then I can get that for you."

Getting to Know Oskar

All the board members are seated as Ruth delivers each one their drink. Oskar smiles as he grabs the coffee she hands him and takes a sip and nearly spits it out. Ruth covers her mouth as Oskar coughs and wipes the dribbles from his chin.

"Oskar, I'm so sorry! I forgot you prefer your coffee black." She grabs his mug, scurries back to the break room and returns in only a few moments. She places his mug on the table in front of him with an apologetic look.

"No problem, I was just surprised." Pointing to the seat next to him, Oskar looks at Ruth. "Go ahead, Ruth, and sit here, and we'll get started."

Once seated, Ruth opens her laptop to take notes.

Oskar starts, "I want to speak to you about a community event I'd like the bank to help sponsor. As you know, there's a Pearl

Harbor Remembrance Day ceremony and presentation each year on the anniversary of the bombing of Pearl Harbor. I had an idea of something we could do that might be a moving gesture and wanted your input. As you all know, I've been building my second wooden outrigger canoe and I should have it finished next month. It could be a nice touch to fill the outrigger with flowers and row it to the Arizona during the benediction. I could even see if my pastor, Kim Zec, would be willing to do it. What do you think?"

No one responds immediately. Sara is on the other side of Oskar, looking at her cell phone.

Ruth timidly asks, "Would the military allow us to do that? I've heard if anyone tries to go into the harbor, they'll get shot!"

"Ruth, I think I've heard that as well. Can you do some research for me to see if it will be allowed?"

Sara gives Ruth the evil eye, and Ruth spills her coffee. While wiping it with a napkin, she says, "I will look into that for you, Oskar."

"Great, what do the rest of you think?"

Frank Jantzen looks off toward the bank vault but says, "I have to say, this may be difficult to get accomplished as the Navy is quite sensitive about anyone else in the harbor since 9/11. This seems a sweet tribute, and it'd be easy for them to check the outrigger before someone paddles it over to the Arizona. A Navy officer could do it, which might alleviate some of their concerns. I think it would be a nice touch. Maybe we could even make it an annual tradition. It would give us great publicity even though I know that's not your main intent. Thanks, Oskar, for thinking of it. Why don't you let me check on the military? I still know a few guys over there and can get the answer pretty quickly."

Ruth smiles, happy that one of her tasks has now been given to another.

Oskar looks at Frank. "I should have thought of that Frank since you were stationed here in the nineties. You were in the Navy, right?"

"Yes. I'll check into it and get back to you."

"You don't think they would let me paddle it, Frank?"

"Oskar, I don't think so, but let me ask. I could be wrong."

"Thanks again, Frank. What does anyone else have?"

No one else speaks up, so Oskar closes the meeting. "This has to be the shortest board meeting yet. We all have lots to do, so I'll dismiss everyone. Ruth and Daniel, would you please wait?"

"Sure, Oskar. We were expecting the meeting to last longer, so we allocated an hour to be here. Do you want us to stay in the conference room to talk?"

"That makes sense. Everyone else, you're welcome to leave. As soon as I hear from Frank, I'll update you."

CHAPTER 9

A Promotion

"I wanted to discuss a decision I've made concerning you two. Daniel, normally I would discuss this with you first since you are Ruth's direct supervisor, but you've been telling me about Ruth's superior performance, and I felt we could discuss together some changes I have in mind for all of us." Oskar turns to them both. "Daniel, Tom Kawahee has been offered a position with another bank, so his last day at the bank was last Friday. I would like you to manage lending for the entire bank as senior vice president of lending. I want to make Mike Cunningham, vice president of lending for the Kailua Branch, and Ruth, branch president of operations."

Ruth almost falls out of her chair. Daniel looks stunned as well. Daniel looks at Ruth, slightly grimacing, but smiles.

"Oskar, you know being an SVP is my dream job. I think Ruth is an amazing employee, and I don't want to offend you, Ruth. But, Oskar, do you think she's ready for this much responsibility?"

Ruth watches Oskar and thinks she sees the beginning of a frown, but it's so brief she decides she's wrong.

"Ruth came to us with years of bank experience, Daniel, and based on your comments about how she has basically taken over the running of the branch, I would answer your question with a yes. Do you have concerns?" Oskar pointedly asks Daniel.

Daniel looks at Ruth with a tentative smile and says, "You know, I'm going to say I don't, now that I have had a minute to think about it. All the employees trust and rely on Ruth's help. I've been out of the office a lot over the time she's been with the bank and all has run smoothly."

"May I say something?" Ruth asks.

Oskar nods.

"Axle has been a great help to me when Daniel's been out of the office, and of course, I've learned from Daniel as well. I can handle this new role and would consider it a great honor to do so."

Daniel looks pensive. "Let's give it a go. Ruth knows I'm only a phone call away should she have questions, plus as she mentioned, Axle is only a floor away downstairs."

Ruth is thinking, *Hmm, I feel confident Axle will be available to help. Knowing Daniel, getting his assistance might prove elusive with all he has on his plate.*

"Great, I appreciate you both and the work you've done."

Oskar looks at Ruth with a smile that does not quite reach his eyes. "Ruth, I like to get away from Honolulu so I can get more work done. I work many days each week in the conference room downstairs because I get interrupted frequently at my Honolulu office. This causes many of my projects to languish. I like to come in the afternoon and evenings so don't be surprised if you see my papers in the conference room. I'll try to remember to take my stuff with me, but I forget on occasion. Daniel, before you move your office to Honolulu, I would like you to review with Ruth all she needs to know to run this branch."

"Will do, Oskar. I can get that done on Monday and be in Honolulu on Tuesday."

"You're sure you can review everything with her in one day?"

"She *is* pretty bright, Oskar."

"So she is. Then I'll leave you both so you can start this process. Daniel, would you like me to tell the branch employees or would you rather do that?"

"I think it would be more significant coming from you, Oskar."

"Let's go upstairs and share the news."

Ruth stumbles as she stands up, still in a daze over the news.

Oskar reaches out and takes her arm. "You okay?"

"Yes, sir."

Ruth steps away from her chair with Oskar's help. She picks up her laptop and papers, and they walk to the elevator together.

As they do so, Oskar smiles with satisfaction.

Kaho Time

(*K*im, *A*xle, *H*anadie, and *O*skar meet periodically at a local hangout to reminisce and catch up.)

The bar is typical of most in the islands—lots of beer, maitais, laughter, and sand. Surf Shack is a typical name; but Windsurfer Shack might make more sense here because the windsurfers are part of the entertainment at Kailua Beach.

Four men sitting outside aren't watching the water activity but are talking and laughing as beer and colas keep coming.

Oskar looks at his three friends with satisfaction. Each has made significant accomplishments here on Oahu.

"Han, how's business at the restaurant? Last time I was there, the line was out the door."

With a quick swallow of shrimp, Han grins. "We had our best month ever, Oskar. I'm actually considering adding an additional location on Maui. What do ya think?"

Oskar and Axle exchange looks. "That's a pretty huge step, Han. I've seen other restauranteurs try that and ended up closing the second location. My advice would be to make sure you have an extremely talented manager and chef or it can't work."

Axle nods. "I agree. Hanadie's has showcased your culinary skills. You just might be able to pull it off! And not to change the subject, but great message at church on Sunday, Kim. Everyone in the congregation was moved. It sure is painful to remember those times, so I was surprised you could even talk about it."

"Yes, Axle, those times were difficult and painful, but God is so good. Look at all He has given us these past few years with Han's restaurant being successful, the church reaching thousands, and the bank providing work for many. It all goes back to Romans 8:28 (NIV), '*And we know that in all things God works for the good of those* who love him, who have been called according to his purpose.' That's why we continue to glorify God in all we do."

With a raise of his drink, Oskar shouts, "Here! Here!"

Laughing, they all click glasses.

Work at the GA

Leek and Mark are covered in dust and dirt. The GA bathroom and kitchen are gutted except for the toilet and bathroom sink. Leek grabs a couple of waters from a cooler and hands one to Mark as he sits on the floor.

"Mey said you and your mom can use the shower in the main house until we get this bathroom done."

"Thank goodness. Mom would have a coronary if she couldn't have a shower every day! I can't wait to show her the bathroom tile. The green glass subway tiles are the perfect tropical touch."

"The perfect tropical touch? You sound like a decorator!" Leek laughs. "You must have been spending too much time with Mey."

Mark blushes as he takes a big sip of his water.

"How are things going with you and your mom? I've noticed lots of tension lately."

Mark coughs and water dribbles down his chin. He searches for something to wipe it and uses his sleeve. "Leek, she works all the time. We argue constantly."

"Is it her work that's a problem?"

Mark mulls over Leek's question.

"Canoe, talk to me."

"Leek, I don't even know what's going on with my mom right now. I can't worry about her. I'm keeping myself together with the remodel work and you taking me to AA, but I'm still not sure I won't relapse. When I'm stressed, it's the first thing I think about. I'm still not completely sure I can live a sober life."

Leek looks at Mark with a calm smile. "You know there is a solution to your worry. It's the same thing that's keeping my life on track."

Mark whispers, "I know what you are going to say, but I'm afraid."

"There's no need to be afraid. I know it's scary to live without your crutch, but Jesus can help you. As it says in the Bible, His yoke is light and He will be with you in all your struggles."

"What does that mean, Leek?"

"Jesus has the ability to carry all our worries and concerns so we no longer need to do so. His love covers all, and He always has your back! What have you got to lose by opening yourself to the possibility of a life with Him?"

Mark closes his eyes. A tear rolls down his face. "I've been hearing this message for years. Finally, I think I'm ready…"

"You'll be surprised how easy it is because he wants us to come to Him." Leek places his hand on Mark's shoulder. "Repeat after me if you believe this. Jesus, I am sorry for my sins."

"Jesus, I'm sorry for my sins."

"Thank you for dying on the cross for me."

Mark whispers, "Thank you, Jesus, for dying for me."

"I believe you died and rose on the third day, and I give my life to you."

Sniffling, Mark clears his throat. "I *believe* you gave your life so I might live!"

Leek squeezes Mark shoulder, and Mark adds, "And I want to reiterate Leek's words." His voice rises in volume, "I do believe you died and rose on the third day. And I know my life will be forever changed." Looking to Leek for affirmation, Mark smiles.

Leek grins and grabs Mark in a bear hug. "Go to Bible study with me tonight, Mark."

Mark calmly looks at Leek and says, "Sure."

Oskar's Night Work

Later that night, Oskar enters the alarm code at the Kailua branch lobby entrance. He rides the elevator down to the basement, steps out, and walks to the conference room. Turning on the light, he puts his laptop on the table, stretches, and walks out to the break room. He can see the coffee machine well enough without turning on the light. Pushing the brew button, he waits for the process to complete. Once the brewing stops, he pours himself a cup of black coffee. He thinks about the mocha Ruth accidentally made him at the last meeting and chuckles. *Luckily, I didn't spit on everyone at the table!*

Walking over to the wall at the end of the conference table, he slides the paneling to the side. An additional vault door lies behind the paneling. He enters the digital combination and opens the door, revealing another room the length of the conference room. A work table stands against one wall of the room while in the middle of the room is a special stand holding a beautiful outrigger canoe, not quite finished.

Oskar hums as he moves a few feet down in the conference room and opens another wall panel, revealing a digital combination lock, which, after inputting the combination, he opens carefully, pulling out an odd bulky item.

I don't know why I look at this thing each time I'm here. It won't have changed any since I saw it last. Glad I've not told Axle about this cabinet. Too much to explain.

Replacing it behind the door, he secures the compartment.

Stepping back to the workroom doorway, he gazes at the far wall and smiles. He thinks about the additional room situated next to the vault store room known only by him and the builder. He feels in his pocket for the only key to this extraordinary panic-room apartment, feeling pleased he created a possible refuge for the future.

Finding his sandpaper, he turns on the Bose stereo and starts sanding. Oskar ruminates on Bosnia and 1994.

The escape happened according to plan except for the Serbian soldier who caught us trying to cut an opening in the fence in Dubrovnik. Kim has been remorseful about killing the man, but it was either Kim or the soldier. Those days were so crazy. The torture and killing done by the Serbian army was appalling, and we're Serbs! Then the NATO forces were a joke! If only the US had made a stand earlier, things would not have gotten so out of hand. Damn them!

Oskar looks down and realizes he has been sanding the same spot too long and throws the sandpaper down. He can't concentrate and decides to head home. He makes sure he turns off all the lights and all locks are engaged. He washes his mug and replaces it in the cabinet as he thinks about his current challenge. As he sets the alarm, he feels confident he will be able to create the perfect solution. He walks out to his car and drives home.

A Change in Circumstances

Ruth backs out of her space at the Port of Honolulu, glad at finally having her own car to drive! She'd received a text earlier that it had arrived, and she can't wait to show Mark. She speeds out of the parking lot, laughing and thanking God for her incredible new job. *All my work actually paid off.* Ruth sees the traffic has finally lightened, so she should get to Kailua in twenty minutes.

Ruth is practically giddy as she steps out of her Beemer. She sees all kinds of construction debris on the lawn and walks into the GA calling out Mark's name. His head pops up from the bedroom.

"Hey, Mom."

"I have some news." She walks over to the bedroom and sees there is now a door to the bathroom from the bedroom rather than from the kitchen.

Leek is doing tile work on the wall behind the tub.

"Wow, that green tile is fab!"

"Canoe said you'd like it. Look at these border tiles we're going to use." Leek holds one up next to the green tile. "Isn't this great? This silvery subway tile is a great contrast to the green. Mey decided this would work best."

Ruth is about to bust to share her news, but she's also pleased with the work Leek and Mark are doing. *Could things get any better?* "You guys have made some great progress, and it looks so-o-o much better. Guess what, you guys? I got a promotion today! I'm now the branch president of operations."

Mark's eyes get big. "Let's celebrate and eat out."

The screen door slams, and they see Mey walk in.

"What are we celebrating?"

"Mom got a promotion at the bank today and is going to make the big bucks so she's taking us all out to eat."

Ruth laughs. "Not quite the big bucks, but I'm happy to take everyone out."

Mey looks over at the big house and says, "Why don't we pick up some fish and steaks, and we can cook them on the grill over at the big house. I have to clean it anyway. Ruth, maybe you could help me clean while Leek and Mark cook the meat."

"I'd be happy to. I've been so out of pocket. You, Mark, and Leek have been doing all the work here. Let me help now because going forward I may not be able to do so."

"Canoe has been a huge help, Ruth. Maria made the right choice with you two. After so long by myself, I feel blessed with all the help now."

"Let me get changed, and I'll come right over. But hey, since Leek and Mark are working in the bedroom and bath, can I instead bring my clothes to change into over at the big house?"

"Sure. By the way, whose car is that outside?"

Mark jumps up and runs outside. Mey, Ruth, and Leek follow.

"Hallelujah!" Mark says as he grabs the car door and opens it.

"Mark, it's just our old car."

"I know, Mom, but it's been so long since we've had our own transportation. It feels like having a new car!"

Ruth nods, "You're right, it does."

"You have a BMW?" Mey raises her eyebrows.

"Yes, a ten-year-old one!"

Mark doesn't waste any time. "Mom, can I use the car tomorrow?"

"Yes, but why don't you come to the branch to pick it up, and I can show you my new office?"

"Okay. Leek, what are we doing tomorrow? Is there anything I need to pick up before you come by at three o'clock?"

"The tile store texted me that the flooring for the entire apartment has arrived for us to pick up. Do you remember where the store is in Honolulu?"

"Not exactly, but I can look it up online. How much will I be picking up? Do you think it will fit in the car?"

"Let's go look, and we can decide. If not, maybe you can get them to deliver."

Ruth goes back inside to pick up her shorts and tee and changes into her rubber slippers. Mark and Leek walk inside.

"Mey said she would see you over at the big house."

"I'm on my way. Mark, I'll text you when we're done. Mey and I'll go to Foodland to pick up the fish and steaks while you and Leek are finishing up." Ruth steps outside and hums "Oceans" by Hillsong United as she walks over to help Mey clean. *Man, I love this song! God is good.*

Ruth steps into the big house and looks for Mey. Hearing the vacuum cleaner, she wanders until she locates Mey in the master bedroom. As Ruth steps over the threshold, Mey holds her hand up as if she's a traffic cop. "Stop! I just finished vacuuming."

Ruth stops, takes a deep breath before responding. "Uh-oh, sorry about that. Where would you like me to start?"

"Sorry, if I came across a little abrupt. I have a lot on my mind today. Would you mind starting in the next bedroom after you change?"

"Will do, boss!"

Mey directs Ruth to each task that needs completing. Ruth steps right in and hurries through them. As Ruth blows the bangs from her eyes, she searches the house for Mey to see if there is any additional cleaning to be done. *I sure hope Mey is happy with the work I've done.*

Ruth calls out and follows Mey's voice to the kitchen.

"Did you finish cleaning the lanai?"

"I did." *What's the deal with Mey today? She sure is being Miss Bossy, which is not at all what I would have expected from her from our few times together.*

"I think we're completely done then. Let's sit and take a break."

Handing Ruth a drink, Mey motions toward the breakfast bar. They sit and say nothing as they sip their colas. Ruth starts a conversation hoping to uncover what may be bothering Mey.

"I haven't seen your folks at church the last couple of weeks. Is everything okay?"

Feeling her phone buzz in her pocket, Mey answers it as she walks out of the kitchen.

Smiling, Mey quickly returns to her stool. "If you had asked me yesterday, I would have had a different answer. Probably, I'd have cried and cried, and I would have had difficulty explaining the issues at my house."

With her attention fully on Mey, Ruth places her chin in her hands and says, "Well, by your expression, it looks like things are better, right?"

Mey doesn't hesitate. "My little sister, Lea, has been fighting leukemia and undergoing chemotherapy with little hope of full healing. Today, the doctor said she's in full remission!" Mey bursts into tears.

Ruth stands and engulfs Mey in a hug. As they cry together, Ruth begins to speak in her own wondrous language. Sniffling and clearing her throat, she looks up and sees tissues on the kitchen counter and grabs two while still keeping an arm around Mey's shoulders.

Wadding up the tissues Ruth gave her, Mey looks up. "Thank you for being here for me. I'm happy today, and I'm quite grateful for Jesus and his great love for Lea. You know who has been a rock for me during this time? Your son. I can't fully express the intensity of the friendship he has given me. Having him in my life has been the most amazing gift that I do not take lightly."

"God sends blessings in unusual ways. Hey, what about the steaks and fish? Should we go get them now?"

Mey stands up, looking around. "You know, I need to get home to be with my family. How 'bout a rain check? Did you see where I put my purse?"

"Actually, I think its sitting over there on the kitchen counter. And, of course, you should get home to your family. I'll finish and lock up."

Mey gives Ruth a quick hug, "Thanks, see you later."

CHAPTER 10

The New Job

R uth's phone alarm goes off at five thirty the next morning. She turns over and groans because her neck is sore from sleeping on it funny. Yawning and sitting up on the couch, she leans back, closes her eyes, and starts her daily prayer.

"Father, thank you for the amazing blessing of this new job. Give me the strength and knowledge to lead the staff well and have everything I do glorify you. Thank you for Mark's continued sobriety and his new friends Leek and Mey. In Jesus's name, I pray, A-A-Amen!"

Finally wide awake, she decides to steal some of Mark's Honey Bunches of Oats and goes to the fridge to get the milk. She looks around for a bowl since the cabinets have been removed, leaving everything piled on the table including food and miscellaneous utensils. She spies an old silverware packet from a tray as well as a bowl from a box on the floor. Pulling up a chair, she devours the cereal before she barely has a chance to sit. As she rinses the bowl, she realizes this will be the last time she uses the sink as Mark mentioned it was the next item to be removed in the kitchen.

Back in the bedroom, she sees Mark sleeping soundly. Entering the bathroom, the beauty of the tile work leaves her in awe and she notices the showerhead has been installed as well.

Darn, I'll have to wake up Mark and see if I can use the shower or if the grout still needs to be sealed. Hm-m-m, I'll just wash my hair in the kitchen sink and do a sponge bath there. The big house bathroom is available, but since cleaning it yesterday, there's no time to shower and clean again before leaving for work. Ruth returns to the bedroom. *Ah-h-h, here are my trusty navy slacks and white blouse in this temporary "plastic bin" closet.* She hums on her way to the kitchen for her morning ablutions. As the hot water comes on, she sticks her head under the faucet and starts the hair-washing process by quickly lathering and conditioning her hair. On go the work clothes, and upon reflection, she decides to finish her hair and makeup at work. With one last glance at Mark, she reminds herself to send him a text about picking up the car.

Ruth closes the door quietly and steps outside to the BMW in the driveway. She opens the door, throws in her purse, and slides into the driver's seat. As she starts the car and backs out the few feet to the street, she thinks about her day ahead.

Daniel will be coming today to help transition me to the new position. I know he'll be impatient to go the Honolulu office, so I better start thinking of all the questions I need to ask him. I've been doing some of the loan processing for Daniel, but Mike has been using a loan assistant in Honolulu. If I no longer have loan processing tasks to accomplish, I'll be able to truly manage the branch more efficiently. I also want to get more detail on Oskar's nightly visits. For some reason, Oskar makes me uncomfortable. Every time I looked up at the meeting yesterday, he was looking at me. Sara is always scowling and making rude comments. It makes me want to take one of her four-inch Manolo Blahniks and throw them at her or out the window. Okay, that isn't too nice either way! I can't wait to see Sara's face when she hears about my promotion. That'll definitely make my day. It'll be a true test of my humility to I keep my mouth shut! What else do I need to ask Daniel? He needs to give me complete access to the online employee files since the annual evaluations are coming due soon. Now that I think about it, I've been doing so much at the branch, I don't have as many questions as I anticipated. I'm pretty good!

She pulls into the branch parking garage and sees Daniel pull in as well.

Daniel must really be anxious to get to Honolulu if he's at the branch at 7:00 a.m. Good, we can get our discussion completed quickly before the day fully begins.

After seeing Daniel put out the all-clear signal, Ruth gets out of the car and walks to the garage branch entrance. She walks inside and goes toward the stairs but quickly makes a detour to the ladies room to style her hair.

Feeling more herself, she walks toward her desk and calls out, "Good morning, Daniel."

Daniel looks up and smiles as he boxes up his personal items. "Listen, Ruth, I know I said we could talk about your new role and the transition, but Oskar called me last night and needs me for a meeting this morning. Can you handle things today on your own? Oskar mentioned he would come by on his way home this afternoon to go over a few things with you."

Ruth keeps her smile pasted on as she's been doing ever since she started working with him. Feeling like her face will crack, she keeps the smile frozen in place. "Daniel, I'll be fine. Could you get me access to the employee online files, or do I need to ask Oskar that?"

"I'll do it, Ruth. I think I have the last of my things. Gotta run, but I'll see you at the next board meeting." Daniel picks up his box and walks toward the elevator exit.

Even this micro conversation is a record for Daniel! A conversation of all of thirty seconds. Now that I think about it, our longest conversations centered around loan files but never about running the branch itself.

Ruth shrugs her shoulders and smiles though because it's her turn to empty her desk and move her items to Daniel's office. She gets her own box and starts the process, continuing to make a mental list of tasks she must complete. When she looks up, she sees Axle walking toward her with a big bouquet of flowers.

"Good morning, Madam President."

"Axle, the flowers are beautiful."

"They are for someone who has received a well-earned promotion."

"Really? Well, Daniel just left for Honolulu. You'll have to take them to him over there."

Axle looks at Ruth, knows she's kidding, but wonders suddenly if she truly doesn't understand the amazing changes she's effected at the branch. He thinks about teasing her but wants her to hear how much she's appreciated.

"These are for the person who has turned this branch into something that works well. I have no plans to go to Honolulu since these flowers are for you, woman! Plus, since you didn't go to Hanadie's when I asked you last, I'm taking you there for lunch today. Got it?"

"Yes, sir! And thanks so much for those kind words. I think Mike will be in the office all day finalizing some of his deals so I should be able to get away at lunchtime."

"Excellent, I'll come by to get you around eleven thirty. Will that work?"

"Yes, that sounds wonderful."

Axle sets the flowers on the desk. "It's early, let's go downstairs and have coffee." He takes the files out of her hands and pushes her toward the office door.

"You're being awfully bossy this morning. I hope this means you're buying."

"I know you mean, am I making the cafe mochas? And the answer is *yes*."

"Good. You don't have to push me. I need the caffeine today of all days."

They walk together to the elevator and ride down to the basement. With his hand on her back, Axle guides Ruth to the break room. "Sit down. It may be your only chance all day." He walks to the machine and opens the top to add the coffee beans. "I bought this new Kona coffee a friend of mine told me about. Be sure and tell me what you think."

"Axle, can I ask you something?"

"Sure, what's on your mind?"

Ruth hesitates because she knows Axle is super close to Oskar. "Why do you think Oskar promoted me so early in my tenure here? I really want to know. It's not that I don't want the job, I do, but I'm still kind of shell-shocked."

"Ruth, think about all the work you've been doing. I've never seen one person accomplish as much in a day as you. I told Oskar as much. You're here from seven to seven every day plus, the tellers love you, the customers love you, you put up with the craziness of the lenders and still keep a smile on your face every day. Oskar needed Daniel's help at Honolulu. That's why you were hired initially, so Daniel could be away from the branch more. Once Tom gave his notice, it only made sense for Daniel to move into the SVP of lending position and to promote you."

"You say the nicest things, Axle. I truly could not have accomplished all I have without your help. I'm glad you will still be working at the branch. Did you know Daniel already left this morning? He said Oskar needed him for a meeting in Honolulu. I believe I am now officially on my own!"

Axle raises his eyebrows, "All by yourself?"

"Well, I do have four employees upstairs. Oh, yeah, and you, silly. Didn't I just say what a great help you are to me? Actually, I think I will go to my new office and take a load off. Putting my feet up sounds pretty good." Ruth looks at Axle impishly.

With a snort, Axle responds, "Okay, let's not go overboard here." Putting his hands on his hips, Axle looks pointedly at Ruth. "Okay, Ms. Big Head, do you feel better about the promotion?"

"You know what? I do. I'm still nervous around Oskar. I know he's your friend, and I don't want to offend you, but he has a way of looking at me as though he knows all my thoughts. It's kind of creepy."

Axle looks surprised. "Really, I hadn't noticed. I'll try and pay closer attention the next time you two are together."

"I'm sure I'm overreacting. Well, this coffee is nirvana, but I have slurped the last drop. Time to go back upstairs, and I truly appreciate the pep talk. Come get me when you're ready for lunch." Ruth stands up and takes her mug to the sink.

Axle takes it from her and rinses it out. "Are you sure you don't want one to go, Ms. President?"

"That would be fabulous, but it will get cold before I can drink it all. Thanks, though, Axle. See you later." Ruth stops suddenly. "Yikes, I better go put my face on before the employees arrive."

With a smirk, Axle nods his agreement. Ruth slaps his arm as she walks past.

More to Know about Oskar

Oskar locks up his Honolulu office and checks his watch. *Hmmm, 4:00 p.m., maybe I can miss most of the heavy traffic. I want to see Ruth before she leaves for the day.* He sees Daniel talking to one of the lending assistants and interjects, "Daniel, I'm going to Kailua. Do you have anything you need me to tell Ruth?"

"Let me give you a file I accidentally picked up there this morning. She called me earlier and asked for it." Daniel walks to his office, picks a folder from his desk, and returns to Oskar. "I'm glad you asked. Now I don't have to send this with the courier tomorrow. Tell her hi for me. She didn't call me with any questions, so everything must be going smoothly there."

As Oskar takes the file from Daniel, he says, "That's good to hear. I'll get this to her. See you tomorrow."

As Oskar drives along H1, he can't stop smiling. *All my plans are falling into place nicely.* He feels excitement and anxiety as he thinks through the next step in this process he's putting together. *Frank called this morning and said the Navy would not give approval for the outrigger to be paddled in Pearl Harbor at the Pearl Harbor Memorial Day. The good news is the outrigger can be displayed at the memorial, filled with flowers. That will work just fine because it will still provide a focus for those in attendance. Maybe I can work on the outrigger tonight. I'll try to get Ruth to go ahead and leave on time so I won't have to stay late. It's important for me to get close to her, so she'll be comfortable with my many trips to the branch.*

Oskar gets a thrill as he drives into the Kailua branch parking garage. *It truly is a beautiful building and an amazing tribute to the skill and perseverance that it took to build it.* Oskar checks his watch again. *It's four forty-five. Good, I'm here before closing, which means the elevator will still be available without using a key.*

Oskar walks into the branch and sees Ruth speaking to a customer as she escorts her to the door. Oskar waves to Katrina behind the teller line as he walks up to her to visit.

"How was it today? Were you busy?"

Katrina smiles nervously. "Actually, Ruth seemed busy all day, but the teller line was a normal steady flow of customers. How about in Honolulu, was it busy there?"

"You know, I didn't even walk into the lobby today, so I'm not sure, but it usually is busy so I'll answer that with a *yes*! Are you the last teller here today?"

"Yes. Brenda called in sick, Daniel left early today, and Sharon is on vacation. That's why Ruth has been so busy."

"Sounds like it was a stressful day. Only a few more minutes. Why don't you and I help Ruth with whatever she needs so she can get out of the branch on time today?"

Katrina sees a car at the drive-through and walks to the window. "Yes, sir."

Oskar looks back at Ruth walking up to him and gives her a hug. "I thought you might need that after your crazy day today."

Ruth quickly disengages from Oskar. "I enjoyed the day. Providing customers and employees with assistance always fills me with satisfaction. I need to help Katrina at the drive-through. Do you have anything you need me to do for you?"

"Do you need my help? I'd be happy to assist. I would like to meet with you a few minutes before you leave. I'd like to update you on the Pearl Harbor idea we spoke about at the last board meeting."

"Katrina and I together can finish up quickly. Thanks for the offer though. I can meet with you in, say, thirty minutes?"

As Oskar walks toward the elevator, he responds, "That will work. Just come down when you're done. I put a file on your desk Daniel sent with me."

Ruth wants to grind her teeth in frustration. She didn't get to go out with Axle for lunch because of the staffing issues, and now she has to stay late to talk to horrid Oskar? Okay, maybe that's a little harsh! Mark should be here to pick her up soon, which will be a good excuse to leave. That's what I get for asking if he needs anything.

"Okay, I will."

Ruth helps Katrina finish the closing duties, then wracks her brain for any additional tasks she can do to put off going downstairs. Nothing. *Drat!*

"Katrina, looks like we're done. Go ahead and clock out, and I'll see you tomorrow. Thanks so much for switching with Daniel on the closing shift. You're a lifesaver."

"Sure, Ruth. See you tomorrow."

Ruth watches Katrina walk out the drive-through side door. Walking over to her office, she glances at the file Oskar laid on her desk. *I could review it,* she thinks, *but I might as well go downstairs and get it over with.* Grabbing her notebook, she heads down the stairs.

As she walks toward the conference room, she sees Oskar sipping from a coffee cup. He looks up and motions her over.

"I have a coffee ready for you. I bet you didn't think I could operate that monstrosity of a coffee maker, did you?"

"I'm impressed, Oskar. It's kind of late in the day for me. Drinking caffeine now may keep me awake."

"I thought of that. It's decaf. I didn't make a mocha, but I did add cream and sweetener for you. Have a seat at the table, and we can discuss this so you can go ahead and leave."

"That sounds good. It's been a long day." Ruth picks up the coffee and takes a sip. "So tell me, what's the latest on the Hawaii Pearl Day?"

"Hawaii Pearl Day? Is that what you're calling the memorial service?"

Ruth smiles. "It seems appropriate since it's at Pearl Harbor. What do you think?"

Oskar smiles as well. "I love it. Let's use that on any marketing materials we print. Frank called to let me know the military will not allow me to paddle the outrigger in the harbor. He did say I could display the outrigger filled with flowers at the site of the memorial. What do you think?"

"That would look amazing. Since you mentioned fliers, what about if you auctioned the outrigger and gave the money to charity? Maybe a veterans group? We could include that info since we are still in the design phase." *I know Oskar puts hours and hours of work into the wood items he builds, but what the heck, that makes it more meaningful.* She looks in Oskar's eyes and waits for his answer.

Returning Ruth's look, Oskar feels a connection he had not expected. She looks down, but he is taken aback. He can let nothing distract him now.

"Ruth, it does sound intriguing, but I have to get used to the idea of it. As selfish as it sounds, it takes me a year to build one of these, and I hate to give one up."

"How much do you think we could get for it at auction? We could advertise the craftsmanship and uniqueness of it ahead of time."

Oskar mulls over Ruth's question, "Probably $40,000 or $50,000. I could even bid on it myself if I want to keep it. I could have Frank ask if we can announce the amount of money generated at the auction during the ceremony. Since the funds would go to a veterans charity, they should allow us to do it. It would be great publicity for them and the bank. I guess I've decided." Oskar thinks through how this will change his other plans. "What other brilliant ideas do you have in that head of yours?"

"I think my brilliance has died for the day. Is it okay if I leave now? Mark's going to pick me up. If he doesn't see me upstairs from outside, he won't know where I am."

"Of course. I'll call you tomorrow after I speak with Frank. Do you mind handling the printing of the marketing piece for me?"

Ruth wants to say no, thinks about it for a second, but realizes even if she wants to say no, she can't and keep in Oskar's good graces. Trying not to scowl, she responds, "I'd be happy to do it. Too bad you haven't finished your second outrigger. It would be even more impressive if we had several that were auctioned."

"Stop, Ruth! Again, that's an interesting idea. I've almost finished the second one. I could still bid on the one so I would have at least one left! Go home, before you come up with anything else of mine to auction off!"

Ruth laughs. Distracted by the amount of work still left for her to do, Ruth thinks through what to say. With some effort, she prevents herself from saying anything sarcastic. *Goodness, I'm letting Sara affect how I think! Getting irritated at Oskar won't help me. Well, maybe it will, ha!* Trying not to guffaw at her own wit, Ruth looks at Oskar. "You don't have to ask me twice. Thanks for the coffee." She walks toward the stairs, and Oskar hears her phone buzz. She looks at it and hurries up the stairs.

Oskar leans back in his chair. *I haven't had time to reevaluate my plan, but I need to do that. I think I'll do some night swimming. It will relax me and clarify my thinking.* He thinks back to Ruth. *Man, she's dedicated and bold when she needs to be. There's a fifteen year age difference between us, plus I think she and Axle may have something going. Well, I don't have time to obsess about Ruth, especially with everything I have on my plate.* He gets up and places his cup in the sink next to hers. Picking up his laptop, he puts it in its case. He decides not to work on the outrigger after all and checks the branch before setting the alarm code. *I don't really need to stay. I'll be completely finished staining the wood in a day or two.*

Oskar walks to his car and sees Ruth has long gone. He smiles though, realizing he has made progress with her help.

CHAPTER 11

GCA Progress

R uth leans her head back on the headrest, listening to Mark explain the progress made on the remodel.

"The new appliances were delivered today and are in the garage, Mom. The stove and microwave combination, fridge, and dishwasher were all delivered by the appliance store. I hope they fit. Leek and I worked on getting the few kitchen cabinets hung today. They're cool white bead board. Did you like them when you saw them?" Mark looks over and sees Ruth is dozing. He stops talking and continues to drive home. He knows she's going to be blown away by the changes that happened today.

The bedroom closet is built out, and the walls are painted. Mey spoke to Maria, and the owners are buying new furniture. Mey knows a furniture store owner in Kailua and has already ordered bedroom and living room furniture. It really is coming together. I wonder if we're staying here after it's done or if we'll have to move? We've never discussed it.

Mark starts to stress, but he takes a deep breath and remembers that Leek told him that being born again by making Jesus his savior gives him the right to ask for anything. He says a short prayer.

Lord, I have to remember what Leek said and not worry! I have to believe you have a place for us! I'm counting on you! I'm thinking the "garage apartment vacation rental" is no longer going to be provided for our use so do your thing, Jesus.

Mark speeds up South Kalaheo Avenue and pulls into the driveway as he touches Ruth's shoulder.

"Mom, we're home."

"I'm sorry, Mark. I think I fell asleep while you were talking."

"Mom, is your new job going to be more or less stressful? I hardly saw or spoke to you before. I'm not complaining, but I'm thinking of your health. It seems all you do is work and sleep."

"To be honest, I think I've got a better handle on things at work all around. My goal is to leave when the other employee leaves around six fifteen. I truly plan to make that happen. If I can't get done with everything I need to in that amount of time, I'll need to delegate more! What shall we do for dinner? I'm happy to have cereal, but what about you?"

Mark gets his backpack from the back seat. "Let's see what the GA looks like, and we can decide from there."

Mark and Ruth walk up to the door and see the lights are still on inside. The door is unlocked, and they walk inside.

Leek greets them from the kitchen, "Mark, you're just in time. Can you help me push this dishwasher into place?"

Mark throws his backpack on the floor and walks into the kitchen. Ruth follows and her jaw drops when she sees an almost completed kitchen in front of her. She's speechless at how much was done in just one day. The gray tile flooring had been installed the day before, but today, the white cabinets are in as is the stainless appliances. The white subway tile backsplash is done as well. She smiles at the transformation.

"Wow, you guys. This is incredible. You even did the backsplash. I love the bar you decided to build that separates the kitchen and living room. It makes the kitchen look much larger. Leek, you're such a lifesaver, helping us with this."

"When I think of all the free meals I've received, I think we're even on the benefits! I'm starving right now. What's the plan for food today, Canoe?"

"Leek, Mom and I were just discussing that. How about some greasy fast food? Now that we have the car, I can drive to the burger joint down the street and get burgers. Would that work?"

Both Ruth and Leek say, "Yes-s-s!"

"Leek, do you want to go with me to get it?"

"It would be good for me to get out of the GA for a little bit. Let me get my wallet."

"Mom, do you want your usual—small cheeseburger, no onions, and fries?"

"Yum, yes! And forget your wallet, Leek, unless you want to drive. Mark and I are definitely buying."

Mark and Leek walk out to the car, and Ruth watches them leave. She goes into the bedroom that is still a mess, but the bathroom is done and ready for her to use. She's made sure to keep as much of the chaos out of the finished bathroom as she can so they can enjoy using it. Her shorts from yesterday are on the foot of the bed, and she takes them with her to the bathroom to wash and change.

Stepping through the living room, she checks out the kitchen again and is mesmerized looking at it. Her mind wanders, and she thinks about work. *Oskar agreed with my ideas. He was less horrid today, so I feel somewhat better about working with him. I think I'll get my laptop out and play with some flier ideas.* She's pleased and amazed at herself for being so bold about the auction idea.

Mark and Leek walk into the GA, calling out, "Food's here."

Ruth is sitting on the bed working on her laptop and doesn't notice the food arriving. A few moments pass though, and the smell registers for her. She closes the laptop and quickly gets off the bed. Walking into the kitchen, she sees Leek and Mark are already unwrapping their burgers. Ruth digs into the bag for hers.

"This definitely hits the spot," Ruth says as she sees a fountain drink on the stove. "Whose is this?"

Both Mark and Leek smile. "Well, I believe it's a Diet Coke."

Ruth picks it up before Leek finishes talking and starts sucking on the straw.

"Mom, you're so predictable."

"That I am. So what's on the agenda for tomorrow?"

Mark and Leek start to answer at once. "Go ahead, Canoe."

"The countertops will be delivered tomorrow. That's why Leek finished framing the bar and putting in the cabinets today. After that's done, the next step is doing some paint touch-up. Leek has some leftover wallpaper from a previous job he did, and it would fit

91

well on one of the bathroom walls. He has a picture on his phone he can show you."

Leek gets his phone out and walks over to Ruth and shows her.

With enthusiasm, Ruth concurs, "I love the big green philodendron leaves. That will tie in nicely with the green tile in the bathroom. Does Maria know we're doing that?"

"Mey was going to show it to her today. I feel confident she'll go with it. It'll give the bathroom that extra special finished look."

Leek eats the last bite of his burger and picks up his own car keys. "Canoe, I'll see you after my shift tomorrow. It should be around four."

"That late, huh? I'll do some clean up and wait for the countertop guys. See you when you get here."

The screen door slams, and Ruth and Mark finish their burgers as well.

"Mom, something came to mind today that surprisingly we haven't discussed. What happens when the GA is fully remodeled? Will we stay here, or will we have to move?"

Ruth sits for a moment and looks at Mark with an uncertain look. "Would you believe me if I said I don't know?"

"Yes, and that's okay, Mom. I hadn't thought of it either. Don't you think Maria will want us to move out? It's a vacation rental after all."

"You're right, Mark. I'm sure she will. Neither one of us mentioned it, but it could be she assumed I understood that. How much longer before the remodel is finished, do you think?"

"Mom, you've seen how much work Leek and I can do now that we've got a spreadsheet with everything we need to follow. I'm thinking a week at most. We'll need to do the rest of the flooring and finalize any painting we missed plus build some shelves for the closet."

"Mark, would you have time to look online tomorrow for rental houses or apartments? I think I can afford $3,000 a month for rent. I know Kailua can be expensive, but all we need is two bedrooms."

"Since I'll be waiting on the countertop guys, if you leave your laptop, I can work on that. Do you think we can find anything for that amount? I know in Austin it would be easy but not here!"

"I'm not sure. We'll have a better idea tomorrow. This has been so nice eating with you and Leek and having time for the two of us to talk about stuff. I think I'll get ready for bed though. Do you mind if I sleep in the bed tonight?"

"Of course not, Mom. Leave the laptop in here. I might start checking Craig's List tonight."

Continued Interactions with Oskar

Ruth goes into her office. With the lobby quiet and all the branch employees at work today, she opens up her e-mail and sees the marketing piece she sent from her personal e-mail last night. She reviews it one more time. *The added picture of flowers makes a lovely touch.*

> *Pearl Harbor Remembrance Ceremony Auction*
> *Two Custom-Made Koa Wooden Outriggers*
> *Available*
> *True pieces of art created by Oskar Soto*
> *Proceeds to benefit Hawaii Veterans Organizations*
> *Friday night, December 6, at 6:30 p.m.*
>
> *Royal Hawaiian Hotel (the Pink Palace) Monarch*
> *Room*
> *Winning bidder to be honored at the December 7,*
> *Pearl Harbor Ceremony*
> *RSVP at 555-472-1122*

Ruth thinks an actual picture of Oskar's outrigger would definitely enhance the piece. She decides to e-mail him to get his input. Attaching the item to an email, she hits Send. She grabs the Daniel file and reviews it for her customer interview at three. The phone rings.

"This is Ruth."

"Hi, this is Oskar. I got your e-mail. The Royal Hawaiian, huh? Nothing like starting with the best."

Ruth responds to Oskar enthusiastically, "Think of the attendees you could get at a place like that. We have to have high roller buyers! I thought I might call the hotel today and see if they would give us a price break on the events room since we're doing this for charity. What do you think?"

"I think we should do it, Ruth, and hopefully, we will be allowed to announce the winners at the Pearl Harbor ceremony. It'll be great publicity for the bank and money for the veterans groups. It's definitely a win-win."

"Oskar, really? That's magnanimous of you."

"Aw, shucks. Honestly, I think we should hold an early board meeting. I'll contact all the members and see if they can meet together Friday afternoon. Hopefully, I'll have more information from Frank. We need to get the details nailed down, or we won't be able to get the auction scheduled before the ceremony. Would you mind calling Sara? I want to see how much money we have left in our donations general ledger account."

Ruth hesitates. "Okay, Oskar, I'll call Sara first. Did you have a dollar figure you wanted us not to exceed for this? The costs could escalate quickly."

Oskar thinks for a moment. "First, let's see how much money we have available. Get an idea of cost from the hotel, then get back to me."

"Okay, Oskar. I'll call both Sara and Royal Hawaiian and keep you posted on what I discover."

"Thanks, Ruth. Gotta go."

Ruth ruminates on his change in attitude. *Oskar has been natural and nice with me lately. Here I was calling him horrid, and he's been like a real person. Except maybe for him asking me to call Sara, ick! Well, at least he and I are getting along better! It makes my work easier since he's my direct boss now. It'll be super cool if we can pull this auction off.*

If Oskar agrees to auction off both of his outriggers, we could possibly get over $100,000 for charity. That's impressive no matter how you slice it!

Ruth looks up to ensure no customer needs her assistance. Since it's early afternoon, the lobby is quiet. Ruth looks online for the phone number for Royal Hawaiian. *It might help if I have the cost estimate before I call Sara.* As Ruth dials the number, she reviews in her mind what to ask.

"Royal Hawaiian, this is Chad."

"Hi, may I speak to someone in corporate events, please?"

"I can help you with that..."

Ruth hangs up the phone. The cost is more than she anticipated even though Chad offered a deal on the refreshments. *I better call Sara before giving the update to Oskar.* Ruth takes a deep breath and dials Sara's extension.

"Wow, Ruth? What could you possibly be calling me about?"

Ruth growls and answers, "Are you always this grumpy, or is it only with me, Sara?"

Taken aback, Sara answers, "Amazing, you have a spine after all. To be honest, I think this is my knee-jerk reaction to anyone that hasn't proven their worth here at the bank. What do you want?"

"Oskar asked me to call and see what funds we have available in our donations GL to use for an auction we are planning. Do you know the answer, or should I call Oskar and let him know you won't help me?"

Sara laughs. "We have a significant balance in that account as it's been a slow year for making donations. Our current balance is approximately $30,000. Is that enough for you?"

"Yes, and hey, what do you mean? Are you saying I haven't proven I can do my job?"

"You must be doing it since Oskar promoted you. Do you want anything else, or are we through?"

Ruth feels a nudge from the Holy Spirit. *Must I really, Lord? An olive branch?* "Sara, it's obvious we got off on the wrong foot. Oh, and speaking of feet, I need help finding some shoes for my dress for the auction. Can you help me?"

"Oh, I can help you, but the question is, *Will I?*"

Ruth is ready to slam down the phone. "Sara!"

"Okay, okay, you've picked the right subject because I adore shoes. Meet me at the Ala Moana Mall after work at six o'clock at the north entrance."

Click.

Ruth leans back in her chair. *Okay, Lord, I get it. I guess going to the mall isn't too much of a sacrifice, ha! Time to call Oskar and get his feedback.*

"Hi, Ruth. That was quick! What did you find out?"

"I got the donations figure from Sara. It's $30,000. I called Royal Hawaiian, and I wanted you to hear the details before we go further with them. They require we pay the full room rental fee, but they will comp us on tea, coffee, and cookies. What are your thoughts on that?"

"First, Ruth, let me give you some good news. Frank called and said it's a go ahead for us to have the flower filled outrigger at the memorial event. He said someone from the bank can also speak a few words since we'll be donating money to a veterans group with funds from the auction. Frank said his contact was enthusiastic about our idea. Pretty, cool, huh?"

"Oskar, I'm super excited about this. Just in case I should forget, thank you for providing the outrigger for the auction. I know it's a sacrifice for you because of the time, sweat, and tears you put into your creation. You could donate one of the surfboards hanging in our lobby as well so we could get even more money!"

"That's something to consider for sure. I believe most people like the uniqueness of the outrigger, so we might get more attendance with more than one. We should include my other outrigger and at least one of the surfboards as well. Let's add that to the fliers we print. We could advertise both are on display at the branch for people to view prior to the auction."

"Wow! This is so fun. Do you want me to check on other hotels? How about the Moana Surfrider?"

Oskar thinks for a minute. "They would be a great choice as well. Yes, please do call them. Go ahead and pick whichever hotel you prefer. Since we have a plentiful GL balance, don't worry about the cost. By the way, I plan to come by the branch on my way home. Do you need me to bring you anything from here?"

"Could you go by the supplies area and pick up some deposit tickets? I'll call and have them packaged for you."

"Sure, Ruth. See you later."

"Thanks, Oskar."

Kaho Time

Oskar walks through the crowd at Surf Shack looking for the guys. He walks outside to the beach front tables and sees Hanadie nursing a beer at a small table near the bar. Oskar sits, eyeing Hanadie as a young woman comes up,

"Something I can get you, Oskar?"

"Hi, Cheryl. I think I'll start with water right now. I've had a long day, and I'm not in the mood for alcohol or caffeine."

"You got it." Cheryl pours water from the pitcher on her tray into a glass on the table and walks away.

Hanadie speaks. "Sometimes I get sick of this so-called paradise. I've got nothin', Oskar. No family, no country, no God, nothin'." He lays his head down on the table while Oskar stares at the sunset. He looks at his phone screen.

"Kim and Axle aren't coming. Do you want another beer, or do you just want to leave?"

Worked up now, Hanadie continues without acknowledging Oskar's question. "I have these fantasies, Oskar. I want this country to feel the same pain I do, you know?"

Oskar sighs, but realizing it helps Hanadie to talk through his frustrations, Oskar says, "What fantasies, Han?"

Hanadie perks up. "Do you watch the news? Each time a terrorist attack occurs, the whole nation goes bonkers. Analysts talk at length about the terrorist and his motivations. He gets his fifteen minutes of fame. That's what I want."

Oskar thinks through what Hanadie said, "I might have to agree with you on that, Hanadie. Cheryl, can we get one more beer here?"

As the night wears on, Han starts to cry and Oskar comforts him. He looks at his watch but doesn't try to convince his friend to leave, waiting as the crier wipes his eyes, blows his nose, and curses. With a sigh, he tries not to but still rolls his eyes.

"Hanadie, I know the pain can be overwhelming at times when we remember the death of Ena and Luka, and especially Sarah, but they wouldn't wish you to suffer so much. Come on, I'll take you home with me and make sure you get to the restaurant tomorrow." After a moment, he leans toward Hanadie and begins to pray quietly. As they prepare to leave, he pats Hanadie's shoulder and pulls him up out of his chair. "Let's get out of here, buddy."

An Unusual Transaction

The man's pupils are constricted and his hands are shaking as he holds a bag out toward his customer.

"Look, buddy, I don't have all day. It's a miracle I could get these bugs as it is. I'm going to have to charge you more this time as I can't get any more. You want 'em or not?"

Without a word, the customer takes the items and replaces them with a stack of bills. He quickly walks down the alley as his supplier counts his money.

Two "Friends"

The strong wind blows one of the tiki torches out. Drugar lights his cigar to give him a tiny bit of extra light on this night of the new moon. The crashing waves match how he feels, anxious and hyper yet fixated on his project. Because of the wind and waves, his visitor is easily able to slide into the additional chair without notice. The friend takes a deep gulp from his beer and throws the bottle into the surf.

"That was pretty dumb. It's just washing back on the sand. What do you have for me?"

With an irritated look, the visitor mumbles under his breath but answers, "I left something on the porch for you. Also, I found out the best time to set up for your little project. Super early is best. Maybe 5:00 a.m. It's so quiet and no one expects anything to happen then. I think I may have to take care of my contact to tie up some loose ends."

"Shut up." Without looking at his companion, he puts out his cigar in the sand. Angrily, he stands up. "No details, remember? I can't tell anything I don't know."

Walking toward his condo, he starts to regret that he trusted this unstable guy with his life's project.

Speaking of taking care of loose ends…

CHAPTER 12

Things Are Heating Up

Oskar walks into the Kailua branch carrying his laptop and the package he picked up for Ruth. He doesn't see her so drops the package on her desk. He walks to the end of the hall where his favorite surfboard is hanging and rubs the inlaid turtle design with his hand to feel the smoothness of the wood. He smells Ruth's perfume as she walks up next to him. The fragrance reminds him of tropical flowers and moonlit nights on the beach.

"Oskar, it's an impressive piece of artwork. I can understand why you hesitate to donate it."

Oskar puts his arm around Ruth's shoulders. "I did hesitate initially, but when I think of the sacrifices of our veterans, it's a small thing. There's something I would like to show you when everyone has left for the day. I'm going to take my laptop down to the conference room. Can you come down when you're done?"

Ruth steps slowly away from Oskar and pats his back. "Sure. It'll be about an hour." The phone rings and Ruth steps over to her desk to answer it.

Oskar walks downstairs to the conference room, and deciding he's coffee'd out, he grabs a bottled water from the refrigerator. His thoughts change direction, and he grins in satisfaction, thinking of the steps he's taking to put this process into action. Since he has most of the details finalized, he sits at the table in the break room and reads his latest e-mails.

"You are nothing if not prompt!"

"Well, Oskar, I was looking forward to sitting down and getting off my feet so I finished quickly. What do you want to talk about?"

"I did say I was going to the conference room but just plopped down once I got here. Not too smart since I need to show you something there. I'm going to ask you to stand back up. Sorry about that."

Ruth follows Oskar and watches him walk to the wall on the other side of the conference table. He presses one of the door-size panels, revealing a steel door with an electronic combination lock. As Oskar inputs the combination numbers, Ruth stands with her mouth open, holding her breath. Once Oskar finishes, he pushes the steel door, which opens into a room similar to a long narrow office. Oskar turns to Ruth and takes her hand.

"Come on, let me show you what I'm working on."

Ruth allows Oskar to lead her into the room, and in the middle is a special stand holding a beautifully carved outrigger.

"Wow," Ruth whispers.

Oskar laughs. "You don't have to whisper. I don't think anyone can hear you. What do you think?"

"It's one of the most beautiful things I've ever seen. Did you really make this? And why do you keep it here? Oh, I see the wood chips on the floor. You built it here?"

"Yes. I guess because I can. And yes."

Ruth tries to process Oskar's answer and isn't quite sure how to respond. "All I can think of to say is, it looks finished. Is it?"

"It is. I only need to put the final finish on it, and it's done. This branch is like my baby. Of all the things I have built since I came to America, it means the most to me. Woodworking has been a passion of mine for a while, and when we moved here, I started working on the surfboards at home. Once I built the branch, I decided it would be nice to work on my projects here in my spare time. Does it seem odd to you that I do it here?"

"It does. It makes a mess you have to constantly clean yourself since the cleaning crew doesn't come in here when you could do it more easily at home, right?"

Oskar thinks through how to answer Ruth. "I still do some work at home. I can't give you an answer that would make sense to you, but in some ways I wanted to keep my work private. Even my Bosnia friends didn't know the amount of work I had accomplished on this hobby until I hung the surfboards in the branch. Now it doesn't seem quite so important. Once I finish this outrigger, I think I'll clean this workroom completely and do future projects at home."

"What will you do with this room? Will you let others in the bank know it's here?"

Oskar looks at Ruth closely. "I could have romantic rendezvous here."

Ruth raises her eyebrows. "Does Axle know this room is here?"

Oskar chuckles with Ruth's attempt to change the subject. "He does since he was involved in the building process. Where is he by the way?"

"He had a dentist appointment this afternoon. He's had a toothache all week and finally decided to do something about it. I do appreciate you showing me this, Oskar. I'm truly impressed with the outrigger. Why don't we display it in the lobby like we discussed?"

Oskar nods, and they exit the room just as Axle walks down the stairs toward the conference room. Axle looks shocked to see Oskar and Ruth leaving the room together. He doesn't say anything but looks askance at Oskar.

"Ruth, let's bring Axle up to speed on the auction idea. He can help us finalize the details."

"Axle, do you have time to talk to Ruth and me for a few minutes?"

"I do. Let me get some water first."

As they settle in the break room with their waters, Ruth asks, "Axle, how was the dentist appointment?"

"I'm going to have to have a root canal. He gave me some medicine today for the pain, and he's going to do the procedure tomorrow. Will you be okay if I'm out in the morning?"

"Sure, but won't you need to be out the whole day?"

"Maybe, but I have a lot piling up, so I may come in if I don't feel too bad. I'll text you and let you know what I decide."

Oskar takes a sip of his own water as Ruth and Axle sit. "Axle, do you remember our discussion at the last board meeting about being involved in the December 7 Pearl Harbor Remembrance Day? Frank followed up with me after he asked the powers that be if we could be a part of the ceremony. I wanted to paddle my most recently finished outrigger through the harbor during the ceremony. They gave me a big fat no on that, but Frank said I can fill the outrigger with flowers and put it on display at the memorial. As Ruth and I were discussing this, she came up with the idea of having an auction for the outrigger and donating the money to a veteran's charity. Isn't that great?"

Impressed, Axle stares at Ruth. "She seems to be full of great ideas lately. So how would this auction work?"

Ruth looks at her notes. "I called both Moana Surfrider and the Royal Hawaiian. I love both of them, but once we discussed dates, Moana had no rooms available for the dates we need. The Royal Hawaiian confirmed a date so we decided the week after Thanksgiving, which is shortly before Hawaii Pearl Day. Oskar, should we provide a cash bar?"

"That might be good. People may loosen up the purse strings after a few drinks."

"Oskar!" But Ruth smiles anyway. "Has Frank given you a list of different veterans groups we should consider for the donation?"

"Not yet. I'll see him tomorrow for lunch and ask him then. Ruth suggests I auction all my outriggers. I have two, Axle, so I plan to bid on one to keep for myself."

Axle laughs. "You guys seem to have this all figured out. It's hard to believe that it's only two months away. It's incredible, Ruth, you could find an event room for us to use at this late date."

"God is smiling on our idea. We have so many details to finalize. I spoke to a printer today, and they only need a couple of days notice to print from our design. Here's a copy of what I worked on today. What do you guys think?"

It shows an outrigger filled with tropical flowers superimposed in front of the Arizona Memorial next to a picture of the Pink Palace.

Providing feedback, Axle responds, "You did this yourself, Ruth? It's impressive. Are we doing a mail out or just handing them out at the two branches?"

He hands the flier to Oskar, who responds, "We definitely need to do a mail out. We can invite all our customers with balances over $250,000, plus we can get a list of those who live in the high-dollar neighborhoods and send them invites as well. I think that'll be enough. How many people does the event room hold, Ruth?"

"They told me two hundred. They can open one of the walls and add additional chairs should we need them, but that will cost more."

Oskar rubs his hands together. "Everything's coming together nicely. I'm loving this!"

Axle and Ruth look at each other and are surprised at Oskar's excitement.

"The last time I spoke to Kim, he was pleased to be asked to do the prayer at the ceremony. We need someone to video the ceremony and the auction so we can show it to everyone at church. Could you do that, Axle?"

"Sure, I'd be happy to. Ruth mentioned you were considering having a special board meeting. Do we need to do that or just send an e-mail to everyone?"

Oskar mulls over Axle's idea. "An e-mail would work. I want to make sure all the board members attend the auction. I'll send the e-mail out myself."

The phone rings, and Ruth stands up to answer the one by the coffee machine.

"Hi, Katrina. Everything, okay? I'll come right up to audit your drawer since you're going on vacation tomorrow. See you in a couple of minutes." She turns to the guys. "I have to go upstairs, guys. Let me know if you think of anything else I need to do. I'll call the hotel and request a cash bar. Anything else you guys think we need to provide at the auction?"

Both Oskar and Axle stand as well.

Axle answers Ruth. "Hmmm, can't think of anything right this minute, but I'll let you know if I do."

"Great, talk to you guys later. Thanks, Oskar, for showing me the outrigger."

"Of course, Ruth. Would you please not share the room location with anyone? I like to keep that private."

"If that's what you want, sure."

Ruth leaves the break room, and Axle looks at Oskar.

"You showed her the workroom?"

"I did. Since she's now the senior officer here, I thought I should show it to her. You don't agree?"

"It doesn't matter to me. You're the one who always wanted to keep it a secret. You and Ruth seem to be getting close." Axle stands to leave, feeling upset.

Oskar grabs Axle's arm. "Is that a problem for you?"

Axle looks at the man who sacrificed everything to get him, Hanadie, and Kim to the US. "If you're really interested in Ruth personally, I'll step out of the picture. But make sure you are serious, because I'd like to pursue a relationship with her."

Oskar looks at Axle. "Thanks, Axle. I've liked Ruth from the beginning. Getting involved with her would be complicated since she's my employee, but I do want to see if it's possible."

"You're the boss, so you can do what you want. Remember, she has a lot going on in her life right now. Her son is early in his sobriety from hard drugs. I found out today she'll have to move out of the place she's living in now as the owner is turning it into a vacation rental. That, along with her new job, is some major stress. If you start putting the moves on her, she might feel compelled to leave the bank. Do you think she may be interested in spending more time with you?"

"Initially, when she and I met, I got the impression I made her nervous. But since she received her promotion, she's acted pleased to spend time with me. That's my thoughts anyway. I'll gradually see if she's open to us getting closer. She may feel it's not appropriate based on our respective roles, and if I think she prefers you, I'll let you have her! Don't get upset, Axle, I'm just being funny. Come on, I love you. I want what's best for everyone. I'll keep you posted." *I must be losing my mind to add one more complicated aspect to my life.*

Axle shrugs. "Fine."

Oskar changes the subject. "You know, the bank has a small foreclosure property in Kaneohe. We could see if Ruth wants to buy it. Why don't you suggest it, Axle? It might look better coming from you."

Axle looks unsettled. "Okay, Oskar."

The Mall with Sara

Finally finding a parking space, Ruth exits her car and notices Sara leaning against hers near the mall entrance. Putting on her best fake smile, Ruth walks toward her nemesis and stops four feet from the fashion diva, saying nothing.

Sara peruses Ruth's outfit and, groaning, says, "You really do need help, Ms. Goodie Goodie. Since it's already 7:00 p.m., we only have time to look at shoes. I'll take you to my favorite store, and hopefully, we can find a pair to match your auction dress. What color is it?"

"Black."

"That's original," Sara mutters. Stopping for a second, Sara remembers something. "What size shoe do you wear?"

"Seven."

"Me too. Well, let's see what we can find. Luckily, the store is near this entrance."

They wait as someone exits and walk into the mall together. Grabbing Ruth's arm, Sara leads her to Neiman-Marcus.

Ruth's mouth drops open as they step over to the shoe department. "Sara, I can't afford anything here. Did you see the price of that pair of shoes, $875!"

Sara picks them up and looks at Ruth. "Would they go with your dress?"

"Well, yeah, but, sheesh, what does that matter if I don't have the money?"

"How about we look at styles and find ones that will work for you to try on. Then we can look online to find them cheaper. How's that sound?"

Totally flummoxed, Ruth looks straight into Sara's eyes. "Perfect."

They both laugh as a sales assistant approaches them. Ruth puts on her best face of sophistication as Sara speaks,

"Please show us all your black pumps."

The assistant fawningly leads them to a glass case further into the department.

Sara sees a spectacular pair with a jeweled heal. "Oh, we definitely want to try those."

While trying not to laugh, Ruth coughs and actually is able to maintain her haughty expression.

Sara scowls and, putting her nose in the air, says, "We need a size seven."

Watching the woman walk to the back, Sara and Ruth look at one another and burst into laughter. They can't seem to stop as Ruth bends over, putting her hands on her knees.

"Stop, Ruth, she'll be back any minute. Whew, I haven't laughed that hard in a long time." Looking at her watch, Sara frowns. "We only have time to try this one pair. That's okay, I have another idea anyway."

CHAPTER 13

The Finished Project

Mark and Leek are giddy with satisfaction. The GA is now fully finished.

"Hey, Canoe, we should send pictures of this place to one of those decorating magazines. This place is incredible, if I say so myself."

"You're right. I wish we'd taken some before pictures. The change in this place is something. What do you like the best?"

Leek thinks for a second. "It's a toss up between the kitchen and bathroom. I think the kitchen edges out with the koa wood bar. I'm glad we switched to that instead of using the kitchen granite. What do you think?"

"About a dozen things are flying through my head right now. I'm stressed about where Mom and I can find a place to live. I've looked online but haven't found anything here in Kailua. I hate for Mom to drive far to work. To answer your question, I think you have done a stellar job of making this place five stars! I like it all. I owe you, man, for all your help."

"Canoe, the best thing that happened during this remodel process was you giving your life to Christ. Nothing else compares! A new Bible study for the youth group is starting up at church. I'm going to lead it and tonight I plan to share my testimony. Do you want to go with me? We can ask Mey as well."

"Well, if Mey's going, ha! I really want to, but I can't tonight because I've committed to going to the five-thirty AA meeting. How about I go to the next one? I have to get a job now that the GA is finished. The house cleaning doesn't quite provide me with enough income to help Mom. Can you drop me at the meeting house before you go to Bible study? It helps keep me on track to go as often as possible."

"Mark, you're like a talking pinball. Let's see, oh yeah, you asked me for a ride. Sorry, I told my sister I would pick up her kids from day care today. I can drop you off at the bank. Do you think your Mom could take you after work?"

"That might work. I'll call her right now."

Mark and Oskar

Mark waits for Ruth to answer her phone while Leek packs up his tools. It goes to voice mail, so Mark tells Leek, "Yeah, it would be great for you to take me to the branch. If Mom can't take me to AA, I can always walk home."

"These are the last of my tools. Let's hit the road, Canoe."

*****

Mark waves to Leek from the branch parking garage and walks inside. He sees someone in Ruth's office, so he veers toward the teller line.

"Hi, I'm Mark Max. Can you tell me who's in the office with my mom?"

"Oh, that's the big boss, Oskar Soto. He offices in Honolulu, but has been coming by the branch every day to talk to Ruth. Have you met him?"

"I guess I did meet him at church once but didn't recognize him from the back. Do you think they'll be long? I was wanting Mom to give me a lift."

"I doubt they will since it's getting so late. It's already 5:10. I think it would be fine to go ask them."

"Thanks!" Mark walks over to Ruth's office. He sticks his head in and waves to Ruth.

"Hi, Mark! You remember Oskar, right?"

Oskar stands and extends his hand toward Mark. "Great to see you again, Mark. What are you up to?"

"I came by to see if Mom would take me to a five-thirty meeting over at the United Church of Christ. It's not my normal meeting, but a friend suggested I try it. Leek dropped me off here on his way to pick up his niece and nephew from day care." Mark doesn't know why he's rambling on.

"Oh, Mark, I'm so sorry. I have to stay and help the tellers balance, so there isn't time to take you and return here."

Oskar grabs his briefcase. "Mark, I'm leaving now. I'll be happy to take you on my way home."

Knowing his face is turning red, he hopes his newly acquired tan will keep it from showing too much. "Okay, Oskar. I appreciate it."

They say goodbye to Ruth and make their way to the parking garage.

Mark whistles when he sees Oskar's maxed-out Chevy truck. "Nice set of wheels, man."

Oskar uses his key to remotely unlock the truck. "Thanks, I find a truck quite helpful when I go out on inspections as well as getting supplies for the carpentry work I do. Are you talking about the church on Kaneohe Street? That meeting is normally at five o'clock. Did they change the time recently?"

Mark is looking at his cell phone. "I'm sorry, Oskar, what did you say?"

"I thought the meeting you mentioned started at five o'clock not five thirty."

"Really? I must have confused the time with another meeting. I have a hard time keeping track of them all! Dang. I think you're right. Let me check real quick. He looks up the schedule for Oahu AA meetings and finds the list for the Windward side of the island. You're right, Oskar. If I go now, it'll be half over. There's one at six o'clock, but it's at Kaneohe Marine Corps Base Chapel. Can I go to that one since I'm not military?"

"I'm not sure. Let me call a friend of mine and ask." Oskar uses his Bluetooth and starts talking. "Hey, Frank. Sorry to bother you, but do you know if nonmilitary members can attend meetings over at the Kaneohe Marine Corps Base Chapel?"

Mark can hear Frank's voice on the phone, "They can't unless they have access to the base."

"Okay, Frank. Thanks for the info."

Mark looks at his phone again for other AA locations without success. "Well, heck. I guess I have wasted your time. Do you mind taking me home?"

"No problem. But, why don't we go for a cup of coffee, and we can have our own AA meeting? What do you say?"

Mark is taken aback. "I just realized that you know I'm talking about an AA meeting."

"Well, I know most of the meeting locations from here to Honolulu and further north from Ewa Beach. Mark, I think we alcoholics have to stick together, don't you?"

"Actually, Oskar, I'm an opiates addict but the meetings help me. You really don't have to take me anywhere other than home."

"I'd love to stop for some coffee. Look, there's the Kailua Coffee Shop. Let's stop here."

"Sure, Oskar." Mark texts his mom. *The meeting started at 5:00, so Oskar and I are stopping for coffee. See ya at GA later.*

"They have this one blend here that's the absolute best. I'm a black-coffee guy myself. What about you, Mark? Do you go for all the froo-froo stuff?"

Mark laughs. "I do. I'm the typical froo-froo drinker. Normally when my sponsor and I meet here, I go the cheap route and get a regular coffee and add lots of sugar! Macchiatos are my favorite. I haven't had one here. Do you know if they make 'em?"

"They certainly do. Let me get you one." Oskar places their order as Mark walks over to sit at a window table. As he waits for their coffee, Oskar watches Mark looking at his phone. *He's a nice looking kid with the same green eyes as Ruth. I wonder what his story is.*

Oskar places both coffees on the table and sits down, "Mark, would you like to hear my testimony? I know I'd like to hear about your experiences."

Marks nods as he takes his first sip.

"Were you aware that Axle, Kim, Hanadie, and myself immigrated to America from Bosnia during the Bosnian conflict? We were able to enter the US on an asylum status. We ran for our lives. In fact, we barely got out alive. My addiction began at the beginning of the war. Are you familiar at all with that part of the world?"

"To be honest, I don't remember much about the war. I'm sure we covered it in school, but I hate to say, I've had too many drugs since then."

Oskar spills his coffee and grabs a napkin as he answers Mark. "That certainly is being honest! Let me give you a brief overview on the Bosnian War. It's confusing, so I am only going to give you a few details so you can see how it personally affected me and my friends."

Focus on Bosnia

Oskar continues, "Well, let me just say that the diverse factions in the area created deep resentments and hatred. You have probably heard of Yugoslavia. It was formed by the allies after WWI. Then additional changes happened after WWII that created more strife, and as the years passed, the government and the economy fell into deep chaos. The divisiveness happened due to the rivalry between the different ethnic and religious groups. The three groups included the Serbs, who were mostly Orthodox Christians; Croats, who were mostly Catholics; and ethnic Albanians, who were mostly Muslims.

"Okay, I can already see your eyes glazing over! I just want to make a few more comments. The Serbians, my own dang countrymen, attacked many of the Bosnian towns near where we lived. And the Bosniaks, who were Muslims, were forced out by any means necessary. And I mean any means necessary including all-out murder. In mid-1995, Bosnian Serb forces perpetrated the massacre of more than seven thousand Bosniak men. There were rape camps as well. The US did not wish to put American troops into the battle. They wanted the United Nations to take care of it. That decision in itself, in my opinion, caused the deaths of many thousands of people including my cousin Luka and his wife Ena, who were Axle's parents

112

and Hanadie's aunt and uncle. Axle and Hanadie are like brothers since Luka and Ena raised Hanadie with Axle. Even though it was extremely dangerous, as Christians, they felt called to create a safe house in Sarajevo for a Bosniak family. Prior to us escaping in 1994, a group of Serb soldiers were doing a sweep of the neighborhood and found this same family at my cousin's house. All were murdered. I mean everyone." Oskar angrily wipes tears that always start to fall when he remembers. "Luka was my best friend. Axle, Hanadie, and I had been out scrounging up some food. When we returned, we found everyone executed including Han's fiancee, Sarah. I'm thankful we were able to get to the US on an asylum visa, but the US's involvement in the war was erratic at best. If they had shown more leadership at the beginning, so much ethnic cleansing and overall killing wouldn't have happened." Oskar takes a deep breath, realizing his voice had gotten too loud with the rage he is feeling. He feels like punching something, but when he looks around realizes he is out of luck. He grunts as he crumples his coffee cup.

Mark is spellbound by Oskar's story. "I had no idea, Oskar. I'm so sorry. It all sounds horrible. I can understand grief because I still get upset thinking about when my dad died, but I don't know how anyone could get over something like what you've experienced."

"Was your grief over your dad's death what started your drug use?"

"I guess so. I felt so lost. My mom was trying to keep everything together with the house, her job, and her own grief. I feel a lot of guilt for adding to her load. My dad was my best friend. We loved doing the same things—motocross, soccer, and wake boarding. While returning from a Christian summer camp where he was volunteering, he was killed by a drunk driver. Ironic, huh? Faith in God didn't mean much to me after that."

"Mark, believe it or not, I can relate to your feelings even though my experiences were different. I'm Serbian and could not believe the atrocities they perpetrated. It makes me sick thinking about it. Most of the violence was against the Muslims, but unfortunately, Axle's family were caught in the crossfire. They were Christians and were trying to help many Muslims, especially at the rape camps. That didn't go over well with the Serbians in our area. When they discovered what was happening, they laid in wait at the house for when Axle's mom, dad, and a Muslim family returned from helping several young women escape a refugee camp and into another safe house. And as I said, all were killed. Most of my friends found comfort in their faith at that time."

Mark shakes his head as he leans back in his chair. "I wish my grief had made me turn to faith for comfort. I'm just challenged by all the bad things that happen in the world like the situation in your homeland. Life can be so hard, can't it?"

"That's an understatement. But that's enough sad talk. Let's get you home. Your mom will be worrying about you."

Drugar Makes a Move

Covering his eyes to minimize the glare of the lights, he gives the panic room apartment a quick perusal.

I wasn't sure if the key given me two years ago would work. Luckily for me, it did. This place will be a good hideout.

Exiting the building and quietly moving through the empty garage, Drugar motions to his driver, and once the vehicle stops, he quickly slides into the back seat. Drugar looks at his wrist. Making out the time and taking a deep breath, he leans back into the seat, satisfied he completed his task with a few minutes to spare. With no traffic, the driver quickly maneuvers through the early morning streets of Kailua and Honolulu. Nervously, Drugar pulls a bag from the floorboard onto his lap and quickly unzips it. He gently pulls an awkwardly bug-shaped item from the bag and makes a few adjustments. Without setting it, his hand gently moves the timer for the correct number of hours. He replaces it in the custom-made vinyl bag that is quickly zipped shut. He wants to rush the driver as there is still one more errand to be accomplished, but he knows they had best not draw attention, so he slows his breathing as the vehicle continues its journey at the posted speed limit.

I'll finish my task once he drops me at my car. With a sigh of satisfaction, he leans back against the leather upholstery, closing his eyes as a slow smile appears. *I'm finally going to achieve retribution.*

CHAPTER 14

Change Is in the Air (Isn't It Always?)

Ruth opens the door to the GA and gasps at the transformation. All the new furniture is in place. As she takes in each new change, she sees Mey at the sink in the kitchen.

Mey speaks first. "Hey, you. Where's Canoe?"

"He went to have coffee with Oskar." Ruth looks at the sparkling kitchen with the darling wicker bar stools pulled up at the koa wood bar. "This place looks incredible! Can you believe this is even the same place we walked into the day we arrived?"

Mey puts the glass cleaner under the sink. "No, I can't. I never knew Leek was so talented. He and Canoe make a good team. I guess you guys will be leaving soon. I'm going to miss you." Mey looks sadly at Ruth.

"Oh-h, Mey, wherever we move, we'll all still be friends! You are so-o-o right. Leek has been a lifesaver. Can you think of anything special we can do to thank him? I can't afford to pay him for his work, but I'd like to do something."

Mey responds, "Let me give it some thought. By the way, where do you and Canoe plan to move now that the GA is fully remodeled?"

Ruth places her purse on one of the bar stools and sits on the other one. "I don't know, Mey. Mark has been researching house rentals in the area, but everything is expensive. I know we need to leave soon. Has Maria said anything to you?"

"She told me to ask you. She didn't give me a time frame, but I think she'll expect you guys to be out in the next thirty days."

"Thirty days?" Ruth exclaims. "Mey, you know that isn't likely to be possible. Is she going to kick us out, do you think, if we aren't out by then?"

"I don't know, Ruth. What does your contract state?"

Ruth sighs deeply, "I'll have to get it out and look at it again. I should have been more aggressive looking for a new place. Dang it! Well, I can't change that now."

Mark and Oskar walk into the GA, the screen door slamming behind them. Both Ruth and Mey look to the door and smile.

Oskar goes over to Mey and gives her a hug. "Hi, it's Meylani, right? I think I remember from that last service project you and I were on that you clean houses. Are you still doing that?"

"I am, Oskar. My life pretty much revolves around cleaning. It keeps me from going to church most Sundays because most vacationers leave on Saturdays, requiring me to clean on Sundays. Canoe has been a big help to me though. As well as doing the remodel with Leek here, he helps me clean."

"Better him than me!" Oskar laughs.

Mey says sadly, "Ruth and I were just talking about how she and Canoe will have to move out of the apartment within the next thirty days. Do you know of any properties she could rent?"

Looking pointedly at Mark, he says, "Canoe?"

Mark moves Ruth's purse to the floor and sits on the stool. "Yeah, that's me. Leek gave me that nickname the first day I met him because he said it's short for the Hawaiian word *kanuha*, which means 'one who sulks.'"

Oskar laughs and laughs. "I'm not laughing at you, *Canoe*. It just sounds so like Leek."

"Actually, Mey, I think I may have something for Canoe and Ruth. The bank has a small foreclosure property in Kaneohe. It's small, but it has the benefit of an *ohana* over the garage. Ruth, you and Mark know an ohana is like a garage apartment, right? It may need some work, but I mentioned it to Axle and I think he was going to talk to you guys about it."

Mark's eyes light up. "Really? Our own place? That would be so cool. Anything bigger than this place would seem like a palace to us. Right, Mom?"

Ruth's eyes tear up, and she reaches for a paper towel. Mey grabs one and hands it to her. Mark puts his hand on Ruth's arm.

"What's wrong, Mom?"

"I'm sorry, Mark. The stress has been rather intense lately. This truly is an answer to prayer." Ruth turns to give her grateful gaze to Oskar. "Oskar, I don't know what to say."

Oskar is touched by Ruth's gratitude. *I feel like crying myself!* "Ruth, why don't you, Mark—I mean, Canoe—Axle and I go look at the house tomorrow? Can you get away from the branch for an hour or so?"

"Katrina is out, but everyone else should be there. Maybe we could take a late lunch and go, say, around one thirty?"

"Let me call Axle and see what he says." Oskar walks outside to make the call.

Mark and Ruth turn to each other in amazement. "Mom, that would be so cool and Kanehoe is not too far. I wonder what kind of shape it's in. Hopefully, it's not as messed up as the GA was when we first moved in."

"Hopefully not, Mark, but I'll be happy with almost anything right now. You'll probably have to take me to work every day so you can take the car to help Mey clean."

"Ugh, I'll have to get up with the chickens. But I'll get the car, so I guess that's a fair trade."

Ruth throws her wet paper towel at Canoe. "Yuck!" He slaps it away.

Oskar walks back inside. "Axle said he can get the key from Mike tomorrow since it was his loan. Meylani, would you like to go with us?"

"No, thanks, Oskar. I have houses to clean tomorrow. I'm anxious to hear about it after you guys go see it, though."

Mark turns to Mey. "Do you mind if I go with my mom to see the house? I want to help you tomorrow, but if you're okay with it, I'd love to see the place."

"Let's start early, Canoe, that way we might be done with your part by one thirty. You need to get in the habit of getting up early now anyway to carpool, right?"

Mark sticks his tongue out at Mey. Ruth rolls her eyes, and Oskar laughs again.

"It's like a sitcom hanging out with you guys. Ruth, I have to go, but I'll come by the branch tomorrow so we can leave at one thirty. See you then." Oskar's phone buzzes, and he answers it as he walks outside.

At Home at Ewa

Oskar sits on a lounge by his pool looking across Mamala Bay at the airport. He thinks about Pearl Harbor, which is only a short distance away.

Everyone thought I was crazy buying a house at Ewa Beach, but it's close to where I need to be. Kailua Beach was the most often suggested location for a beachfront estate, but it's just too far from the bay.

He lifts the glass of Jack Daniels and swallows a big gulp. In fact, he finishes the whole glass in two gulps.

Mark would definitely question my sobriety if he could see me now.

He stands up and pulls on his wet suit and steps over to the diving equipment.

I've been allowing myself to get directed away from my main focus with all the changes I'm making at the bank. Why did I tell Axle I was interested in Ruth? I can't begin to go down that road right now.

He looks over at the next house and sees his neighbor doing laps in her pool.

If I want a distraction, Julie next door would make more sense. She and I have "spent some time" together already. I don't need to put my focus on anything but the Hawaii Pearl Day Remembrance ceremony. Relationships are not part of the equation.

While putting on his scuba gear, he looks out again toward the water. Making sure he has his underwater flashlight, he walks over the beach and into the water. If Julie had been looking, she would've noticed a dark form slowly slide into the ocean.

Drugar Again Comes into the Picture

Everything is going so well, I can't believe it. Coughing, Drugar thinks about where he dumped his gear and feels confident it won't be discovered at the hiding place in the harbor. He goes to the bar refrigerator as he muses over what he has accomplished so far and continues on outside stepping out to his lanai. He seems mesmerized as he watches the waves continue to crash against the shore and the tiki torches near the beach provide enough light to give sporadic glances of the rhythmic surges.

Picking up a beach chair, he goes to sit near one of the tikis. He places his White Mountain Porter beer in the sand as he opens his chair. He has a few moments to relax before he leaves to finish his task. His mind is at peace as he sits and watches the waves. At 9:00 a.m. on *the* Saturday, the world will change forever, and he looks forward to his well-planned solution.

Going Uphill

"Mark?" Ruth looks at Mark sleeping on the new sleeper sofa. She steps over his new laptop and taps him on the forehead. He opens one eye. "Do you want to walk over to the branch around one o'clock?"

"Sure." Mark closes his eyes.

Ruth chuckles and walks outside. The sky is overcast, and it starts to drizzle as she quickly opens her car door and gets inside. She can't stop smiling.

Things have been going well in spite of the flurry of activity I'm managing.

Starting the car, she reviews her tasks for the morning.

Okay, with Katrina off, Sharon will be coming in early. I have to get the Hawaii Pearl Day Memorial ceremony fliers confirmed today to get them ready tomorrow for couriering to the branch. The invitations should also be ready, so I can get both Daniel and Brenda working on addressing them. Axle was getting me the list of customers with over $250,000 on deposit. I can't wait to go to Kaneohe today. Her mind wanders. *Buying a house right now is a big step and it means Mark and I will be here for a while. This is such a permanent change. Thank goodness he seems good with it. That will certainly make it easier for both of us to adjust. What else do I need to do today? Hmmm, starting the car might be a good beginning!*

Mark hears the BMW as it backs out of the driveway. He looks at his phone, and since it's already 7:00 a.m., he decides he should get up and take a shower. He needs to meet Mey down the street at the new rental. As the warm water pours over him, he also takes stock of his day. *I'll need to be super speedy when cleaning today so I don't leave too much for Mey to finish.* Washing quickly, he steps out of the shower and hears someone in the kitchen. He puts on his work shorts and sticks his head out the door, calling out, "Is that you, Mey?"

"Yep, it's me. Would you like me to pour you some coffee? Your mom made a full pot."

"Please!"

Mark finds a ratty old T-shirt and pulls it over his head. Grabbing his rubber slippers, phone, and sunglasses, he walks into the kitchen as Mey adds cream and sugar to his coffee.

"Hey, you." He looks at Mey affectionately.

Mey hands Mark his coffee. "Hey to you. You ready to get started? Maybe you should give me a key to this place so you guys don't have to keep it unlocked for me."

"Good idea. During the remodel, Mom and I were so accustomed to keeping the place unlocked, we haven't thought about or discussed keeping it locked now. I should be able to go to the hardware store tomorrow and get a copy for you."

"Good deal. You ready to head out?"

"Now that I have my coffee, yeah."

As they leave the GA, Mark locks up and they start down the street toward the first cleaning job. They walk in comfortable and companionable silence, each lost in their own thoughts. Mark and Mey have spent significant time together and rarely feel the need to talk to fill in the quiet. Mark's daydreaming about the new house he and Ruth may be buying, and Mey is daydreaming about Mark.

Mey looks surreptitiously over at Mark. "Canoe, you looking forward to checking out the Kaneohe house today?"

"I feel like I have ants in my pants. I'm so excited to see the place. With our own place, it'll feel more like home. Sometimes I feel like we're on an extended vacation and not living a normal life. I wish you could see it with us. I know you could give us some good insight on updating or remodeling."

"I wish I could go, but I have two other cleaning jobs today, which means I'll barely have enough time to finish them before the first vacationer shows up this afternoon."

"Mey, as soon as I get back from looking at the house, I'll help you finish up. What's the third house you're doing?"

"Back here to clean the big house."

He reaches over and takes her hand. "That makes sense. I did notice the last renters left yesterday. I should easily be able to help you, I promise."

She squeezes his hand back. "I'm going to hold you to that. So your mom works for Oskar? I knew he owned the bank, and I've seen him at church a few times, but for some reason I didn't think about the connection to your mom."

"She works directly for him now since her promotion. They seem to have a great working relationship. Now that I think about it, that seems kind of odd to me. When she started working at the bank, she tried to hide it, but I got the distinct impression Oskar made her nervous. When we would see him at church, she would greet him but not go up and visit. You know that's not like her at church, right?"

"Well, I haven't attended much lately, but I'll agree Ruth is friendly. I've always found Oskar to be friendly too, which I think is one of the reasons he's been so successful. I'm usually watching Kim during the service, so I don't interact with Oskar as much. What are your thoughts about Oskar? You had coffee with him the other day, right?"

"He and I connected pretty quickly because he let me know he's a recovered alcoholic. When I went by the bank and Mom couldn't get away to take me, he offered to drive me to an AA meeting. The meeting I chose was only for military personnel, so Oskar took me to Kailua Coffee where we had a nice chat. I thought he was pretty normal, and I didn't get any weird vibes. I'll watch them today and let you know this afternoon. You know the first time I met him at church, I told Mom he looked like a Mafia guy."

Mark and Mey both laugh. "He does at that. Here's the house. Let's hope the last group of vacationers didn't make too big of a mess!"

Chapter 15

Kaneohe

Ruth looks out from her office and sees Mark and Oskar walking in the door at the same time. She picks up the phone and buzzes Axle.

"Mark and Oskar just showed up. You ready to go?"

"Yep. Is Mike back from his inspection? I still haven't gotten the key from him yet."

"He is. You want me to go ask him?"

"No, I'll ask, but don't let him leave again. He's as slippery as an eel to get hold of when I need him!"

"Roger that."

Ruth steps over to Mike's office. "Hi, Mike. Are you going to be here for a few minutes? Axle needs to ask you for something."

"Do you know what he needs? I have a lunch date in fifteen minutes."

Axle walks up to the door. "Mike, Oskar wants to show Ruth the Kaneohe foreclosure property. Could you please get me the key? He and Mark are coming in the door now."

Mike's eyebrows rise about two inches as he pulls a file from the cabinet next to his desk. "Ruth, have you seen this house yet?"

"No, I haven't. In fact, I don't know anything about it other than it's in Kaneohe. Mark and I need to move quickly, and Oskar thought the house would be a good option for us."

Mike thinks for a second as he hands Axle the key. "It's about 1,400 square feet, but there's also a tiny ohana above the carport. The previous owners started doing some remodeling but ran out of money. You might be able to make it work. I'd certainly love to sell it, so keep me posted. I gotta go though." He steps out of his office and hurries out to the lobby, greeting Oskar and Mark as he runs toward the elevator.

Axle shakes his head. "That guy is always running somewhere. Hi, Canoe. Hi, Oskar."

Mark steps up and shakes Axle's hand as does Oskar.

Ruth steps over to her office and gets her purse. "Let me give the tellers a few instructions, and I'll be ready to go."

Axle looks at Oskar. "You know where we're going, right?"

Oskar looks at Axle and laughs. "I don't know the address, do you?"

"No, but I did see Mike pull the file. Let me see if I can find it. Otherwise, I'll have to call him." Axle goes over to the file cabinet, shuffles through the files, and finds one sticking out from the others. He pulls it and hands it to Oskar. "Is that it?"

Oskar looks at the info in the file. "Yep, this is it. I know exactly where this house is located. Let's take the file though, it might provide helpful information about the place." He looks up as Ruth walks toward them.

"Daniel isn't feeling well, but said he'll stay until we return. We need to make this trip a quick one."

Oskar frowns and mumbles under his breath. He starts to say something, then stops himself. "Let's go." He quickly starts walking to the door as the others watch.

Axle shrugs. "We're taking my SUV, so he can't go anywhere without us, but we better go since he doesn't seem too happy. You guys ready?"

Mark and Ruth nod, and they all walk outside. Oskar is leaning impatiently against the SUV, so Axle quickly uses his remote to unlock it, and Oskar gets in on the driver's side.

"I guess that means he's driving," Axle murmurs. He opens the back seat door for Ruth as Mark gets in on the opposite side.

Ruth tries not to frown but is frustrated with Oskar's attitude. *It's not as if Daniel can help that he's sick. I want to ask to look at the file, but I'm afraid to say anything for fear Oskar may cancel the trip.*

Mark looks at Ruth, and they shrug their shoulders at the same time, laughing at themselves and relieving the tension. Axle looks in the rearview mirror and sees Ruth and Mark smiling. He's glad because he was afraid this trip might get awkward real fast. Oskar doesn't say anything. Since Oskar had laid the file down between them, Axle picks it up. Leafing through it, he sees some interesting information about the house.

It's a two bedroom house built in 1954 with a living, kitchen, and loft area. It faces the bay, which is a nice benefit. It's on Kamehameha Highway, which could be good or bad. Hopefully good.

Axle watches for the house number as Oskar slows down. "It's the next house, Oskar."

Oskar quickly pulls into the driveway, which takes them around to the carport. He looks in the rearview mirror, and Ruth and Mark are holding hands as Ruth prays, "Father, thank you for this door opening for Mark and me to own our own home. If it be your will, have this be the place you have chosen for us to live. In Jesus's name, we pray, Amen."

Both Axle and Oskar say, "Amen," as well.

Oskar relaxes and takes a fortifying breath. *My worries are starting to affect my work, and that can't happen! Daniel being sick is such a stupid thing to get irritated about!*

All exit the SUV, taking in every detail of the property. The house is a small A-frame house with a deck around the upstairs perimeter. Attached to one side of the house is the carport that includes an ohana on the second level. The lot is filled with a variety of trees including two coconut palms that frame it on each side. Cook pines line up and down one side, separating the house from its neighbor, and a producing mango can be seen behind the carport.

Mark walks around outside the carport where he spots an outdoor staircase. "It looks like this is the way to get to the ohana. Shall we start here? Axle, do you have the key?"

"Yep, let me open it up."

Mark, Ruth, and Oskar take the stairs; and all huddle behind Axle as he approaches the ohana door. As the key clicks in the lock and the door opens, Mark and Ruth peek over Axle's shoulder. Once

Axle steps inside, all four stumble into the room together and Axle places his hand on the wall to keep from falling. "Whoa, guys." He moves further in so everyone can get inside. They are surprised to find bare stud walls in an area that could be a living room and kitchen, but is difficult to tell with no finishing details just *naked* plumbing showing! They all stop to look out a big picture window with a spectacular view of the bay.

Oskar steps next to Ruth. "You should buy this house for no other reason than for this view!"

Ruth nods and sees there's a doorway on the other side of the kitchen, which opens into a bedroom-and-small-bath combination. Oskar answers a phone call and leaves the ohana, taking the stairs two at a time. Mark, Axle, and Ruth all sigh in relief without realizing they have each done so.

Ruth takes a moment to visit with Mark. "It looks like the ohana will make a great rental. What do you think?"

"I agree. Axle, are you ready to go back and see the house?"

Axle nods agreement as they return outside and down the stairs. Walking through the carport, Mark points to the side door of the house. "Axle, will your key open that door?"

"Let's see."

The key works, and they carefully follow Axle inside. No stumbling this time. This entrance takes them directly into the kitchen where Ruth's eyes move to every corner. Here, the previous owners had made headway in the remodeling process, so the top cabinets have been removed and are on the floor in the small breakfast nook. The bottom cabinets are painted white, and gray granite countertops have been installed. The walls are painted a pale blue. A new refrigerator, dishwasher, and stove are still wrapped in plastic, protecting them from paint and saw dust. Ruth's smile shows she isn't intimidated by the lack of completion in the kitchen. The kitchen doorway opens to the family room with a ceiling that goes all the way to the top of the A frame. The staircase on the far side of the room leads up to a loft.

Ruth says, "I love this whole look. The two-story ceiling gives the place a greater feeling of space. Since the floor is only concrete, do you think it was going to be stained or was some other floor covering going to be installed?"

Axle opens the file he brought with him. "I don't see any notes on that other than it says there's tile stacked in the carport. I didn't notice it when we drove up though. Before we go to the loft, it looks like there's another room downstairs by the kitchen. Let's look at it first."

Almost simultaneously, Mark calls out, "There's a bedroom next door to the kitchen!"

Axle and Ruth follow Mark and exit the kitchen into the family room and see an open doorway into another room. It's a white-painted bedroom and features a rather large window with jalousies and an attached bathroom. The bathroom has been gutted, and the vanity and toilet have been installed but the tub has not.

"Hm-m-m, this might be considered the master bedroom. It will look pretty darn good when the remodel is finished," Ruth adds as she fiddles with the jalousie window mechanism.

"Let's go check out the loft. The stairs are back in the other room." Axle leads the group back into the main downstairs living area.

They troop to the stairs and follow Axle up as if he is their Pied Piper. Once at the top of the stairs, they view the small loft. The ceiling of the loft is taller than it looked from downstairs, probably at least nine feet. There's older beige carpet on the floor.

Ruth opens one door and sees a small closet. "Well, at least there's a closet!"

Mark opens the other door, which reveals a small newly remodeled bathroom that includes a pedestal sink, toilet, and subway tiled shower.

Ruth puts her hands on the mirror edge. "This is nicely done and one less thing to finish."

"Yeah," says Mark. "You don't need to worry since I'm the one most likely to do the work!"

Ruth slaps Mark playfully with her purse strap. Ruth notices another door in the small bathroom and opens it to reveal another bedroom. So in addition to the sitting area, the loft contains a bedroom and a bathroom.

Axle looks out the front of the loft and sees Oskar is still on the phone in the driveway. "Okay, kids! Let's check out the carport and see if we can see any building supplies."

Reentering the kitchen, they walk through the exterior door that takes them directly into the carport, and looking to the backside, they see a few boxes.

Ruth picks up a tile from one. "This pale aqua subway tile is prettier than the white in the other bath. It will be more interesting with a different-colored tile for each bathroom.

Mark comments, "I think this place has definite potential. I could do most of the finish work myself with some assistance from Leek. I guess the floor tile for downstairs disappeared so that might be the biggest expense."

Ruth tries not to get too excited. The place looks like the perfect Hawaiian home to her. "Mark, is this a place where you could see yourself living?"

"It works for me if it does you, Mom."

"Axle, what would be our next step in the purchase process?"

Oskar walks into the carport. "Did you see the entire house? What are you thinking, Ruth?"

"Oskar, I was just asking Axle what the next step would be for Mark and me to purchase the house. It would be perfect for us. The most important information I need to know is the price!"

Axle looks at Oskar. "Has the price been determined and do all employee loan applications go through you, Oskar?"

"Hand me the file will ya, Axle?" Oskar peruses the file and looks up to see Mark and Ruth looking at him anxiously. "First, based on the appraisal in the file, the price should be $435,000 since there is still work to be done. Secondly, I have recently delegated employee loan processing to Daniel. In fact, I was just speaking to him on the phone and gave him a heads-up in case Ruth decided to buy. He knows it's critical to make this a speedy process. Ruth, you and Daniel can discuss down payments and monthly mortgage figures once you complete a loan application. Why don't we return to the branch so you can start the process."

Mark interjects, "Oskar, could Mom and I start doing some of the construction work in the meantime? I might be able to get Leek to help me."

"I feel pretty confident Ruth will qualify for the loan, so I don't see why not. Axle, go ahead and give Ruth the key."

Axle hands it over, thinking Oskar is going way out of his way to make this happen. He grinds his teeth and hopes Oskar is sincere about his feelings for Ruth because he has never known Oskar to take any relationship seriously. He looks over at Ruth. Tears are falling down her face as she walks over to Oskar and gives him a big hug. Oskar hugs her back but doesn't extend it.

Mark's on the phone speaking to Leek. He turns his head from the phone. "Guys, Leek's in the area and is going to detour over here to see the place. Mom, can I have the key? Leek said he'll give me a ride home after he looks at the house."

Ruth excitedly hands the key to Mark. "You're on top of things, Canoe. Thanks so much!"

Mark laughs, as does Axle. Oskar's already outside on the phone again as Axle and Ruth move to get into the SUV.

As Ruth opens the door to the back seat, Oskar waves her and Axle to the front. He hands over the keys to Axle as he looks over and sees Mark wave and go back to the main house. Turning out on the main street, they see Leek drive by in his cab. Ruth waves furiously, and Leek smiles and returns her wave.

"Axle, I can't believe what God is doing for us. I feel so blessed. I'm trying to think what all I have to do when I return to the branch so I can find time to complete the loan application. I think I have a safe deposit box customer coming in at four o'clock." Ruth looks at her watch and then at Axle and says, "It's 3:35 p.m. now..."

"Ruth, I'm happy to help the customer while you do the loan ap."

"Axle, are you sure? I know you don't like paperwork much."

"You know I don't mind. What does the customer need?"

"The Yamamotos want to add their son to their contract. I could do the new contract quickly when we get to the branch if you want to meet with them for their signatures."

"You know I won't argue with you doing the paperwork! Buzz me when you have it done, and I'll come get it."

Ruth turns to the back seat. "Oskar, thanks so much for providing us the opportunity to get this Kaneohe house. I'm so excited, I can hardly sit still. Wow, I think we just bought a house in Hawaii!"

Oskar looks distracted but answers Ruth. "It sounds like a win-win to me. We get the house sold, and you get a nice place to live."

Axle pulls into the Kailua branch parking garage, and Oskar quickly steps out and tells Axle and Ruth, "I have some urgent issues to address guys, so I'm not coming into the branch. Ruth, I'm excited for you and know it'll all work out. Talk to you both later." Oskar walks quickly to his truck.

Ruth is already out of the SUV as Axle picks up the file and locks the vehicle. They walk inside quickly and separate at the elevator.

"Axle, I'll call you about the contract in a few minutes. I want to check on the tellers before I start on it."

"Hey, why don't you bring it and the customers to my office when they arrive?"

"Great idea. Thanks, Axle, for coming with us." She walks to him and gives him a hug as well. She holds it a little longer, and Axle's heart beats double time. He pats Ruth's arm, pulls back, and looks at her.

"Okay, Ruth, see you in a few."

CHAPTER 16

Unexpected Results

"Look, Lonnie, you're not in a position to demand more money from me. I've paid you plenty."

Slurring his words, Lonnie whines, "Come on. Since I got kicked out of the Navy, I can't seem to get any work. You have plenty of dough. 'Sides, you want me ta keep your secrets, don't ya?"

"You're pathetic." Stumbling in the surf, Drugar grabs Lonnie's arm and jabs bills into his pocket. He shoves Lonnie further out of his way. "Don't ever contact me again. No one would believe we knew each other anyway."

As Lonnie trips over a volcanic rock, a big wave crashes the shore simultaneously. The "friend" shakes his head in disgust. He waits for Lonnie to surface, but after a minute, he nervously jumps into the surf, calling Lonnie's name. The friend is a strong swimmer, but the undertow is scary strong. After looking for over thirty minutes, he realizes a continued search will be fruitless. He drags himself onto the beach, breathing heavily. Sitting down in the sand, he can't believe this turn of events.

The first casualty of my plan. Stupid, Lonnie. He didn't even try to swim. Surely he knew how! No one could get in the Navy without being able to swim, right? Of course, all the alcohol flowing through his veins probably didn't help. Damn!

Hawaii Pearl Day

Oskar throws his keys on his desk, closes his door, and sits down. He dials a number and starts talking as soon as the person answers.

"Frank, what's the problem? Did I understand your e-mail correctly? The military is waffling on allowing us to have the outrigger at the ceremony?"

"Settle down, Oskar. They told me they're nervous about doing anything outside the normal with all the recent terror attacks."

"But, Frank, those attacks weren't in the States. You know what they say, if we change our lives, the terrorists win."

"I agree with you, but I also understand their concerns as well. In fact, they had an incident happen yesterday. They found a man's body washed up on Iroquois Lagoon Beach. You know where that is, right? Outside of Pearl. That stepped up their anxiety. But they didn't give me a total no. Actually, they'll allow you to display the outrigger but not allow you to speak. I hate to mention it, Oskar, but in addition, they were concerned about your Bosnian background. They told me they're going to rescind their offer to Kim on the benediction as well."

Oskar almost throws his phone across the office but takes a deep breath. "Kim and I have been in the States for over twenty years. We're upstanding members of the community here. For heaven sakes, Kim's a pastor! I can't believe this. What about if someone else from the bank speaks? Would they approve that?"

"You know, they might. We'd have to get the name to them ASAP though, so they can do a background check. Who were you thinking of doing it?"

Oskar quickly makes a mental list. *Axle won't be approved either since he is also from Bosnia.* "Frank, what about you? They certainly could not complain about your background. You're on the board of one of the veterans groups after all."

Agreeing with Oskar about the importance of being involved in the ceremony, Frank acquiesces. "Sure, Oskar, I'd be happy to do it. I'll call them and get back to you. You're taking this better than I anticipated. I guess one reason you're so successful is that you don't let your emotions dictate your decisions. I'll call you as soon as I get an answer. Later."

"Bye." Oskar now takes the opportunity to throw his phone across the room. It hits the wall and falls to the floor unbroken. *If Frank only knew. I should have anticipated this response. There have been concerns about terrorists from Eastern Europe. So for instance, what's the point of doing the auction if we can't make the presentation at Pearl Harbor? In fact, I better call Ruth right now because I think she was mailing the invitations this week.* Oskar dials his desk phone, and it rings once.

"Hi, Oskar. Long time no see."

Oskar tries to put a smile on his face but doesn't bother with chitchat. "Ruth, I just got off the phone with Frank. The military isn't allowing me to speak at the Pearl Harbor Remembrance Day ceremony. I didn't pass their background check because I'm from Bosnia. Frank has agreed to ask them to allow him to do it, but we won't know for a few days whether Frank will be approved. Have you mailed out the auction invitations yet?"

"No, Oskar, we're finishing addressing them today. We won't mail them until we hear from you." Ruth tentatively says, "We'll still do the auction if Frank is not approved, right?"

"What would be the point?"

Ruth is shocked. "The money we'd get for charity. I thought that was the main point of the auction."

Oskar breathes in and out two times before answering. "You're correct, Ruth. I'm letting my frustration get the best of me. Also, I wanted the added publicity from the ceremony. We could still do an auction but maybe dovetail it with some other event."

"I have an idea, Oskar. What if we have the auction the day after the ceremony, and Frank could mention it there since the outrigger will be on display."

"Ruth, again, you never cease to amaze me. I like it. I'll e-mail you as soon as I hear from Frank. Can you check with the Pink Palace and determine if they can accommodate a date change?"

"Will do. Don't worry, Oskar. I'll say a prayer that everything goes according to God's plan."

"Thanks, Ruth."

An Okay House

Leek and Mark search outside the Kaneohe house looking for the additional tile listed in the loan file. Leek pushes his hat up on his head.

"Canoe, I'm thinking somebody lifted the tile right out of the carport. Let's measure the space to see how much we'll need, and we might as well make a list of all the other items required to finalize the finish out."

Mark looks toward Leek. "Do you think tile would be best? I was wondering if bamboo flooring might work."

Leek opens the door to the downstairs. "I think anything light would work since the house has so much dark wood everywhere. In fact, we might want to consider completely painting the downstairs white."

"That sounds *A-okay* to me. What about the cost? I'm not sure how much money Mom has, but I can see a lot of paint is going to be needed to cover the dark brown currently on the wall and ceiling beams."

"We can always check on the paint store for some estimates. You know, you always name everything. Why not name this the A-OK house? It is an *A* frame, and it is in Kaneohe."

Mark lights up. "I love it. What the heck. Let's make our wish list, get our estimates, and we can pare it down after talking to Mom. Leek, what would I do without you?"

"You know, Canoe, from what I have seen over the last few months, I'd say you would do quite well without me, but I don't want you to find out yet! By the way, the church bought a bunch of Bibles so I brought you one. It's in the cab, so don't let me forget to give it to you."

Mark walks out to the back of the yard, looking at the bay in the distance. Seeing a couple of plastic chairs leaning against the back of the carport, he walks over and drags them to the middle of the yard where the view is best. "Leek, let's take a load off."

As they sit and watch the boats on the water, Mark looks at Leek. "Thanks, Leek. I've been borrowing Mom's Bible, but having my own will be much better."

"Sure, Canoe. Wow, this is a great view. God's handiwork never ceases to amaze me."

Mark shakes his head. "Leek, you're an amazing guy. You work for the cab company, you're a worship leader at church, you conduct a Bible study, plus you help me with remodeling! How do you keep up with everything?"

"My stock answer is my faith, Canoe. Believe it or not, my life before my salvation mirrored yours. My coming to Christ was so dramatic. *Everything* changed. Would you like to hear my story?"

"I wanted to ask you when you prayed for me but became distracted by my own experience!"

"Sit back, Mark, and hear how God made this miraculous change in my life."

Leek sits for a few moments, absently playing with a plastic piece dangling from his chair. He reaches up to brush the hair from his eyes and starts to speak.

"I've always been drawn to the supernatural. You know Hawaii has an amazing history of dedication to our spiritual life from the distant past, but it didn't focus on Jesus as they had no knowledge of Him. They did know a greater power than themselves created this wondrous 'pearl' we call Hawaii. I have an uncle that's educated on, and dedicated to the *heiau* ceremonies, and he taught me what he knew. I still hold our history in great esteem, but I had a supernatural experience that led me to the life I lead now."

Leek stretches his legs out, leaning back in the chair as he closes his eyes. "Explaining my salvation is an emotional journey for me, so I need to sit for a minute to think through what I want to say."

Mark nods even though Leek doesn't see it. All is quiet except for the wind blowing the tree branches and the chirping of the birds moving from tree to tree. Mark mirrors Leek's movements by leaning back and stretching his legs. The sound of nature settles him as he waits to hear Leek's explanation of his coming to Christ.

"Several of the schools here conduct a Hawaiian language immersion program. One particular day, I was asked to do a school presentation on Hawaiian ceremonies performed at the ancient heiaus or temples. Explaining to those small children our heritage in our own language was emotional for me and really emphasized to them why it's important not to forget our past. I was feeling quite proud and decided as I was leaving the school to reward myself by smoking a joint I had stashed in my backpack. I drove to a secluded beach, walked near the water, and dropped my pack on the sand. I finished my smoke and dropped the little bit left from my joint and watched it swirl in the water. I felt so incredible and became motivated at that point to take a swim. The undertow at that beach is strong, but I swim there all the time and know it well.

"The swim was refreshing, but I started to get tired. I stopped, and treading water, I looked around and saw the shoreline quite far away. I wasn't concerned and started to swim toward shore but realized I wasn't getting any closer. I started to panic, and with some marijuana still in my system, I wasn't thinking straight. If I had been, I would've remembered to relax and go with the current but I didn't do that. The more I struggled against the current, the more panicked I became. You know how strong I am, but soon my legs were beyond moving. I took a deep breath and just stopped and lay on my back. I cried and cried knowing there was no way I could swim any longer. I was at least a mile from shore, and in my current shape, I wouldn't make it back. As I looked toward the sky, I thought through my life and knew I still needed to accomplish more. What that was I didn't know but felt it deep in my bones. What do you think happened next?"

Startled that Leek has asked him a question at this point, Mark blinks a couple of times and blurts out, "You cried out to God?"

"Good answer, but no."

"No?" Mark asks. "What then?"

"I hear a lapping of the waves and look over and see a bearded long-haired man sitting in a small wooden boat." Leek starts to cry and pulls a handkerchief from his back pocket and blows his nose. He smiles though, and Mark looks confused. "I felt relieved, a chance to be saved. The boat was about fifty yards from me, and I knew I didn't have the strength to swim even that far. I tried to cry out, but my voice was hoarse and made little sound. The man kept looking at me without moving, and the boat stayed exactly in the same location.

"Then the man spoke. 'Alika, do you know I love you?' As you can imagine, being fearful and exhausted, I was taken aback by the question. I didn't answer, and again the man asked, 'Alika, do you know I love you? Let me save you.' Suddenly, I felt a strange yearning, and as I looked at this man, he smiled and held his hands out to me. 'Alika, come to me. Let me save you. My yoke is easy and my burden is light.'

"I was in an extremely confused state, but a powerful peace came over me, and I started to swim toward the boat. I didn't think about it at the time, but the swimming came easy, and it seemed with only a few strokes I was at the boat. As I grabbed the boat, the man again asked me, 'Alika, do you know I love you?'

"My mind became completely clear, and I looked the man straight in the eyes, and said, 'Jesus?' He smiled and reached his hand toward me and pulled me into the boat. The next thing I knew I looked up and realized I was no longer in the boat but my hands felt sand."

Mark is dumbfounded by Leek's words. Looking at him, Mark doesn't speak but waits to hear the rest.

"Mark, I rolled over in the sand and got up on my knees and kissed the sand and said out loud, 'I am bowled over, Jesus, that you would save me, but I am not going to question it! Thank you for showing me you're real! I can't wait to see what comes next!'"

Leek's phone beeps at him. "Looks like I have a fare. Let's go do the measurements lightning quick so I can get you home before I pick my fare up outside Kailua, but before I do, I have one last comment. As I mentioned earlier, I still highly respect our Hawaiian culture and continue to do presentations at the schools, but I present the ceremonies in a historical way not a religious way."

Knowing time is of the essence, Mark runs out to Leek's cab to open the trunk to get the measuring tape. After measuring the floors that need to be replaced, Mark locks up quickly and he and Leek get into the cab. Holding his new Bible, Mark sits quietly ruminating over Leek's testimony. *It's a lot to take in.*

Mark's thoughts move to the work to be done at A-OK and returns over and over in his mind to Leek's earlier comments that

Mark could do well without help. He can't quite place the feeling he's experiencing, but finally realizes it's joy. He relaxes and puts his head against the headrest and closes his eyes to experience fully the joy in his heart.

A-OK or Not?

Oskar sits in his office stewing about the authorities blocking his participation at the Pearl Harbor Remembrance Ceremony.

This puts a real damper on my plans. How long will my Bosnian background be a shadow over my life?

He's feeling an unbelievable amount of anger. Rage is probably a better way to describe it.

I probably need to leave the bank, or I may say something that will trigger some concern by the employees. An afternoon with my neighbor Julie might settle me down.

He picks up his phone and starts texting. A moment later he gets a response.

"No."

He takes the phone and throws it against the wall. His face is red, and his heart rate is off the charts. Rising to pick up his phone, he's surprised to see only the back popped off. He puts it back together and checks to make sure it's working. *I seem to be making a habit of this!*

What's wrong with me? I can't do anything right now to jeopardize my long-term plans. Right now I need to get Ruth's loan application finalized.

Checking his e-mail on his laptop, he sees that she has e-mailed a completed application to him and Daniel. He picks up his phone again, glad that it's in one piece, and dials Daniel. It goes to voice mail, so he leaves a message.

"Daniel, please put a rush on Ruth's application for the Kaneohe house. The sooner she qualifies, the sooner we get that foreclosure off the books. If you see anything troubling in her credit or ability to qualify, talk to me first before speaking to her. If you could get back to me by day's end, I would appreciate it." *I know Daniel isn't going to like the rush I'm placing on this loan for Ruth. Who cares?*

Back at GA

Mark rushes into the garage apartment hoping Mey is inside. Finding the door locked, he's anticipating, no. He still gets a "rush" each time he looks inside the place he and Leek remodeled.

I learned so much working with Leek. I know I can do a lot with the Kaneohe house with minimal direction. I'm excited to get started.

Mark looks at the calendar on the kitchen counter. Mey has notated her schedule and the days Mark will be helping, so he traces his finger across the page till he finds today's date. Mey is down the street at the new vacation rental. As he grabs a bottled water from the refrigerator, he looks down at his clothes.

Hmmm, I think I need to change to my work shorts. Jeans will be too hot for cleaning.

He peels off the jeans as he walks into the living/bedroom. The cabinet with the TV is his dresser, and he takes a pair of shorts from the bottom drawer. Transferring his wallet from his jeans, he quickly changes, remembering to pick up the water before exiting the GA. He locks up and starts to jog down the street. Making it to the house in record time, he bends over to get a breath, waiting a few seconds before walking up to the house. Hearing the water running in the kitchen, he walks in that direction. He peeks around the door and sees Mey wiping down the counters.

"Boo!"

Mey keeps wiping. Mark has a puzzled look, then sees her ear-buds. He decides he better not scare Mey and waits until she turns toward him. As she does, he waves to her. She is still startled and drops her rag. She smiles though and pulls her earbuds out of her ears.

"Hey."

"Hey to you."

"Okay, don't keep me waiting. What did you guys think of the Kaneohe house?"

"You mean, the A-OK house?"

Mey rolls her eyes, still smiling. "O-o-okay. I'm going to assume that means you guys liked it?"

"Yep, Mom's probably completing the loan application as we speak. Oh, Mey, we have to go by there later so you can see it. I know you'll love it. It's an older A-frame home, but some remodeling has been done. I called Leek, and he came by so we could measure everything like we did at the GA…"

"Whoa. Did you take any pictures with your phone?"

Mark looks at Mey blankly. "Ugh, no. That means for sure we have to go see it today. How many more homes do we have to clean today?"

"One more."

"That doesn't leave any time because I told Leek to pick me up for the five-o'clock AA meeting. You want to go with us? We could go by the house afterwards."

"Mark, it'll be dark by then. Is the electricity turned on? If not, we won't be able to see much."

"You're right, dang it! I'm going to work at a supersonic speed today to see how much we can get done. Let's see, it's two thirty. How much more do we have to do here?"

"Today I'm doing the kitchen last so we can go out the kitchen door when we leave. I'm done here. Let's go to the Lanikai house. We've never done it before, but we may finish it quickly enough to go to Kaneohe today."

"Perfect. I'll get your cleaning supplies."

They walk out to Mey's Mazda 3.

Mark feels his phone buzz in his pocket and takes it out. "It's Leek. Hi, Leek. What's up?"

"Canoe, I forgot to mention earlier, but since my boss wants me to work an extra shift, I won't be able to take you to the meeting. Is that okay?"

"Sure. Mey and I were thinking of going over to the A-OK house to check it out if we can do it before it gets dark."

Leek laughs. "Be careful. The neighbors may think you guys are breaking in or something."

"We will. Thanks for calling."

Mey starts the car. "Change of plans?"

"Yep, we may have time to go to the house after all. Even though I should go to a meeting."

"Mark, I'm happy to take you to your meeting. We can go to the house another time. I don't want to stay at the meeting though. Do you think your mom could pick you up?"

"I'll text and ask."

Mark's fingers fly across the face of his phone and Mey is amazed at his speed. *My clumsy fingers could never go as fast.* "Okay, let's get to the Lanikai house."

Mark salutes Mey. "Yes, ma'am."

CHAPTER 17

Things Go Awry

Mey pulls up to the building entrance where the AA meeting is being held. "I'm sorry we have to delay seeing the A-Ok house. The new rental was way bigger than I expected. Is your mom picking you up?"

"I'm sure she will. I haven't heard from her yet though."

"Mark, it's already five o'clock. You texted her at two thirty. Are you sure she hasn't gotten back to you? I hate to leave you if you don't know she's picking you up."

"It's okay, Mey. I can probably get someone here to drop me off. It's not far to the GA."

"You sure?"

"Absolutely."

"Text me when you get home?"

"Sure." Mark slams the car door and sprints to the building entrance and goes inside. There are about ten people standing around. Heading to the coffee pot, he drops a dollar in the basket, fills his cup, and moves out of the way for the next person. Looking around, he notices someone he knows.

"Hey, Matt. I think my mom is picking me up, but if not, could you give me a ride home? I live on South Kalaheo Avenue."

"Wow, the high-rent district, huh?"

"Yeah, but my mom and I live in a tiny garage apartment, so we aren't in the *rich league*, just live among 'em."

"Sure, that's so close I'd be happy to take you home if you don't mind a detour. My roommate works at that dive, Surf Shack, and she asked me to bring her work shirt."

Mark doesn't hesitate. "Thanks, Matt. I'll wait in the car while you go inside the place. I normally try to avoid all bars."

"I know what you mean. Me too."

They move over to the folding chairs and sit as the speaker stands up. When the speaker begins, Mark pulls out his AA Big Book and looks for the chapter on step 4, "Make a Moral Inventory." Matt leans back and stretches his legs. Mark pays close attention, but Matt has closed his eyes and is taking a nap. Mark finally notices and gives Matt a nudge. Matt opens the lid of one eye.

"I like to close my eyes and meditate on the speaker's words."

Mark looks at Matt. "Sure you do." He doesn't say anything else as he listens.

The speaker finally finishes. Even Mark is finding it difficult to pay attention. He looks toward Matt to say so and sees Matt is snoring away. Mark nudges Matt again.

"Why do you come if you aren't going to listen?"

"It's better than being at the Surf Shack, right?"

"That's true."

Mark looks at his phone and still does not see a response from Ruth. That puzzles him. *When was the last time she didn't respond to him? Like never!* For the umpteenth time, he redials Ruth's number.

Ruth and Axle

After hanging up the phone with Oskar, Ruth relaxes in her desk chair as she reviews all that needs to be done. She closes her eyes momentarily and after a few minutes feels a presence in the room, and her eyes pop open.

"Can't a girl get a nap around here?"

Axle grins as he hands Ruth a smoothie. "I was taking Mike his smoothie to his office and overheard you on the phone with Oskar, so I figured you needed a break. I decided five minutes was long enough."

"Gee, thanks," Ruth mumbles as she takes a long drag on the drink. "Yum, yum, yummy! Just what I needed. Probably doesn't have caffeine, huh? After this day, I think I need some kind of stimulant!"

Pulling up a chair close to Ruth's desk, Axle responds, "I'm sure you do. I can make coffee if you feel you still need it after your smoothie. So what was Oskar all worked up about?"

"He's thinking of canceling the auction because Frank called and told him the military denied the request for Oskar to speak at the ceremony. He didn't pass their background check because of his Bosnian background."

"Whooee! I bet he was boiling!" Axle swipes his hand across his forehead, pretending to wipe nonexistent sweat from it.

Ruth laughs. "You got that right!"

Axle's demeanor changes, and he sighs. "He is sensitive about Bosnia. He seems to have become more so since we moved to Hawaii. He and Han both."

Ruth puts her chin in her hands, "I can understand about him being sensitive about Bosnia, but why more so here?"

"You've never heard the whole story of our escape, have you? Just the bit Kim described on your first visit to Ho'o. Maybe you better get that cup of coffee after all, this may take a while. Do you have time to go to the conference room so we can visit there?"

Ruth glances at her computer for the time and sees it's after five o'clock. "The bank lobby is closed, so I can go downstairs for a little while. Let me check real quick and see if Katrina needs anything in the drive-through, then I'll meet you downstairs."

"Sounds like a plan." After standing, Axle stretches and exits the office.

Two Hours Later

"So there you have it. That's why Oskar and Han become upset when Bosnia is discussed. You asked an interesting question. Both

Han and Oskar have let their bitterness increase over time, so I think it may not be because we're in Hawaii but just them not forgiving and putting the experience behind them."

Ruth grabs a tissue and blows her nose. As she does so, she glances at her watch. "Yikes, it's 7:00 p.m.! I didn't realize so much time had passed since Katrina left." She grabs her phone and glancing at it sees several texts from Mark. "I think I'm in the doghouse because it's so late. Mark's been looking for me. Thank you for sharing your story, Axle. I was moved by the sufferings each of you experienced." She picks up her mug to take to the break room. "I should have been watching the time. Mark and I have been at odds lately, and this won't help."

Axle grabs her mug, "Here let me take care of this so you can go. Don't worry, I'll lock up. See you in the morning."

Back at ACA

"Come on, Mark. I gotta get this shirt to my roomie. Let's get out of here."

Mark jumps up with the phone at his ear and runs after Matt as he walks toward the door. They see the sun has already set as they get into Matt's small Camry.

As they drive, Mark sees they are in one of the less affluent areas of Kailua. Pulling into a space at the oceanfront bar, Matt says, "Come on, Mark. Go inside with me and you can meet my roommate, Cheryl."

"I'd rather not, Matt. You said you won't be long, right?"

"Sure. Suit yourself."

Mark rolls down his window, so the breeze will keep the car cool. He watches as Matt walks into the bar behind other patrons. He looks at his phone, hoping for a text from Ruth, but there is none. He tries calling her once more, but she doesn't answer and her voice mail comes on.

"Hey, Mom. I'm on my way home from my meeting. See you soon."

He doesn't bother to tell her he had texted her earlier. *No point now.* Mark looks at the time and realizes he's been sitting in the car for fifteen minutes. *There's no way it takes that long to drop off a shirt to someone.* Mark thinks for a second. *Matt wasn't carrying anything when he went inside.* Mark twists around and sees the shirt in the back seat. He grabs it and exits the car. He tries not to be irritated, but *gee, I told Matt I don't like going into bars.* He steps inside the bar with the usual dark and smokey atmosphere. Mark smells the alcohol. He looks around and doesn't see Matt. Mark starts grumbling to himself but walks out to the back deck bar. He sees Matt talking to a young woman behind the bar. Matt reaches for a glass and knocks the drink back in one gulp. *Uh-oh.* Mark hesitates but walks over to Matt.

"Hey, Matt. What're you doing?"

Matt looks at Mark as if he doesn't recognize him. "Ahh, it's my buddy, Mark, from AA." Matt throws his arm across Mark's shoulders. "Cheryl, pour my friend here a Shirley Temple. He's trying to stay sober."

"Don't bother. I need to get home." Mark turns toward the young woman. "Matt left your shirt in the car, and I thought I'd bring it in for you." He hands the shirt to a tall woman who is preparing several drinks at once. She looks at the shirt and then at Mark. "He was supposed to bring that hours ago."

"Hey, Mark, are you going to drive Matt home?" Cheryl asks pointedly.

Mark takes a deep breath. "I'd be happy to if you can give me directions. But who's going to take me home from Matt's house?"

"I get off in fifteen minutes. I'll follow you and take you home."

"Matt and I'll wait for you in his car. Do you have any coffee around here? Maybe I can sober Matt up while we wait."

"Good idea." Cheryl turns around and sure enough there is a pot behind her. She picks up a paper cup and pours it half full. Adding cream and some sugar to the cup, she hands it to Mark. "I'll find you in the parking lot in a few minutes."

Mark takes the cup and takes Matt's arm to lead him around the side of the bar to the parking lot. Matt's quiet and walks with Mark docilely toward the car. Mark puts the cup on the roof of the car as he sees Matt's key chain dangling from his pocket. He gently helps Matt into the passenger seat. Grabbing the coffee and placing it into the cup holder, Mark slides into the driver's seat and leans back to wait for Cheryl. Seemingly only a few moments later, a knock on the car window startles him and he opens his eyes to see Cheryl. Checking the dash clock, he realizes twenty minutes has passed. "I must have fallen asleep. Where's your car?"

"The employees park down the street. Can you give me a lift to my car so I can lead you to the house where Matt and I live?"

"Okay. The car's unlocked."

Cheryl opens the door to the back seat as Mark starts the car. He pulls out and asks, "Which direction?"

"Go south a block, then stop."

Mark turns the car south and sees several cars parked in a vacant lot. He pulls into the lot.

"My car is the silver Chevy Cruz. Pull over there a little bit so I can drive out first. That way you can follow me." Cheryl steps out of the car and hurries to hers. As she pulls out of the little lot, Mark follows closely.

Cheryl turns right at the next intersection, then an immediate right again. She stops in front of a tiny home two houses down on the right.

Right, right, and right. That's easy to remember.

Mark steps out of the car and moves to the passenger side. Opening the door, he kneels down to awaken Matt. "Hey, wake up, guy." Mark gently shakes Matt's shoulder. No response.

Cheryl walks over. "It's probably best to leave him in the car. I'll take you home and check on him when I get back. When he wakes up, he'll go inside the house."

"Are you sure? I hate to leave him outside like this."

"I've had to do this on many occasions. Don't worry."

Mark sighs. He lowers his head, "Jesus, you know Matt's struggles. Tell those crazy, evil spirits, go! No more cravings for Matt, and even though I'm new at this, help me to help him! Thanks, Jesus."

Cheryl steps back with an amused look, "You ready now?"

Mark smiles. "More than ready."

As Cheryl drives the short distance to the GA, Mark ponders his experience with Matt.

I have been rather selfish. Now that I have Jesus, He gives me strength in my sobriety. There are so many who attend the meetings who don't even know Him. It's time for me to spend more time sharing how Jesus keeps me sober. Where would I be if Leek hadn't been persistent in witnessing to me?

"There's our driveway up ahead. Thanks for the ride, Cheryl. Do you mind giving me Matt's number? I'd like to call and check up on him tomorrow."

"Give me your number so I can text you Matt's." Cheryl pulls up in front of the GA. Mark looks at his phone and realizes it is only seven thirty. His phone beeps, and he sees Cheryl's text with Matt's number. "Thanks again for the ride and helping with Matt."

Mark waves as Cheryl drives away. He's happy to finally be home. He hurriedly steps up to the screen door, hoping his mom is home so he can tell her about his new idea about the A-OK. He realizes a trip to the house is out of the question tonight. He's okay with that. *Tomorrow is another day.* He guffaws at his statement.

"Ugh, I can't believe I just quoted *Gone with the Wind*." With a shake of his head, he walks inside. "Mom?"

Sara Unearths a Bank Secret

Sara Chin reviews the bank's balance sheet as she taps her French manicured fingernails against the desk. Steadily over the last six months the bank's cash position has increased.

What would Oskar's intent be here? Is he thinking of selling the bank? I guess if I want to know the answer, I'd better just ask him. Sara smiles as she slips her shoes back on. *They look amazing on me, but they are killers on the feet.*

Sara steps to her doorway and looks down the hall to see Oskar's door is closed. Sara harrumphs but walks down the hall and knocks.

"Come in."

Sara opens the door. "Oskar, may I speak to you about the balance sheet? I've got a couple of questions."

Oskar closes his laptop. He appraises Sara and smiles at her short Michael Kors skirt and stiletto heels. His adrenaline kicks into gear as it usually does when a sexy woman appears.

"I bet I can preempt your questions by saying we do have an interested buyer. I haven't discussed any of this with the board or investors because I'm still evaluating what would be best overall. With that in mind, I've been holding off on some big loans, making our cash position look uncharacteristically large." Oskar leans back in his executive office chair. "Sara, sit. You're giving me a crick in my neck with those shoes you're wearing."

"If that's all you're going to share, there's no reason for me to sit. Is that all you're going to tell me?"

Oskar uses all his acting skills to hide his irritation. He thinks about Sara sitting and bending over the desk, and he smiles. "Sara, sit."

She does so and leans toward Oskar. Her v-neck blouse slips, and he sees her expansive cleavage. He sighs in satisfaction as he looks up. "Tell me your concerns."

Sara is surprised Oskar has asked her opinion, so she pauses to think. "Honestly, my job protection. I don't own any stock, so I wouldn't make money on a sale. If a bigger bank buys us, my job will be in jeopardy. What do you think the odds are that a sale is imminent?"

"Fifty-fifty."

"Ouch. Can you include job protection in the sale?"

"Possibly. Why should I?" Oskar looks pointedly at Sara.

Sara is taken aback by Oskar's obvious innuendo and narrows her eyes. *This could be construed as sexual harassment. Maybe I can get something out of this yet.* "Obviously my job is important to me. I make an excellent wage, and my chances of acquiring a similar position in Honolulu are slim. I'm happy to help in this process, and whatever I can do to ensure my job, I'm willing to do." Sara looks innocently into Oskar's eyes.

Oskar stands up and walks around the desk.

Sara gulps but also stands.

Oskar puts his arm around Sara's shoulders. "You're a real trooper. Let me think about the best way to proceed. Please keep this to yourself, and I'm sorry I didn't discuss this with you previously, Sara. You are the comptroller after all."

Sara is relieved Oskar wanted nothing more than a hug. She briefly returns the hug and slides out from under his arm. "Thanks for being honest with me. Call me if I can help you further."

Oskar moves back closer to Sara, pushing her into his desk. He points his finger along the neck of her blouse, stopping at the end of the *v.*

Sara's heart rate increases substantially.

Oskar looks Sara in the eyes, "Oh, you can be sure I'll be calling you."

Sara tries to replicate her normal witchy smile, but it comes out more like a grimace. She doesn't respond but steps around Oskar and walks down the hall. As she walks, she wonders if this situation might get out of hand. Her eyes narrow again confident she can handle Oskar.

Oskar's Take

Oskar watches Sara walk away.

Now that my neighbor Julie is ignoring me, maybe Sara might be a good substitute. She thinks she's smarter and can outmaneuver anyone, but she has a surprise in store for her. Oskar sits back down and chews on the end of his pen. *All this extra-curricular stuff is getting in my way. I haven't done all this work over the years to get distracted by a pair of big, uh, blue eyes.* Oskar laughs at his own one-track thoughts.

He opens his laptop again and goes to the file labeled "Loose Ends" and opens it. He updates the outline and sits thinking. Time to put in place the next stage of his project. He picks up his cell phone and finds the number he needs in his contact list and pushes it.

"Kim, I'm surprised you answered. I've got some stuff I need your help with for a project connected to Pearl Day. Do you have some time today or tomorrow for us to catch up? Great, let me pick you up for dinner tonight. Hanadie's, okay? I'll be at your office at six o'clock. See you then."

CHAPTER 18

Back to Normal?

Mark hears Ruth in the shower and drags himself from the sofa bed. He wants to ask her if he can borrow the Beemer today to take Mey to the A-OK house. The coffee maker beeps that it has finished brewing. *Nice.* Mark steals Ruth's mug and pours himself a cup of black coffee. He looks in the cabinet for another mug for Ruth, finds an old Waikiki beach mug, checks it for dust, and takes it over to the sink to rinse out. *Looks okay, but just in case...* Mark sticks the mug under the running water and looks up as Ruth grabs his cup and takes a sip. She spits it out.

"Yuck, no sugar!"

"Mom, wait just a second, and I'll poor you a cup. I poured the first cup for me, sorry."

Ruth grimaces. "You know I'm rather grumpy until I get my first jolt of caffeine."

Mark hands her the cup, and he points to the sugar on the counter. "Doctor up your coffee before you have a coronary. Geez!"

Ruth chuckles, "What are you doing up this early?"

Mark picks up his mug and turns it around to sip from the opposite side and says under his breath, "Ick, Mom, germs! Hey, could I take you to work so I can borrow the car? I want to take Mey to the A-OK house since I wasn't able to do so yesterday."

"I don't see why not. Are you okay missing an AA meeting today? I'll need you to pick me up at 6:00 p.m."

"Yes, I'll tell you my experience last night later, but I think I need to reevaluate my attendance at those. I was sure glad to see you when I got home. I was beginning to wonder if something had happened to you."

"I'm sorry, about that. Did you try to call me? I got involved in a long conversation at work, and time got away from me. As I was leaving, I saw you had texted me a few times. I figured you would call if it was urgent. Go get dressed then. I'm going to have a quick bowl of cereal, then we can go."

Under his breath Mark mumbles, "I actually did call you." So as not to start the day on the wrong foot, he says, "Thanks, Mom!" He quickly texts Mey that he'll meet her after taking his mom to work.

Is It A-OK?

Mark waves to Ruth and steers the car back to the GA. *I checked the cleaning calendar, and it looks like there's only one house to clean today. Unfortunately, tomorrow there are three, but that will give Mey and me plenty of time today to see the A-OK house.* Mark pulls into the driveway and sees Mey in the kitchen. *Great, she's here already. I can go over my plan for an afternoon trip to A-OK.* Mark slams the car door, but it doesn't catch. *Piece of junk.* He opens the door again and slams it harder this time.

Mey sticks her head out the screen door. "You trying to wake up the neighborhood?"

"I guess." Mark quickly makes his way to the door. "I noticed we only have one house to clean today, so how about we go to see the A-OK house? Mom let me keep the car, so we have plenty of time for lunch on the way. What do you think?"

"I love that. Can't think of the last time I was able to do something in the middle of the day. You buying lunch?"

Mark grins, "Sure, as long it's somewhere cheap."

Mey pulls a rag out of her back pocket as if to snap Mark with it, but he steps back. With hands raised, Mark says, "Okay, I get the message. I'll try and think of something fancier than McDonald's."

They both laugh as they walk back inside.

Bad, Better, and Best News?

Oskar steps into the Kailua branch searching for Ruth, but seeing her in her office with a customer, he walks down the stairs to find Axle in the break room typing on his laptop. "Hey."

Axle looks up as Oskar walks into the room. Axle's not really in the mood for a long drawn-out conversation with him but closes the laptop and waits for Oskar to speak.

"I need to talk to you about something."

Axle barely avoids showing his exasperation as he responds, "I figured. You look worried. Is it something serious?"

Oskar sits facing Axle. "It might be but probably isn't. I was approached by a syndicate about purchasing the bank, and I've been entertaining the idea for the last several months, so I began increasing the cash position of the bank."

Axle's jaw drops, "You're just now telling me? I am a stockholder, you know."

Oskar waves his hand as if he's knocking an unseen fly away. "No decisions have been made, and I'd intended to introduce the idea at the next board meeting. I decided to mention it to you now because Sara questioned me about it after working on our balance sheet, and I didn't want you to hear it from someone else."

"Gee, thanks."

"How about some good news, Axle? Daniel approved Ruth's loan application today. He took to heart my encouragement to do the paperwork quickly!"

"Yeah, I can just imagine what type of 'encouragement' you gave him. Does he still have all his fingers?"

"Axle, Axle, we are no longer in Bosnia so those tactics won't work here." He laughs.

Axle decides to ignore Oscar's comments. "Either way, that's good news. Does she know yet?"

"She was with a customer when I walked into the branch, so I haven't spoken to her yet. That's why I'm here, as well as to speak to you, of course."

"Of course," Axle says sarcastically.

"Tsk, tsk. Don't get your briefs in a wad now." Oskar laughs again at his own joke.

Axle shakes his head.

Oskar stops laughing. "Now that I'm thinking about it, I want you to tell Ruth about the house. I might as well tell you I have decided not to pursue Ruth romantically since as you may have noticed our personalities don't mesh."

Axle doesn't question Oskar but feels better already. "I'll tell her. I do feel Ruth and I have a connection and am hopeful she feels the same."

Oskar looks Axle in the eye and answers him, "I wish you both the best. Look, I gotta go. I'll pick a date for the board meeting and e-mail everyone."

"Sounds good, Oskar."

Oskar leaves, thinking, *How did I let my life get so complicated?*

Good News Is A-OK

Ruth waves to her customers as they leave her office. Her desk phone buzzes, and she picks it up.

"Hi, Axle. What's up?"

"I need to speak with you. Can you come downstairs?"

"Sure. I'll be right down."

Axle can't sit still, so he paces the break room but stops to make coffee to keep his hands busy. As he completes the process, he feels almost giddy. *Oskar actually has decided not to pursue a relationship with Ruth.* Bowing his head, he prays, "Lord, you're so good and continue to answer prayers. Thank you, Jesus. This is definitely an answer to my prayer! Thank you for softening Oskar's heart, and I ask you to lead Oskar to a woman right for him. Hallelujah! Amen."

A fragrance surrounds him. He stays bowed for a moment, enjoying the experience until he feels a hand on his arm and hears,

"Lord, thank you for my friend, Axle. He has been a true blessing to Mark and me, and I ask you to provide him the desires of his heart."

Axle turns around and envelopes Ruth in a hug that lasts for a few seconds. Ruth places her head on Axle's chest and hears the escalated beating of his heart. She sighs and steps back.

"Ruth, when would you like to move now that your loan has been approved?"

Ruth's eyebrows rise, and her mouth becomes a big *O*. She whispers, "For real?"

Axle laughs and says, "Yes, it's for real. Oskar just came by and asked me to tell you. Isn't it great?"

"Axle, I can hardly take it all in. I have a house! Whoopee! I don't know where to start. I have a million questions, but I need to get back upstairs."

"Ruth, how about if I call Mike and have him tell me the next steps. He's an old hand at this stuff and can give us all the information we need. Also, I'm not going to take no for an answer. We are going to lunch today to Hanadie's to celebrate. Got it?"

With a salute, Ruth smiles and says, "Yes, sir. I'll be ready to go at one thirty."

"Well, okay then. I'll come upstairs and get you." Axle grabs Ruth for another hug, then hands her a cup of coffee and pushes her to the stairs.

She laughs as she takes the stairs two at a time. She checks the lobby and sees all customers are being assisted, so she runs to her office and picks up her cell phone. She taps it against her chin, trying to decide if she should call or text Mark. She smiles to herself, thinking that she can't resist hearing his reaction and pushes his number. As she waits for him to answer, decides to use the same strategy that Axle used when she tells Mark the news. Mark picks up, and Ruth hears a vacuum in the background.

"Hi, Mom. What's up?"

"When would you like to move?"

No response.

"Mark?"

Mark takes a moment, grins, and decides to tease Ruth. "Mom, I forgot to tell you. You know that AA guy I spoke to you about, Matt? His roommate is moving out, so he asked me to move in with him. I'm going to move there tonight. That's okay, right?"

Ruth is totally flabbergasted. She takes a deep breath. "Mark, are you serious?"

"Nope." He laughs.

Ruth gripes, "That isn't funny."

"Well, turnaround is fair play and all that."

"Yeah, yeah. Isn't this exciting? The house is ours. I'm still in shock. Hey, Axle and I are going to lunch at Hanadie's today. Do you want to go with us to celebrate?"

"Sounds fun. But you know what? I spoke to Mey about going to A-OK after we finish our cleaning job today, and she's onboard as long as I buy her lunch. You and Axle have fun though."

"Thanks. If you have time, do you mind making a list of everything we need to get done before we can actually move into the house?"

"I will, Mom. Congratulations, by the way."

"Thanks, honey. You know, we've both been so incredibly busy we haven't talked about the long-term aspects of this. Buying a home is setting down roots and making a long-term commitment. I know we don't have much time to talk right now, but how are you feeling about that?"

"Believe it or not, Mom, I'm okay with it. I really like Leek and Mey. I enjoy the church more than I thought I would, and I enjoyed the work to remodel the GA. I'm ready for this next adventure. Thanks for making me come."

Tears appear at the edge of Ruth's eyes and start a slow fall down her face. She swallows, sniffles, and says, "You're the best son, ever."

Mark clears his throat, "Ah, shucks. Don't get all mushy. I'll get all snarky again before you know it. Especially moving. Ugh."

"Gotta go, sweetie. See you tonight. Love you."

"Ditto, Mom. Later."

CHAPTER 19

Change in Direction

Oskar takes an elevator to his office in Honolulu thinking about Axle's joy in finding that he had decided not to pursue Ruth. As he steps off the elevator on the floor to the executive offices, he sees Sara on the phone through the glass wall of her office. He steps inside and sits down. Sara turns her chair away from Oskar and continues to talk. Oskar laughs, crosses his legs, and waits Sara out. Sara realizes Oskar is not going to take the hint and leave, so she ends the call. She turns her chair back around and stares at Oskar. He stares back with a huge grin. She sees no malice there, which surprises her. She's still irritated. *Who wouldn't be with the high-handed tactics Oskar uses?* "Okay, Oskar. What do you want?"

"Let's do lunch today. I feel like celebrating because Ruth's loan was approved. Did you know she's buying one of our foreclosure properties?"

"No, I don't seem to be in the loop these days," she says pointedly. "And why would I care what happens to Ruth anyway?"

"Tsk, tsk, Sara. This rivalry you have with Ruth is unattractive. If for no other reason, you should be happy we're taking the foreclosure loss off our books. See, it is good news!"

"Poo! Whatever."

Oskar restates his invitation more firmly. "I insist on lunch. We'll go to Hanadie's. How about one o'clock?"

"I'm here to do as you command," Sara responds.

"Exactly. I'll come by your office around twelve thirty to pick you up. I expect you to be here ready to go."

Sara doesn't bother to respond and answers her ringing phone instead.

Annoyed, Oskar knows that Sara thinks she has won this skirmish somehow, but he doesn't care. He steps out of her office and walks toward his own a few doors down.

Sort of a Showdown at Hanadie's

Hanadie himself takes Axle and Ruth to their table, and as they walk through the restaurant, they see Oskar and Sara at a corner table.

Axle points to them and asks Ruth, "Do you want to say hi?"

Ruth looks over to where Axle is pointing and says, "Of course."

Surprised, Axle tells Hanadie, "We want to say hi to Oskar and Sara. Can we make a detour on the way to our table?"

Hanadie changes direction, and they walk to the corner.

Axle speaks first. "Hey, guys. We didn't expect to see you here. We're celebrating Ruth's first Hawaii house purchase." He looks at Oskar, expecting to hear why he and Sara are there and notices Sara's expression is irritated, as usual.

Oskar places his arm over the back of Sara's chair. "We're celebrating the same thing. We'd invite you to join us, but the table is too small."

Sara moves her chair away from Oskar's arm.

Oskar looks like he doesn't notice. "Are you excited, Ruth?"

"I don't think excitement even covers it, Oskar. Mark is thrilled as well and plans to make a trip to the house this afternoon to make a list of everything that needs to be done before the move-in date. How are you, Sara?"

Sara looks at Axle and notices he has his hand on Ruth's back. "Obviously, not as good as you. I hope you're sure you can afford this house because I'd hate to see it show up on the foreclosure spreadsheet again."

"I think it has as much chance of that as you wearing Payless shoes, Sara," Ruth says with a smirk.

Both men laugh, and Sara says with irritation, "After our little shopping expedition, Ruth, I think you know I wouldn't get near that store. Unlike you, I wouldn't be caught dead in those."

Oskar is amused at this turn of events because it's like watching a soap on TV. "Okay, ladies, you can both put your claws back. You guys enjoy your lunch. It looks like our food is here, so we will bid you *adieu*."

As Axle and Ruth walk to their table, Oskar turns his steely gaze on Sara. "I've let you get away with your witchy behavior for too long, Sara. You're attractive and good at your job, but you can't get away with talking to Ruth that way now she is the president of that branch. Got it?"

"Yeah, well, I could drop a sexual harassment lawsuit on you in a minute, so don't be telling me what to do. You have a lot of gall, you know it?"

Oskar scoots his chair next to Sara and places his hand on her shoulder, squeezing it until she says, "Hey! Stop! That hurts!"

"Do you think I can be threatened by you, Sara? All my employees love me, plus I'm considered a pillar of the community. Who would believe you, the evil witch of the Pacific, if you file a complaint against me? Our relationship can be pleasant or not so pleasant. You choose."

Sara suddenly drops her combative attitude, and a wary woman looks at Oskar. She thinks back to the previous day in the office when she felt confident she could handle Oskar. She's not so sure anymore.

"You've hidden this side of you well, Oskar. Of course, I'll do as you say."

Oskar lessens his grip on Sara and scoots his chair back. "Let's eat, shall we?"

Looking over where Axle and Ruth are sitting, Oskar enviously watches their animated discussion. *About Ruth's house, no doubt.* Sara follows Oskar's gaze and sees he's watching Axle and Ruth, and the proverbial light bulb goes on for her. *Mmm, I see why Oskar's defending Ruth, but Axle obviously has her attention.* Sara almost chokes on her salad as she tries to keep from laughing. Her witchy look returns, but Oskar is too busy looking across the room to heed Sara.

Has Anyone Noticed It's Hot in Here?

As they leave the restaurant, Oskar detours over to speak to Ruth as Sara lags behind.

"Ruth, we need to meet about Pearl Day plans. With all the Kaneohe house stuff, I got distracted. I'll drop Sara in Honolulu and meet you at the branch so we can finalize all the details today. Do you have time for us to do that?"

Axle states, "I can help out at the branch, Ruth, if you need it. I know this project is important to you."

Ruth looks between both men and responds to Axle, "Thanks, you're a lifesaver. Oskar, I want this finalized as well. Let's do it!"

With disdain, Sara grunts. Oskar pinches her back. Her face immediately takes on a bland expression.

"Great," says Oskar. "I'll see you in about an hour. Will that give you enough time to finish your lunch?"

Ruth looks at Sara and for some reason feels a pull to pray. *Lord, please help Sara in whatever struggle she may be facing.* "I think that's a great idea, Oskar. Sorry, I've been distracted by all the excitement of the house. The invitations with the new approved date have gone out, and I have the staff scheduled to call the invitees for a head count on attendance a week before the event. We can go over all that when you get to the branch." Ruth looks at Sara and again feels a pull toward her. Ruth takes a deep breath. "Sara, it is good to see you. Sorry about teasing you earlier."

Surprisingly, Sara's face softens and she tears up. Ruth muses, *Something is definitely not right here.*

"I accept your apology, Ruth, and submit my own. I'm letting the stress of the bank get to me too much lately."

Oskar smiles, thinking his little pep talk had a positive effect on Sara. Of course, that wasn't the case at all. Someone way more powerful than Oskar is at work here.

161

"Oh, I know exactly what you're talking about, Sara, and, yep, Oskar's certainly a slave driver no doubt about it. I have an idea. Let's you and I do a spa day this coming Saturday. I'm not taking no for an answer. Maybe Oskar would even consider paying for it." Ruth smiles at Oskar, daring him to disagree. Oskar feels like the conversation has gotten out of his control.

"Now, Ruth…"

"No, Oskar, I mean it. You've helped me immensely with the house, but Sara works just as hard as I do. Sara, where shall we go?"

To her surprise, Sara immediately agrees. "What a great idea! The Bamboo Spa near Diamond Head is my favorite, so I'll make the reservations and e-mail you with the time."

She looks satisfied, and Oskar looks like a man who has had his arm twisted. Sara regards Ruth with more respect.

Axle is not sure about all the tension going on among everyone but decides he has had enough.

"Are you finished, Ruth? You and I need to review what you want me to do while you and Oskar meet. Oskar, see you later. And, Sara, it was actually good to see you today."

Hanadie Watches from the Wings

Peeking around the kitchen door, Hanadie watches the fireworks. *Oskar seems to have gone a little nuts lately. I've never seen him so overwrought and acting like such a jerk! That's not like him. I wonder what's going on with him.* Shrugging his shoulders, he smiles. *As long as he doesn't get in the way of my work, why do I care?*

What's Oskar Really Up To?

Walking into the Kailua branch, Oskar sees Axle in Ruth's office, steps to the door, and knocks on the glass. Their heads are together as they review a file, so they don't hear Oskar's knock. Oskar tries again, louder this time.

Axle and Ruth look up simultaneously.

Oskar can't believe how quickly the two seem to have established a close relationship.

"Ruth, you ready for us to meet? Shall we go downstairs? Oh, and, Axle, I need to get your help also. Can you come down when you have a few moments?"

"Sure, I'll send Ruth down with you now," Axle says as he hands Ruth her file on Pearl Day. "See you guys in a little bit."

Accepting the file, she says, "Thanks for your help, Axle. Okay, Oskar, let's take the stairs. I need the exercise after that wonderful lunch at Hanadie's."

"Me too, Ruth. What did you have?"

"I had the perfectly cooked tuna entree of the day, and you?"

"My steak was excellent as usual. Shall we sit in the break room?"

Oskar turns on the light and goes to the refrigerator. "Would you like a bottled water?"

"Yes, I would."

Oskar walks back with the waters and unscrews the lids, handing one of the bottles to Ruth. "We have to get these auction and Pearl Day items finalized today. I can't stand all this hanging over my head, so let's call Frank to find out exactly what we're allowed to do on Pearl Day."

Ruth nods. "Sounds good."

Oskar chooses the speaker function on his phone and calls Frank.

Frank picks up immediately, "Hi, Oskar. What's up?"

"Frank, I have you on speaker, and I'm sitting with Ruth. We want to get everything associated with Pearl Day, including the auction, finalized today. I wanted to double-check with you on what we're going to be providing at the ceremony. What's the latest?"

Frank has an immediate response, "Once I told them I'd be happy to do the benediction and auction announcement, they became more accommodating. They did say it's okay to mention the auction since the proceeds will go to veterans groups. So here's what's going to happen. The outrigger, filled with flowers, will be placed in the Arizona Memorial next to a podium. I'll be first on the agenda since I'm doing the benediction. After I finish it and the auction announcement, I'll step aside and the admiral will get up and talk about the sacrifice of those entombed in the Arizona. There will be reporters from all the major Honolulu stations and newspapers and even some national news organizations as well. We should get some great media coverage."

"Frank, that sounds great. How long do you think the ceremony will last?"

"Hmmm, probably forty-five minutes at the longest."

"May I interject?" Ruth asks.

"Of course, Ruth. What's on your mind?" Frank replies.

"What if we have the flowers in the outrigger arranged in such a way that those in attendance can take a flower home with them? They could be arranged with loose flowers easily accessible for anyone to choose."

Oskar smiles, waiting for Frank to answer.

"I think that would be great. There will be some veterans at the ceremony, and I'm sure they'd love to take flowers home to their spouses. Works for me."

"Frank, Ruth is our little marketing guru because she has a new idea every time we meet. So do you need special permission for that as well?"

"I will, Oskar. Let me put you on hold. I'll call my contact right now."

As Ruth and Oskar wait for Frank, Oskar looks at Ruth and shakes his head.

Ruth looks sheepishly at Oskar. "What?"

"You honestly never cease to amaze me."

"Oskar and Ruth?"

"Yes, Frank?"

"The person I spoke to told me that would be fine. Just as an FYI, make sure the florist places a plastic liner in the outrigger. You wouldn't want it to get water damaged."

"Good point, Frank. I'll make sure the finish is perfect so that won't be a problem. Thanks for all you're doing on this. I can't tell you how much I appreciate it."

"Oskar, you know veterans are near and dear to my heart, especially since I'm one! I guess the next time I see you will be at the ceremony."

"Actually, I want to have an emergency board meeting this week. I'm thinking about Thursday. Would morning or afternoon be better for you?"

"Let me get back to you on that."

"Thanks, again, Frank."

"Later, Oskar."

Oskar turns back to Ruth, "Well, that's good news. So, tell me now about the auction."

Ruth pulls out her file, grabs her notes, and reads through them. "Okay, the date decided for the auction is the day after the ceremony, December 8. That's great because it's Sunday night. God is definitely smiling on our plans. The invitations have been mailed, and we've received a few RSVPs. Next week, plus the week before the event, I'll have the staff start calling those who haven't responded yet. The Pink Palace is serving their specialty pink iced Christmas cookies as well as other specialty hors d'oeuvres. They'll make a nonalcoholic wassail, coffee, and ice tea. There will be a long table with seating at the front for the auctioneer and anyone else from the bank who wish to attend."

Oskar asks, "Who'll be doing the emceeing and the auctioneering?"

Oskar sees a phone call is coming in on his cell. "Ruth, I think I should take this since it's Frank." Speaking into the phone, Oskar says, "Hey, Frank, what's up? I hope it's not bad news."

"No, just the opposite. You're not going to believe this. When speaking to my contact, he told me the admiral first heard of our involvement today, and he suggested we do the auction prior to the ceremony so the winning amounts and those who donated could attend the ceremony and be announced. Isn't that exciting?"

Both Ruth and Oskar look at one another.

Ruth speaks first, "I think we can get the hotel to change the date, but how would that look with those who have received invitations? We can try calling each one to get their opinion."

Oskar quickly responds, "Ruth, why don't you guys get on the phone today and see what you can find out. Frank, can we get back to you later today?"

"Sure, Oskar. I can see how this complicates things. But if it can be changed, I think we should move heaven and earth to do so. It'll create some great publicity and goodwill with the people running the ceremony and the admiral, of course."

"Sounds like a time for prayer for sure," Ruth states.

Oskar wraps up the call. "I sure appreciate your help, Frank. I'll get back to you later."

Ruth picks up her file. "I better start calling. I'll double-check with the hotel first. If they don't have an open date, there's no point in calling those invited to the event. Luckily, we haven't handed out the fliers yet, so I'll call the printer for a reprint."

Oskar grabs Ruth's arm. Surprised, she leans away and turns her head to look at him.

"Ruth, just do what you can. If we can't change it, we can't. It'll be great if we can. I appreciate you not complaining and just offering to do the work. I knew there was a reason I promoted you."

Ruth smiles and steps away from Oskar's grip. "Thanks, Oskar. Your words of encouragement are appreciated. I'll send Axle down to talk to you."

As Ruth walks away, Oskar provides one last direction, "If we don't have an emcee yet, why don't you ask Kim? He tends to draw crowds so that would be another way to get attendees. I'll e-mail you his phone number."

As she steps away, Ruth responds, "I was thinking of someone with the initials O. S."

Oskar takes a moment to realize to whom she's referring and smiles without commenting.

Exiting the elevator, and almost running into Ruth, Axle quickly steps aside and nods as he holds the door for her. He walks toward the break room. *I feel like I spend half my time in that room.* "Is this about the emergency board meeting?"

"No, I want to move the outrigger out to the lobby tonight. Are you up to helping me?"

Axle nods. "Sure, Oskar. What time?"

Oskar stands, "How about 7:00? That way we can do it after everyone leaves tonight."

Axle stands as well. "Yes, that should work. I'll bring the vacuum cleaner and the broom from upstairs so we can clear out all the wood shavings on the floor."

"Excellent idea." Oskar looks at his watch. "I need to run a quick errand and pick something up at the house. I'll be back before seven o'clock."

Are We Going Forward or Backward?

Quickly stepping from his house, Oskar jogs to his pickup. Out of habit, he looks next door and sees Julie by her pool talking on her cell. *She does look amazing. I wonder how I can get back into her good graces?*

She looks up, and Oskar waves. Julie hesitates but waves back without smiling.

Well, that's an improvement. I might get back with her one way or another.

Oskar whistles a tune while sliding into the driver's seat and clicks on his seat belt. He pulls out of his driveway and hums an old Bosnian folk song as he reminisces back to the long walk he and the guys made to leave Bosnia in February of '94.

I wish we could put all this behind us, but the hurt stays fresh.

Chapter 20

Drugar Prepares for the Worst

Slowly the man's head breaks the surface of the water. He pulls the regulator from his mouth and looks to the shoreline for any movement. He watches closely concerned he saw something but realizes it's only a fish jumping for bugs. He vacillates on his next move, deciding to take a rest before his long swim home. With one flip of his fins, he moves to the edge and pulls himself up onto the dock. He softly lays his backpack down and using it as a pillow, he stretches out on the dock, breathing heavily for the next few minutes.

Drugar thinks back on the last few days. He obsesses over the "accident" at the beach. He worries about the repercussions of having worked with Lonnie. There was no other alternative to getting the "bugs" needed. Lonnie being stationed at Pearl before he was dishonorably discharged meant he had lots of information that helped move the plan forward. Cringing as he remembers their last meeting, he thinks about the fall into the surf and Lonnie never resurfacing! Even though there has been some scrutiny around Pearl after the body washed on shore, things have died down so he should be able to complete his plan.

With a snore, he jerks his head almost falling back into the water. He quickly peruses the area and sees nothing amiss as his breathing slows to a normal rate.

"That could have been bad if anyone had seen me. I better get going."

Replacing his pack on his back, he slides into the water.

Step 2: Outrigger Removal
Hey, What Happened to Step 1?

Oskar walks inside the darkened branch. He sees someone behind the teller line, and thinking it's Axle, he walks over and says, "Hi."

The teller knocks over the notebook he's writing in, and it falls to the floor. Daniel turns around, sees Oskar, and nervously picks up the notebook. Hesitantly, he says, "Hello."

Oskar is taken aback to see an employee still in the branch. "I'm sorry, I didn't mean to scare you. I'm Oskar Soto, the president of the bank. I'm here to see Axle and thought you were him." Oskar extends his hand toward Daniel, who places the notebook back in its normal slot in the cabinet and wipes his hands on his slacks before shaking hands.

Daniel speaks up, "I'm not normally at the branch this late, but right before closing I had a commercial customer with several large cash deposits come through the drive-through. Axle was with me helping count until just a few minutes ago. Once we finished counting, we put the cash in the vault and closed it for the night. I was finalizing my closing duties when you walked up."

"I bet it was Kailua Coffee Shop. Was it?" Oskar asks.

"Wow, you're right. They hadn't been in all week, so they had four deposits they wanted me to process now rather than putting them in the night drop."

Axle walks up, "Hi, Oskar. Did you give Daniel a fright?"

"I did startle him and myself! I thought he was you!"

Axle can tell Oskar is anxious for Daniel to go, so he turns to him. "You ready to leave, Daniel? Is there anything else you need to complete tonight?"

"I'm finished, Axle. I better leave. I don't want Ruth to freak out over overtime hours." Daniel picks up his backpack. "I'll see you tomorrow, Axle. It was a pleasure meeting you, Mr. Soto."

"Oh, please call me Oskar."

"Yes, sir."

The door clicks behind Daniel as he exits the teller area.

Oskar shakes his head. "I do think I scared the poor boy to death. I wasn't expecting anyone but you in the branch."

Axle turns from watching Daniel walk to his car. "He does seem to be pretty jumpy lately. I'm beginning to wonder about it, to be honest. Every time he sees me, he acts surprised, almost as if he is hiding something."

"Have you audited the vault lately?" Oskar asks jokingly.

Axle laughs. "Ruth has, but that wasn't what I was thinking about. I was thinking more about drugs."

"Drugs! Talk to Ruth tomorrow. We can't have any scandals at this bank. Are you serious?"

"It's just a gut feeling, Oskar. Don't get so worked up because it's probably nothing."

Oskar takes a couple of deep breaths. "I don't like it, Axle. I'm serious. Does he have any performance issues?"

"He has been out of balance several times lately. One was $100 last week."

"You and Ruth need to put him on probation and get him out of here. We could do a surprise drug test. It's part of our policy to do random drug tests, though we haven't done any."

"Oskar, don't you think you're overreacting? Like I said, it's probably nothing. I'll stay on top of it. Come on, let's get this outrigger monstrosity into the lobby."

*****

Daniel pulls out of the parking garage and drives by the lobby window, watching as Oskar and Axle awkwardly carry something large through the branch. Daniel turns around and drives up to the side of the building to get a second look. He stops, exits his car, and peeks inside. His eyes widen as he sees Oskar and Axle gently set a large wooden outrigger on a stand in the lobby. Daniel remembers the invitations he and Katrina worked on today, which did note an outrigger would be on display in the branch lobby for those who would like to see it before the auction. Returning quickly to his car,

Daniel puts it in drive and speeds away. He can't help wondering where the heck in the branch they had stored the outrigger.

I've looked at every square inch of that branch where I have access, and I've never seen that thing. It's so big. Where could they possibly have kept it? I'll have to do some snooping tomorrow afternoon or possibly during lunch. Most likely Ruth and Axle will be working together in her office, so I can slip downstairs. There's something kind of fishy about this whole thing. They're bringing it out after hours when they know the branch would be deserted. I know we're doing the auction, but it just seems like something is a little off here.

Daniel looks down at his shaking hand. He rubs it on his pants leg, grabs his water bottle from the drink holder, and takes a big swig. The vodka is soothing to his throat, and he takes another gulp. He doesn't pay attention and swerves the car, almost running into a bicyclist, who shoots him the finger. He puts his hand on his chest and can feel it pumping furiously. He takes a deep breath to calm himself, and an idea pops into his head, and he mulls it over while he drives toward his apartment. *A friend has been pushing him to go to AA meetings. Is now the time to do it?*

Sara and Oskar

As Oskar drives home, he speaks into his Bluetooth. "Dial Sara."

On the third ring, Sara answers, "Oskar."

"Sara, how about I come by and have a drink?"

There's a long silence.

"Sorry, Oskar, my mother's here on a visit. You're welcome to come by and meet her if you like."

Oskar wonders if Sara is bluffing but decides he's too tired to challenge her tonight.

"That's fine. We *will* make it another time. Have a good evening."

"You too. See you in the morning."

Oskar is too tired to even dredge up any anger. He pulls into his driveway, and as always, he looks at his neighbor's house and sees her swimming laps. Removing his clothes as he walks through the house, he steps into the utility room and finds his swim trunks on the washer and puts them on. Grabbing a bottle of Jack Daniels and two glasses from his poolside bar, Oskar quickly walks over to Julie's house, entering the backyard as she steps out of the pool. He puts the bottle and glasses down on her lanai table, picks up her towel, and puts it around her shoulders and rubs her down. She doesn't say a word as he dries her off. He pours the Jack into the two glasses and hands her one, which she downs quickly. She puts the glass down and removes her towel. Oskar appraises her tan nude body with appreciation, picks her up, and carries her into the house, getting what he wants after all.

Later, feeling energized, Oskar steps outside Julie's gate and enters his garage through the side entrance, looking through his scuba gear to pull out his wet suit, fins, mask, and tank.

I need to make one last trial run. If I swim deep, I may be able to get all the way to the spot I mapped out earlier. Time's running out, so I can't put this off any longer.

Oskar pulls on all his gear, checks the oxygen levels of his tank to make sure he has enough, and steps out to the beach. For some reason he feels an unrelenting sadness.

I have to follow through and ensure this plan ends perfectly. If I don't get this done ASAP, there's no telling what may happen.

For the next to last time, Oskar puts on the rest of his gear and quickly steps into the surf. He concentrates on his swimming and doesn't think beyond that.

This Is Heavy! Let's See What Canoe and Mey Are Doing

Mey and Mark lean on the second floor lanai railing of the A-OK house. Mey puts her arm around Mark and gives him a hug.

"Mark, this is the perfect house for you and Ruth. I'm so excited for you both but sad I won't be able to walk into your house all the time."

Mark slips his hand through Mey's. "Me too. You know, we should probably car pool since trying to find parking spaces at the vacation rentals can be a challenge. The days I take Mom to work I can pick you up, otherwise, I can have her drop me off at the first house. Would you be able to take me home on those days? I know it's a drag to spend that much time with me, but I could contribute gas money." He smiles and lifts his eyebrows.

Mey turns toward Mark and leans closer. Looking directly into his eyes, she says, "I would not call our time together a drag! I thank God I get to see you each and every day." She reaches out and touches Mark's cheek.

Neither says a word. For some reason, Mark's eyes water. He asks, "Is it okay if I say a prayer?"

Mey nods, and both bow their heads.

"Father, I am so sorry for being mad about moving to Hawaii and how mean I was to my mom. Thanks for the most amazing experience of my life—meeting new friends, learning remodeling skills, strength in staying sober, and these new feelings I have for Mey. Help me to honor her during our relationship by seeking you at every step. Love you, Jesus. Amen."

Mark slips his arms around Mey and lowers his head for their first kiss. They touch lips, and the wonder of it is almost painful. Their foreheads touch, and they stay that way for some time.

"The prayer was beautiful, Mark. The kiss wasn't bad either!"

They both laugh, lightening the mood.

Mey moves first and backs away a small distance. "Shall we go back to the GA now? How about if we stop at that storage facility we saw driving here and pick up some boxes? Between house cleanings tomorrow, we could start packing for you and your mom."

Mark laughs. "I love your work ethic. You help me stay on track!"

They hold hands as they go down the ohana stairs. Mark checks and locks the house door. "Did we lock all the other doors?"

Mey thinks for a second. "I'm not sure, let me go check." She returns up the steps.

Mark realizes it's locked when he hears her rattle the door. As Mey comes down the stairs, she says a silent prayer herself, thanking the Lord for sending Mark to her.

What's Next?

The sunrise over Kailua beach is a perfect example of God's hand-iwork. Ruth takes a sip of coffee from her Waikiki mug as she walks along the beach through the surf. *I'll miss this when we move to the A-OK house. Living here has been a blessing, and all part of God's plan. It'll be nice to have the spa day today with Sara. I can't believe I had the courage to ask Oskar to pay for it, but I'm glad I did! I think I misjudged Sara. I wasn't feeling or acting very Christian toward her when she was being so insulting. After spending more time with her at the mall, I'm thinking that's her defense mechanism so she won't get hurt. Okay, Dr. Ruth, don't start psychoanalyzing again. But why not, I'm so-o-o quali-fied!* Ruth looks down and sees something in the sand. *A sand dollar! My first shell find here!* Ruth picks it up. *Wow, it's perfectly formed and beautiful.* Holding it gingerly, she turns back toward the GA.

Ruth checks her watch: 8:00 a.m. After washing the sand off her feet with the house hose and stepping through the screen door, she walks inside, smiling as she sees Mark snoring on the new sleeper sofa. Walking over to the coffeepot, she tops off her mug and writes a note to remind Mark she's going to the Bamboo Spa.

Spa Day, Here We Come!

Just as Ruth finishes dressing, she hears a honk. Picking up her purse, she blows Mark a kiss and runs out to Sara's car. Ruth is dressed casually in a sleeveless polo top and walking shorts. As she slides into Sara's car, she decides she most likely looks shabby compared to Sara's mega designer outfit.

"Sara, were you ever a model? You always dress impeccably, and your hair and makeup look professionally done."

"Why, thank you, Ruth. I actually did some modeling in California when I was a teenager. I had big plans to be an actor as well, but once I saw how competitive and cutthroat it was, I decided to go to college and become a CPA."

Ruth looks puzzled. "That seems like the direct opposite career wise. Why that choice?"

"Believe it or not, math was my favorite subject in high school, so it seemed like a good fit. My grades were good enough to get me into Cal State and since I was the study queen, I graduated summa cum laude. After graduation, I had my pick of jobs and became an internal auditor for Bank of America. Eventually, I was promoted to VP of auditing. A year ago a recruiter acquaintance of mine called me about the comptroller position here at Oahu National. I did a phone interview with Oskar, and here I am."

"Sara, your accomplishments have been impressive for someone as young as you."

Sara looks at Ruth as if she can't believe she's for real. "Okay, Ruth, stop with the compliments. I've been rude and catty to you from day one, even when we went shopping. In fact, I thought you had designs on Oskar! Why're you being so nice to me? I hate to say it, but I don't deserve it."

Ruth thinks about how to answer Sara, "Do you want the truth?"

"Yes. Don't worry about me because I definitely have thick skin."

Ruth takes a deep breath. "When I saw you with Oskar the other day at Hanadie's, I saw a vulnerable side to you. I know he can be difficult at times, but you always seemed able to handle him with aplomb. That day was different. You seemed human, and I truly related to you. I didn't want Oskar to get away with his bullying, so I jumped into the conversation with the spa idea, so thanks for agreeing right away. This'll be fun. And I can't believe you thought I was interested in Oskar!"

As Sara listens and watches Ruth, something strange happens to her. *I'm relating to another person.* She relaxes and smiles. *It feels a little odd but great! Could it be I've made a friend?* "Okay, Ruth, I agree that you with Oskar is a pretty far-fetched idea!"

"Come on, Sara, let's forget work, Oskar, and anything else unpleasant. Let's enjoy this day. So tell me what treatments you picked for us at Bamboo Spa."

Sara lists out the services as they pull into the spa parking lot. "I'm getting a Brazilian wax but figured you were not quite ready for that, so while I get mine, I scheduled you for a stone massage. Next, they will serve us lunch, then on to mani-pedis."

Ruth looks confused. "What's a Brazilian Wax?"

Sara laughs, "It's almost a complete wax 'down under' so you can wear the skimpiest of bikinis."

Ruth makes a face. "Ugh."

Sara laughs again. "You sure you don't want me to change your treatment from the massage to the wax job?"

Still making a face, Ruth says, "Funny, funny. *No.* I really need the massage. I'm totally fine 'down under' since I wear a one piece."

Sara says with a straight face, "Is that just the bottom or only the top? You go bottomless, huh?"

Ruth pushes Sara in the arm as they walk into the spa. "So now you're a comedian? I wear a maillot, goof. Do you go bottomless?"

"No, but there have definitely been times I've gone topless, especially when I was on the French Riviera."

Ruth sticks her nose up into the air. "I want there to be an air of mystery around me. I don't want anyone to see my body until I marry them, so there!"

"Okay, Miss Goody Two-shoes, don't get your panties in a wad." Sara can't get over these pleasant feelings she has spending time with Ruth. *Who knew having a friend could be fun? Amazing!*

CHAPTER 21

Mark, Matt, and Daniel

M ark walks into the GA, exhausted from helping Mey clean four houses. He checks the time on his phone.

If I hurry, I can get to the five o'clock AA meeting. It'll give me a chance to see how Matt's doing. Mark looks in the fridge for anything to eat and sees a to-go food container, opens it, and sees a couple of pieces of pizza. He smells it and shrugs his shoulders.

"It smells okay to me."

He takes a couple of bites and quickly walks toward the bathroom for a shower. He finishes the first piece quickly and takes the last piece, throwing the container on the bed.

I better remember to throw that in the trash, or I'll never hear the end of it from Mom.

*****

Twirling the BMW keys around his finger, Mark walks into the meeting room and, as usual, goes directly to the coffeepot. He looks around to see if Matt is there and notices there's already a pretty big crowd. The community center has a good-sized room for the meeting, and thirty chairs are lined up in the center of the room in six rows of five chairs each. The room is plain with a nondescript linoleum floor and a large podium at the front. The plainness doesn't negate the fact that it's Mark's second home, and he has some special feelings about the place. As he picks up a Styrofoam cup, he feels a push from someone. He looks over, and Matt has his usual bored expression.

"What's up, dude?"

Mark is thinking, *Who says dude anymore?* "Matt, I'm great. Good to see ya'. Did you get my phone messages?"

"Sure, sure. Just busy, ya know?"

Another young man walks up and takes a cup. "Matt."

Matt answers, "Hey, Dan. This is Mark."

Daniel looks at Mark with a perplexed expression. "I feel like I know you. Have we met?"

Mark grins, "You work at Oahu National here in town, right?"

"Yes-s-s."

"My mom is Ruth Max. I come to the branch occasionally to talk to her."

"Oh, yeah. I remember seeing you there." Daniel pours coffee into each of their cups.

Mark motions towards the chairs, "Looks like the meeting is about to start and tonight is the speaker meeting. You know, where people stand up and give their testimony? It's my favorite meeting. How 'bout you guys?"

As they sit, Daniel takes a big gulp of coffee. *Some Jack in this would sure taste good.* "This is my first meeting."

As usual, Matt leans his head back in his chair, but Mark leans toward Daniel.

"Congratulations, you've made the first step to recovery. I know a great sponsor. Let me introduce you after the meeting."

Daniel puts up his hands as if warding off an attack. "Whoa, thanks, but it's a huge step for me even to be here." He stops for a second, takes a breath, and quietly says, "I almost had a wreck last night which scared the heck out of me. Give me some space, but I do appreciate the offer."

Mark nods. "Of course, I get it."

As the speaker presents his story, Mark is attentive to each word. Hearing Matt snoring, Mark sighs. *Oh, well, it can only be a good thing he's here rather than the bar!*

As they finish the serenity prayer at the end of the meeting, everyone stands to leave.

Mark looks at Daniel. "What did you think?"

"I'm still trying to process it all, but based on what I heard, I'm glad I came."

"I would say that's a good start. I come to these meetings almost daily. I can give you my phone number, and we can meet up for future meetings. In fact, how about lunch sometime? Actually, tomorrow would work great for me. How about you?"

Daniel hesitates but responds, "I work late most days, but I get off at two o'clock tomorrow. If you buy, we can go then."

Mark nudges Matt. "Daniel and I are going to lunch tomorrow. I'll text you the location in the morning so you can go with us."

Matt mumbles what could be assent.

Daniel informs Mark, "Everyone calls me Daniel at work, but I prefer Dan."

Mark nods, "I'll remember."

Are We Selling the Bank or What?

Ruth gets ready for the emergency board meeting by preparing the usual coffees and cookies for everyone. She sees Axle walking toward the conference room and calls out to him as she counts the coffees. "Hey, you. Do you mind helping me with these?"

"Your wish is my command!" Axle returns back to the break room and takes the tray from Ruth.

"Wait a minute. I'm missing a coffee." With a puzzled look she counts them again. "Oh, I forgot Oskar's." Hearing the elevator door open, she sees Sara and Oskar walk into the conference room.

"Here, Ruth, take the tray. I'll make Oskar's coffee."

"You're the best, Axle!"

Ruth watches the tray closely as she walks slowly out of the break room almost running into Sara. Sara laughs and reaches toward the tray as the cups wobble back and forth. They settle, so Sara grabs her own coffee and follows Ruth into the room.

Axle returns to the break room as Sara and Ruth chat.

Ruth whispers, "Are you sore, you know from the, ahh…thing you had done Saturday?"

Sara laughs and whispers back, "No, today it feels fine. I tried on my new bikini yesterday, and I have to admit I look pretty fabulous."

"I certainly feel fabulous after my massage. Look at my toes. Don't they look great?"

Sara squints as she looks at Ruth's feet, "Those sandals look way better on you than me. You're really stylin' today."

"Sara, I can't believe you gave me these Jimmy Choo shoes. I love the wedge look, and I think they go great with my shirtwaist dress."

"I don't know about the dress, but I agree the shoes work on you. Looks like all the other board members are here. Are you staying for the meeting?"

"Yes, Oskar asked me to take notes."

The drinks are passed around as Oskar clears his throat, looking at each person in attendance. He takes a gulp of coffee and grimaces. "Umm, Ruth…"

Axle smacks his forehead and reaches for Oskar's coffee cup. "Sorry, Oskar, I don't know what I was thinking making you a mocha. I forget. How do you drink it now?"

"Black would be great, Axle. Thanks."

Within only a few moments, Axle returns and sits next to Ruth. Oskar returns his gaze to those at the table that includes Axle; Ruth; Sara; Frank; and Daniel, Ruth's former boss.

"Thank you for arranging your schedules to meet on such short notice. Sara noticed the bank has increased its cash position over the last few months and asked me about it. I'm glad she's keeping a close watch on our books."

Axle looks at the others, anxiously waiting to see their reaction as Oskar shares his news about the bank. Turning his attention to Oskar, he takes the last gulp from his own cup and, in the process of setting it down on the table, knocks it to the floor.

With a look of impatience, Oskar frowns but ignores Axle.

"I'm going to get right to the point. A couple of months ago I was approached by the largest bank in Hawaii asking me if I would be interested in entertaining a buyout offer of Oahu National. I responded negatively, but they continue to call me. The cash received for those of us who are stockholders could be substantial. If we were to decide to accept an offer, I'll try and negotiate job protection clauses for officers who are not stockholders. These are all the details I have at the moment. I asked Sara to do some research on the viability of this opportunity, and she put together the bank's current balance sheet as well as a spread sheet with some initial information."

Sara hands out the spread sheet and balance sheet and glances at Ruth, gauging her reaction. Ruth's head is down, and she's typing furiously, so Sara can't tell what Ruth's thinking. Sara sits down, but before she can explain anything, Frank pipes up.

"Oskar, I'm a little taken aback about this. I feel like I'm getting a mixed message here. On the one hand, you're saying you're not pursuing it, and on the other hand, you're talking job contracts for the officers and increasing our cash position. I can tell you your customers will not like the bank being sold to a huge conglomerate. One of the reasons they like us is our hometown community feel."

"Ruth, please don't add that to the minutes. Frank, let me share my thinking before we all jump to conclusions. I wasn't even going to mention it, but Sara asked me about it. I'm not looking for a buyer, but we should always look at offers to see if there are fiscal benefits for all of us."

Frank crosses his arms, "Ruth, please keep my comments in the minutes. There's no need to hide our conversation since that's the whole reason for the meeting."

Ruth types them back into the document, and Oskar looks frustrated but does not argue with Frank.

"Sara, would you please explain the bank's current financials and how the sale would benefit or hurt the bank?"

Sara does not acknowledge Oskar. "As you can see, the bank has been extremely profitable this year. Daniel and the loan officers have been doing a spectacular job with loan production, and Ruth has been doing an amazing job keeping costs down here in Kailua. We're recovering nicely from the huge expense of building this branch. On the balance sheet, you will see we are currently cash rich making us prime for additional loan production."

Frank interjects, "Sara, thank you for putting this together. I'd like Oskar to give us his reasons why we would or would not want to do this."

Oskar takes a deep breath. "I'm not sure, Frank. I love this bank, but as you see by the numbers Sara has put together, we're ripe for a buyer to pursue us. Tell me your thoughts."

Frank throws the papers on the table, takes a deep breath, and pointedly asks, "Oskar, is there an actual offer on the table? I have not done any research on the buyer, but they do have the majority presence on the islands."

Oskar pulls out the spreadsheet and points to the last line, "Frank, our share value is $35. They called me just yesterday with a tentative offer of $42. You personally own 200,000 shares, so with the sale, you would receive $1,400,000. Now tell me what you think."

Frank drops the spreadsheet on the floor and leans back, almost falling from the chair. Axle grabs the armrest to keep the chair from tipping over. Frank picks up his water and takes a big gulp.

"Okay, Oskar, you have my attention. I had no idea the shareholders could receive that big of a payout. I obviously would love the money, but is this our best option moving forward?"

Looking toward Ruth, Axle jumps in, "I propose a motion that all officers of the bank be provided a minimum of twenty thousand shares of stock with the amount they receive based on seniority."

Frank quickly responds, "I second the motion."

Both Daniel and Sara do a high five.

Ruth looks hesitantly at Axle, who nods and mouths, "That includes you."

Sara turns to Ruth and raises her hand. Ruth hesitates and realizes it's her turn and slams Sara's hand. They both laugh as Sara shakes her hand. "For such a small person, Ruth, you have a lot of strength! Remind me not to make you mad!"

Oskar relaxes, content that this meeting has ended on a positive note. *Now all my people will be in good shape financially for the future. Now I can turn my focus on my own future plans.*

*****

Daniel walks over to Ruth as she and Sara grab their papers to go.

"Ruth, may I speak to you for a few minutes?"

"Sure, Daniel, what's up?" Ruth responds as she waves goodbye to Sara.

Daniel points toward the break room. "Do you mind if I get a water to go?"

"Of course not. I'd like one myself."

Ruth places her papers on a table and turns as Daniel hands her a bottled water. He unscrews his and takes a long drink. Ruth sets hers down and waits for Daniel to speak.

"Wow, I'm still in a daze over Oskar's revelation at the meeting." He shakes his head and, looking at Ruth, says, "Your loan for the A-OK house closing is scheduled for the thirtieth of this month, and Oskar said you can move in anytime. Hey, do you guys have any more snacks around here? I'm starving. By the time I arrived at the meeting, all the cookies were taken." Daniel opens each cabinet door.

Ruth goes to the refrigerator. "I keep extra cookies on hand for those last-minute meetings Oskar schedules. We have chocolate chip or oatmeal left. Which do you prefer?"

"Both, of course." Daniel grabs both bakery boxes.

Ruth laughs and shakes her head. "Daniel, I can't tell you how much I appreciate the quick turnaround in processing my loan since I'll need to move from my current place in the next few days. I plan to have a house warming once we get settled, so I hope you'll come."

Daniel has a mouth full of cookies, with two in one hand. He gives her the "okay" hand signal as he walks out.

Ruth picks up her papers, phone, and water to head upstairs. She stops for a moment and places a call.

"Hi, Mom, what's up?" Mark yells over the sound of construction noise in the background.

Ruth holds the phone away from her ear, "What are you doing?"

"Leek is using the drill to stir the grout for the ohana bathroom. I'll walk downstairs so I can hear you better."

Ruth waits a few seconds. "Mark, Daniel told me today we can move into the A-OK house. The closing will be on the thirtieth, so when would you like to move? The thirtieth is only ten days away."

"What about furniture, Mom? I don't think you'll want to sleep on the floor."

Groaning, Ruth responds, "You're definitely right about that. I'd forgotten about the small issue of no furniture!"

"Mom, I see I have a call coming in from Mey. You know she has those friends that own the furniture store in Kailua. Would you like her to look for some stuff for us?"

"Great idea, Mark. I can transfer some money into your account. You pick out your bedroom furniture and have Mey choose some for my room. If you guys see a recliner sectional you think would work for the loft, would you text me a picture of it?"

"I think Mey would love to do that. I'll see if she can go tonight once Leek and I are finished with the grouting."

CHAPTER 22

Searching for Sobriety and the Outrigger Closet

Mark leans against the teller counter as Ruth picks up the teller work. "Hi, Mom. Dan and I are going to lunch today with my friend Matt. Is he getting off soon?"

"Hi, Canoe. Dan, huh? Hm-m-m, we call him Daniel. I believe he's done for the day and will be coming to the front in a few minutes. I didn't realize you and he knew each other."

"Mom, I don't think you've ever called me Canoe! It sounds kinda odd." *Not sure Dan would want Mom to know he's a drinker and that I first met Dan at an AA meeting.* "Yeah, Matt introduced us."

Daniel walks up beside Ruth, "I put my drawer away. Is it okay if I leave now?"

"Yes, Dan, thanks for opening with me today. Tell me, how did those you called about the auction respond to the date change?"

Dan gives Ruth a concerned look as he puts on his glasses to read his auction attendance tally sheet. "Actually, I would say only half told me they could come. I called twenty-five people and thirteen said yes."

Ruth frowns, "Ugh, that's more declining than I anticipated. Did Katrina say how many she was able to call?"

"She was busy with drive-through customers, so it's probably not many, but I didn't get a specific number from her." Daniel hands his tally sheet to Ruth.

"Did I hear Ruth call you Canoe?" Dan pointedly asks Mark.

Mark laughs, "Yeah, let's go, and I'll tell you the story."

Mark waves as the elevator door closes, and they descend to the garage. They quickly walk to the Beemer.

Dan speaks up, "Why don't I drive my car? That way Ruth will have her car to drive home."

Mark hesitates, "Okay, thanks."

They change direction to the next parking space, and Dan unlocks his Toyota. As they sit, Mark speaks up.

"I'm glad you agreed to come, Dan. There's a new burger truck at Lanikai beach. Are you up for a burger? Matt's gonna meet us there."

Dan takes the water bottle from the drink holder and throws it in the back seat and takes a deep breath. "I'm not dressed for the beach, but I guess I'm game." He starts the car and slowly exits the parking lot.

"I know you're going to ask me about my drinking, so I'll go ahead and tell you. I'm sober today. Thank goodness. That bottle I just threw in the back seat? It has water and vodka in it. I took a swig from it right before I almost ran over that bicyclist. That's what drove me to take off work early and go to the meeting last night. It was long overdue for me to do something!"

Mark ponders his response. "How did the drinking start?"

"In high school, I was on the football team and attended the after game parties. Everyone drank at those parties, so I did too. At first, I only drank there, but by the time I was a senior, I drank at home. My uncle lived with us for awhile, and he'd buy alcohol for me. My parents don't even know I drink too much. I'm careful to hide it from them."

"Are you sure they don't know? I'm surprised. Of course, many parents don't want to accept the idea their children could be alcoholics. My mom was in absolute shock when she discovered my heroin use. I'll tell you what my friend Leek told me when I moved here, the solution is accepting Christ as your Lord and Savior. My response to him was basically, 'Sure, whatever.' He was right though. I gave my life to Christ recently, and my life is so-o-o much improved. Yours can be too."

Dan shakes his head, "You don't beat around the bush, do you? I didn't know you were a Jesus freak. I mean, you come across so normal."

Mark feels amazingly comfortable witnessing to Dan. "It changes you, man. You'll see. Hey, look there's a space right ahead. Pull in before someone else gets it."

Quickly pulling into the space, he looks over at Mark, "What's next? An ocean baptism?"

Mark grins, "I'm up for it if you're ready."

Dan shakes his head again and laughs. "Not quite. Now where's this burger truck you were telling me about?"

"Let's find Matt, then burgers, in that order."

"If you say so." He then thinks to himself. *What the heck have I gotten myself into?*

They look up and down the beach. Mark uses his hand to shade his eyes. "You know Matt's probably already at the food truck waiting for us." Mark stops someone passing them, "I hear there's a great new burger food truck here. Do you know where it's parked?"

The girl grins, "Look up, it's about 200 feet south of here."

Dan says, "I see it and Matt too."

"Thanks for your help. As they say, if it'd been any closer..." Mark and Dan take their shoes off to walk in the sand and quickly head over to Uke's Burgers. Greeting Matt, they step in line with him. As they wait for their turn to order, Mark speaks up.

"Matt, so glad you came. Have you checked out the menu?"

Matt smirks, "Yep, I'm gettin' a burger."

"Funny, funny, Matt. Why don't you and Dan tell me what you want, then you can grab us one of the picnic tables over there."

Matt responds, "Oh goody, with you buyin' I know just what I want, the Shrimpy and a beer."

Mark is looking up at the menu painted on the side of the truck but jerks his head back to Matt at the last comment. Mark grimaces. "You could be a comedian, Matt, how about a Hawaiian Sun drink instead?"

"Sure. What about you, Dan, you gettin' a beer?"

Mark frowns, "Matt, I know you think that's funny, and it was the first time, but now it's not. Sheesh!"

Matt looks at Mark, "You take life too seriously, bro. Take a chill pill."

Dan shakes his head and is happy he's getting a free burger out of this.

Mark says a silent prayer for patience. "Matt, how do you want your burger cooked?"

"Medium."

Mark turns to Dan and silently mouths, "Sorry."

"And you, Dan, what do you want?"

Trying not to sigh, he says instead, "The same as Matt is fine. Come on, Matt, let's go find that table."

A light bulb goes off for Mark. Not just a light bulb but a message from the Holy Spirit. *Matt is trying to push my buttons to see if I'm serious in my sobriety. I can't let his comments make me mad because I can't help him if I get frustrated. I guess I do need to loosen up some and let God handle it!*

"Sir, what can I get you?"

Mark looks up, smiles at Moe, and places his order. "Three Shrimpys and three liliquoi Hawaiian Suns."

"You got it, man. That'll be $50.72."

Mark slowly hands the man his debit card, looking at the menu again to check the prices. The Shrimpy is the most expensive burger at $12.98. *I know the burger has shrimp on it, but the price sure isn't shrimpy!* He shakes his head as he looks over at Matt.

"Here's your receipt. I'll call your number when it's ready."

Mark accepts the receipt, tells Moe thanks, and jogs over to Matt and Dan. He takes a deep breath as he sits down.

Dan looks at Mark, "Thanks for buying lunch. I have something going on that's really bothering me. I need to talk about it, but I need you to keep it to yourselves."

Matt doesn't seem to be paying attention as he is checking out the girls on the beach.

Mark responds, "Of course, Dan. That's understood when working on our sobriety."

Dan responds, "It's not about AA Mark, it's about work. It's bugging me, and I need to know what I should do."

Mark's eyebrows couldn't move much higher. "I'm not sure I'm the person you should speak to about work, Dan. Wouldn't my mom be a better choice?"

"No, hear me out, then you can give me your ideas on what I should do."

"Number 32!"

Matt jumps up. "Is that ours? I'll go get it."

Mark looks at his receipt. "Yep."

Matt quickly walks toward the truck as Mark looks over and notices Cheryl in line.

"Dan, I think we may have another at our table. Matt's roommate, Cheryl, is in line at the burger truck."

Dan frowns. "The more the merrier, I guess. I have met Cheryl, but I don't know her well."

"Understood, but Cheryl seems to be cool. It's up to you what you decide to share."

Dan doesn't look convinced as he uses his hand to wipe the sand off the table.

Matt walks up to the table with two large bags with Cheryl next to him carrying the drinks.

"Hi, guys. Mind if I join you?"

Mark scoots over and responds, "Hi, Cheryl, this is great. How've you been?"

Cheryl looks at Matt as she hands out the drinks, "Good, now that Matt is going to AA almost every day."

Mark knocks over his drink, which luckily was not open. He looks over at Matt. "Wow, man, I'm so proud of you. Next is Jesus."

Dan says, "Don't worry, Matt, Mark's already had the Jesus talk with me today. Hi, Cheryl. Long time no see. I work with Mark's mom at Oahu National."

Cheryl smiles as she sits down, "Really? I didn't know that."

Matt takes the paper off his burger and takes a huge bite, completely ignoring everyone as he closes his eyes and chews with a look of pure nirvana on his face. Cheryl, Mark, and Dan all laugh.

Mark grabs his burger. "I take it the Shrimpy is not disappointing you, Matt."

Matt smiles as he continues to chew.

Mark looks at Cheryl. "Dan was about to share something serious about work that has him concerned. I told Dan you would keep what he shares confidential."

Cheryl looks over at Dan. "Of course, I will. But, Dan, if you're uncomfortable speaking about it with me here, I can get my burger to go."

He ponders her words, looks at Mark who nods his head, and starts to speak. "Cheryl, no need to leave. My concern is that everyone understands we need to keep this between us." Dan thinks back to the night he saw Axle and Oskar carrying the outrigger in the lobby. "I'll give you guys a little history so you can get a feel for the bank and what's been happening there. Cheryl, I'm a part-time teller at the Kailua branch. Do you know the one? It's next to the elementary school."

Cheryl nods. "Sure. That's the bank that shares a wall with the school."

"It does." Dan takes his napkin and wipes his mouth. "I have to agree this burger is unbelievably good. About a month ago, the bank decided to sponsor the Arizona Memorial ceremony on December 7. Ruth, Mark's mom and my boss at the bank, came up with the idea to have an auction to raise money. This ties in with the memorial because the amount made at the auction would be donated to veteran's groups and announced at the ceremony. The owner of the bank, Oskar Soto, is an expert in woodworking and building. He makes wooden surfboards and outriggers and has three of his surfboards on display in the branch. You should see these things. They are off the charts incredible in detail with the most amazing artistic carvings and inlays. I've never seen anything quite like them. Ruth mentioned they could bring thousands of dollars at the auction. As I said, in addition to surfboards, Oskar is auctioning two of the outriggers he's built."

Mark's face lights up, "I've seen the surfboards. They're extraordinary!"

Dan takes a gulp of his drink and continues his story. He looks at Matt, who continues to watch the tourists, but Mark and Cheryl are giving Dan their undivided attention.

"Here's where the story gets a little weird. The night I almost ran over a bicyclist, I had stayed late at work. I was out of balance, and Axle, the security officer at the branch, was helping me because Ruth had already left for the day. Right before I left around seven o'clock, Oskar shows up at the branch. That in itself isn't unusual, but he seemed anxious for me to leave. He was super surprised I was still at the branch, and even though he was talking to me, I could tell he was nervous. He was sweating and drumming his fingers on the counter."

Matt jumps in with impatience, "Come on, Dan, get to the point."

With a look of frustration, Dan continues his story. "This all sounds innocent so far, but you haven't heard everything yet, Matt! Anyway, I left and went out to my car, and as I drove around the building, I looked inside the branch and saw Axle and Oskar carrying this huge outrigger I've never seen before into the lobby." Dan crosses his arms and looks at Cheryl and Mark.

Matt says, "And?"

Dan continues, "I've been everywhere in that branch before and since then. There's nowhere inside to store that outrigger. I know Oskar didn't bring it with him as his truck had no trailer attached. So-o-o, today I asked Axle about it." Dan takes a bite of his now cold burger.

Matt leans forward as do Cheryl and Mark.

"Don't leave us in suspense, Dan, what did Axle say?" Mark asks.

Dan takes the last bite of his burger and talks with his mouth full. "First, he seemed shocked I had seen him and Oskar carrying the outrigger since they had seen me leave the branch fifteen minutes earlier. All that time I sat in my car drinking. Of course, I didn't tell him that. He gave me this cock-and-bull story—sorry, Cheryl—about the outrigger having been delivered earlier by a boat-moving company and left in the parking garage. The stairs are wide from the garage to the first floor, so they are big enough to move the outrigger up to the lobby, and it could have been delivered to the garage, but I know it wasn't. That day I worked an all day shift at the drive-through, and I could see all the cars that came into the parking garage. There's no way it was delivered without me seeing it. Plus, it would have been a big deal and everyone would have been talking about it. Why wait until everyone has gone to move it if the explanation is that simple?"

Matt starts to speak, and Dan raises his finger to stop him. "I'm not through. The next time Oskar came to the branch, he went downstairs to Axle's office. I had finished balancing for the day and said goodbye to Ruth as she left. Once she was out of the building, I slipped downstairs. I heard them talking in the break room. I'll give you an idea of the layout so you can get a better picture of it before I tell you what I found out. From the stairs, you make an immediate right towards the restrooms, but before you get to them a left hallway takes you to Axle's office. Once they were in the office, I slipped into the restroom, which shares a wall with Axle's office. I wasn't sure I would be able to hear anything, but I did that nifty thing you see on TV using a glass against the wall, and I could hear them!"

Matt throws up his hands. "You're driving me crazy, man. Please just tell us what they said!"

Mark lays his hand on Matt's arm and squeezes it.

Dan ignores them both. "Here goes. Axle asks Oskar what plans he has for the extra space beside the conference room." Dan looks at each of his audience and realize they don't get the significance of his comment. "Guys, there's a secret room in the branch that can be accessed from a hidden door in the conference room."

Matt looks like he has used his last bit of patience. Before he can say anything, Cheryl gently says, "I'm not sure why you're concerned about this, Dan."

"Yes, well I'll get to that, just hold on. Axle suggests he and Oskar check out the space to see how it could be used. They move out of the office and walk over to the conference room. I am thinking to myself, *How can I follow them without being seen?* I'm shaking like crazy and drop the glass I'm holding, and it breaks! It sounds like a gun going off. I was pretty sure I was done for, but the walls are so thick they never heard a thing."

Matt starts to stand up, but Mark pulls him back down and looks at him, shaking his head. Matt sighs and sits.

Dan takes a deep breath. "Once they step into the conference room, I slip into the break room. I can hear them clearly, good thing too since I broke my glass!" He laughs nervously. "I heard something like a cabinet door sliding open and some beeps as a combination was input. I was dying of curiosity at that point, so I sneak over to the conference room door and peek in and see Axle walk into this large room that was hidden on the other side of the conference room. As Axle talks and walks further into that room, Oskar walks toward a wall panel in the conference room, which he slides open to reveal another combination unit. While he keeps tabs on Axle, he quickly inputs the number sequence until the door pops open. I noticed there were no beeps from this lock as I heard with the first safe. Oskar lifts out a backpack, opens it, and takes out a metal rectangle with several protrusions. It looked like a big bug! He returns it to its hiding place and barely gets the panel closed when he sees Axle walk back toward the conference room."

Dan takes another drink from his Hawaiian Sun and looks at his audience for a response. Mark and Cheryl exchange looks, but as Matt starts to comment, Mark interjects quickly, "Dan, I don't want to sound James Bondish, but are you thinking there's something sinister about this item from Oskar's backpack?"

"Well, what do you think?" Dan asks.

Matt stands up. "I think you're paranoid, man. It's probably just some piece of equipment for the bank or something. You're losing it. I recommend you work out or something to clear your head so you don't let your imagination go wild. Cheryl, I think I heard your number being called, so I'll go pick up your burger." Matt stomps over to the burger truck.

Mark lays his hand on Dan's arm. "I know you're under a lot of stress while you stop drinking. I'm not sure what I think, but maybe you can keep your eyes and ears open, and I'll pray for direction for you. In fact, can I pray right now?" Mark doesn't wait for an answer but grabs Dan and Cheryl's hands and bows his head. "Jesus, please help. Dan needs you to direct him with this issue he's facing at work. Help him to listen for what You want him to do. Give him a specific sign, Jesus. Thanks. Amen."

Matt walks up with Cheryl's food. "Cheryl, I hitched a ride here so do you mind driving me home?"

Frustrated, Cheryl says, "I guess, but I'm finishing my food first." She quickly takes a big bite and then another.

Grumbling, Matt sits.

Dan turns to Mark. "I really need to study. Is it okay if we leave now?"

Crumpling her food bag, Cheryl stands and turns to Dan and Mark. "It was good seeing you again, Dan. Mark, I'll see you around."

As they leave, Mark says, "Dan, be honest with me. Do you think something serious is going on at work? Maybe Matt's right, and it's just a piece of bank equipment or something. I mean, why would Oskar want to do anything horrible? He's rich and seems to have everything he could possibly want."

Dan looks straight into Mark's eyes. "If it's all so innocent, why did he hide it from Axle, Canoe?"

Getting Away from It All with Mey

Mark walks into the GA, drops his keys in a dish on the bar, and reaches for the cleaning calendar. Feeling anxious, Mark checks his phone for the time and looks to see which house Mey is cleaning. He sighs, happy she is right behind him at the big house. Slipping into the garage entrance, he walks from room to room, ending at the large family room facing the beach and sees Mey hurriedly sweeping the lanai.

Pushing the big slider to the right, he waves as Mey looks up with a smile. Mark takes the broom from Mey, leans it against the house wall, and takes her hand. He kisses her cheek and leads her out toward the water. Kicking their shoes off at the edge of the lanai, they wander a little way down the beach and sit, Mark still holding Mey's hand.

"How was lunch, Mark? Did both guys show up?"

"Hmmm, yes, they did. Do you mind if we just sit for a while? I'm feeling a little unsettled and just need your calming influence."

Mey leans her head against Mark's shoulder as he places his arm around her. The mesmerizing motion and sound of the waves slapping the shoreline lulls them into a sense of peace. Mey actually dozes off, and Mark feels contentment as he holds her close. He takes a deep breath and reviews the recent conversation with Dan.

Does Dan have an overactive imagination, or is there really something to worry about at the bank? What should I do? Should I tell Mom? Axle? No one?

Glancing down at Mey, he sees she is awake and staring at him.

"It's obvious something's bothering you. Do you want to talk about it?"

"Mey, I would, but it was told to me in confidence. What would you do if someone told you something and you felt the situation could be dangerous? Would you tell someone or contact the authorities?"

Mey sits up. "Whoa, Mark. You can't just drop something like this on me and expect me to give you rational advice! You're scaring me."

Mark laughs. "I'm probably being overly dramatic. Dan shared something about the bank today at lunch, and he was being super dramatic too. I'm sorry to upset you."

"Mark, if it's about the bank, you should tell your mom. Especially if you think her life could be at risk. Is it that serious?"

Shaking his head, Mark watches some windsurfers walk into the water. "Maybe we could pray together. Would that be okay?"

Mey reaches for both of Mark's hands. She looks into his eyes, "Jesus, what a blessing it is to have you with us. We seek you in this situation. Please, Holy Spirit, provide Mark with a sign on how he should respond. Mark truly wishes to know your will and to follow it. We wait upon you for his next step. In your holy name, we pray. Amen."

Mark adds his "Amen" and helps Mey stand up. Smiling, Mey says, "Dad's grilling tonight. Come with me."

"Sounds perfect. I've been wanting to meet your folks. Are you done cleaning?"

"Yep, just let me put a few things away, and we can leave. Don't even go back to the GA. We can take my car."

Meeting the Family

Mey parks her car down the street from her parent's house as there is absolutely not an inch of parking anywhere near their property. Mark gets Mey's tote from the back seat, and they walk hand in hand toward the smell of grilling burgers. Mey walks faster and leads them through a fragrant side yard of plumerias and to the back where a huge crowd is gathered. Grabbing a blossom from the nearest tree, Mark puts it behind Mey's ear. As they step closer to the grill, Mark locks eyes with a man he suspects is Mey's father.

Mark stops abruptly, but Mey pulls him forward.

"E comomai, keiki."

With a swift kiss to his check, Mey responds, "Mahalo, makuakane."

"Who's the *haole*, Mey?"

"Father!"

Mark nervously reaches his hand out. "Hello, sir. My name is Mark Max. I'm a friend of Mey's. We work together cleaning houses."

"Mark, this is my father, Sam Kalili."

Sam hesitates but wipes his hand on his apron and grabs Mark's hand in a crushing grip. With little preamble, Sam spits out, "Mey, go help your mom in the kitchen while I visit with your *coworker*."

Mey opens her mouth to speak, but with one look at her father, quickly closes it and, shooting an apologetic glance to Mark, turns around and jogs to the back steps.

Sam hands his spatula to another relative manning the grill. "Okay, Marky Mark, let's go for a walk so we can get to know each other."

Mark looks longingly at the grill but says, "I'm no Mark Wahlberg, Mr. Kalili. Just plain ol' Mark will do."

"You look just like him to me. One street over is the North Shore so let's go look at the waves for a minute. If I take much longer than that, Mey's mom won't be happy. Why don't you define for me your relationship with Mey," says Sam with a steely gaze. "You might want to think through your answer."

Taking a deep breath, Mark says a quick prayer and responds, "I highly respect, Mey. She has been a true friend to me and my mom since we moved here a few months ago. My intentions are only honorable, sir."

"Call me *Sam.* That sounds good so far. How about long term?"

"Sir, I'm seeking the Lord's guidance on that."

As they turn the corner, Mark's mouth drops open at the magnificence of the waves crashing in the distance. Sam waits a moment, then softly places his hand on Mark's cheek and pushes it back toward him.

"Well, you've said the right thing, Mark. I was worried there for a minute. Let's go back now, so Mey won't worry, and her mom won't be too mad."

With a grin, Mark says, "Yes, sir!" and they walk at a brisk pace to return to the women in their lives.

Chapter 23

From GA to A-OK

Mark looks around the GA one last time. He sent his mom ahead to A-OK with their clothes and a few kitchen items while he and Mey did a final once over of the place. He hands her the keys and smiles.

She asks, "Bittersweet leaving, huh?"

He nods as Mey locks the door, "It's because I have so many memories here. This was the hub of our lives for these first few months, and of course, it's where I met you." He grabs her hand as they walk to her car. "We're starting a new chapter of our lives, so I'm excited but also a little scared."

"Scared? Why is that?" Mey asks as she drives away from Kailua.

"I've kept busy remodeling the GA and the A-OK plus helping you clean houses and going to AA meetings, but now I need to figure out what I should do next. I love working with you, but cleaning houses isn't my long-term career goal. In fact, I have no idea what I should do."

"You know I want you to continue to work with me, but I can understand your dilemma because I have that same thought myself on occasion. You know what I think you should do?"

"No, but I'm pretty sure you're gonna tell me." Mark laughs as she sticks her tongue out at him.

"Okay, I'll tell you," Mey says seriously. "Mark, I've listened to you tell me about your AA buddies. You keep up with them and are helping them in their sobriety. Have you thought of becoming a counselor?"

Mark doesn't immediately respond to Mey's question but gives it some thought.

Mey takes her fist and knocks on Mark's head, "Hey, you in there?"

Mey turns into the A-OK house driveway and parks behind the Beemer. Mark answers her question, "It's an interesting idea, Mey, but the schooling would take me forever. I went to a community college right after high school, but I only lasted a year."

As they walk into the kitchen, Mey comments, "Give it some thought, Mark. I think you'd be an amazing counselor."

Mark bumps into Mey's back as she stops short on the threshold of the kitchen. He smiles as he watches Mey's eyes circle the changed room.

"Just wait until you see the rest of the place. It looks incredible if I do say so myself."

Mey walks over to the gray granite countertop, rubbing her hands along the smooth surface. She does the same to the ice-blue mosaic backsplash tile. Walking over to the built-in nook, she sits in the booth and looks at Mark in awe. "You did it, Mark. You worked magic here."

He scoots into the booth, pushing Mey further in. Taking her hand, he plays with her fingers. "I'd like to take all the credit, but I'd never have gotten all this done without Leek. My mom and I really have to come up with something cool as a gift for him. I wish I could afford to give him one of Oskar's surfboards, but alas, they're way out of my price range."

Mey mulls over Mark's statement. "I've never seen Oskar's surfboards that everyone raves about. You know I've never even been to the bank. We should make a special trip there to check it out."

"The auction is coming up soon, and you're my guest, so if not before, you can see them there," Mark responds. He scoots back out of the booth with his hand out toward Mey. "Come on, let's see the rest of the place. Mom should be around here somewhere."

As they walk into the downstairs living space, they see Ruth sitting in a rattan club chair talking on her phone. Mey looks at the furniture placement, smiling in satisfaction.

"Canoe, you did good on the arrangement. This is exactly how I pictured it, and the rug ties everything together nicely."

Ruth finishes her call and walks over to Mey, giving her a big hug. She places her hands on either side of Mey's face. "You are a talented decorator, my dear. I feel so blessed to have your expertise in setting up our home. The house looks like a million bucks, literally! In fact, I think you should consider doing this as a career!" Ruth gives her a big kiss on the cheek, and Mey's face takes on a thoughtful look.

Ruth goes to the buffet on the opposite side of the room and opens a bottle of sparkling grape juice, filling three glasses. "Let's do two things—one, make a toast to our new home, and two, Mark, I would like you to pray a dedication to bless our new house." Ruth holds her glass up. "To a home filled with joy and the love of the Lord."

All take a sip of their drink, and Ruth points her finger toward Mark.

They bow their heads.

"Father, we are awed by all the gifts you've provided us on this Hawaii journey. Thanks for all our new friendships, Mom's job, my work with Mey and Leek as well as this new amazing home. All this comes from you, and we give thanks and dedicate this place to you, asking for divine guidance in using it for your glory. In Jesus's name, we pray, Amen."

Ruth's face is glowing as she says, "Mark, thank you. That was lovely. Why don't you show Mey the rest of the house while I put together a salad for us? I bought some fajita chicken for a taco salad. Oh, and by the way, I want to talk about the housewarming I want to have because I'd like to do it soon. We can talk dates and other details while we eat."

Mark and Mey nod as they walk to the master bedroom. Ruth hums "How Far I'll Go" from the movie *Moana* as she goes into the kitchen.

All Together

Already moved in and settled, Mark and Ruth are enjoying an open house with all their Hawaiian friends. Mark sips his soft drink as he watches the shish kabobs on the grill. Dan walks up with his own drink and reaches his hand toward a kabob on a platter. Grabbing Dan's arm, Mark laughs.

"And what do you think you're doing?"

Dan snickers, "Hey, I thought I could get away with getting a head start on the food!"

Mark snorts, "Forget it, man! They'll all be done soon so you can wait with everyone else. Why don't you tell Mom they're almost ready? I think she was going to announce dinner once these are done."

"Your mom is stuck at the door with a bunch of guests." Dan continues as he takes a piece of meat that fell onto the plate and pops it in his mouth.

Mark raises an eyebrow. "So how is it?"

Dan closes his eyes as he chews. He opens his eyes and says, "It's okay."

Mark punches Dan in the shoulder. "Go tell Mom these are done, goof."

Dan continues to laugh as he goes into the house, picking up a napkin from the counter and looking for Ruth. A pretty young woman is setting the kitchen bar buffet style with all the plates and flatware. Dan thinks for a moment, *Oh yeah, this is Canoe's girlfriend.* "Hey, we haven't met. I'm Dan."

Mey looks up, "Hi, Dan, I've heard about you. I'm Mey."

As they shake hands, Dan responds, "I feel like I know you. Your name comes up frequently." Dan slaps his forehead, "I forgot what I came in to do. Mark says the kabobs are practically done. I see a crowd doing a tour of the house. Should I wait to announce the food is ready?"

"We better not, or the food will get cold. I'll get her if you will put the drinks in this bucket of ice."

Dan opens the fridge, thinking of last night at work. *If Mark knew what I did, there would be hel—heck to pay.* Dan hears footsteps and puts one last drink in the bucket before he picks it up and places it on the booth table.

Mark walks in from outside with a huge platter of kabobs and puts them on the end of the kitchen counter just as Sara, Kim, and Oskar walk into the kitchen. Bringing up the rear is Leek.

Mark yells, "Here he is, the man of the hour, the man who made this house what it is, Leek Ihohali!" Mark starts clapping, and everyone else does the same.

Leek yells over the clapping, "I'd like to take full credit for this beautiful transformation, but alas, I cannot."

Mey shakes her head and laughs.

Leek walks over and places his arm around Mark. "This guy did most of the work. I may have spent a day total helping, and Mark did the rest." Leek picks up a drink and lifts it. "I want to propose a toast to a super friend and a great Christian example for me, *Canoe!*"

Mark's face turns three shades of red as the group continues clapping and choosing drinks. "For you that don't know, we called our little garage apartment, GA, and this A-frame Kanoehe house, we call A-OK. Leek, I am super thankful for all your assistance with both houses." He quickly moves to the pantry and pulls out a scuba tank tied with a huge red bow. Turning to Leek, Mark excitedly says, "Anyway, as a small token of our appreciation, we bought you a scuba tank so you don't have to rent one anymore. And I can borrow it once I finish my scuba lessons!" Mark hands the tank to Leek, who holds it like a baby, and gives it a big kiss.

Everyone laughs while Leek shakes hands with Mark and gives Ruth a quick kiss on the cheek.

Ruth yells over the noise, "Hey, everyone, before we eat all this amazing food, Kim, would you please say grace for us?"

Everyone quiets as Kim steps forward. "Ruth, would you and Mark please step in front of me?"

Ruth takes Mark's hand, and they walk over to Kim. He places one hand on Mark's shoulder and the other on Ruth's.

"Lord, thank you for providing this food for the nourishment of our bodies. We are immensely grateful to you for bringing these two special people into our lives. We ask for divine protection of this home, and that it would be a sanctuary for those seeking you. For any here tonight who don't know you, Lord, draw them to your unconditional love. In Jesus's name we pray, Amen."

Mark and Ruth add their own amens. Ruth reaches over for a plate and hands it to Kim, who smiles and immediately grabs the tongs for the kabobs.

Sara leans against the doorjamb, observing skeptically as Axle walks over to Ruth. *These people, their whole lives are caught up in this Jesus business.* Sara hears the doorbell and, seeing no one else paying attention, goes to answer the front door. She opens it to an extremely tall and handsome man who looks vaguely familiar.

"Hi, my name is Sara Chin. I work with Ruth at the bank. Come on in, everyone's in the kitchen getting food." Looking closely at the new guest, Sara is pretty sure she has met him before. *It will come to me in a minute.* Sara steps back to let Hanadie come inside.

"Well, hi yourself. I'm Hanadie Besic, also a friend of Ruth's, who I met through my best friend, Axle. I'm sure you know him as he also works at the bank."

"Yes, I do know Axle." Sara grins mischievously. "I used to have the biggest crush on him, but I think I'll switch to you. You aren't married, are you?"

Hanadie laughs with delight. "Girl, I'm not married, but the day's not over yet. Take me to the food!"

Sara takes Hanadie's hand and leads him to the kitchen. The crowd has diminished, with most sitting at the big table on the lanai. Axle and Ruth remain in the kitchen talking, and they look up to greet Hanadie and Sara. Ruth looks pointedly at Sara and Hanadie's clasped hands. Sara smiles and shrugs her shoulders. Hanadie gently drops Sara's hand and hugs Ruth.

"Congrats, my dear, on this lovely home. This is a fantastic location. I know you and Mark will be happy here."

Ruth looks over Hanadie's shoulder, making faces at Sara, who again shrugs her shoulders and throws her hair back. Hanadie moves toward Axle, shaking his hand.

"Hey, guy. How're things?"

"Great, Han. I see you met Sara, our resident fashion diva."

Sara narrows her eyes as Hanadie looks back at her. "Yes, I have and I'm intrigued. Sara, have you eaten? Why don't we get something and join those outside?"

Sara picks up a soft drink and pops the top. "I'm game. Mark made some killer-looking kabobs. Ruth, are there any left?"

Ruth hands Sara a plate filled with a steaming kabob. "Here you go, *dar*-lin-g. Mark just took the last batch off the grill. Hanadie, here's a plate for you. It may not match the gourmet choices at your restaurant, but it will definitely be filling."

Sara looks with surprise at Hanadie. "Now I know where I've seen you before. You were introduced to me when Oskar and I went to Hanadie's for lunch a couple of weeks ago. I don't know why it took me so long to remember. I'm definitely losing my touch!"

"I wouldn't say that at all, Sara. I remember that now as well. How could I forget?" Han shakes his head in disbelief. "Come on, let's go outside." Taking Sara's plate, Han waits as she opens the door.

Axle sighs as he watches them leave. "Ruth, let's make our plates and eat in here. It's quiet, and I'd love to be able to visit with you for a few minutes. Sit while I make your plate."

Ruth sits at the booth with a glass of water, taking a long drink and blowing her hair out of her eyes. *It feels great to sit for a few minutes. This has been a wonderful day with all my new friends here. God is good.*

Axle brings two plates to the table, setting one in front of Ruth as he slides in next to her. He hands her a fork and knife, and they dig in.

Axle takes his first bite of steak kabob. "Mark has another skill to add to his list. The seasoning as well as the grilling flavor is top notch. Are there any left?"

Ruth stabs a piece of steak and transfers it to Axle's plate. "I'm pretty sure this is the last of it. He plans on making ice cream sundaes later, so you should get enough to eat."

"Really? I'll help him with those," Axle says with a playful grin. As he takes his last bite of kabob, he says, "Were you able to move the date for the auction?"

Ruth nods her head, "Believe it or not, the hotel had the date we needed available because of a last-minute cancellation, but I haven't had a chance to tell Oskar. I'll catch him when he comes inside. The problem is, we're having difficulty contacting some of those invited to tell them the date change. Should we expand our invitation list?"

"Let's see, today is the twentieth and the date of the auction is December 6, approximately two weeks away. Could you possibly mail date-change notifications as well as sending invitations to a new group? Maybe the admiral could give you some names you could invite. If you do it tomorrow or the next day, you might get some additional responses."

"Here comes Oskar. Let's ask him!" Ruth runs to the back door to open it since Oskar is carrying several plates. "Oskar, do you have a few minutes to talk about the auction?"

Oskar places the plates in the sink and turns around. "I was just about to ask you about it. What's the latest?"

Ruth steps to the sink to rinse the plates as she answers Oskar. "I was just telling Axle the hotel actually had that date available. Good news there, but we've gotten quite a few negative responses from those we called plus there are many we haven't been able to speak to personally. Axle and I were discussing the idea of mailing a notification to those invited of the date change as well as sending out new invitations. What do you think of that idea?"

"Who else would you invite?"

Axle chimes in, "How about asking the admiral who he would like us to invite?"

"Excellent idea. I'll call Frank right now and have him call Admiral Martinez." Oskar pulls his phone from his back pocket. "Ruth, go ahead and mail the date-change notifications, and once we hear from Frank, mail the new invitations. Let's place an ad in the paper that announces the date change, opening it to the public. At this late date, we're not likely to get hordes of people coming, but I think we should have enough at this point. I'm planning to hire a mover to take the outriggers and the surfboards to the hotel. What other details do we need to cover?"

Ruth finishes filling the dishwasher. "I think that's enough! I want to thank you again, Oskar, for your part in helping me get this house. Mark and I are both loving this place."

Distracted, Oskar pats Ruth on the shoulder, "You're welcome, my dear, but I gotta go. See you guys later. Ruth, will you please continue to update me with the RSVP numbers?"

"Yes, sir."

Ruth and Axle walk Oskar to the door and wave as he drives away.

They return to the kitchen as Mark pulls the ice cream from the freezer. Mey sets the scoop and bowls on the table. Sara and Hanadie walk back inside and eye the ice cream preparations with interest.

Leek walks inside with his ukulele and pulls a chair over to the corner and starts to play "Over the Rainbow." All activity stops as Ruth, Sara, and Mey stand by Leek to sing along. Mark drops his scoop as he looks up and sees Matt at the doorway to the kitchen. The clatter as the scoop hits the floor causes everyone to look up, and the music stops.

Matt smiles apologetically. "Hi, I knocked for some time, but no one answered. Hope you don't mind me letting myself in."

Mark picks up the scoop and rinses it in the sink. "Of course not. It's great you could make it. Let me introduce you quickly so Leek can continue playing. Everyone, this is my friend Matt."

Hanadie and Axle step up to shake Matt's hand, and Leek begins playing again with the ladies as backup. Mark lays out ten bowls and piles the ice cream, chocolate sauce, whipped cream, and cherries in each. Mey hands bowls and spoons to Hanadie, Axle, Matt, Kim, and Dan. When the song ends, everyone claps and Mark and Mey hand the singers their sundaes.

Dan, Matt, and Mark lean against the kitchen counter, eating their sundaes; and Dan says, "I saw Oskar leaving when we drove up, and remind me to tell you about work. Mark you have to tell Matt and me the *Canoe* story."

Laughing, Leek places his bowl in the sink. "You can blame that on me." Leek places his arm around Mark's shoulder. "I consider Mark my best friend, but our first meeting was a little rocky. Mark and I met upon his arrival in Hawaii when I was the cabbie picking up him and Ruth at the airport. He was whining and complaining in general and giving his mom a hard time. I became frustrated and told him I was changing his name to Kanuha."

Dan interrupts, "Kanuha? I'm confused."

Matt shakes his head. "Don't pay any attention to him, confused is his usual state."

Leek ignores Matt and responds to Dan, "Immediately after I told Mark he had a new name, I shortened it to Canoe and it stuck."

Dan still looks uncertain. "But why Kanuha? What does it actually mean?"

Mark responds, "It means 'one who sulks' in Hawaiian."

Dan and Matt laugh while Leek walks back to his chair and ukulele and starts his next song, "It's a Wonderful World."

Everyone else finishes their sundaes quietly as they listen to Leek's song, and each one in this diverse group feels the companionship of the moment.

CHAPTER 24

Snooping

"D an, do you need anything from me before I leave?" Ruth asks as they finish the cash vault audit.

"I'm good, Ruth. Say hi to Canoe for me." Dan grins as he twirls the combination dial.

"You really get a kick out of that, don't you? I think you and Leek are the only ones who consistently call him that. I can't believe everything fell into place for the auction, and that it's almost here. Tomorrow's the big day! Oskar is having the outrigger and surfboards picked up at two o'clock tomorrow to deliver to the hotel. Thanks for helping me finish the last audit. I'll see you in the morning." Ruth waves as she goes to her office to pick up her things to leave.

Dan watches her leave and sits on his bar stool in the drive-through, contemplating how he can sneak into the conference room and check out the cabinet where Oskar placed the backpack. He checks the drive-through for customers. It's empty so far, so he quietly walks downstairs, preparing himself in case he runs into Axle. Dan hears voices coming from the break room; so he tiptoes to the entrance, peeks inside, and sees Axle and Oskar talking as Oskar gets a water from the fridge. Dan mulls over his options and decides to listen to the men's conversation.

"Oskar, are you going to be here for a while?" Axle asks.

"Yeah, do you mind?" Oskar asks as he sits and opens his laptop.

"Of course not. Do you mind closing up with Daniel, I mean, Dan? Ruth and I are going on our first formal date tonight."

"Well, good for you guys, Axle. Have fun. So Daniel goes by Dan now? Have him call me when he's ready to put his cash away."

As Axle leaves the break room, he squeezes Oskar's shoulders. "Thanks. Tomorrow's the big day, right?"

Oskar nods. "I hope we have a good turnout. Since it was Ruth's idea, I want it to have a successful conclusion."

"Me too. Thanks again and see you tomorrow," Axle responds as he quickly walks out of the break room toward the garage exit.

Dan stumbles as he backs up in the corridor, knowing he won't be able to hide from Axle. "Any waters left, Axle?"

Surprised, Axle raises his eyebrows. "You better hurry. You don't want to leave the drive-through for too long. Oh, and Oskar asked me to tell you to call him when you need to put your cash box away. He's staying tonight."

"Yes, sir, I will."

The door slams behind Axle. Dan cringes, *we need to get that fixed.* Dan notices Oskar never even raises his head but continues to scroll through his laptop. Dan quietly backs up further and climbs the stairs to check on the drive-through.

Dan finishes with his last customer and turns off the customer drive-through lights. He quickly balances his drawer and places the lid on it for vault storage.

I'm going to go downstairs one last time. Maybe I can still check on the conference room if Oskar is still in the break room. Am I crazy? If he sees me snooping around, I could get fired or worse! Okay, don't get dramatic. Just go downstairs. It's no big deal. If Oskar notices you, just mention you came down to get a water and tell him you're done for the night.

Sneaking downstairs, Dan notices the break room is empty so he walks to the edge of the conference room and sees Oskar standing by *the* panel. Just as Oskar starts to turn to check the hallway, Dan jumps back, breathing heavily. He waits a few moments pressed against the wall and glances back inside to see Oskar slide the panel to the right. Dan watches closely as Oskar inputs the four-number combination. Dan waits a few moments as Oskar pulls out the backpack for a quick inspection but seeing Oskar swiftly replace it in the cabinet, Dan runs back upstairs. He slides to Ruth's old desk and picks up her phone to call the conference room. When Oskar answers, Dan explains he's ready to put his cash drawer in the vault.

CHAPTER 25

Auction or Bust

R uth is mesmerized by the setting sun on Waikiki beach. The ocean sparkles in the waning light as the final few swimmers leave the water. *Sunset must be why Royal Hawaiian is painted pink since it literally glows among the lush landscaping.* Ruth pulls her car up to the valet area of the hotel, and as soon as she stops, the car door is opened and the valet reaches his hand toward her. Loving the attention, Ruth smiles as she steps from the car, handing Steve her keys. She ruins the moment by tripping in her new shoes, and Steve catches her before she falls. *Nice, my new name is grace.*

"Thanks for your help. I'm not accustomed to tall heels."

"My pleasure, ma'am. Are you okay now?"

"Other than embarrassed, I'm great. I'm here to meet with Chad for the auction."

Steve grins. "I believe he's waiting for you at the entrance."

Looking at the hotel entrance, Ruth sees Chad waving. She smiles back at Steve and thanks him for his help. She awkwardly walks in her four-inch heals to meet Chad. *I wish I had practiced in these darn things before wearing them.* Chad walks toward her, offering his arm, which Ruth gratefully takes.

"Ruth, wait until you see the room. It looks beautiful with the outriggers on display. I'm glad you're here early so you can see the room in all its glory."

They walk inside the hotel lobby, and Chad leads the way to the auction room. Ruth nods her approval, seeing the chairs lined up in two sections of ten rows with eight chairs in each row. There's a lectern on the stage with a draped table next to it. A huge tropical flower arrangement sits on one end of the table; and three chairs are arranged for Oskar, Frank, and Admiral Martinez. The pièce de résistance is the incredible oceanview outside the big glass doors.

She looks to the left, and her jaw drops at the sight of one outrigger on its stand filled with flowers. Ruth quizzes Chad, "Who authorized the flowers?"

Chad pulls out his phone and scrolls through it. "Oskar Soto called me two days ago and told me a florist would be delivering flowers today. Don't they look amazing? There are some on the sign-in table as well."

Ruth looks toward the room entrance past the entry stairs and notices a long table she missed when first entering and sees where another impressive arrangement rests. She calculates the cost in her head and whistles. "I agree. They truly add the perfect touch. We're sponsoring the Arizona Memorial Ceremony tomorrow and plan to take the outrigger there, filled with flowers, to give to the veterans in attendance. It was smart for Oskar to get them delivered today so we can enjoy them at the auction as well."

"Oh, that reminds me, Ruth, I have something for you and Sara Chin," Chad says over his shoulder as he walks to the lectern. Reaching behind it, he brings out two boxes, one of which he hands to Ruth and the other he places on the table. Ruth opens the box and catches her breath as a beautiful white phalaenopsis orchid wrist corsage is revealed.

"Here, let me do it," Chad says as he removes the orchid gently from its layers of tissue. He places it on Ruth's wrist and nods approvingly. "It's the perfect accessory for your little black dress."

Axle walks up quietly and touches Ruth's shoulder. Startled, Ruth again wobbles in her shoes. Both Chad and Axle reach for Ruth, but Axle gives Chad a look that changes Chad's mind.

"Ruth, I'm sorry I surprised you. Wow, I've never seen you so tall. Uh, nice shoes," Axle awkwardly says.

Ruth steadies herself and laughs. "I know I'll be regretting wearing these before the night's over. The valet already had to save me earlier as I was getting out of the car."

Again, Axle looks toward Chad, who quickly tells them, "Ruth, I'll go check on the refreshments and be back momentarily." He scurries out the doorway, and Ruth looks sternly at Axle, "You're making poor Chad nervous. Are you getting jealous on me or what?"

Axle kisses Ruth on the cheek. "I didn't like the way he looked at my girl, that's all. By the way, you look stunning."

Ruth looks down at her dress and in her best Texas twang voice says, "What? This little ol' thing?" She and Axle both giggle, and luckily, he has his hand on her arm to keep her from falling again.

"Really, Ruth. Did you bring another pair of shoes?"

Ruth straightens her dress and determinedly stands on her own. "I'm going to get used to these, Axle. They go perfectly with the dress, and Sara gave them to me."

They both look up and see the topic of their discussion walk in on Hanadie's arm. Axle whistles as Sara steps away from Hanadie and twirls to show off her outfit. Ruth punches Axle in the arm and walks over to get a closer look at Sara's Japanese silk dress.

"Hi, Hanadie. Sara, my goodness, you've outdone yourself, if that's possible. This look is chic and spectacular at the same time. The red-and-black print is perfect with your coloring. Are those chopsticks in your hair?"

Sara touches her hair. "They're not falling out, are they?"

Ruth looks closely at the elaborate hairstyle. All of Sara's glorious hair has been arranged on top of her head in a geisha style. Ruth says, "It looks like the chopsticks are firmly in place."

Sara notices Ruth's hand. "Is this the prom, or what?"

Ruth looks down. "Oh, yeah! There's one for you too." Ruth walks carefully to the table and grabs the corsage box and brings it back to Sara, who opens it to reveal another wrist corsage, this one made from deep red roses. "Those are perfect with your dress! You have to wear it! Oskar would be disappointed if you didn't." Ruth takes the corsage and places it on Sara's wrist. "Guys, look at the outrigger on the other side of the lectern."

All their heads turn, and they walk toward the huge flower arrangement. Hanadie speaks first.

"Whoever did this arrangement is a true artist. I don't believe I've ever seen so many flowers in one place. These are great choices too, orchids, anthuriums, ginger, and bird of paradise. Pretty impressive, I must say."

Ruth looks at her watch. "The auctioneer should be here any moment, plus our guests will be arriving in about thirty to forty-five minutes. I better check with Chad and see what's happening with the refreshments." Ruth's attention is drawn to the entrance of the room. "Hi, Oskar." Ruth grabs Sara's hand and drags her over to the doorway. "Oskar, Sara and I want to thank you for the lovely wrist corsages. As you can tell, they work wonderfully with our ensembles."

Sara raises one eyebrow, "Yeah, they look great with our *ensembles*. Thanks."

Before Oskar can respond, Ruth chimes in, "Come see the outrigger, Oskar. Your florist outdid themselves on the arrangement. Are you having this delivered to the ceremony tomorrow with all the flowers?"

Oskar nods as he steps up to the flowers and reaches in and picks one of the smaller orchids, pinches the flower off, and places it in his lapel. They hear a commotion at the doorway and see Chad and the hotel staff bringing in carts of Christmas delicacies and coffee. The bartender is setting the bar at the end corner of the room.

Following the employees, Kim walks in with a woman Ruth recognizes from church. She steps over to greet them, reaching her hand out. "Kim, a pleasure as always. Let me introduce you to my coworker. Sara, I would like you to meet the pastor of Ho'o Church, Kim Zec. Sara is our comptroller at Oahu National. I don't think you guys met at my party a couple of weeks ago."

Kim takes Ruth's hand into both of his. "Ruth, it's wonderful to see you. Sara, a pleasure to make your acquaintance. This is my wife, Lily."

"I do remember seeing you at church, Lily. I'm so happy you could attend our little soiree."

They smile and shake hands.

Sara stands by, idly playing with the chopsticks in her hair. Ruth gives her a look, and Sara reaches her hand toward Lily as well.

Lily responds, "Hi, it's a pleasure to meet you, Sara. Your dress is stunning."

Sara peruses Lily's outfit and decides the cream satin sheath works well with her blond hair. *The blue opal necklace sparkles against the dress and brings out the blue in her eyes.* Sara grudgingly compliments the outfit. "Quite the *ensemble* you have on, Lily. Is that a Donna Karan?"

Ruth links arms with Lily. "Don't pay any attention to Miss Fashion Plate over there. She's making fun of my earlier use of the word *ensemble*. She's right, though, you look lovely. Come see the outrigger."

Hanadie, Sara, and Kim trail Ruth and Lily as they inspect the outrigger, oohing and ahhing the entire time.

As Oskar and Axle stand by the door, discussing work, a gentleman walks up to them.

"Is this where the auction is being held?"

Axle speaks up, "Yes, you're in the right place. I'm Axle Besic, and this is Oskar Soto, the executive president of Oahu National as well as chairman of the board."

"Hi, I'm Charles Knox, the auctioneer."

They shake hands.

Ruth excuses herself from the group and walks over. "Hi, I'm Ruth Max. So glad you're here tonight. Would you like to see the items up for auction?"

"Indeed, I would. I think I see an outrigger already, and wow, the flowers are spectacular. Where are the surfboards?" Oskar snaps his fingers. "I built an elaborate display stand to showcase them that I only finished last night, so I had the movers pick them up today. Let me call them to make sure they're on their way with the surfboards and the second outrigger." Oskar steps out into the hall to make his call and pulls his phone from his jacket pocket. It rings, and he practically jumps out of his skin, but noticing it's from the movers, he takes a deep breath. "Hello, where are you guys? The auction starts in thirty minutes."

Continuing to stand in the hall, Oskar takes a moment to analyze his plans for the evening and the next day. *I suppose I should be praying, but my faith has taken a nosedive lately. Do I really think I can get this done by myself?* Not answering the question, he takes a deep breath to calm his nerves. He doesn't want anyone to be concerned once he steps back into the room.

Outstanding Turnout!

After Ruth greets what appears to be the last auction guest, she tells Sara, "I'm so pleased at the turnout. Chad's even gone to get more chairs for seating. Aren't you impressed?"

Sara uncharacteristically takes Ruth's hands in her own, "Ruth, everything you do is impressive. This is just another success to add to the list."

Ruth turns three shades of red, shocked at Sara's compliment as well as her touch. Moved, Ruth returns Sara's squeeze. "What did I do before you became my friend? Thank you. *But* the night isn't over yet. Let's get something to eat and drink and find our seats. It looks like Oskar is about to introduce Admiral Martinez."

Heads together, they approach the food table, each grabbing a plate and choosing from the large selection of mini fruit kabobs and specialty cookies. As they fill their plates, Hanadie walks up and touches Sara's shoulder.

"I'm sorry, but I have to leave because my manager just called and said two waiters called in sick. The restaurant is packed, and they need my help. Ruth, do you mind getting Sara home?"

Ruth looks up to Hanadie. "It would be my pleasure, Hanadie. I'm sorry you'll miss the festivities though."

"Walk me out, Sara?" Hanadie tucks Sara's arm into his, affirming his apology as they move toward the room exit.

As Sara returns to find her seat, she sees Ruth across the room speaking to Axle as he adjusts his video camera. *Oh, yeah, Oskar wanted Axle to tape the auction.*

Looking at the room entrance, Ruth sees Mark and Mey walk into the room. Ruth's breath catches in her throat at the star quality of her son and his girlfriend. He's wearing a navy suit, and Mey has on a Hawaiian-print sarong and orchids in her hair. They wave, and Ruth points to the food table, and they change direction. *They make an amazing couple. I'm so proud.* Ruth feels a tear forming and takes her napkin to blot it.

Oskar steps up to the lectern, and the room becomes quiet.

"Good evening, all. I thank each of you for attending Oahu National's Veterans Auction. Tomorrow is a solemn occasion for us in Hawaii, and it's important for us to take every opportunity to recognize the incredible sacrifices of our soldiers and veterans. I know each of you will be thinking of this as you dig deep into your significant resources when bidding knowing that every dollar will go to support the veteran's organizations listed in your programs. Now I would like to introduce Kim Sec, the pastor of Ho'o Church to do the benediction."

Kim walks over and shakes Oskar's hand. Oskar steps back as Kim steps up and bows his head.

"Lord, we thank you for all those here tonight who willingly give up their time and money to bid on Oskar's art to benefit veterans who gave their all so we may sit here tonight in freedom: freedom to do as we choose and to worship you. We thank you for this beautiful island you created for us. Amen."

Kim steps away and walks back to his seat. Oskar introduces Admiral Martinez, who also speaks on the veterans groups who will benefit from the auction dollars spent. As he finishes his speech, Mark and Mey slip into the two seats next to Sara and Ruth. The audience claps as Admiral Martinez sits down. Frank goes to the lectern to introduce the auctioneer, who steps up behind Frank.

"As you can see the money we raise tonight is going for a very good cause. I hope you had an opportunity to inspect the items, but if not, the brochure handed to you gives you details on each one. These hand-built outriggers and surfboards took years for Oskar to create and each is a unique work of art. I have my eye on one of the outriggers, and I know you can see it's outstanding and one of a kind. Remember these are fully operational boats, which I know firsthand as Oskar has taken me out on the first one going up for auction."

Chapter 26

Success at the Auction

The audience erupts in applause as the last item, the most elaborately carved outrigger, has received a bid amount of $50,000. In a booming voice, Charles states, "Do I hear $51,000?" He waits several seconds. "Sold for $50,000!"

The clapping is thunderous, and the audience stands as they continue clapping. Oskar moves to stand beside Charles, and they chat for a few minutes as the audience continues to clap. The audience slowly stops clapping, and Oskar addresses them. "I would like to thank Charles for his amazing auctioneering skills." He shakes Charles's hand before Charles steps away from the microphone.

"Are you ready for the final total received today?"

The crowd yells, "Yes!"

"Our grand total is $148,000! Admiral Martinez, please come stand with me."

Admiral Martinez has his handkerchief in his hand, wiping his eyes as he walks up to Oskar.

Oskar places his arm around the admiral's shoulders. "I feel confident the admiral joins me in our profuse appreciation to those of you bidding tonight. Enough can't be said for your generosity in helping those who have done so much for us." Oskar looks directly at Ruth with a nod, and he continues, "Please stay and enjoy each other's company and the bar, which I have directed to be reopened at the bank's expense. It will only be a few moments for the hotel to accommodate our request."

Ruth jumps from her seat and runs from the room with her phone looking for Chad, who luckily is just outside the door talking to the cleaning crew.

Kaho Time Ends

Oskar walks to his pickup while the valet holds the door with his hand out. Without acknowledging him, Oskar steps into the vehicle, putting the truck into gear. Driving off, he leaves the valet with a look of chagrin on his face as he looks at his empty hand.

After having praised the US military in his speech, Oskar finds his mind full of reels and reels of scenes depicting the past horrors of Bosnia. He relives each experience, but also thinks of life he has experienced in the US. Unbelievably, he smiles, thinking of his three friends and what they have accomplished in the years here in Hawaii. His next thought generates a frown. The last Kaho get together was not a pleasant experience. There was much arguing, and an agreement was made to suspend the boys' nights out. *The argument is always the same.* Oskar curses, thinking of the differences of opinion about the war and the aftermath. *I suppose it's time to move on, but it's so hard thinking about Ena and Luka. I hate it that our differences are taking a toll on our friendships. Maybe my efforts tonight will change some opinions.*

Finalizing the Details

Oskar stands in the waiting area of the airplane charter company.

"Mr. Soto, we're doing the final checks on the plane, then we'll be ready to takeoff. I'll come get you in a few minutes."

Oskar nods. "Thanks, Stan. I appreciate your willingness to do a late-night plane ride for me."

Stan opens the door to leave. "I'm happy to do it. I love to fly at night but rarely have anyone request night flights."

Oskar looks at his watch. *I'm running out of time. It's 11:00 p.m., and the ceremony starts at 9:00 a.m. Am I going to get this all done by then? I have to get it done. That's all there is to it. I'm hoping my research tonight will help me tomorrow.*

Stan sticks his head back inside. "We're ready now."

Oskar picks up his backpack and rushes out to the plane. He steps in right behind Stan and buckles himself into the copilot seat. Stan starts the engine and requests approval for takeoff from the tower at Honolulu International. Once he receives the go ahead, he slowly directs the plane to his designated runway. It takes only a few minutes for the small plane to take off and do a fly over of Oahu.

As the plane makes its turn over the north shore, Oskar speaks up. "Stan, would you mind flying over Ewa Beach? I want to see if I can see my house from here."

"Sure." Stan redirects the plane toward the south side of the island, and after ten minutes or so, the lanai lights of Oskar's house come into view. Oskar picks up his high-powered binoculars and focuses on his house to get the view as clear as possible.

"This is so cool. I'm glad I left my outside lights on. Wow, I can even see my patio furniture."

Stan laughs and makes another circle. "Have you seen enough?"

Oskar sighs. "Yep, this has been great, but all of a sudden I'm pretty beat. Let's head back."

"No problem, we're close." Stan changes direction toward the airport.

Eyes to his binoculars again, Oskar becomes hyper focused as the plane passes over the harbors near the airport. As he can see the lights of Pearl Harbor, he thinks anxiously, *This is where everything changes.*

Stan calls the air traffic controller, "This is flight 9274, requesting permission to land."

"Flight 9274, you are second after Hawaiian Air 902."

Oskar sits back in his seat with the binoculars in his lap. Closing his eyes, a look of nostalgia settles on his face. *I'm glad to have gotten this one last view of the island…* It's quickly replaced by a look of grim determination.

"Did you see what you came for?" Stan asks.

"I certainly did. The beauty of the island from the air will stay with me for a long time. Again, thanks for flying with me tonight."

"Not a problem," Stan responds as he taxis to the terminal.

What Happened Tonight at the Bank?

Dan locks his cash drawer and steps outside the teller area, looking toward Mike's office. He has his feet on his desk with his phone glued to his ear. *Okay, I can go downstairs now and check out Oskar's cabinet.* Dan avoids the elevator and walks down the stairs, heading directly to the conference room. He moves around the table and places his hands on the paneling as he pushes each panel, looking for the correct one to access the secret room.

He gets nervous as he moves from one end of the wall to the other without finding the movable panel. As his heart pounds, he starts over and after checking a few, he finally feels movement in one panel. It slides to the right, revealing the electronic push pad. He stands there for a few moments, thinking through combination options. He enters 3394 and is shocked when he hears a loud click, and looking to his left, he sees a part of the wall pop inward. *Amazing, Oskar used the same combo he used for his pack cabinet.* Dan pushes the secret door open further so he can step into the room and is surprised and disappointed to see the room is empty. He realizes he needs to hurry in case Mike comes looking for him. The door clicks shut behind him as he leaves the room. Starting to count, he searches for the panel covering the back pack cabinet. He slides it open and enters the same combination, and again, the safe door pops open. With a deep breath, he grabs the pack for a quick look inside and stands in shock at what he sees.

It's Time to Take a Stand

After worrying all evening, Dan mumbles under his breath, "I have to do something." Glancing at his phone, he sees it's midnight. As he backs out of his driveway, he calls Mark.

"Hi, Dan, what's—"

Dan interrupts, "Canoe, I looked in that cabinet not too long after we talked about it at Lanikai beach. I haven't told you this because I didn't know what to do, and I needed to do more research, but I am pretty sure the backpack in the cabinet had a bomb in it. I took a picture of the device and went to the library to use their computers to do an online search for bomb types. I found one that looked similar to the one I saw. Listen to me, tomorrow is the memorial and that's a perfect venue to do something dramatic."

Mark pulls over and feels like he is hyperventilating. "Dan, this is scary. Shouldn't we call the authorities and let them handle it?"

Dan shakes his head, not thinking Mark can't see it. "Just listen," Dan says. "We're running out of time. Before leaving work tonight, I looked in Oskar's pack cabinet at the bank, and it's gone. That means he's moving forward with whatever plans he's put together. I've been agonizing over it all night and decided I couldn't *not* do anything! I'm afraid we don't have time to bring the authorities in. You know those government entities work at snail speed. By the time they figure out what to do, it'll be too late. I think we should confront Oskar at home. Call Matt. If the three of us go over there, one of us should be able to take him out."

Mark's hand is shaking as he tries to keep the phone to his ear. "We don't know where Oskar lives or if he's even home. How do we find his house?"

"One advantage of working at the bank is I have access to Oskar's information, not his accounts but his personal address. I already Google mapped it, and I'm ready to drive us there. Give me Matt's address, and I'll pick you both up there. Look, Canoe, if it's nothing, I'll get fired and everything will go back to normal. But if I'm right, we will stop something horrific from happening. If you don't go with me, I'll do it by myself."

Without realizing it, Mark mirrors Dan's head shaking. "Dan, you know I can't let you do that, so I'll text you Matt's address. It will take me about twenty minutes to get there since I'm almost home after dropping Mey off at her house. I'm still feeling uncertain about all this since my mom works with Oskar. Her job could be affected by what we do. I want to see your picture of the bomb research to see if my interpretation matches yours."

"We can discuss it when I see you, Canoe. Text me Matt's address quickly so I can drive in that direction."

"It's on its way."

Back at Ewa

Oskar sees a light on next door and runs to the backyard to see if Julie is in the pool. She isn't swimming. *Why would she be swimming so late?* He walks to the back door and opens the slider and lets himself inside.

"Julie? Julie?"

Julie is putting on her robe as she walks from the kitchen to the open family room.

"Oskar? I'm sorry I couldn't make it to the auction…"

"Julie, I don't have time to talk. I've heard some scuttlebutt that there may be some gang members trying to burgle some of our beachfront homes tonight. I'll call the cops, but I want you to leave, so you won't get hurt. Can you stay at your condo near Waikiki?"

Julie's expression changes quickly from remorse to fear. Without questioning Oskar, she grabs her purse. "Let's leave from the front so I can set the alarm. Will you check the slider to make sure it's locked?"

After locking the door, Oskar walks her outside to her car and opens the driver's side. "I have to get some things from next door. Be safe, okay?"

"Oskar, why don't you come with me? We both can stay at the condo."

Oskar kisses Julie on the cheek as she buckles her seat belt. "Thanks for the offer, but I have to warn others. If I can, I'll meet you there later."

Julie nods as she starts her Lexus and backs out of the driveway. Oskar waves as he hurries back to his house, going immediately to the garage. He looks up as he slips inside and sees the headlights of a car coming down the street. He moves to his scuba gear without further thought of who would be driving in the neighborhood at two in the morning.

CHAPTER 27

The Three Stooges Arrive Now What?

Mark scrolls through bomb designs on Dan's notebook computer as Dan speeds down 76. Dan looks over from the driver's side and points to the notebook. "Look on page 2."

The car swerves right, tires squealing as Dan returns to the lane. Mark drops the notebook and snaps at Dan, "Watch where you're going, sheesh!" As he picks it up from the floorboard, he buts his head on the dash coming up and almost drops it again. As Mark rubs his head, he opens the notebook, checks the screen, and scrolls the page down with a shaking hand. "Is this the one you mean, Dan?" Mark shows the picture to Dan who briefly looks and nods. Mark grabs Dan's phone and compares pictures of the two bombs. He whistles, "You're right. It's the spitting image of it."

It's quiet in the car as it speeds along and for several moments all that can be heard is the heavy breathing of the passengers with Mark the first to speak.

"We have to have some kind of strategy when we get to Oskar's place. What if he isn't there? We have no idea of his plans."

Dan careens around a corner and slams on the brakes, almost hitting the curb when he realizes he's close to Oskar's house. "I can't see the house number. Is this the place?"

Mark opens his door as soon as the car stops and kneels down to read the number on the curb. He jumps up and starts running toward the house. Matt curses from the back seat, and he and Dan also exit the car and follow Mark. With the new moon, it's pitch black and the two stumble into Mark. The heavy breathing continues, and Mark finally speaks.

"No lights are on at the house. He's either asleep or not here…"

They hear a squeak, and Mark sneaks toward the sound and sees a dark shape moving toward the water from the side garage door.

Before Mark can do anything, Matt runs after the shape in the darkness. As the shape moves into the water, Matt dives toward it and tackles it in the water. Dan turns on the flashlight ap on his phone and shines the light onto the two figures and sees Matt has hold of Oskar! Matt grabs the item in Oskar's hand and steps back through the water as Oskar lunges toward him, screaming, "Give it back. You don't know what you're doing!"

As Dan continues to shine the light on the three figures, Matt hands the item to Dan, turns around, and he and Mark grab both of Oskar's arms. Oskar continues to struggle and Dan shouts, "Stop, Oskar! There are three of us and only one of you." Oskar's chest heaves as he stops struggling and says again with a hoarse voice, "You guys don't know what you're doing…"

Matt and Mark drag Oskar out of the water as Dan looks into the pack taken from Oskar. All he sees are tools. He looks up confused and hands the pack to Mark, who digs into it as well.

"Where's the bomb, Oskar? Have you already placed it?"

Oskar looks in shock at Dan recognizing him from the bank. "Dan-n-n, what are you talking about?"

"Don't play dumb with me, Oskar! I've been watching you and Axle at the bank and doing a little recon when no one was around. I saw the bomb was removed from your secret cabinet at the bank. We knew you were going to do something tonight and came after you and caught you in the act!"

Oskar's head drops to his chest, and Matt and Mark have difficulty keeping Oskar upright. After only a few moments, he looks up. "You have it all wrong. I'm not the perpetrator here."

Jerking Oskar away from Mark, Matt drags him back toward the water. "If you don't tell us, I'm going to drown you!" Once he gets Oskar to the water, he pushes his head into the water.

Mark and Dan are frozen with shock, but Mark recovers first and runs the few steps to pull Matt off Oskar. "Are you crazy? Stop!"

Everyone is heaving at this point, and Dan finally says, "Oskar, you have ten seconds to tell us where the bomb is or we call the cops!"

Oskar shakes his head. "I'm double checking tonight to make certain it's not there, but it could be."

Dan growls, "You're not making sense! You mean you already put it out there? Where is it? Tell us where it is, or I'll let Matt drown you, and I mean it!"

Oskar shouts, "Just shut up for a second. I'm the good guy here. What you saw at the bank wasn't the real bomb. It was only the decoy I made to switch with the real one. I don't have time to explain everything, but I did already make the switch earlier in the week, but just to make sure another live one wasn't placed, I returned last night and the decoy was gone. Nothing was there! Since tomorrow is Pearl Day, I want to go back tonight to ensure the perp didn't place an additional real bomb. If he did, I have sort of figured out how to adjust the timer to prevent it from setting off the explosion. Or heck, I can just remove it completely! You have to let me go look or the whole Pearl Harbor may blow up during the ceremony tomorrow."

Mark wipes the hair out of his eyes. "Oskar, why should we believe you? Why haven't you gone to the authorities? Who's the mystery perp here?"

Oskar looks toward the water, "It'll take too long to explain. It takes me an hour to swim out to the area where the Missouri ship is docked. Do any of you scuba? One of you could go with me for insurance. One of you can even notify the authorities, let's say at 6:00 a.m. Tell them to cancel the event. That way if there's a real bomb already in place and I can't fix the timer, fewer people will get hurt. I will remove it either way, but the goal is to still try and stop the timer."

Dan says, "I'm calling 911 right now!"

Oskar raises his hand. "Wait, Dan, if you tell them now, things will get messed up. I'm trying to stop it before anyone finds out, so it won't get in the papers and people won't see that a terrorist got through US security systems here. I know who it is. It's a friend of mine, and I have the greatest chance of stopping this. To explain to the authorities will take time, and that's time we don't have."

Mark starts disrobing and says to Oskar as Matt and Dan look on in shock. "Do you have extra scuba gear?"

"Mark, you can't go with Oskar! Your mom will have a coronary!" Dan sputters.

Mark looks pointedly at both Matt and Dan. "Do either of you scuba dive?"

They both say no at the same time, so Mark looks at Oskar who starts taking off his own gear. "Take mine. It's ready to go. I'll go get another set while you dress."

Oskar jogs back to the garage while Dan peppers Mark with questions. "Mark, this is crazy. Have you ever gone night diving?"

"Help me with the tank, guys. No, but I'll stay close to Oskar, and I'll be okay. What do you expect me to do, stay here and hope for the best? That's not how my dad raised me. Leek has been helping me learn, and last Saturday I took a diving class."

Matt kicks the sand. "One class, dude? You're about to go out and save Hawaii and you have taken one class!"

"We're wasting time talking about it. Here comes Oskar. We need to get answers from him for questions the authorities will ask you."

As Oskar puts the additional tank on and adjusts his mask to the top of his head, he looks sternly at the two young men staying on the beach. "I'm going to explain to you how this is going to work. We have one window to stop this, and any hiccups could be catastrophic. Are you willing to listen and follow my instructions?"

Both Dan and Matt gulp and whisper, "Yes, sir." They step up to Mark and assist him with putting on the tank, and Dan gently places the mask on Mark's head. He looks closely into Mark's eyes and mouths, "I'll be praying for you." Mark's expression changes from fear to peace as he nods in agreement. Before Oskar positions his mask and regulator, he explains, "Good. I'm going to make this quick because Mark and I need to get going."

Mark gulps as he listens to Oskar explain what needs to occur. Once he lays it all out, he steps up to Mark. "You ready?"

"Yes, sir."

"Let's get going then."

Mark grabs Oskar's arm while he looks at Matt and Dan. "Let's pray." Everyone stops as Mark bows his head. "Lord, we know you are with us. We ask that you lead Oskar and I there super quick and help us to stop anything bad from happening! Help Matt and Dan to explain everything to the cops so they can help stop this threat. In Jesus's name we pray, Amen."

As they both walk back out of the water, Dan says to Matt, "I'm going to call Leek so he can help us explain this catastrophe to the police. He gave me his number at one of the AA meetings. Let's sit on Oskar's patio so we don't have to talk over the sound of the surf." Without them noticing, Oskar leans down toward the water, picking up another pack and stuffs it with his tool bag.

Leek Takes Charge

Matt has his hands over his face and his shoulders shake as he succumbs to the aftermath of his body being flooded with adrenaline since he rushed to tackle Oskar in the water. Dan is talking to Leek and grips Matt's shoulder as he tries to explain the dire circumstances the island is facing.

"Leek, Oskar explained what we should say to the police, but I'm wondering if we should be helping Oskar and Mark. They just left swimming toward Pearl Harbor from Oskar's house here on Ewa Beach. It's a long swim from here to the Missouri near the Arizona Memorial. I'm worried about Mark and his lack of scuba training."

Leek is pulling up his jeans as he grabs his cab keys from his bedside table and starts running out his house door. He stops for a moment, not sure where he should be going. He takes a deep breath. "Stop talking for a minute, Dan. I need to ask the Lord."

"Haku, only you can save us. Guide me to make the correct choices to save peoples' lives and protect our memorial from desecration."

All that can be heard is a dog barking in the distance.

After a full minute, Dan is ready to scream when Leek says calmly, "Don't worry, I know what to do. Here's what I need you guys to do. Dan, that admiral guy that I heard attended the auction. What's his name?"

Dan answers with confusion, "Martinez."

"Do you have any way of getting in touch with him?"

Dan thinks for a moment. "I believe one of our board members, Frank Jantzen, knows him. I know Frank owns Jantzen Security. I think I have their number in my cell to call in emergencies. I could call and have them get Frank to call me."

"Good, have him call me ASAP. Tell him it's a matter of national security and the island may be under a terrorist attack. Do not tell the operator that unless they won't transfer you to this Frank guy."

Dan takes a deep breath. "You know, Ruth probably knows Frank better than I do since she goes to all the board meetings. It might be better for her to call him. I'd ask Axle, he's our security officer, but for all I know he's the planner. Oskar never told us which 'friend' was doing this horrible thing."

Leek makes a split decision. "Dan, good intel. I'll call Ruth myself."

Dan's eyes get big. "You know she'll flip out if she finds out Mark's with Oskar."

"Under the circumstances, I'm not sure if I'll tell her. Too much is at stake. I'll get back to you as soon as I find out anything. Don't call the authorities until you hear from me. But if for any reason you don't hear from me in the next hour, you call them anyway. One hour, got it?"

As soon as Dan says, "Yeah," all he hears is the crashing of the waves as he realizes Leek is no longer on the line.

Dan mutters, "I feel like I'm in a Tom Clancy novel." He grabs Matt and gently shakes him. "Get it together, man. Let's drive to Pearl to see if there is anything we can do to help Leek."

Next Step

Axle parks in the A-OK carport as Ruth reaches toward the floorboard for her purse, glad Axle drove her home even though she will need to return tomorrow for her car. Her phone buzzes, and puzzled, she pulls it from its pocket and looks at the screen. Seeing it's Leek, she answers, "Wow, Leek, this is pretty late for calling. Missed you at the auction tonight…"

"Ruth, I don't have time to talk. Something terrible is going to happen, and I need to contact this admiral guy you know. Dan said you know Frank Jantzen who can contact the admiral. Can you call Jantzen and tell him to call me? It's a matter of life and death."

Ruth looks at Axle but responds to Leek, "You're not making any sense, Leek. I can contact Frank, but you need to give me more info. Our security officer, Axle, is with me. He probably can get to Frank right away."

Leek is driving like a bat out of you know where, not caring if the cops try and stop him. "Listen, Ruth, how well do you know Axle? My understanding is he could be part of our problem. This is really urgent. We have to get a hold of this admiral. If we don't, all heck is going to break loose. I'm serious."

Ruth hears the squealing of Leek's tires and responds quietly, "I trust Axle with my life. Whatever you're talking about, I can't believe he would be a part of it."

Axle gently takes Ruth's hand and mouths, "May I?"

She nods as he takes her phone from her. "Leek, this is Axle. What's going on?"

Leek looks up and says a prayer and waits.

Swimming toward Pearl

Not seeing Oskar, Mark tries not to panic. He feels the flashlight in his hand and clicks it on. The water is murky, but he can see a big body swimming further ahead. Hoping it's Oskar and not something else, Mark increases his speed, catching up quickly. He feels less panicked when he sees Oskar's tank. Mark knows he has to keep up with Oskar. As a novice diver, he knows he could drown before he finds the shore by himself. He certainly can't afford to get lost at this point.

Oskar clicks on his flashlight and motions for them to swim to the surface. Oskar removes his regulator and lifts his mask, and as he and Mark tread water, Oskar looks up to watch a jet flying overhead. He looks at Mark and motions him to lift his mask and regulator as well. "We're close to the entrance of Pearl Harbor. As you can see, toward the east are the airport lights. How are you holding up?"

Mark takes a big breath as he keeps himself above water. "Okay, I think."

Oskar knows Mark can't see him well, but inputs urgency into his words, "Mark, I'm going to ask you to do something very dangerous. Our next step is to swim over to where the Missouri battleship is anchored. If I determine the real bomb is attached, then I'll use a cutting motion across my neck. You will need to swim up to the surface near the battleship, quickly make it to the shore, and contact the authorities in any way possible, maybe even start screaming. Got it? Stay close to me. If the water is too murky for you to see, I'll give you a push so you'll know what to do."

Mark thinks about his dad and knows he may be joining him soon. Oskar can barely make out Mark's features but surprisingly sees a grin. "Yes, sir, I can do it."

Oskar nods as they both return to the water.

CHAPTER 28

Can the Pearl be Saved?

*L*ord, *only you can direct my path. Please give me a sign that Axle
can be trusted.* Leek takes a deep breath and, without realizing, slows down his cab as he looks at the sky and after a few
moments sees a falling star. *Okay, Lord, I trust you.*

"Axle, the three stooges—Mark, Matt, and Dan—found out
about a terrorist attack on Pearl tomorrow during the ceremony.
I can't get into all the details, but they thought it was Oskar and
confronted him at his home and actually determined it wasn't him.
He and Canoe have gone to retrieve or reset a bomb Oskar feels is
attached to the Missouri battleship near the Arizona Memorial in
Pearl Harbor. They're swimming all the way from Ewa Beach to the
vessel. Don't tell Ruth, I'm afraid she might freak knowing Canoe
is getting that close to the bomb. I'm hoping if you can contact this
Frank Jantzen guy, he can contact the admiral that Dan mentioned,
and we can get this thing stopped. What do you think?"

Axle responds without hesitation. "I agree. I'm on it. Where are
you going?"

"I put my scuba gear in my trunk and plan to drive closer to
the Missouri. Maybe I can intercept Canoe and Oskar to see if I can
help. Canoe isn't experienced enough with diving to help Oskar, so
by the time they swim from Ewa to Pearl, he's going to be exhausted.
Once I get to them, I can send Mark over to the shoreline. My plan is
to drive to the parking lot near where the Arizona Memorial Visitors
Center is located. I wish I could cross the Ford Island Bridge, but I

don't have a Navy military pass to get across. That would take me straight to the Missouri. Well, that can't be helped, but at least parking near the Visitors Center minimizes the walking I'll need to do to get to the water. No one will be around this early, but I'll be noticeable carrying my gear."

"Leek, why don't I meet you at the parking lot? I can help with your gear and be a lookout for you and wait on the shore to help with Mark. If I leave Kaneohe now, I should get there in thirty minutes."

Leek thinks for a moment. "It's going to take me another ten minutes to get there and ten minutes to put on my gear. I'll wait for twenty minutes but not a moment longer. Thanks, Axle."

Ruth looks anxiously at Axle as he explains, "Ruth, I need to go. I'll call you as soon as I can to let you know what's happening. Your son and Oskar are working to stop a major terrorist attack from happening at Pearl Harbor."

"You're crazy if you think I'm waiting around here to hear from you! I'm going too. Don't bother arguing, but instead get this big fat SUV on the road!"

Axle does as she says and burns rubber as he backs out of the driveway with his phone on speaker.

Ruth and Axle wait anxiously as they hear four rings on the phone.

"Axle, this better be good. It's after three in the morning! Is something wrong at the branch?"

"Thank, God! Frank! I don't have much time so just listen and make your questions count. Oskar discovered a major terror attack is happening at Pearl Harbor today. Specifically, the Missouri battleship. What I know is a bomb has been attached to it and is set to go off during the ceremony. Oskar is swimming out to it to try and remove it. Can you call Admiral Martinez and get the ceremony canceled and all the necessary people out there to stop this catastrophe? Mark and Leek are there as well. Warn the authorities not to harm them. They're trying to help Oskar. Honestly, that's all I know. I found out two minutes ago."

"Holy crap! Are you serious? The admiral, the admiral…oh, yeah, he gave me his cell during the auction planning. I'll call him right now. If he doesn't answer, I'll have to call the police."

Axle thinks for a moment. "Frank, text me if you don't talk to the admiral. Let's give the guys some time to fix this thing. We have to think through the best resolution here. I have Ruth with me, and she will beg you not to send in the cavalry with her son in the cross-fire. If you get a bunch of cops swarming over there, someone could get hurt. Give them till six to get that bomb out of there."

Axle floors the SUV as he enters the H3 highway. Ruth's eyes get as big as saucers, and she immediately starts praying, "Father, you know that Mark and Oskar need your protection. Mark is a mighty warrior for you and knows you're with him. Please put an army of angels surrounding them as they work to keep others from harm. Jesus, Jesus, thank you for your love and be with the person who has done this horrible thing and have that person change the plan here…"

Frank abruptly says, "Can't argue. I'll text if I can."

"Wait! Quick, can you tell me where on the Missouri the bomb could be attached?"

"Haven't a clue."

Click.

Axle looks apprehensively over at Ruth. She has her head bowed, and her lips are moving. Axle decides to say nothing and increases his speed to 85 mph. He sees his exit and whips over to leave the freeway. As he speeds through the city streets, he adds his prayers to Ruth's.

The Plot Continues

The beer didn't hit the spot as he had hoped. He crumples the can and drops it, watching it land near the tiki. Feeling more anxious, he decides to call his best friend.

He'll have the right words to help me though my anxiety, which reminds me, I need to get my prescription refilled.

The call goes to voice mail, but he doesn't leave a message.

I'll go to Oskar's place. He won't care if I bunk with him for a couple of hours. I need a distraction. My thoughts are so chaotic and I just don't want to think about the future tonight. It's too uncertain and my fears are taking over my brain. Oskar always helps me when these feelings come over me.

Feeling better immediately, he heads inside to the kitchen, picks up his keys from the counter, and quickly walks to his Corvette.

With so little traffic on the road, the trip to Oskar's house is a quick one. He pulls into the driveway and is glad to see a light glowing from the front porch. Exhaustion starts to take over, and he slowly walks the few steps to the door. He pulls out his own key to the house and unlocks the door. As he walks toward the guest room, he stops to peek into Oskar's room but in the dark cannot tell if anyone is there. Not totally understanding why, he steps quietly into the room, moving next to the bed. After a few moments, his eyes adjust to the dark and he realizes it's empty. He turns on the table lamp and sees the sheets have not been disturbed.

Puzzled, he thinks for a moment. *Ahh, I bet Oskar's spending the night with Julie.* Again, the puzzled look resurfaces. *Oskar told me he was taking a break from Julie, that he doesn't need a relationship complicating things right now. Maybe he's in his workshop in the garage.*

Trying to make up his mind, he decides to get a drink from the fridge and check to see if Oskar is outside. He grabs a soft drink this time and steps out to the lanai and walks over to the garage, thankful the lanai light enables him to find his way. Seeing the side door open, he walks toward it.

"Hey, Oskar, what are you doin' up so late?"

With only a small light glowing over the workbench, he turns on the center garage light and looks inside. No one is there. He does see a car in the garage and notices a bunch of gear scattered on the floor and recognizes it as miscellaneous scuba paraphernalia.

Surely, Oskar didn't go scuba swimming at this time of night. He checks his watch. *Wow, 4:10 a.m. What's that crazy guy up to now?*

He sees an underwater map on the work bench and recognizes many of the areas it showcases. As he studies the map, the proverbial light bulb goes off, and he realizes where Oskar has gone. His anxiety

235

ratchets up as he picks up a bunch of Oskar's gear, deciding it's better to use it than drive to where his own is located. With his exhaustion forgotten, he sprints over to his car, leaving the house unlocked and the lights on.

The Confusion Gets Worse

Leek pulls into the lot near a big tree and notices another vehicle a few spaces over. Leek's eyes get large when he sees two people exit the vehicle. He takes a relieved breath when he realizes it's Axle and Ruth. As Leek exits his cab, Axle quickly steps close.

"How can I help?"

"Grab my tank from the trunk. Once I have it on, all I need is my flashlight and speargun, and I can get in the water. Ruth, how are you holding up?"

Unbelievably, Ruth responds calmly, "I'm believing the Lord has this, Leek. How 'bout you?" She steps closer and touches Leek's face. Her serene expression bowls him over.

"I'm determined to stop this thing, and your confidence is encouraging. Continued prayer is good too." Turning from Ruth, Leek quickly grabs his wet suit from the cab and pulls it on.

Axle places the tank on Leek's back. "How does that feel?"

Leek moves his shoulders around. "Good. Walk me to the water. I haven't seen anyone around, but you never know."

"Sure. Ruth, why don't you wait in the car? You can call me if you see any activity or people in the area."

Ruth agrees that Axle's words are a good suggestion so doesn't bother to argue or disagree. Instead, she grabs his face and lays a big kiss on his lips. "Bring my boy back to me, okay?"

Axle hugs Ruth tightly. "Will do. Leek, let's get this show on the road."

They walk quickly across the street to the Pearl Harbor Visitors Center, taking a route around the building to the water.

"Have you thought what you're going to do when you get to the ship?" Axle asks as he nervously swings the turned off flashlight back and forth in one hand while holding Leek's fins in the other. The few street lights are enough to light their way.

Leek says with confidence, "Here's my plan. When I see the two guys, I'll approach Mark first and flash my light at him twice so he won't get scared. That's our agreed upon signal when diving together. I'll motion to him to tap Oskar and give a thumbs up to indicate we should swim to the surface. I'll explain Mark needs to swim over here to the shore, and I'll be assisting Oskar in finding the bomb. Since I'm a skilled diver, I can cover a lot of ship area looking for the thing."

"I guess there aren't many options here, but I hope you don't spook Oskar before you have a chance to talk to him, and he ends up doing something crazy like knock you out thinking you plan to intervene in removing the bomb. I mean, we don't really know if Oskar is the good guy here."

Leek looks puzzled but shakes his head. "Axle, don't worry, the Lord is with me." Smiling, Leek says, "And, just in case, I have my speargun." Leek steps to the water's edge, hands his speargun, and flashlight to Axle who returns the items to Leek once the mask and fins are in place. Nothing is said as Leek sits on the water's edge and slips down slowly.

Keeping her eyes peeled, Ruth hears her phone buzz. The screen shows Axle's message: "Leek's in the water." Ruth repeats the Twenty-Third Psalm continuously as she continues to watch for any human activity.

Missouri Search

Leek swims quickly from the Pearl Harbor Visitors Center toward the Missouri. His mind keeps replaying his plan for when he finds Mark and Oskar. He uses the flashlight just enough to help guide him to his destination, and after some time, he sees another flash of light near the stern of the ship and swims toward it. As he gets closer, he sees two swimmers, one larger than the other, and assuming the larger lead swimmer is Oskar, he swims toward the other one. Both are so focused on the ship, neither see him as he swims close. Leek is almost upon the swimmer he assumes to be Mark, who, sensing something, jerks his head in Leek's direction. Leek immediately flashes his light twice and can see the terror on Mark's face. Leek waits a moment and feels the water move around him and reaches out. It's pitch black, but he senses the change in the water. Mark is swimming toward him. Leek's hand finds a body and finds Mark's hand. Leek manipulates Mark's hand into a thumbs-up position and, still holding the hand, starts swimming to the surface. Oskar never notices as they leave the ship.

Once the two reach the surface, Leek removes his regulator and, reaching toward Mark's, removes his as well.

"Hi, Canoe."

Mark takes two huge breaths. "Boy, am I happy to see you. How did you find us?"

"It's a long story, but I'm here to relieve you."

"I think you're saving my life, Leek. I would say I'm dead on my feet...ha!"

Leek snorts. "Okay, I need you to do one more thing before swimming over to the water's edge by the Visitors Center. Axle is over there, and he can help you get out of the water since there's no beach there. Do you think you need to return to the water with me so Oskar will know I'm now the one who will help him? He probably can't tell the difference between the two of us underwater. If you think he won't freak out, that will save us some time. You can leave, and I can go back down and help Oskar with the bomb."

"Even though he freaked when we first confronted him at his house, I think he's so focused on making sure this situation gets remedied, he won't care who's helping him. He placed a decoy earlier in the week, but he checked last night, and it had been removed! He decided he would have to keep checking to ensure another bomb doesn't appear, and that's the reason for all the activity tonight."

"This isn't making much sense. Are you sure he's the good guy here, Canoe? Dan told me the story, but it's not adding up to me."

"Leek, if he was the bad guy, why would he return to remove the bomb? His pack only has tools in it, nothing else."

Mark is having difficulty staying afloat and feels as if he is getting a leg cramp but continues to answer Leek's question. "He did say he can adjust the timer so the bomb won't go off, but it's too time consuming. Easier to just take it. In this case, he just wants to make sure the bomb isn't on the ship. If it is, he will remove it. I guess I could have just said all that for my benefit. Dan was convinced Oskar was the bad guy initially but changed his mind after we spoke with Oskar. What do we do if he's the bad guy? I'm going to have to move to the shore, Leek. My leg is killing me."

"Go then. I'll figure it out." Leek slips under the water; and Mark, shining his flashlight once to locate the shore, sees a figure sitting on the ground. Assuming it's Axle, Mark starts the swim to return him to solid ground.

Another Player in the Mix

Ruth is having difficulty keeping her eyes open but looks at the vehicle clock for the fifty-seventh time and sees it's now 4:40 a.m. Suddenly, a sporty car whips into the parking lot, driving toward her section of the lot. She immediately locks all the doors and texts Axle. The car parks right next to Leek's cab, and the occupant exits to walk toward Ruth.

With her heart pounding, she has her finger on her phone emergency button as she watches the person get closer to her. He puts his face right in the window, and Ruth jumps. She immediately recognizes him and opens her door. "Hanadie, what are you doing here?"

"That's my question for you, Ruth. What are *you* doing here?"

Glad to see a friendly face, she smiles in relief. "Waiting on Axle and Mark. You still didn't say why you're here. Did Oskar call you?"

"No, but I think I know what's happening after stopping at Oskar's house. I'm going to put some scuba gear on. Can you help me?"

Still uncertain, Ruth answers, "Mark, Oskar, and Leek are in the water. Are you certain you need to go in?"

"Yes." He steps back to his car and drags the gear he needs out onto the ground. He removes his shirt and puts the wetsuit on over his shorts. He grabs the regulator, dive mask, and tank.

Ruth texts Axle, "Everything okay, just Hanadie."

Axle had started quickly for the parking lot, but seeing the text, he stops, and immediately returns to the shore. Hearing something, he kneels down and listens closely.

"Axle? Axle?"

"Mark, I'm right here."

"Thank God. Can you help me? I can't figure out how to get out of the water."

All of Axle's six-foot-five frame stretches out on the grass with his long arms out on top of the water, and he tells Mark, "Grab onto my arms, and I'll drag you out."

One at a time Mark throws his flashlight, mask, and regulator on the shore and grabs Axle's arms. With little effort, Axle drags Mark onto the shore, the wetsuit protecting Mark's body from the rough shoreline. "Your mom is going to be so happy to see you're okay."

Mark stays flat on his back, breathing heavily and holding his leg. He and Axle both look up as a dark form comes toward them. Holding the flashlight as a club, Axle stands close to Mark. "Who's there?"

"Axle, it's me, Hanadie."

Repeating Ruth's question, Axle asks, "Hanadie, what are you doing here?"

Without answering, Hanadie steps next to Axle. "Where's Oskar?"

"He's in the water trying to remove a bomb from the side of the Missouri."

"I'm here to stop Oskar from placing that bomb on the ship."

"What the heck are you talking about, Hanadie? Have you been drinking?"

Mark interrupts Axle, "Han, I've already had this conversation with Leek. Oskar only has tools in his pack. He's not placing a bomb. He mentioned he knew the real bomb maker and his plan is to remove any bomb placed on the ship."

Without addressing Mark's comment, Hanadie says, "Oskar and I've been complaining about the shameful US lack of involvement at the beginning of the Bosnian conflict. Both of us have harbored extreme hatred because of the deaths of our loving family. Axle, you know counseling has helped me immensely and I've been able to forgive and move on. But it hasn't been the same with Oskar. I didn't know what he was planning, but several of his comments and actions have led me to believe he might do something extreme. He misled you to think it was someone else so you wouldn't stop him. Come on, Axle, help me get my tank on. I have to stop Oskar."

Axle shakes his head in disbelief. "I've heard Oskar say some critical things about the lack of US help, but I'm shocked he would go this far."

Mark slowly gets to his knees, grimacing at the pain. "I have to go with you, Han. Leek is down there with Oskar, and I can't let anything happen to Leek. He thinks Oskar is the good guy."

Axle grunts. "Mark, you're not in any shape to return to the water. Give me your gear. I'll go down with Han."

Mark immediately starts removing his suit and fins. With only his boxers on, he takes Axle's shirt and slacks and puts them on, holding on to the waist to prevent losing the slacks to gravity. Forgoing the wet suit and only in his boxers, Axle finishes dressing in the rest of the scuba gear and turns to Mark. "Did Oskar give you an idea where the bomb has been placed on the Missouri?"

"There was no time for a discussion, but we were at the stern when I met with Leek. I'm worried. Oskar thinks Leek is me because we didn't have time to tell him we switched places. By now, they may have already reached the bomb and no telling what Oskar plans."

Axle places his hand on Mark's shoulder. "Go to your mom in the parking lot across from the visitors center and pray, pray, pray. Hanadie and I will fix this. And just in case Frank didn't get through to the admiral, call 911 in twenty minutes no matter what happens."

And at the Ship

Oskar senses Mark behind him but continues to the spot near the propeller where two bug-shaped metal containers have each been attached by a magnet.

Two? Previously, there was just one. The two together would make a huge hole in the Missouri probably sinking it and preventing future visits to the area. And the Memorial is sacrosanct! What if something happens to it! I know I only have a small window of time to get these out of here. The sun will come up soon, and we can't afford to be seen coming out of the harbor. It's a good thing I brought an additional bag in which to carry these things. I've got to get these things off and on shore so I can try and adjust the timers!

Touching the ship, Oskar turns on his flashlight and seeing the two attachments, slowly removes one. Leek treads water, watching Oskar place what's in his hand in his pack so they can swim to the shore to get the thing out of the area. Perplexed, Leek sees Oskar reach back toward the ship.

Oskar feels a tap on his shoulder and turns, assuming it's Mark. He's shocked to see that it's someone else. Scared, he automatically jerks back, hitting the ship and even though dazed, he grabs the swimmer by the neck and starts to squeeze. Oskar knocks the spear-gun from Leek's hand. There is no time to grab for it in the struggle.

Both strong swimmers, Hanadie and Axle arrive at the ship in record time. Nearing the stern, they see two figures struggling in the water. Hanadie understands the situation immediately, and sensing which one is Oskar, he grabs him as Axle pries Oskar's hands from Leek's neck. Gratefully, Leek takes a couple of strong breaths from the oxygen in his tank, recovering quickly. He takes a couple of additional breaths to calm his nerves. Watching the scuffle, Leek sees Oskar's pack fall from his shoulder and slowly drift through the water. After grabbing the falling pack, Leek swims back to the ship curious to see why Oskar had reached toward it the second time. Hanadie and Axle pull the struggling Oskar to the surface. Frantically, Leek moves his hand over the surface of the ship until he feels the edge of the propeller and, continuing his search, finds nothing. Feeling compelled to check Oskar's bag, he is able to open it enough to slide his hand inside and feels two separate items!

Once at the surface, he notices it's still dark but knows the sun will soon rise. Trying to decide his next move, he sees the three men nearby. With a solution in mind, he closes and adjusts the heavy pack and slips back underneath the surface, quickly swimming away from the ship.

Woozy and seeing he's unable to escape Axle and Hanadie, Oskar quits struggling. He's exhausted from the swim and the late hour. He smiles though, convinced he averted disaster by removing both bombs.

Axle is distracted by some movement in the water and sees Leek break the surface. He's confused when he sees Leek turn the opposite direction and return beneath the water. "Hanadie, I just saw Leek, but he returned to go under the water. What do you think he's doing?"

Still holding on to Oskar and treading water, Hanadie looks across the harbor. "Is he trying to remove the bomb?"

"That's it! Can you handle Oskar if I go help Leek?"

"Yeah, I don't think he's going to give me any more trouble. We're running out of time. What should happen to it once it's removed? Oskar, when's it scheduled to detonate?"

Oskar refuses to answer and starts humming a Bosnian folk song. Shaking his head, Axle responds, "We'll have to let the authorities handle it. Let me go help Leek, and you take Oskar and return to shore. Oh, and make sure Mark called 911."

Knowing time is of the essence, Axle dives below the surface as Hanadie swims away with Oskar.

Axle quickly swims to the ship's stern but doesn't see Leek or anything attached to the ship. Using a small flashlight attached to a wrist cord, Axle searches frantically around the stern of the ship, but can't find anything. Trying to determine where Leek might have gone, Axle swims away from the ship and toward the surface to get his bearings. When he notices some movement in the water, he swims quickly in that direction and, seeing a swimmer, flashes his light twice. The other swimmer continues on, so Axle flashes the light again. At touching distance, he grabs Leek's shoulder while putting the light on his own face. Leek jerks his head toward Axle and, seeing a light on Axle's face, recognizes him and gives the thumbs up. Axle motions toward the surface, and they swim to the top.

Removing his regulator, Axle sees the pack on Leek's back. Before he can comment, Leek says, "We don't have time to try and figure out how to keep the bombs from detonating. This isn't a movie, and we can't just cut some wires and hope we make the right choice or adjust the timer if that's what needs to be done. I'm a fast swimmer, so I'll swim out as far away as possible so when it detonates, it will do minimal damage."

Axle's mind quickly runs through several solution scenarios in his head, but none improve on Leek's. "I'll go with you."

"No! You have a family back there with Ruth and Mark. They would never forgive me if anything happened to you. Swim back and pray the entire time."

Without further comment, Leek quickly replaces his regulator and kicks away from Axle. And as Axle swims back to the shore, he prays, "Jesus, you are the only one who can save everyone involved in this horrible situation. I trust in you to bring Leek home safely. Be with him as he chooses the place to drop the bomb and keep him safe upon his return…" Noticing a faint light in the sky, Axle goes underwater to lessen the chance of anyone seeing him.

CHAPTER 29

Is the End Near?

Military and local police swarm the Pearl Harbor Visitors Center, and roadblocks have been placed to prevent anyone, including military personnel, from coming onto the Ford Island bridge or near the visitors center across the bay. Admiral Martinez questions Ruth and Mark who has a towel wrapped around his middle to keep Axles slacks in place. They hear a commotion and loud voices near the water. Ruth hears Axle's voice and starts to run over to the shore as Mark grabs her arm.

"Wait, Mom. Admiral, that's my friend Axle I told you about. He's been trying to stop this thing. Can we go over and help him out?"

Mark follows the admiral as he moves to intervene and keep the authorities from arresting Axle. While Admiral Martinez questions Axle, Mark hands him his towel. Wiping his face, Axle explains Leek's strategy of swimming the bomb far away to minimize damage when it detonates.

"How far would you estimate he's traveled? Can you lead our guys to him?" Admiral Martinez asks before he turns to another officer nearby. "Lieutenant, where's the boat with our dive team?"

A boat motor is heard, and all turn toward the water as the two men and Axle walk to the shoreline.

"Quiet! Men, we have a good guy swimming out of the harbor with our bomb. He's been swimming for ten minutes so should be about a mile out. This man here, Axle, will lead you to him. Get there as quickly as possible so you can prevent this thing from blowing up, now *go!*"

Axle jumps into the boat, which speeds to find Leek.

Where's Oskar?

Admiral Martinez turns to Mark and Ruth. "Okay, where's the slimeball that's behind this?"

Mark thinks back through what has occurred over the last few hours and answers, "Sir, I believe it's a man by the name of Oskar Soto. It's a long story, but Axle and Hanadie swam out to stop him and remove the bomb placed on the Missouri, but I only saw Axle return."

Turning to Ruth, Mark asks, "Mom, did you see Hanadie and Oskar?"

With impatience, Admiral Martinez barks, "Yes or no?"

"No." Ruth responds as she looks around as if to see if Hanadie and Oskar are hovering nearby.

"Crap! Commander, get over here!" Immediately, a naval officer steps beside the admiral. "Our suspect has escaped, and no one saw him. The only person that can help us is out on that boat trying to get to the bomb. We have to find this guy!" Looking at Mark and Ruth again, he said, "Is there anything you can tell us that will help us find him?"

Mark answers, "We can tell you the location of his home and business and who he's with, but I'm not sure where they'd go. Oskar's home is on Ewa Beach, and he owns Oahu National Bank. He's with his friend from Bosnia, Hanadie Besic."

The admiral looks meaningfully at the commander. "Looks like we definitely have a terrorist in our midst."

"Admiral Martinez!" A man wearing a government-issue jacket jogs over and, breathing heavily, says, "I'm Stan Muhic, with Homeland Security. I've brought several of my guys as well as FBI agents with me. What do we know so far?"

As the admiral turns to the new arrivals, Mark pulls Ruth away from the group. "Mom, Oskar and Hanadie have to be around here somewhere. I want to search for them."

Ruth takes a deep breath and tries not to think of what's happening with Axle and Leek. She grabs Mark's arm. "Hanadie's car is in the lot where Axle parked. Let's go see if it's still there."

"We should have told the admiral that. Let's check it out now because if it's still there, we'll know they have to be in the area."

Having given up his towel, Mark holds on to Axle's slacks to keep from tripping on them as he and Ruth hurry over to the parking lot. They cross Arizona Memorial Place drive, and Ruth looks for the big tree to find Axle's SUV. She looks perplexed by the number of vehicles in the lot.

"All the FBI and Homeland Security people must be parked here. There it is. Over by the tree, Mark."

Mark suddenly stops, and Ruth runs into him. She starts to grumble, but in the light of dawn, she makes out two figures approaching them. Mark's mouth drops as he sees his two friends get closer.

Matt speaks first. "Wow, dude, you made it. I'm shocked."

Dan guffaws as Mark responds sarcastically, "Gee thanks, Matt. Your vote of confidence is overwhelming. How'd you guys get in here? The place is crawling with cops, Feds, and military."

Dan responds first. "We've been here awhile but were afraid to get out as all these guys showed up. Boy, was I glad I didn't have to call the authorities. Wasn't feeling too good about how to explain everything. We wanted to see you so we decided to sneak around and see what we could find out. Hi, Ruth."

"Dan. We need to check to see if Hanadie's car is still parked in the lot. Walk with us." Ruth speeds up and sees Axle's SUV and, nearby, the sporty car belonging to Hanadie. She slowly walks up to it and looks into the window. Not seeing anything she backs up as the guys reach her. Dan raises his hand, showing he's carrying a flashlight. He shines it into the vehicle and sees it's empty.

"No one here."

Mark jumps in. "Dan, do you have any clothes in your car I can borrow? Axle's pants are driving me nuts."

They walk over to Dan's car on the other side of Hanadie's, and he removes a pair of work khakis and a T-shirt from the back seat and hands them to Mark, who divests himself of Axle's clothes.

"Much better. Okay, you guys listen up. Hanadie and Oskar are around here somewhere. Let's find them before the Feds do." Mark turns to Ruth. "Mom, I know you're exhausted after the auction and being up all night. Why don't you sit in the SUV and rest? I'll text you from Dan's phone when we find out something. Oh, yeah, and pray for us and Axle and Leek."

"I think you're right, Mark. I'll be in the SUV praying. You guys be careful. Listen to the Lord. He'll guide you."

Mark reaches toward his mom and gives her a tight hug. "You're the best, you know it? Axle and Leek will be fine. The Lord is with them too."

Mark walks Ruth to the SUV and opens the door for her, and she steps inside and leans her head on the headrest. "I love you, Mom."

She smiles and says, "Ditto."

Softly closing the door, Mark steps away from the vehicle and looks at his two partners. "You guys ready?"

Matt rubs his hands together. "You bet, scuba boy. Where do we start?"

Mark laughs and pushes both guys back away from the parking lot toward the street. He stops for a moment and lowers his head. Matt starts to speak, and Dan shakes his head. They stand still while Mark's lips move. Dan lowers his head as well and speaks.

"Jesus, I don't know you, but Mark, Leek, Ruth, and Axle do. They pray all the time, and I know you listen to them, and I'm just a regular guy, but I know you have to be out there somewhere or they wouldn't rely on you, so please guide us to find these two men so nothing bad can happen. Amen."

Mark feels a strong impression, and a vision comes upon him. He hears Dan's words but is focused on his vision and in a mesmerizing picture he sees Hanadie and Oskar sitting together in a large stadium. It only takes him a moment to understand. "Guys, I know where they went. We have to go over to Aloha Stadium, but I don't think we can drive over there with all the cops around, so we have a walk ahead of us."

Dan questions Mark, "That's a bit of a walk. Do you really think Oskar and Hanadie would go that far without a car?"

Mark doesn't bother to explain. "Yes, 'cause the Lord showed it to me. Let's hurry." He starts running toward Makalapa Park and his two sidekicks follow.

They leave the park and walk between buildings so as not to be seen and stopped by the police. They cross over into a neighborhood on the edge of Salt Lake Boulevard, which sides the stadium. Once they get behind the driver's license building, they stop. Traffic is non-existent since the roads have been blocked off.

Mark sees a tree across the road. "Let's walk from tree to tree." He looks at his watch. "It's 6:15 and pretty cloudy, so we might not be seen. After I go, each of you follow me separately. Got it?"

They nod.

"Dan, hand me your flashlight."

Keeping his head down, Mark steps into the road and, bending over, walks purposefully, hoping he will be less noticeable. He finds a tree and kneels at it. He motions to the others. Matt and then Dan follow Mark's lead. They stay at the tree for a minute to see if they are spotted.

Seeing no one, Mark says, "I'll find trees to cover us. Watch me and follow me to each tree I choose." He doesn't wait but goes to the first one and waits a moment for Matt and Dan to catch up, then goes to the next one, eventually making it to the stadium parking lot.

"Oskar mentioned to me that when the church originally met here, he always went in the door that was opened early for the weekend market days. Leek told me the worship team used the same entrance. I'm not familiar with this place, but based on what Leek told me, I believe it's the one closest to us so let's check it first." Mark looks at the sky. "Even though it's not quite light outside, let's stay close to the trees and hope no one notices us. There is a restaurant at this entrance, so be careful no one sees you even though I doubt anyone would be here yet."

Mark continues to find trees in the parking lot to use as cover, and they quickly make it to the entrance. Seeing the gate is open, they walk into the arena.

"Thank goodness the gate is open. I was afraid it might not be with all the activity in the area. We'll start with one section at a time 'till we find them."

All turn their heads in the direction of the seating and are surprised to see two men sitting about halfway up.

Dan whispers, "What's the plan? Are we sure who the bad guy is? Do you think they're armed?"

Mark looks toward the two men in question. "I think it's Oskar, but we should be alert till we are sure. After all Oskar said he knows the bomber. Oskar wasn't armed at his house. Remember, his bag was filled with tools and nothing else. Hanadie was in the water and didn't have anything with him, but he did bring his car and could have stashed a gun in it."

Matt grabs and pulls his hair. "You guys are driving me nuts. Let's figure out a way to jump them and worry about everything else later. I say Mark goes up to them bold as you please and acts like he thinks everything is on the up and up. Dan and I can climb down to the seats from the back and sneak up behind them and knock their heads together."

Dan snorts, but Mark looks pensive. "That's not a bad idea except the knocking their heads together part. I have an idea that could work. Let's go back behind their seats so we can make this happen."

Who's on First?

Skimming on top of the water in the Navy's Zodiac, Axle grips the ropes and narrows his eyes against the spray as he looks out for Leek. The water constantly washes over the men as the driver pushes the boat's speed to its limit.

Axle shouts, "I think we're about a mile past where I left Leek. Will we be able to see him underwater?"

"Ensign, get that spotlight and aim it on the water and slow it down. We may see the bubbles from his tank." The commander watches closely as the boat moves smoothly across the water.

In the distance, Axle sees Leek's head pop from the water. "There he is right in front of us!"

The boat returns to its highest speed as Axle waves his hands back and forth.

Leek hears a boat motor as he again has to pull his regulator from his mouth. He turns around and sees a boat coming straight for him, and as he fumbles to replace his regulator, he sees Axle crazily waving his hands. "Dang! I don't have time for this!"

The boat almost drives over Leek, but he's able to keep away from the motor as Axle reaches out to him.

"Leek, these guys can help us with the bomb. Do you still have it?"

Without speaking and grabbing the side of the boat, Leek hands the heavy pack to Axle.

Axle and one of the Navy guys help Leek into the boat as the commander opens the pack, revealing two separate items and another man shines a light onto the top one.

"Ensign, both are Maindeka limpet mines. I'm not familiar with these timers, but I can see there is still an hour left before detonation. I need assistance on stopping them. Everyone, listen up. There's a Navy vessel moored a few miles outside the harbor. I think we should motor out there and have them stop the timers from setting off the mines. Let's head that way while I call Admiral Martinez and get his approval."

Back at Aloha

Mark walks the stadium steps near Oskar and Hanadie, who seem in a trance and don't notice him. Once Mark is at the correct row, Hanadie looks up and calmly greets him.

"Mark."

"Hanadie, I was worried about you guys. Is everything okay? Oskar, you're the hero of the day going out to get that bomb removed from the Missouri. Did you know that, Hanadie?"

Hanadie's expression is perplexed as he looks at Oskar. "Mark, what are you talking about?"

Mark focuses on Hanadie, giving him a significant look that includes a slight wink. "Leek found a dud at the ship, so Oskar was right. He took care of it."

"The authorities want to thank him. They sent me to tell you so they can recognize him for saving the Missouri."

In the hallway outside the section of seats where Mark is speaking to Hanadie and Oskar, Dan is on the phone with Ruth.

"Can you send the admiral? Tell him not to bring the full cavalry just a few men who can arrest these two guys."

"Okay, Dan, I'll walk over there and see if I can get close. Please make sure Mark is okay."

"Yes, ma'am. Call me when you know something. Please hurry!"

While still holding her phone, Ruth steps out of the vehicle and runs over to the visitors center where she is stopped. "Ma'am, you cannot be here—"

"Quick, I need to talk to Admiral Martinez. It's a matter of life and death!"

With a long look at her, the man gets on his walkie-talkie. "I have a woman here who says she needs to talk to the admiral. What's your name, ma'am?"

"Ruth Max. I work with Oskar Soto."

Can This Please be Over?

While waiting, Ruth feels her pocket buzzing. She doesn't want to answer her phone, but seeing it's Sara feels compelled to. "You're calling early, Sara. What's up?"

"Ruth, I saw on Facebook some chatter that something is going on at Pearl Harbor. Have you seen that? I don't know why I bring that up. Something else is bothering me. Hanadie was going to come by early this morning so we could go on an early hike, and I haven't seen or heard from him. Do you know if Axle has spoken to him?"

"Uh-h-h, yes."

Perplexed, Sara says, "And?"

Ruth is beyond tired and decides not to prevaricate. "I'm at Pearl Harbor where a terrorist attack is being attempted. I don't know all the details only that Oskar and Hanadie are somehow involved."

"What? There's no way Hanadie would do anything like that! What are you doing down there?"

"Sara, I'm exhausted and not sure I even have all the facts. I only know that a bomb was put on the Missouri by Oskar who went to the ship last night to check on it. Mark and his friends, Dan and Matt, found out about it and tried to stop Oskar, who convinced them he was not the bomber. Mark swam out to the Missouri last night with Oskar thinking he was going to help remove the bomb. While he did that, Dan called Leek, worried about Mark swimming so far in scuba gear. Leek called Axle, who called Frank to notify Admiral Martinez. Once we arrived here, Hanadie showed up worried Oskar was the bad guy. Ugh, this is a mess! In the process of helping Mark and Oskar, Hanadie disappeared with Oskar and now everyone thinks Hanadie is involved."

"That's bull, and you know it!"

"Sara, think a moment. How well do you really know Hanadie?"

"Ruth, I don't have to think. The man has a business here. He's gentle and fun loving. I've never even heard him raise his voice. This can't be happening!"

Ruth calmly responds, "Sara, this place is crawling with authorities of every type. Mark, Dan, and Matt have gone to look for Oskar and Hanadie. There's nothing we can do at this point but pray."

"No, we have to do something, Ruth. What can we do? They'll throw Han in Guantanamo, and we'll never hear from him again!"

"Ma'am? Admiral Martinez wants me to bring you to him."

"Sara, I have to go. I'll call you later."

"R-u-t-h!"

Back Again

Mark sits in the seat next to Hanadie. "I don't know about you guys, but I'm exhausted. It feels good to sit." Looking into Hanadie's eyes, Mark asks, "What do you think, Han, should we walk back over to the visitors center?"

Without answering Mark's question, Hanadie leans back and looks off into the distance. "For years, decades really, Oskar and I haven't moved past the horror we experienced in Bosnia. Every time we got together, all we could discuss was my aunt and uncle, my fiancee, and friends who were massacred in the conflict. Oskar has done many good things, but the suffering has destroyed him. Some of his comments recently have been extreme even for him, and when I saw that underwater map on his work bench, I felt like I saw the last piece of the puzzle. He kept saying, 'I wish I could show this country the awfulness of war on their home turf.' I truly didn't think he would go this far. He's so screwed up in his head, and after this last incident, I'm afraid of what is going to happen to him."

Mark drops his pretense after hearing Hanadie's words. "You have to turn him in, Han. There's no other alternative."

Hanadie sighs and looks over at Oskar who is slumped in his seat fast asleep. "Mark, do you know what happened to the bombs?"

"All I know is Axle went out to help Leek remove it from the Missouri. Why don't I call Mom and have her bring Admiral Martinez over here? Just one person might be less disturbing to Oskar. I know you're concerned, but he has done something terrible and will have to pay the price."

New Information

Dan stops his nervous pacing and says, "Matt, I'm going back to the stadium entrance so I can grab any authorities that show up and direct them over to where Mark is talking to Hanadie and Oskar. Don't move, okay?"

"Duh, where would I go? Get outta here."

It takes Dan several minutes to arrive back at the restaurant near the entrance to the stadium. He steps outside and sees it's still overcast and fairly dark considering the time. As he looks at his watch, he hears a rustle in the trees and looks up to see several men approach. Dan raises his arms.

"Admiral Martinez?"

"Who's there? Step out in the light so I can see you."

"My name is Dan Barlow. I work at the bank with Oskar, and I'm the one who discovered the plot. Oskar and his friend Hanadie are inside the stadium with my friend Mark, and my other friend Matt is keeping a watch on them so they don't leave."

"Son, the plot isn't exactly as we believed. Will you take me to them?"

"Yes, sir."

CHAPTER 30

A New Discovery Explained

L eek and Axle are sitting on the ground after returning from their taxing boat trip to the Navy destroyer, sipping on bottles of water while warming themselves with towels. While Axle and Leek discuss the most recent turn of events, Ruth sits down and hands Axle a pair of sweats she found in his SUV. While he pulls them on, Axle asks Leek, "Were you as blown away as I was, Leek?"

"Yeah, I still can't quite get my head around what the commander told us. Did you have any idea?"

"Heck, no! What do I know about bombs? All I know is I was operating on full-scale adrenaline."

Ruth adds, "Well, you certainly could have knocked me over with a feather when you called this morning, Leek. I always thought Oskar was different and kind of creepy, but it never entered my mind he could do anything like make a bomb to destroy an important piece of American history."

"She doesn't know, Leek."

Ruth, knowing her mind is fuzzy with lack of sleep, agrees she must be missing something here. "There's lots I don't know. Anything new I haven't heard about?"

Leek takes a long swallow of water. "Ruth, when the commander had one of the bomb experts on the Navy vessel open the bomb container, this is what he said, '*Wait, these bombs aren't fully functional. The timers on the two devices were set to stop working after 100 hours.*' I never gave it a thought that there was no ticking with all the waves and commotion. The bombs were never going off! What do you think about that?"

Axle reaches over and gently pushes Ruth's two lips together. "You're gonna start catching flies."

They all laugh with relief. The worst is over.

Is the Worst Over?

Axle removes his arm from around Ruth to answer his phone.

"Hi, Frank. Have you heard the latest? What?" Ruth and Leek look at Axle with questioning expressions. "Okay, I'll get over there right now to check it out."

"Frank said he went into his office this morning and while there felt compelled to review the cameras from the Kailua branch and noticed someone went into the branch immediately after the auction. From his quick review, he feels it was Oskar. Plus, the alarm wasn't reset. He thought I should look into it considering what's happened here."

Ruth asks, "Do you think it was Oskar?"

"Yes, and that's concerning. Leek, do you want to go with me to check it out?"

"Sure."

Axle turns to Ruth. "It's probably nothing, but under the circumstances I better make sure all is okay at the branch. Please stay here and wait for Mark. I'll call you as soon as I know anything." He groans as he stands up and stumbles but keeps from falling. "I know I shouldn't complain considering how far you swam, Leek, but my legs and arms are killing me!" He leans down and kisses Ruth's cheek. "I'll try to call you as soon as possible."

Leek stands without any problem, and Axle says a few choice words under his breath as they quickly make their way over to the parking lot to Axle's SUV. Axle notices there are fewer cars in the lot. "I guess once they figured out the bombs' timers had stopped, the authorities didn't need so many people here. Hopefully, that means we won't have any problems leaving."

Waiting for the End

Ruth sits cross-legged under the tree reading Facebook posts about Pearl, and hearing a car pull up next to her, she looks up. She sighs as she recognizes the driver and doesn't bother to stand up. In fact, she continues to view her phone as she hears steps getting closer to her. She sighs and looks up at Sara standing with her hands on her hips. Thinking she is about to receive a tongue lashing, Ruth gears herself up for it but is surprised by the movement beside her as Sara makes herself comfortable, scooting close and giving Ruth a sideways hug.

"Sorry for freaking out on the phone. You're a true friend and don't deserve such poor treatment. Whew, now that I have that out of the way, please update me on Han. This place is busy, but I was able to drive over here. What's the latest?"

Axle Goes to the Bank

As he directs his SUV into the branch parking garage, Axle articulates his thoughts about the last few hours. "Boy, once they realized that the bombs' timers were dysfunctional, many of those crawling around the visitors center cleared out except for Admiral Martinez and a few FBI guys looking for Oskar. That's a relief, plus Frank said they are canceling the ceremony." He parks near the door and notices Leek is sound asleep in his seat. Axle grins. *Ha, Mr. Macho is tired after all.* Grabbing his branch keys from his glove box, he decides not to disturb Leek.

The door to the SUV barely clicks as Axle closes it. He looks to see Leek wasn't disturbed by the noise and makes his way over to the branch door. Quickly unlocking it and stepping to the alarm panel, he starts to enter in the code but remembers it's not set. Strange that Oskar forgot to reset it. He pauses a few moments to look and see if anything seems out of place.

I haven't thought this through. Why would Oskar come to the branch before swimming out to the Missouri? He loves this branch. Would he really do anything to harm it? I can't think. Maybe a cup of coffee will help. Do I have time for one? Since I haven't had sleep in twenty-four hours, I think I need the jolt it will give me.

He walks to the break room and continues his thoughts as his hands automatically go through the motions of operating the coffee machine. Not waiting for the brewing to finish, Axle moves the carafe out of the way and places a mug under the streaming coffee. Once the mug is full, he switches it with the carafe and walks toward the conference room. His eyes go immediately to the wall panels and finds the one that covers the electronic combination lock to the extra room behind it. Once the door is open, he thinks, *Everything looks normal. Great, that was a bust. What was Oskar doing back here? Frank said he came in here for about ten minutes. That's more time than he would need to get the bomb if this is where he was keeping it. Hmmm, it's obvious Oskar came here for a reason. There must be something I'm missing.*

Operating on a caffeine high, Axle stalks from the extra room to his office. He turns on his desktop and opens the security system to review the branch cameras to see if he can determine what Oskar did while at the branch. He reviews from 11:00 p.m. on until he finally finds Oskar entering the branch around 11:42 p.m.

Man, I didn't realize Oskar had gained so much weight. His suit jacket is so tight on him.

Oskar is purposeful in his movements, doing as Axle just did, walking into the conference room, and moving on to the workroom outside the view of the camera. After only a minute, he is seen reentering the conference room. Since no camera is placed there, Axle doesn't know what Oskar did while in there. He continues reviewing the camera footage, seeing Oskar buttoning his jacket as he finally leaves the branch at midnight empty-handed. Leaning back in his chair, Axle closes his eyes and thinks through everything he knows about Oskar, the branch, and even thinks back to their escape from Bosnia.

How Many Twists Can There Be?

Waking up, Oskar stretches as he watches Mark and Hanadie talking about Bosnia. Hanadie says with emotion, "I had a fiancee in Bosnia, Mark. I held her in my arms when she died. You know what her last words were? '*Han, I see Jesus.*' As I have dwelled on those words all these years, it's selfish I know, but I wish she had said, '*Han, I love you.*'"

Speaking as if he's a child needing direction from his parent, Oskar says as he stands up, "Han, I need to go to the bathroom."

Mark stands up, blocking the two men from leaving.

Hanadie tiredly takes Oskar's arm. "Okay, I'll walk you to the bathroom." Before Mark can protest, Hanadie says, "It'll be okay, Mark. You can go with us if you want. Oskar is beyond any problematic behavior at this point."

Mark steps back, giving a thumbs up to Matt to let him know all is okay as he lets Hanadie and Oskar exit the row of seats. The three troop down to the exit as Oskar leads the way straight to the restrooms.

Matt texts Dan, "Mark's taking Oskar and Han to the can."

Stopping for a moment, Dan looks at his phone. "The can?"

Admiral Martinez stops, "Is something wrong?"

"I received a text stating Oskar, Hanadie, and Mark are all going to the can."

"There are many restrooms in the stadium. Do we know which one? Sergeant, you go east, and Dan and I will go west."

"Yes, sir."

So Much Drama in the Can!

Mark stands outside to guard the men's restroom door as the other two men walk inside. As he leans against the door, he finds himself nodding off. After what seems only a few minutes, he jerks awake feeling anxious, and looking at his watch, he realizes it's been over five minutes since Hanadie and Oskar went into the restroom. He opens the door to peruse the room and does a double take.

"Dang it. Han? Oskar?" Mark quickly looks in each stall, finally accepting both Han and Oskar have given him the slip. "This is just great, I can just hear Admiral Martinez now…"

Mark rushes down the hall, calling out for Oskar and Hanadie. Up ahead, he sees two men coming toward him but jerks his head the opposite direction when he hears Matt yell from behind him, "Where are you going?" Matt reaches Mark the same time as two FBI agents.

"Stop. Which one of you is Mark?"

"I am, sir," Mark says breathlessly as he raises his hand.

"What's the problem, son? Where are Oskar Soto and Hanadie Besic? I heard they were with you."

Mark's face turns beet red as he stutters, "No-o-o, s-s-ir." Looking at the lanyard hanging from the agent's neck, Mark continues, "Agent Muhic, Oskar and Hanadie gave me the slip by going out the second entrance to the bathroom. I didn't think to watch it."

Without responding to Mark, Agent Muhic turns to see Admiral Martinez, his aide, and Dan catch up to them. "We have a problem, Admiral. Those two guys have slipped away from these *citizens*, so we need to conduct a search before they escape the Pearl area."

Mark pipes up, "I can't understand why Han would help Oskar escape. I thought Oskar was the problem, but now that they have both disappeared, I'm not sure."

Is Oskar Going to Win after All?

Axle jerks awake and hears a noise coming from the break room. He begins to stand and sees Oskar walk to him carrying a cup of coffee. Axle chuckles from either exhaustion or nerves. "Well, here comes the man of the hour."

Oskar, still in his swimming trunks and a University of Hawaii T-shirt with his silver hair sticking up in all directions, falls into one of Axle's guest chairs. "Yep, that's me, and we have a problem."

"Amazing deduction, Watson," Axle answers acerbically as he sits hard in his chair. "If I wasn't so exhausted, I'd beat the living daylights out of you. Did you chicken out at the last minute? Is that why the timers weren't working on the bombs?"

"Shut up, Axle, and listen."

With a burst of energy, Axle stands up abruptly, causing his chair to slide back against the wall. "I'm done listening to you. I've been listening and following you my whole life and look where it's gotten me! I'm calling the Feds."

In a surprisingly strong voice, Oskar says, "Sit!"

After that one burst of energy, Axle's body automatically responds as he plops back into the chair. Nothing is said for some time as they both try to gather their thoughts. Neither notice the click of a lever or scratch of a panel sliding open or the soft tread of feet coming toward them from the conference room. A familiar voice greets them.

"I knew you would show up here, Oskar. That was pretty slick, slipping out the stadium bathroom without me hearing you. I suppose you can still sneak around with the best of them after all your experience back home. I'm amazed I beat you to the branch. Of course, you are an ol' geezer." Hanadie's laugh has a desperate sound to it.

Oskar's bloodshot eyes stare with confusion at the newcomer. Axle is taken aback to see Hanadie step into his office.

"Where the heck did you come from, Han?"

Hanadie responds contemptuously, "You know, Axle, you think you know Oskar, but he has secrets that don't include you. You want to know where I was? I was really close, just beyond the workroom wall. Check it out."

Axle twists around, ignoring the two men, and makes his way to the workroom where he sees revealed behind another door a small hideout room to enable a person to spend time away from prying eyes. There's a rolled-up sleeping bag against the wall, a small table, chair, wall cabinet, refrigerator, and a door he opens to reveal a tiny bathroom. He looks closely at the metal door to the room and maneuvers the lever that opens it. Shaking his head in amazement, he wonders how Oskar kept this secret.

In Axle's office, Oskar is confronting Hanadie. "How did you know about the panic-room apartment? I've never told a soul. In fact, I had a separate construction crew from Salt Lake finish out this area of the branch so no one local ever knew about it."

"You always did underestimate me, *cousin*. Good news for me, I ran into them at Surf Shack one evening and was able to get 'close' to a sister one brought with him. I'm quite perturbed with you after hearing what you did with my special project. You and your partner here."

"So all that Salt Lake construction detonation knowledge came in handy, huh, Han? I don't know how you got access to those mines, and I don't care. All that drunken babel you spewed at the Surf Shack was serious? You've gotten me in some trouble, and I don't like it!" Oskar spits out as he jumps from his chair.

Hearing Oskar's raised voice, Axle returns to his office determined to find out what's the real story here. While stepping back into the room, he hears Hanadie laugh.

"Don't be so melodramatic and self-righteous. Some of the hatred I've heard you speak rivals mine any day. I'm so glad you built this fun little apartment. It was the first place I thought about when I escaped Pearl Harbor. Now that you guys are here, I can leave. My next step is to finish what I started. I have more mines at the condo, so I'll just leave you guys to your conversation I interrupted."

"Do you think we'll really let you leave?" Oskar demands.

Hanadie immediately stalks over and grabs Oskar by the arms. "You can't stop me, and you know it! After witnessing the tortures of the Bosnians, I think I can *convince* you to not interfere as I leave, but for old time's sake, I'd rather not resort to such unpleasantness."

In shock, Oskar doesn't move, but once realizing Hanadie's intentions, he tries to jerk away.

Han frees one hand and jabs his finger on Oskar's right eye. "I can do this in the blink of an eye…" Hanadie eerily laughs at his own sickening humor.

Their words penetrate Axle's consciousness as he looks back at the two men. With the last vestiges of his strength, Axle stands to push Hanadie away from Oskar but instead pushes him forward. Axle uses his arms to put a choke hold on Hanadie, lifting him off Oskar, who falls to the ground, hitting his head against Axle's chair. Axle's anger takes over, and with superhuman strength, he drags Hanadie down the hall to the panic apartment and, with one last shove, lands Hanadie face down on the floor. Seeing a landline phone in the apartment, he grabs the cord and ties Hanadie's hands. Leaving Han, Axle slams the panel door closed and since he doesn't have a key to the apartment, he closes the conference room door and with a quick input of the combination, locks Hanadie inside. Heaving, Axle staggers to his office and falls to his knees. Turning his head, he sees Oskar groaning and lying in a pool of blood. Confused, Axle drags himself over and turns Oskar on his back and sees a bloody mess where Oskar's right eye used to be.

"Oh-h, Oskar…" And with a tear running down his cheek, Axle grabs desperately for his desk phone and dials 911. With a choked voice he tells the 911 operator an ambulance is needed and drops the receiver as he staggers to the restroom to find some paper towels to stop the blood. He returns and kneels and gently places the towels on Oskar's eye. A desperate prayer rises from his heart. "Lord, what a mess we've made here. Instead of trusting you, we have used our own selfish anger to dictate our actions. I ask forgiveness and seek your full healing for Oskar's eye. Jesus, you are the great healer. Please heal this man who needs you. Jesus, in your name, I pray."

A siren is heard in the distance, so Axle stands up to let the EMT's into the branch.

CHAPTER 31

Three Months Later

Walking toward the conference room, Dan lifts the coffee tray high over his head with one hand as he carries the cookie basket in his other. Already ensconced in her chair at the conference table, Ruth jumps up and opens the door.

"Wow, Dan, I'm impressed by your serving skills. Here, let me take the cookies."

With savoir faire, Dan lays the tray with the drinks on the table, bows, and backs out of the room.

With a cookie already in her hand, Ruth reviews the five mugs, grabbing hers as she returns to her seat. It's quiet but for the clicking of Sara's nails as she writes an e-mail. Ruth places her hand on top of Sara's. The clicking stops as Ruth lowers her head.

"Father, you say in your word that you work all things together for the good of those who love you and are called according to your purpose. We need you desperately as we recover from the Pearl tragedies. I seek Shalom peace for myself and Sara. Please be with Hanadie as he goes through the legal process and trial, and open his heart to you so he may understand the seriousness of his actions. We plead for your intervention. Fill Hanadie with the Holy Spirit to help him lose his bitterness and feel the peace only you can provide."

Again it's quiet, but this time sniffles and hiccups occasionally break the silence. Ruth notices Sara's perfectly applied makeup smeared by the tears that continue to fall. Sara takes a deep breath as she stands.

"I'll be back in a minute."

Ruth leans back and keeps her mind blank as she watches out the glass door for the other board members. The first to arrive is Axle who fixes the door in its open position and moves to the chair by Ruth. He leans down and kisses her forehead as he grabs his own coffee. Frank and Daniel walk in next, and behind them is Sara looking more herself. Only Ruth would notice the puffiness around Sara's eyes. It's quiet as each grabs a coffee. Ruth sees Dan has forgotten to bring Frank's water and steps out to get it. She returns and gives Frank the bottle and a glass. Sara hands each person an agenda, and as she hands out the last one, she realizes she has one left.

"I'll take that one, Sara."

All eyes turn to the new arrival. In the time since the Pearl incident, he's changed much. His hair is shorter to accommodate his eye patch. He's much slimmer, and the spark in his eye has dimmed. With Oskar is Kim who pulls out a chair, helping Oskar to sit. Ruth's lips quiver, but she stands up.

"Oskar, may I get you a *black* coffee?"

Daniel and Frank look confused, but Axle and Oskar laugh.

"You know, Ruth, I'd love one. How about you, Kim?"

"Water is fine for me, Ruth."

Sara clears her throat, but before she can speak, Oskar interjects, "Before you start the board meeting, I have a few things I would like to say."

After handing out Oskar's coffee and Kim's water, Ruth slips back into her chair as Sara says, "Please, Oskar, go ahead."

Oskar looks at each individual for a moment prior to speaking. "I'm in awe of what each of you has accomplished during my absence. Sara has been updating me weekly on the bank's status, and your efforts to continue the good work here under intense publicity is impressive. I want to speak today for the last time of what occurred three months ago. We must continue to move forward, but I feel those in this room deserve to know the full truth. What you hear today can never be repeated outside this room."

Kim opens his water and pours some in a cup, handing it and a pill to Oskar.

"Each of you know bits and pieces of the story, but to ensure you know everything in its entirety, I will start at the beginning. My best friends, my *drugari*, are sitting at this table, Kim and Axle. You are both welcome to add information that you feel relevant. It all started back in 1992 when the Bosnian conflict began. With the breakup of the old Yugoslavia, several diverse groups mobilized to take over their piece of territory starting an armed conflict. Axle's Bosnian father, Luka, and mother, Ena, were devout Christians. As many of you know, Luka was my first cousin and my best friend. Their little home supported Axle, Hanadie, Kim, and myself. Once the ethnic cleansing of the Muslims in Bosnia started, Luka and Ena provided sanctuary for many. Their house had a basement, which seemed the perfect hiding place. That's where I learned how to construct a secret door! No one could detect the door to the basement or so I thought. The men took on the job of scrounging for food. I was a contractor and still able to do some work, which provided our group with enough income to buy rice and bread and other essentials.

"For you to fully understand the atrocities that occurred, I have to relate one specific story to you. Hanadie fell in love with a young woman he met before the war started. She and her family owned a wonderful bakery in town that we all enjoyed on a regular basis. Wednesday night Bible studies were held at Luka's house, and one week Hanadie brought Sarah with him. It was obvious Han was smitten as we all came to be since she had the sweetest disposition, quite unlike our own Sara."

All laugh as they look at Sara tapping her nails on the table.

Kim adds, "After attending several weeks of Bible study, Sarah gave her life to Christ. The next week, we baptized her in the family tub. I thought Han would burst from happiness that night."

"Yeah, I thought so too," Oskar continues his tale. "Several weeks after that, her family bakery was burned to the ground. With nowhere else to go, the family was taken in by Luka and Ena as well. Sara's parents were Muslim, and Sarah had not told them of her conversion. Once they moved into Luka's house, it became obvious Sarah had become a Christian, but after experiencing the kindness of Luka and Ena, her parents never condemned Sarah. During this same time, Han sought out Sarah's father and asked for permission to marry his daughter. It was unheard of for a Muslim to approve of a Christian marriage, but that's exactly what happened. Once Sarah accepted Han's proposal, big plans were made for the wedding. It was wonderful to think of something besides roaming soldiers and lack of food. Unfortunately, this story doesn't have a happy ending. Only a week before the wedding, Han, Axle, and I went on a food hunt. We knew another Christian group eight miles away had extra provisions to share so, since we had no gas, we started early in the morning to walk to our destination. It took us the entire day to get there and return. Once we arrived back at the house, we stopped outside for a moment as it was eerily quiet. Axle even said, 'Where is everyone?' I remember thinking at the time, *Maybe they went to help out another family in the neighborhood we had heard needed assistance.* We trooped into the house and immediately saw Luka and Ena on the floor, dead from gunshot wounds to the head. Axle ran to them, kneeling to check for a pulse that wasn't there." Oskar looks to Axle. "I'll never forget them as long as I live. They are in my thoughts each and every day. We heard a scream from downstairs, and I rushed through the destroyed basement door to see Han sitting on the side of a bed crying and holding Sara, rocking her back and forth. Her body was covered in blood and bruises, and her clothes were torn, barely covering her. Unbelievably, she was still alive. She whispered in his ear, and her eyes fluttered closed as she took her last breath. I'll never forget the look in Han's eyes. I've never seen such suffering in my entire life. Never. He gently laid her down and pulled the blanket over her body. We found her parents in the next room, also dead."

Oskar stops talking and all sit quietly. No one moves. The elevator opens, and Dan exits with a customer. Axle notices and leaves the room. Whispering a few words of sympathy, Ruth slips a tissue to Sara.

Nothing else is said until Axle returns.

Oskar states, "Once we buried our friends, we started in earnest planning our escape. Han changed dramatically and, initially, just went through the motions of survival each day. But over time that changed to anger and bitterness. He rarely spoke though he mumbled constantly, and honestly, we didn't want him to speak as the perverse words that sprang from his mouth were immeasurably disturbing.

"It took us almost two years to plan our escape, and by that time Hanadie was sullen but not as vocal with his anger. We arrived in the US in late 1994, initially moving to Salt Lake City. Eventually, after working for other contractors, I started my own company. We worked together to build the business and after several years, we were making boat loads of money." Oskar laughs, which starts him coughing, but after taking a sip of water, he is able to continue. "After all our hard work, we rewarded ourselves with a trip to Hawaii, and that was all it took for us to desire a final move here."

Kim whispers in Oskar's ear.

"I'm okay, Kim. Once we moved here, Hanadie spent all his energy establishing his restaurant, Kim went to seminary, and Axle and I started Kaho Construction. Since the old gang didn't see each other as often, we set up a sort of guys night out we called Kaho Time using the Hawaii construction company name comprised of each of our initials.

"Kaho was intended to be the third Thursday of the month, but because of everyone's busy schedule, there were many of those nights it was only Hanadie and myself attending. I'll confess I allowed myself to become embroiled in Han's anger against the US concerning their slow involvement in the Bosnian conflict. We talked a lot of trash, especially after we had several drinks. There were many times I took Han home with me because he drank too much. It may seem odd that Han directed his anger at the US, but you have to understand the full intensity of his grief, plus it makes a small amount of twisted sense. President Clinton didn't want to be entangled in a foreign conflict, so he let the hostility among the different parties boil out of control until finally the US did get involved, and with organized and skilled communications and military strength brought the war to a halt.

"So I will tell you, I sympathized fully with Han's position and thus made myself believe his talk was just that. But there came a time when I realized Han had gone beyond the talking stage."

Noticing Sara's expression moving from shock to sorrow and finally resignation, Ruth reaches under the table to clasp Sara's hand.

No one notices Ruth and Sara moving closer to one another as Oskar continues to speak.

"Hanadie was spending more and more time at my house. I have a great computer and game system, and Han took full advantage of the gaming setup but always brought his own laptop. I offered him the use of mine, but he always responded he was more comfortable with his own. One day Han got a call from the restaurant and had to leave in a hurry. I was thinking at the time, *Oh good I can watch the new James Bond DVD now*. As I sat to watch, I noticed Han had left his laptop open on the desk behind the couch. As I started the movie, I decided to close the laptop but as I clicked to close it, for a split second I saw a quick view of a schematic of some device. Wanting to see it again, I started thinking of password options and entered Han's nickname for Sarah, "sarahlove" which actually opened the screen. I saw a note written on the bottom of the schematic. The notation was *Maindeka*. I wasn't familiar with the term *Maindeka* and looked it up online and discovered it was a type of limpet mine used by the military to sink enemy ships."

Axle starts in his chair and all look at him as he stands. Nervously he says, "Who wants a refill?" Without waiting for an answer, Axle gathers the mugs and moves to the break room.

Frank starts to speak but stops and waits for Oskar to finish.

"Axle, Hanadie, and I became experts in using a special explosive product for construction called ANFO, which we used in excavating holes for our commercial construction projects. Hanadie was the true expert, but in addition, he trained himself in using C4. In Salt Lake, he spent hours and hours learning the process and was diligent in ensuring the explosions happened safely and accurately. When I bought the bank, I sold Kaho Construction, so seeing this schematic, I was confused. Hanadie had not worked at the construction company since opening the restaurant four years ago, so why would he be researching explosives? That confused me, but I assumed he was keeping himself educated on the newest devises, so I shut down the laptop. I had intended to ask Han about it, but quickly forgot to pursue it."

The room was deathly quiet, and Oskar starts to speak but is interrupted by Kim.

"Let's take a short break, Oskar. You need to eat something. Ruth, could you order some sandwiches for us?"

"Of course."

Kim helps Oskar up as they walk to the rest room. Ruth uses the conference room phone to call Dan.

"Please order a sandwich platter from that place we used last week. Can you place a rush on it? Thanks."

Back to the Story

Surprisingly, Oskar seems relaxed as he puts down his sandwich.

"At the next Kaho get together, some of Hanadie's comments reminded me of the schematic I had seen, so I asked him about it. He told me he heard about the Maindeka from a Navy friend of his and decided to look it up to satisfy his curiosity. That made sense because he was always interested in explosives, but for some reason, I couldn't get it out of my mind. Hanadie spent more and more time with me, and I tried on several occasions to access his computer but was unable to do so until about six months ago. One day while he was passed out on my couch, I searched his laptop for that same schematic, and after a long time looking, I opened a file he titled, 'Bosnia Solution.' I was looking at all his files and wasn't expecting to find anything in this one, but there it was! There were three pages, one for the Maindeka design, one for instructions for placing the device, and the last page was a picture of the Missouri."

Flabbergasted, Axle says, "Oskar, why didn't you tell me?"

"Axle, I didn't want you dragged into the situation. I wasn't sure how it would turn out."

Frank asks, "What did you do after that?"

"I felt confident there was no way I could change Han's mind on whatever plans he had decided upon. I still wasn't sure what he had planned, so I started asking him over to the house and eating at the restaurant more frequently to see if I could get him to tell me anything. The conversations always deteriorated into a 'bitch' session—sorry, ladies—and finally, a couple of months ago, I said,

'What the heck, Hanadie, we might as well bomb this place to get even.' I was expecting a full denial, but all he said was, 'Sounds good to me. I feel like I'd get final resolution for Sarah.'

"I laughed, pretending he was talking trash. Hesitantly, I said, 'What could we do?' Han immediately responded, 'I've been fantasizing about a bomb in the Pearl area. That Navy friend of mine had been stationed at Pearl and bragged and bragged to me one night about all he knew which got me to thinking about how an attack would work. I'd never do it, but it would certainly get this country to sit up and take notice.'

"I laughed again, and said something inane like, 'That it would.' I quickly changed the subject. He left, and of course, I put two and two together and realized his plans for his Maindeka ship bomb."

Oskar stops talking while he eats a cookie and takes a large gulp of water.

Axle is still dumbfounded by Oskar never letting on about Hanadie's plans.

"Oskar how did you find the Maindeka bombs Hanadie acquired?"

"I didn't figure it out right away. Both Han and I've been avid scuba divers since arriving in Hawaii. He and I would go diving from the Ewa Beach house on a regular basis, but all of a sudden I'd get home and Hanadie would be putting gear away. It surprised me he would be scuba diving without me. I asked him about it, and he muttered something about increasing how far he could swim on his own.

"Three weeks prior to the incident, I found an underwater map of Pearl Harbor near my game station. I tried to convince myself it didn't mean anything, but I hid it in the garage anyway." Oskar hesitates and takes another sip of water. "I decided I needed to become more comfortable swimming long distances as well and daily began training myself to last longer and longer. My suspicions of Han actually doing something dire escalated. It took me two weeks, but I was able to swim the entire way to the Missouri. As you can imagine, I was exhausted, but I still had to swim back! No one was around, so after considerable effort, I pulled myself up on shore and rested for a long time with my back leaning against a tree by the Missouri. I started preparing for my swim back and heard movement in the water. I was terrified and jumped to my feet. I know the Navy takes a dim view of people in the harbor and will shoot on sight if they see you. Even though it was pitch black outside, there were area lights shining on the Missouri. I couldn't believe what I was seeing. Hanadie was pulling himself up from the water not ten feet from me. I didn't want him to see me, so I quietly moved to the other side of the tree as I tried to figure out what he was doing. He carried a large canvas backpack, and he struggled with the zipper and was having difficulty opening it. Finally, after several tries, he moved the zipper enough to pull out a small flashlight. He placed his hands to partially block the light, but I still was able to see the additional item he maneuvered from the bag, and even after all I thought Han might be up to, I was still shocked he had a Maindeka with him."

Jumping from his chair, seething, Frank slams his mug down on the table.

"I can't believe you didn't call the authorities immediately. Do you know how many people might have been injured or killed? So you put your loyalty to this insane friend of yours over your loyalty to a whole community?" As if leaving, Frank steps away from the table.

"Frank," Oskar says firmly. They lock eyes, and Oskar says emotionally, "I would have done the same for you."

Frank opens his mouth but closes it as he seems uncertain what to do and looks at everyone else at the table. No one moves or speaks. Frank looks directly at Oskar, "I wouldn't have wanted you to do that, Oskar, or *ever* have put you in that position."

"Frank, please sit down. I can understand your anger and distress, and once I finish what I came to say, I'll accept your resignation from the board if that's your wish."

Frank sits, but the tense set of his shoulders indicates he may not stay long.

Oskar's phone buzzes, but he ignores it as he finishes his story. "I knew I had to figure out what Hanadie was going to do with the bomb thus I continued to watch as Han made an adjustment and placed the item back in the bag. He pulled his mask down and moved to slide back into the water. Once he was in the water, I quickly followed him in and saw he was swimming to the Missouri. Keeping well behind, I kept Han's flashlight in sight as I followed to see what he would do. Hanadie stopped near the stern. He was there only a few moments and swam away. Waiting until I no longer saw the flash of his light, I used my own and swam to the spot where he had stopped. Once I was in front of the bomb, my mind went through my options. I could take it down now, and hopefully, the whole thing would be averted. I was running out of air, and I still had a long swim. My mind was a mess, and I couldn't come up with a solution so I started praying and seeking God's guidance. The first thing I saw was the Arizona Memorial Ceremony. I knew at that point Han's goal was for the detonation to happen at the ceremony which was almost eight days away! I knew the bomb was specifically designed for ship destruction with only a seven day timer, so since he wouldn't have set it, I knew it was safe to leave it. I turned away to swim back home, but I just couldn't leave the device there and returned to remove it. My mind worked diligently on a solution as I carried this inconceivable object back to my house."

Oskar looks directly at Frank. "My thinking may be flawed, but you have to remember Hanadie is like a son to me! Upon returning to the Ewa Beach house, I disengaged the device's timer, placed it in my home safe, and fell into bed. As soon as I awoke, I knew my course of action and put it into place. I determined a decoy would work, so should Han return to the Missouri, he would assume the original live bomb was still in place. I have a key to Hanadie's condo, so went snooping when he wasn't at home. I found several additional Maindekas in a shed on the property. I guess he figured since he had a license to buy explosives, he didn't need to hide them. I took a couple of them and spent a lot of time figuring out how to set the timer to ensure it would stop working at one hundred hours without detonating the explosive. It took me some time to make one of the devices unable to detonate. I must say it was very nerve-racking, and I don't think I could replicate it now if I tried. I returned to the Missouri four days later and left the decoy on the ship. Luckily for me, Han didn't check on it during those four days.

Hanadie's behavior during the auction made me nervous. Some time after he left, using the restaurant as an excuse, I checked up on him. The restaurant manager explained they hadn't seen Han since earlier in the day. I knew I couldn't leave the event until it was over, but as soon as I could get away, I left. My worry was either Han had discovered the decoy with the adjusted timer and would get a replacement or figure out how to readjust the timer to make it explode.

"After leaving the auction, I took the original bomb from my home safe and brought it to my secret safe in the branch in case I needed to show it to the authorities later. I felt it was safer here if anything went wrong as Han knows about my safe at home but not the one here."

Axle speaks up at this point. "The one thing I don't get, Oskar, is how Hanadie got into the vault here at the branch? I thought you had asked him to give you his branch key."

"I'll get to that in a minute. When Canoe and I arrived at the ship, I saw two bug-shaped Maindekas! I knew my original next step was to check the timer to make sure it wouldn't detonate before I could get it out of the area. But now there were two! I felt a tap on my shoulder, and thinking it was Canoe, I turned and saw a much bigger body. Assuming it was Han, I started attacking him. Of course, there was an underwater scuffle, and I was jerked away from the man I thought was Han but who turned out to be Leek. Almost immediately, another hand reached for me and dragged me away from the scene. Leek saw me drop the bags containing the Mains and grabbing them, swam outside the harbor. This time it was Han! When Axle swam after Leek, Hanadie pulled off my regulator and put a pill down my throat. He was gentle and said, 'It's okay, Oskar. This'll make you feel better.' That's why I became loopy."

Everyone is transfixed by Oskar's story. Sara is anxious to find out about the future of the bank, but at this point, is as spellbound as everyone else to hear the rest of what Oskar has to say.

"Hanadie dragged me to the shore and pulled me out, and from what I remember, we lay on the ground and didn't get up for I don't know how long. We were out of the view of the authorities, and once Han felt like we had enough rest, he anxiously dragged me to my feet. As we shuffled to the stadium, he practically had to carry me. It was amazing there were so few police types there. I think I saw a few in the parking lot, but since it was still overcast, we managed to sneak into the entrance by the restaurant unnoticed. We walked to what once was our normal Sunday morning service spots and just sat there. I was becoming more aware but still unable to focus or go anywhere on my own. Hanadie never said anything, just sat there. I think he was waiting for the drug to wear off so he could question me about the bombs when Canoe and the guys showed up. Han hadn't seen me remove the additional Main. It would not have mattered on one anyway because I had adjusted the timer so it would stop at one hundred hours. Later, I found out Han had discovered the timer had been set for one hundred hours, ending the morning of the ceremony. No reason then for him to bother to change it. Of course, he didn't realize it would stop and not detonate. Thank God! The oddest thing was that the second Main I had put in the pack had the same adjustment, and I never even touched it. All I can figure is that it was divine intervention."

Oskar looks at Axle. "Bud, you're my hero. Without your quick thinking, I'm pretty sure I wouldn't be here to tell the tale. You asked about how Han got into the bank. I hate to tell you, but I never got the key back or asked Frank to delete him from the security system. I had given Han the workroom combination when I originally gave him the branch key. You would think once I discovered Han's plans, I'd have retrieved his key first thing, but I never thought of it. Honestly, I quite forgot I ever gave him one. What I didn't know is he was able to get a key for the special branch panic apartment from one of the locksmiths who no longer has a job! Unbelievable how many contacts he had.

As I started to become more coherent, I came up with the brilliant idea of going to the bathroom, and knowing if I pretended to be out of it, I could sneak away from Hanadie. It all worked perfectly too until Hanadie showed himself here at the bank while Axle and I were talking. Once I left the stadium, I dragged myself over to the Auto Zone on Salt Lake Boulevard. I managed to talk the employees there into calling me a cab to pick me up. Luckily, I had a twenty in my swim trunks pocket. I looked pretty bedraggled in my swim trunks and T-shirt. It had taken me some time just to get to the Auto Zone, and on top of that I had to wait on the cab. I'm assuming that's why Hanadie arrived at the bank before I did. Believe me, I was sweating bullets thinking Hanadie would find me, but he was totally focused on finding his extra Mains I had taken from his condo so he could replace the bombs removed from the Missouri that day. He most likely deduced the bank was the easiest place for me to hide the extra Mains. As you all know, there was a scuffle with Han, Axle, and me at the bank, and the upshot is I lost my eye."

Oskar leans back in his chair obviously exhausted. Oskar places his hand on Kim's arm. "I'll be okay in a minute." Sighing, Oskar looks at Sara. She returns his stare unblinkingly. "Sara, I want you to know, I've hired the best defense attorney on the island. He feels confident he can use the insanity defense for Han. I feel responsible and will do everything in my power to help him."

Everyone is transfixed by Oskar's story, and for the first time, Axle notices the loud ticking of the conference room clock. He nervously plays with his coffee cup as he glances at Ruth. Without changing position, Oskar states, "What I haven't told any of you yet is my plan to resign from the bank."

A small crash is heard as Axle bends down to pick up the broken pieces of his mug off the floor.

Oskar doesn't even take a breath and says, "This has been on my mind for quite some time. I want to make a return trip to Bosnia to finally move beyond my past demons and anger. I don't know how long I'll be gone or even if I'll return to Hawaii. I'll get back to that in a minute, but I bring it up because I had already planned a night flight after the auction to get one last look at this island I love. I thought of canceling the trip, but felt I had time before having to check on Hanadie. Of course, in retrospect, many of my decisions were poorly thought out, and I can't fully explain why I did what I did. Once I got home to Ewa Beach, I immediately suited up to go check on the Missouri. As many of you already know, that's when I was accosted by my three buddies Canoe, Dan, and Matt. I wish they were all here. They were instrumental in saving Pearl.

"And in saying that, I feel my presence here at the bank is a hindrance to its future growth. I've already made plans to leave Honolulu after the trial. In the meantime, I'm appointing Sara as interim president."

All heads turn to Sara who stands and walks over to Oskar. "Oskar, we've had a rocky relationship over the years, but even so, I love my work here and going forward, I will work diligently to continue your vision." She reaches out her hand, and Oskar takes it in both of his. "Thank you, my dear, that means the world to me."

"Frank?"

Grimacing, Frank answers Oskar's unanswered question. "I guess since you're leaving, Oskar, I can work with Sara." He stands to shake Sara's hand as the rest of the group follows his lead.

With a huge sigh of relief, Oskar looks at Axle. "There is one small piece of the puzzle I want to share with you. I never told you why I went to the branch after the incident. I really needed a place to evaluate my next steps. I wasn't sure it was safe for me to return home, so I came here. Crazy, huh? Luckily, I keep an extra set of keys to the branch in a utility cabinet in the garage. Did you ever wonder why I came here that day?"

"I did. And now I know! You mentioned earlier about returning to the branch after the auction. That's why I came to the branch after the incident because Frank mentioned you had been here the night before, and he was concerned about it. While I watched you on the security footage, I kept looking at you." Axle snaps his fingers. "Ah-ha! You had the Main hidden under your jacket, didn't you?"

Oskar nods. "I had been keeping Han's live Main in my house safe. I was concerned he may figure out a way to get to it there, so I brought it to the bank."

With a chuckle, Axle comments, "I even commented to myself how fat you looked with your jacket buttoned."

They both laughed.

After a few coughs, Oskar asks, "You okay with my decision to resign from the bank?"

"Absolutely. I've been thinking of leaving the bank myself, and this is perfect timing. I'll help in the transition, but I've accumulated some wealth as you know, and I want to spend some time exploring the islands. Hopefully, I can encourage a close friend of mine to accompany me." He looks at Ruth as she congratulates Sara.

Oskar looks as well. "You might want to make that a permanent arrangement."

With a smile, Axle agrees. "All in good time, all in good time. Well, in God's time, I should say."

CHAPTER 32

And Everyone Else?

Mark walks into the Big House by the GA and wanders room to room looking for Mey. Seeing her in the laundry room with the washer going and a pile of sheets on the floor, he stops for a moment in the kitchen doorway.

Father, I know I've only known Mey for a few months, but I care deeply for her. I've been praying and feel you are with me on taking the next step in our relationship. I spoke to her dad yesterday. Whew! Thanks for giving me the courage to have that conversation! It was nerve-racking, but he's a kind man and obviously loves his daughter. Give me the words to share my feelings for her.

Stepping from the kitchen to the laundry room, Mark surprises a delighted Mey who grabs him for a hug. She lifts up a diet soda. "You want to take this home to Ruth?" Mark doesn't answer, but takes the soda from her hand, placing it on the counter. He leans in for a swift kiss. "How's my girl?"

"Well, and you?"

"Better. Can I borrow you for a minute? Do you have time to sit on the beach for a little bit?"

Taking Mey's hand, the two walk outside to find an open spot and sit quietly watching the windsurfers.

"Mey, I know this has been a crazy time, and your friendship and support have meant the world to me. You are the best friend I've ever had. It may sound corny, but I want to ask you to go steady with me."

Mey laughs. "I think it goes without saying we're going steady, right?"

Mark smiles. "I mean like, real steady." He pulls a chain from around his neck and pulls a ring from it. It's a small princess-cut diamond in an antique setting. Mark takes Mey's left hand as her mouth opens into a big *O*.

"I, Mark Max, take you Meylani Kalili, as my steady, permanent girl. I will love and cherish you for all my days. Do you agree to this long-term commitment so we may take time to know each other and be guided by our Lord and Savior, Jesus Christ, to the next step in our relationship?"

With tears in her eyes, Mey says, "I do."

With a click, she and Mark look over as Leek takes their picture with his cell.

Laughing, Leek shows them the picture, and he oohs and aahs with Mey as he looks at her ring. "Canoe wanted me to take your picture as he gave you the ring. I'm not staying long though. I want you guys to have plenty of time for privacy." Leek raises his eyebrows a couple of times.

They all laugh as Mey keeps her eyes locked on her hand.

"Canoe, you gonna tell her where the ring came from?"

"It's the ring my dad gave my mom when they became engaged. My mom wears her wedding band, not this one. When I told her my intentions, she asked if I wanted to use her ring, and I knew it would be perfect. What do you think, Mey?" Mark asks hesitantly.

"I agree, it's perfect." She grabs Mark in a big hug as they all laugh and talk about the future.

It's amazing how God takes disparate souls and intertwines them into His best work. In this case, a perfect *Hawaii Pearl*.

Authors Note

I ask your indulgence when you are reading the detailed explanations included in Hawaii Pearl. My internet research provided the bulk of the information provided. My imagination also was the driving force of the narrative, so adjustments to actuality may have occurred to increase the intensity of the story. Thank you for taking the adventure with me as I put in print all the ideas swirling in my head. God bless you!

Oahu National Basement Floor Plan

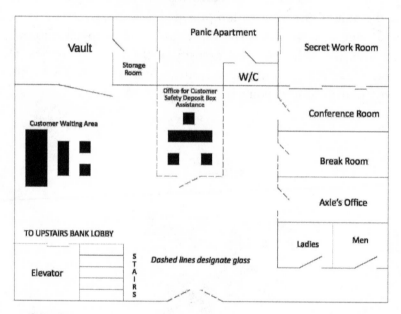

About the Author

J ena Nix is a long-time Texas resident who considers Hawaii her second home. After nineteen visits to the Hawaiian islands, she highly honors the people and culture of that exceptional place. This inspired her to set her novel, *Hawaii Pearl*, in the magnificent setting of the islands. Because she herself is a voracious reader, it was true joy for her to use her love of the written word and the mesmerizing scenery of Hawaii to create her first story. She presently lives in Austin with her husband Michael and son Matthew but plans a move permanently to Hawaii in the near future.

CPSIA information can be obtained
at www.ICGtesting.com
Printed in the USA
BVHW081631210721
612419BV00004B/76

9 781098 084424